The Quest for Anna Klein

Books by Thomas H. Cook

FICTION

Blood Innocents

The Orchids

Tabernacle

Elena

Sacrificial Ground

Flesh and Blood

Streets of Fire

Night Secrets

The City When It Rains

Evidence of Blood

Mortal Memory

Breakheart Hill

The Chatham School Affair

Instruments of Night

Places in the Dark

The Interrogation

Taken (based on the teleplay
by Leslie Boehm)

Moon over Manhattan
(with Larry King)

Peril

Into the Web

Red Leaves

The Cloud of Unknowing

Master of the Delta

The Fate of Katherine Carr

The Last Talk with Lola Faye

The Quest for Anna Klein

NONFICTION

Early Graves

Blood Echoes

A Father's Story
(as told by Lionel Dahmer)

Best American Crime Writing
2000, 2001 (ed. with Otto Penzler)

Best American Crime Writing
2002 (ed. with Otto Penzler)

Best American Crime Writing
2003 (ed. with Otto Penzler)

Best American Crime Writing
2004 (ed. with Otto Penzler)

Best American Crime Writing
2005 (ed. with Otto Penzler)

Best American Crime Writing
2006 (ed. with Otto Penzler)

Best American Crime Reporting
2007 (ed. with Otto Penzler)

Best American Crime Reporting
2008 (ed. with Otto Penzler)

Best American Crime Reporting
2009 (ed. with Otto Penzler)

Best American Crime Reporting
2010 (ed. with Otto Penzler)

THE
QUEST
FOR
ANNA KLEIN

Thomas H. Cook

AN OTTO PENZLER BOOK
MARINER BOOKS
HOUGHTON MIFFLIN HARCOURT
Boston • New York

For Susan M. Terner, first reader, editor extraordinaire,
and in all ways, my secret weapon

First Mariner Books edition 2012

Copyright © 2011 by Thomas H. Cook

www.hmhbooks.com

Library of Congress Cataloging-in-Publication Data
Cook, Thomas H.
The quest for Anna Klein / Thomas H. Cook.
p. cm.
"An Otto Penzler book."
ISBN 978-0-547-36464-3   ISBN 978-0-547-75040-8 (pbk.)
1. Quests (Expeditions) — Fiction. 2. Missing persons — Investigation — Fiction.
I. Title.
PS3553.O55465Q47 2011
813'.54 — dc22   2010042696

Book design by Brian Moore

Printed in the United States of America

DOC 10 9 8 7 6 5 4 3 2 1

And hence one master passion in the breast,
Like Aaron's serpent, swallows up the rest.

—ALEXANDER POPE

PART I

The Slenderness of Bones

Century Club, New York City, 2001

The question was never whether she would live or die, for that had been decided long ago.

Danforth had said this flatly at one point deep in our conversation, a conclusion he'd evidently come to by way of a painful journey.

It had taken time for him to reach this particular remark. As I'd learned by then, he was a man who kept to his own measured pace. After our initial greeting, for example, he'd taken an agonizingly slow sip from his scotch and offered a quiet, grandfatherly smile. "People in their clubs," he said softly. "Isn't that how Fitzgerald put it? People in their clubs who set down their drinks and recalled their old best dreams. I must seem that way to you. An old man with a head full of woolly memories." His smile was like an arrow launched from a great distance. "But even old men can be dangerous."

I'd come to New York from Washington, traveled from one stricken city to another, it seemed, a novice member of the think tank that had recently hired me. My older colleagues had manned the desks of what had once been called Soviet Studies. They'd been very assiduous in these studies. There'd hardly been a ruble spent on missiles or manure that they hadn't recorded and scrutinized. But for all that, not one of them had foreseen the abrupt collapse of the Soviet Union, how it would simply dissolve into the liquefying fat of its own simmering corruption. That stunning failure in forecasting had shaken their confidence to the core and sent them scrambling for an explanation. They'd still been searching for it years later when the attack had come even more staggeringly out of nowhere. That had been a far graver failure to understand the enemy at our gates, and it had sharply, and quite conveniently for me, changed their focus. Now I, the youngest of their number, their latest hire, had been dispatched to interview Thomas Jefferson Danforth, a man I'd never heard of but who'd written to tell me that he had "experience" that might prove useful, as he'd put it, to "policymakers" such as myself, "especially now." The interview was not a prospect I relished, and I knew it to be the sort of task doled out to freshman colleagues more or less as a training exercise, but it was better than standing guard at the copying machine or fetching great stacks of research materials from the bowels of various government agencies.

"I remember that line of Fitzgerald's," I told Danforth, just to let him know that, although a mere wisp of a boy by his lights, I was well educated, perhaps even a tad worldly. "It was about Lindbergh. How 'people set down their glasses in country clubs,' struck by what he'd done."

"A solo flight across the Atlantic that reminded them of what they'd once been or had hoped to be," Danforth added. Now his smile suddenly seemed deeply weighted, like a bet against the odds. "Youth is a country with closed borders," he said. "All that's valuable must be smuggled in."

I assumed this remark was rhetorical and found it somewhat condescending, but our conversation had just begun and so I let it pass.

Danforth winced as he shifted in his chair. "Old bones," he explained. "So, what is your mission, Mr. Crane? The grand one, I mean."

"Our country's good," I answered. "Is that grand enough?"

What remained of Danforth's smile vanished. "I was young like you." His voice was even, his tone cautionary, as if he regarded my youth as an animal that could easily turn on me. "Clever and self-confident. It was a very good feeling, as I recall."

He'd been described to me as reticent, distant, somber, and his experience in what my senior associates still called "the great game" had been brief and long ago. For these reasons, I'd concluded that in all likelihood he could offer little of value to the present situation. But in the still-settling dust of the Towers' collapse, every corner was being searched, every source, no matter how remote and seemingly irrelevant, gleaned for information. The gyroscope at the center of our expertise had been struck by those planes—so the thinking went—and it had wobbled, and now all its movements had to be recalibrated.

And so, after reading Danforth's letter, Dr. Carlson had decided that Danforth might have something to add to our intelligence. He'd told me that Danforth did not give interviews, so it was quite surprising that I'd been singled out for this audience.

"Have you ever met the old buzzard?" he asked.

I shook my head.

"Then why you, Paul?"

"I don't know," I answered. "Maybe he saw that little piece I wrote in *Policy Options*."

"Oh, well," Dr. Carlson said. "At least you'll get to see the Century Club."

Which was indeed something of a treat, I had to admit, as I glanced about the room in which Danforth and I now faced each other, its bookshelves lined with works written by the club's members.

"A very impressive place," I said.

"If one is easily impressed," Danforth replied with a slight smile. "I read your article on the current crisis. You seem very certain, I must say, in regard to what should be done."

5

I shrugged. "It's not really a very prestigious publication," I told him with slightly feigned modesty. "More of an opinion sampler where graduate students attempt to get noticed. Which I did, evidently. By you."

"Your father was a professor of foreign affairs," Danforth said.

My father's position at a rather modest little college had been mentioned in the brief biography that accompanied my article, so I wasn't surprised that Danforth was aware of it. Still, there was an air of clandestine knowledge in his tone; he seemed to carry, almost like a mark upon his brow, the faded brand of a spy.

"Yes, he was," I told him. "He never made policy, of course . . ."

"Which is clearly what you hope to do?"

"Yes."

"Hmm," Danforth said. He drew a piece of paper from his jacket pocket and read: "'Our response should flow from passion as much as policy, and should bear with it a hint of the paranoid.'" He looked at me quite seriously. "So there should be no irrationality gap between ourselves and our enemies."

His remark held no mockery, it seemed to me; Danforth truly appeared to be considering what I'd written.

"My point is that now is not a time for half measures," I replied. "Not in the face of these medievalists."

"The target is all," Danforth said. "Picking it and destroying it. Which is where true intelligence comes in."

Comfortably seated amid the old-fashioned opulence of the Century Club, Danforth looked very much the worldly intelligence officer who'd once sipped cognac and smoked cigars with the sort of characters one might find in Graham Greene or Somerset Maugham. His suit had passed its prime, and his tie was unstylishly wide, but I could imagine him as a figure from a bygone age, a handsome young man in a white dinner jacket, lounging on some tropical veranda, watching a steamer move out of the harbor. There would be riotously colored birds in the long green fronds of the nearby trees, and on that ship, a woman in a satin dress would be standing with a champagne glass in her long white fingers, lifting it to him silently, *Adieu, mon amour.* He was part of a vanished time, I thought, a lost world, and because of that, my current mission seemed even more a matter of giving the new boy something to do.

"You're an Ivy Leaguer," Danforth said. "Columbia." His gaze softened, and I saw the wound we shared. "A fellow New Yorker."

A familiar wave of kill-them-all rage passed over me at the barbarity that had been inflicted upon what had always seemed the most American of cities, but I tamped it down with a crisp "Yes."

Even so, it was clear that Danforth had seen the flame that briefly lit my eyes.

"Hatred is a very legitimate emotion," he said. "Believe me, I've known it well, and certainly at this moment we have a right to our ire."

This was a different position from the self-loathing justifications for the attack that had lately wafted up from various quarters, and I was relieved to hear it.

"Anyway," Danforth said, "I'm sure the best think tanks are bloated with boys like you."

I didn't like the term *bloated* but nodded anyway, now a little impatient to get on with the interview, write up my report, and head back to Washington. "So?" I said hastily. "Shall we go on?"

Danforth noted my impatience. "You are a very focused young man." His expression was quite gentle, perhaps even a bit indulgent. I might almost have called it Socratic.

"Crane," he said. "An English name."

"Yes, but I'm really of German stock," I answered. "At least, for the most part."

"So a name must have been changed along the way," Danforth said. "What was it before?"

"I don't know," I answered. "My grandfather changed it during the war." I offered a quick smile. "I suppose he didn't want to be blamed for things he hadn't done."

Danforth nodded. "Quite understandable. No one would have wanted to be accused of things like that."

"And which he couldn't have done because he left Germany before the war," I added.

Danforth smiled. "Do you speak German?"

"Not since high school."

"That's a pity," Danforth said. "Certain words in that language often come to mind. *Rache*, for example. It has a rough sound, don't you think? Kind of a snarl. It sounds like what it means: 'vengeance.' But others don't sound anything like what they mean, of course. For example, *Verrat* doesn't sound like what it means at all."

"What does *Verrat* mean?"

"'Betrayal.'"

Before I could respond to this, Danforth turned toward the window, beyond which a gentle snow was falling. "There was a lot of fear after the Crash of Twenty-nine," he said. "People were desperate." His gaze turned searching. "I'm sure you've read about it in your history books."

"Of course," I answered.

In fact, I'd read a great deal about that instability: streets filled with the angry dispossessed. Rallies, protests, mobs that surged and withdrew in enormous, roaring waves. Communists gaining influence. Fascists too. Those had been interesting times, no doubt, but Danforth's backward drift smacked of the mental vis-

8

cosity common to people of his age, and I simply had no time for it.

"Your activity before the war," I said. "How did you —"

"We called it the Project," Danforth corrected firmly. "I later came to believe that the name lacked resonance, that it gave no sense of what had actually been involved. Not like *Nacht und Nebel*, certainly. Which sounds pretty scary and said what it was."

I looked at him quizzically.

"'Night and Fog,'" Danforth translated. "The German policy of sending prisoners to camps where they would disappear into, as it were, night and fog." He smiled in a way that suggested not only that my understanding of the Project might be less than accurate but also that he would not be rushed into his discussion of it. "And do forgive me for drifting into modal verbs. *Would* this and *would* that. It's a habit I have, reflecting on things while I talk about him." He laughed softly. "I also tend to drift into asides."

"Asides?"

"For example, there's a castle in Vincennes, on the outskirts of Paris," he said quietly. "Diderot was imprisoned there. So was the Marquis de Sade. Just think of it, Mr. Crane —"

"Paul," I said, to establish a slightly less formal mood. "Please, call me Paul."

"Very well, just think of it, Paul," Danforth went on. "The two poles of human thought within a few yards of each other. The reasoning of a philosopher and the ravings of a psychopath."

"Why did you happen to think of this aside just now?" I asked.

"I suppose because the castle was used for executions as well as a prison," he answered.

He went on to discuss the various times he'd been to the chateau at Vincennes, what he would have felt on his first visit had he known of the ones to come, what he would have made certain to see and recall, because these small things would speak to him eloquently and with great poignancy at a later time.

"We act in the present tense and recall in the past tense," he said at one point. "But we reflect in the conditional and regret in the subjunctive."

"I'm aware that you are a very gifted student of languages," I told him, in case he'd been laboring to impress me with that point. I drew a notebook and pen from my jacket pocket and pretended that his answer to my next question was worth recording. "What languages do you speak?"

He spoke quite a few, as it turned out, and as he listed them, I took the opportunity to look him over as I'd been trained to do, evaluate and assess his fitness as a source.

Thomas Jefferson Danforth was ninety-one years old, but his eyes were sharp, and, save for the occasional wince of discomfort, there was little of the creakiness of age in the way he shifted his body or reached for his glass. His mind was obviously quite clear, and his voice never faltered. He might go off the beaten track, but so far his asides had remained tangentially connected to the topic of discussion.

"You mentioned Vincennes," I reminded him when he reached the last of his languages.

"Mata Hari was executed at Vincennes," Danforth said with deliberation, the way an etymologist might turn a phrase over in his mind, review the origin of each word, ponder its many facets and vagaries. "And the Germans executed thirty people there in 1944. I once went through the list."

"Why?"

"Looking for a name," Danforth said. "And do you know, Paul, the feel of a murder site changes when you know someone who was murdered there."

"You knew someone who was killed at Vincennes?"

Danforth shook his head. "No, but I thought I might have," he answered almost casually. "At Vincennes, I was just looking. I did a lot of that after the war."

"After the war," I said coaxingly. "So that had nothing to do with the Project?"

"Not all things end abruptly," Danforth said matter-of-factly. "And some things never do. Acts of war, for example. They ripple on forever."

This line of talk seemed not at all germane, and so I said, "You were in the army, I believe?"

"Working in London," Danforth said. "Translating intelligence reports from all over Europe." He appeared to scan those years for a relevant memory. "I remember a particular contact. A priest, as it happened. His communiqués about Drancy were quite heartbreaking. What happened to the children there, I mean. He claimed to have heard their cries from the steps of Sacré Coeur."

"But that wouldn't have been possible," I said in a rather too obvious effort to show that, for all my youth and limited travel, I was at least familiar with Paris and its environs. "The distance would have been too great."

Danforth's smile seemed indulgent, a worldly old man educating an unworldly youthful one. "No distance is too far for guilt to travel." He shrugged. "But yes, the priest was no doubt speaking metaphorically."

Despite his faintly pedagogical, didactic air, I had to admit that a certain gravity emanated from Danforth, an intense centeredness; reason enough, I decided, to play it his way a few minutes longer, go at things a little less directly than I'd planned, allow him the occasional digression. Such mental wandering was typical of advanced age, after all, and besides, it was always possible that some little jewel of useful information might be gleaned along the way.

Still, I wanted to hoe a more or less straight row, which is why I made my next statement. "They all spoke several languages. The people recruited for the . . . Project."

"How do you know that?"

"Robert Clayton's report to the State Department," I answered. "I have to say it makes for rather interesting reading, all that cloak-and-dagger business."

"How old are you, Paul?" Something in Danforth's voice was at once hard and tender, both the scar and the flesh beneath it.

"Twenty-four."

Danforth nodded. "At around your age, I was a callow young man, running the family business. Picture me, if you can." He seemed to disappear down the long tunnel of his own past. "A young man with plenty of money and a lovely fiancée, dressed to the nines, having dinner at Delmonico's."

Delmonico's, New York City, 1939

A burst of flame swept up from the pan as the tableside chef splashed brandy onto the steak, and the people at the surrounding tables joined them in laughter and applause that seemed to circle 'round the dining room and linger in the drapery, lending yet more sparkle to the light.

"That's the show," Clayton said happily, and in response they all lifted their glasses, Clayton and Caroline, his wife of six months, Danforth and Cecilia Linnartz, his fiancée, blond, with dazzling blue eyes, who seemed still not quite used to the glint of her engagement ring.

"Confusion to the French," Clayton said as a toast.

Danforth looked at him, puzzled.

"It's an old Anglo-Saxon toast," Clayton explained. "My oh-so-English uncle taught it to me."

They'd driven to Beaver Street in Clayton's spanking-new car, a gift from his father on his most recent birthday, and during the trip they'd cruised past the remnants of a late-afternoon riot. There'd been a few overturned cars, a couple of them set on fire and still smoldering, and the streets had been strewn with placards. Caroline had looked unsettled by the scene, but she was a nervous girl, Danforth knew, and he liked the way Cecilia, calm and cool, had quickly soothed Caroline's rattled nerves.

Once they arrived at Delmonico's, the incident had fled their minds, and for the past few minutes they'd looked very much the happy foursome they were, Clayton talking at full tilt, stopping only to sip his six-olive martini.

"The marble portal out front, did you know it came from Pompeii?" he asked.

"That's the story that went out," Danforth said. "But my father doubts it."

"Why?" Clayton asked.

"Because it would have been very hard to get it out of Italy," Danforth answered. "Even out of Naples, corrupt though that city is."

Clayton laughed. "Then it must be a fraud," he said. "But Danforth Imports can get anything out of anywhere, right, Tom?"

"Right," Danforth said confidently.

Something sparked in Clayton's eyes. "A great skill, that," he said. "A very great skill. You must have many secret devices for spiriting objects of great value in and out of exotic ports of call."

"That's a rather grand way of putting it," Danforth said, "but yes, we do."

The dinner progressed as it usually did, though it struck Danforth that Clayton often returned to the subject of the family business, the contacts Danforth Imports had throughout Europe, particularly in France and Poland but also in the Balkans, where, as Danforth rightly informed him, order could be found only after one understood the structure of disorder.

They went through the courses and finished off the meal with yet another fiery display, this time baked Alaska. It was ten o'clock before they piled back into Clayton's car for the drive uptown, where, some fifteen minutes later, Danforth and Cecilia at last found themselves alone in the lobby of Cecilia's building.

"Caroline's frightened of everything," Cecilia said. "I can't imagine what Clayton sees in her."

Danforth shrugged. "Men like Clayton often marry women like Caroline. I don't know why." He laughed. "Stanley did, you know. The great explorer. His wife rarely left London, and she seemed mostly interested in hats."

Cecilia said nothing in reply to this, but Danforth could see that she was turning it over in her mind, a thoughtfulness he liked in her and that he considered important in the life they would live together. Had he been asked at that moment if he loved her, he would have said that he did, and he would have believed this to be true. Many years later, as he searched through old papers and followed distant clues, alone in rooms so spartan nothing hung from their walls, he would recall that once he had loved a woman named Cecilia and that if it weren't for a single, decisive choice, he would have married her and lived his life with her. She would have been the full measure of what he knew of love, their life together a glass that — because he knew no other — he would forever have taken to be full.

Finally, as if something about him had troubled her, she said, "You're happy with me, aren't you, Tom?"

"Of course I am," Danforth assured her.

A few minutes later, in a taxi going home, he recalled that moment, and it returned him to his earlier life: how he and his father had traveled over the wildest terrains, eaten things that could scarcely be imagined, part of his training to run the family business. The actual running of it had eased him into a far more comfortable world, however, and now those earlier times were like dreams from childhood or stories he'd read in a boys' adventure book. Lately he'd begun to wonder if everything had been experienced too early, absorbed by a mind too immature to provide much resonance to the man he later became. In fact, on those occasions when he couldn't prevent a certain uneasiness from creeping over him, he suspected that time was slowly dissolving all save the most harrowing episodes of those dramatic years — the stormy ferry ride to Cozumel, the wind that had nearly blown him off the Cliffs of Moher — and that since his youth he'd added nothing to his ever-dwindling store.

He felt a familiar discontent and turned to work, his no less familiar route of escape. He'd brought the usual briefcase of papers home with him earlier that day, and he now set about going through them.

He'd completed about half the evening's tasks when the phone rang.

It was Clayton.

"Do me a favor, Tom. Go to your front window and look to the right, the northwest corner of Madison and Sixty-fifth."

"What?" Danforth asked with a faint laugh.

"Come on, just do it."

Danforth put down the phone, walked to his front window, drew back the drapes, and looked out. The streets were deserted at that hour; he saw only a single figure, a man wearing a dark hat pulled down low, slouching against the corner of the building at Madison and Sixty-fifth.

"All right, I looked," Danforth said.

"And saw a man, right? Leaning against the corner building."

"Yes," Danforth said warily. "How did you know?"

"I know because I'm in the bar across the street from that corner. I can see him very clearly."

Danforth looked at the clock across the room. "That bar closed an hour ago, Robert."

Clayton's laugh was entirely relaxed. "I thought you'd know that. It's good to be aware of your surroundings."

"I have no idea what you're talking about," Danforth told him.

A steely seriousness came into Clayton's voice. "How about we meet at the Old Town Bar tomorrow evening?" he said. "Say, seven thirty?"

Century Club, New York City, 2001

"So, Clayton was looking for certain characteristics in you," I said, a banal question, I knew, designed merely to keep Danforth talking, since I would never return to my bosses in Washington without completing an assignment, even one as ultimately unenlightening as I expected this interview to be. "That you were a man who observed his surroundings."

"A penetrating glimpse into the obvious, Paul," Danforth said.

I gave Danforth no indication that his "penetrating glimpse into the obvious" remark offended me, though it did. Still, I could see that the real purpose of this statement had been to warn me against indulging him with even the most glancing flattery.

"He was evaluating you though, wasn't he?" I asked. I once again positioned pen and paper in a way that gave the impression that Danforth's answers were important. "Your strengths, I mean."

Danforth shook his head. "No. He was looking for my weaknesses. Not of character, however. He was looking for cracks in me, little places he could enter. He already knew what he wanted me to do. He just didn't know if I would do it. That's what that little trick with the man on the corner was all about. It was like a scent he released in the air."

"A scent of what?"

"Mystery, what else?" Danforth answered. "He wanted me to know that he had something on his mind. He wanted me to be curious about what it was. It's the simplest way to draw someone into a plot. You make them want to know what you know." He shrugged. "Anyway, Clayton was just working a bit of a shell game with that guy on the corner. A touch of legerdemain."

"Did it work?" I asked. "Did you meet him at the Old Town Bar?"

Danforth nodded. "Of course I did," he said. "I thought I could hear whatever was on his mind and not be in the least seduced by it." His smile emerged like a tiny ray from the belly of a cave. "But I wasn't prepared for what happened there."

Old Town Bar, New York City, 1939

Danforth brushed the snow from the shoulders of his overcoat and slapped it from his hat. The interior of the bar was dark in a way that mirrored the times, at least insofar as he had come to see them, everything dimly lit and faintly threatening, a sense of an old world dying, the new one as yet uncertain, inevitably forming but perhaps misshapen, "a monster-making age," as Clayton had recently called it. Yet another rally had ignited more street violence that very afternoon. A few cars had been overturned and set ablaze on Tenth Avenue, according to the radio, and the whole city was on edge. Danforth had seen a company of mounted police make their solemn way toward Union Square as he'd walked from his office, all of them grim-faced and expecting the worst, if not tonight, then sometime soon. There was a sense, everywhere and in everything, of lives ripped from the old bonds of steady work and stable families, a great cloth unraveling.

As he always did in an unfamiliar setting, Danforth took a moment to locate himself, take in his surroundings. He noted the hours of accumulated cigarette smoke that had gathered and now curled beneath the bar's pressed-tin ceiling. The smell of bar food hung lower and more heavily: grease, ketchup, a hint of onion. A group of regulars occupied the stools at the front, manual laborers clothed head to foot in flannel, broad shoulders slightly hunched, big hands curled around mugs of beer. Danforth could not imagine what they talked about in the gloomy light. But at least these men had jobs, unlike those who'd taken up residence in the city parks or erected shantytowns along the river. There was an explosive quality to the enforced idleness of unemployed men, Danforth thought, something both inert and volatile, like a damp fuse drying. They would rip down a forest to make a campfire, and who could stand in the winds that blew then? Certainly not himself, Danforth knew, nor any of his well-heeled kind.

The barman gave him a quizzical look.

Danforth nodded toward the empty tables at the back.

"Anywhere you want," the barman said, then returned to the regulars, who were clearly more his sort — wore caps instead of hats, frayed woolen jackets rather than Danforth's immaculate cashmere.

Clayton had suggested the place and Danforth hadn't bothered to question it. Eighteenth Street wasn't far from Union Square, the offices of Danforth Imports. Still, the Old Town Bar seemed a strange choice, and he was surprised that Clayton even knew about it. And yet that was precisely the part of his friend that he both enjoyed and admired, that from out of nowhere he would demonstrate a knowledge or familiarity he'd previously kept concealed. He gambled in back-alley crap games, that much

Danforth knew, and seemed to enjoy an occasional excursion into the edgier reaches of the city, Harlem dance clubs and the basement bars along the waterfront. At college, he'd regularly smuggled bootleg hooch into their fraternity house, cases of it borne up the stairs by men who scarcely spoke English and dealt only in cash. The man who had slouched at the corner of Sixty-fifth and Madison had no doubt been one of Clayton's shadowy army of demimonde contacts.

He walked back toward a table he'd selected almost the instant he'd come into the bar, in much the same way a hunted man might locate the nearest exit. He knew that there was something primitive in this, something not altogether rational, something he thought might serve a soldier better than an importer. For that reason, he'd found a secret anticipation in the rattling rumors of European war, even an obscene but reflexive hope that they might prove true. It was the hope of a young man, he knew, and a foolish one at that. The two uncles buried in the American cemetery at Romagne reminded him that war could prove fatal, so any time he allowed himself to anticipate it with anything but dread, he also made himself recall the long rows of white crosses he'd seen in that sweeping burial ground. But even in this memory, a glimmer of war's romance managed to peek through: he also recalled the visitors' book at Romagne, how in so many distinctly different hands, the French had written the simple, elegant *merci.*

A barmaid swam out of the gloom a few minutes after he took his seat, a woman clearly recruited from the kitchen staff. The greasy apron proved that, along with the damp washcloth that hung around her neck.

"What can I get you?" she asked.

The Old Town Bar was no place for a dry martini.

"Scotch," Danforth said. "Straight up."

While he waited, Danforth went over the day's usual business problems: delays in shipments, boats waylaid by storms, and always, always, overland disruptions in Manchuria. In the Orient, the actual nature of the obstacle was rarely clear, but then what did it matter if a mountain pass was blocked by a blizzard or by the thievish whim of some local warlord? In the importing business, his father had taught him, one learned to accept the inscrutable. There was no other enterprise on earth, according to the elder Danforth, that more fully and continually confronted hazard: shipments inundated by swollen rivers or buried in avalanches, trains seized by starving mobs or expropriated by revolutionaries, and if the merchandise did not fall victim to any of these, then it was held captive by greedy functionaries intent on expanding bribery's already more than generous largesse. Importation operated like the universe, as Danforth had come to see it: irrationally and violently, with something vaguely criminal at its core.

The bar door burst open and Clayton came through it, stopped, stomped the snow from his shoes, then peered about expectantly.

Danforth lifted his hand.

Clayton nodded briskly and headed toward him, rubbing his glasses with a white handkerchief. He'd returned them to his face by the time he reached the table.

"It's like the Blizzard of Eighty-three out there," he said.

Clayton worked as a photography archivist for the library on Forty-second Street, a job secured for him, no doubt, by the large annual contribution his family made to the library. He specialized in New York City history; his head was filled with black-and-white images of its storied past. Danforth knew with certainty that at the mention of the 1883 blizzard, Clayton's mind had instantly offered up striking pictures of that peculiar disaster: a city locked in great drifts of ghostly pale; horses buried in harness, their heads protruding from white mounds, stiff as bookends.

"Have you been here long?" Clayton asked.

"Only a few minutes."

He pulled off his coat and draped it over an empty chair but left his red scarf around his neck and shoulders. "This place seems quite cozy, don't you think?"

The barmaid lumbered over. Clayton ordered a vodka tonic with lime.

"So," he said once it was just the two of them again, "how are things in imports?"

"A family business is a family business," Danforth answered. "I liked the training better than the mission."

"Imagine how bored you'll be at thirty," Clayton said with a quick smile.

Both of the drinks came a moment later. They lifted them but toasted nothing.

Clayton put down his glass firmly. "What's the most frightened you've ever been, Tom?"

It was an odd question, Danforth thought, and yet he instantly recalled the incident quite vividly.

"I was seven years old," he answered. "My father and I were in Romania. The train suddenly stopped very hard, so you knew the brakeman had seen something unexpected up ahead. In this case it was a man hanging from a cross."

Clayton's gaze intensified. "A cross?"

"Yes," Danforth answered. "As in Calvary. It had been raised beside the tracks at the end of a mountain pass, and several men with rifles were standing on the railroad bed. A bandit with a dagger ordered us out of the train to see it. There was never a word after that. Other bandits came out of the woods and simply walked among the passengers, taking whatever they liked. They nodded toward your pockets and you emptied them. They nodded toward your watch and you gave it to them. I noticed that my father's fingers were trembling. I'd never seen him frightened, and I said to myself, 'Well, I guess you don't fool around with men who nail other men to crosses.'"

"That's quite an experience," Clayton said.

Danforth recalled the flat look in the bandits' eyes, how lightless they'd been, utterly without sparkle. "Dead souls are very scary, Robert."

"Dead souls," Clayton repeated. He was silent for a moment, then his gaze took on an unexpected urgency. "All your travels, the nature of your business, your command of several languages. It struck me last night at Delmonico's that you'd be the perfect man for a secret mission."

"A secret mission; I can see it now," Danforth said with a laugh. "Sipping a kümmel at the Hermitage. Meeting shadowy figures on a park bench in Vienna. Learning how to make invisible ink."

"That would be equal parts baking soda and water," Clayton said matter-of-factly. "Write with a toothpick on white paper. Then hold the paper to a heat source, and your message will appear in brown."

"You're kidding me," Danforth said.

"Not at all," Clayton said quite gravely. He took a sip from his drink. "So now you know how to make invisible ink, Tom."

Danforth waved his hand dismissively. "Forgive me, Robert, but this all sounds like play-acting."

"Believe me, it's more serious than that," Clayton said solemnly. "It might even have an influence on history."

"An influence on history?" Danforth asked. "That's an ambitious project, even for you."

"Project," Clayton said. "That's a good word for it. We'll call it that from now on. The Project." He glanced at his watch. "Seven forty-five," he said with a quick smile. "Our lives pass so quickly, don't they, Tom?"

Danforth gave no response to this deadly familiar philosophical aside and instead took a sip of his drink.

At the front of the bar, a few more customers came in: a couple of men who were obviously regulars, and a bedraggled young woman who seemed unsure if she was in the right place.

"We have so little time to make lasting memories," Clayton added.

Danforth watched as the men huddled up to the bar and left the woman to stand alone, looking frazzled and forlorn, like an animal cut from the herd because it was sick or wounded. In the woman's case, it seemed due to some mental confusion or disorientation. She stared about almost vacantly, her gaze wandering the room in uncertain fits and starts, as if she were following the flight of an invisible butterfly.

There was something poignant in the scene, Danforth thought. "We're like animals, really," he said, almost to himself.

"Animals?" Clayton asked. "In what way?"

The woman now seemed to be overtaken by the throes of a manic seizure, her movements very quick and contorted. A few people at the bar had begun to watch her. Some were grinning in a cruel way that completely undercut the great Communist romance; these noble workers were no more generous to this fellow lost soul than they would be to one another when the wolf was at the door.

"In the way we have no mercy for the weak," Danforth said as he watched the scene play out at the front of the bar.

Clayton laughed. "You're a sentimentalist, Tom. What the Irish call a harp."

"Maybe I am," Danforth admitted.

The people at the bar were now entirely taken up in cruel amusement, watching with jagged smiles as the woman pulled off her wool cap, dropped it, picked it up, worked to find a place for it, found that place in the pocket of her coat. Her every movement betrayed her solitary vagabondage, how in this teeming city, she was wandering alone.

"Maybe I am," Danforth repeated.

By the time Clayton turned around to face her, the woman had unwound a ragged scarf from her neck and was tromping back toward the rear of the bar.

"The city is full of nuts," Clayton said. He appeared mildly annoyed that Danforth continued to be distracted by the woman. "If she comes this way, just give her a few coins." He drew a pack of cigarettes from his jacket and thumped one out. "They're everywhere now," he added irritably. "These goddamn nuts."

Century Club, New York City, 2001

"You must be thinking that Clayton was not exactly a man of the people," Danforth said with an arid chuckle.

"He does seem very old-school," I admitted. "But the intelligence agency recruited pretty much exclusively from those ranks back then, didn't it?"

"Yes, it did," Danforth said.

"The good news is that our boys weren't like those upper-class Brits who ended up so disloyal, spying for Mother Russia," I added. "Philby, Burgess, and the rest. Traitors all."

"And all equally to be condemned," Danforth said.

"Of course," I agreed.

"Even if they believed in their cause?" Danforth asked.

"I wouldn't care what they believed," I answered.

Danforth's gaze betrayed a curious complexity, as if the memory of something won or lost had suddenly returned to him.

"Indeed," he said softly, as if reviewing an old decision or coming to a new one.

"Of course, most of them were fools," I said, determined to show Danforth that I knew my espionage history, could recite a few details. "The Cambridge Five. Imagine that group, dashing around Europe, delivering a codebook on Gibraltar, like Philby did." I laughed derisively. "They always struck me as buffoons."

"Or posing as such," Danforth said. "There is a lot of acting in this business. Pretending to be afraid. Pretending to be brave. Even pretending to be in love."

"That would be a cruel pretense, wouldn't it?" I said.

"Yes, it would," Danforth answered firmly. "Perhaps as cruel as pretending to believe in something when you actually believe the opposite."

I sensed that this last remark had returned Danforth to his subject.

"Did Clayton believe in whatever he was doing?" I asked.

"Clayton believed absolutely in what he was doing," Danforth answered. "There was never anything confused or addled about him, nothing in disarray."

"Not like that woman in the bar, then," I said, to demonstrate that I'd been listening closely to his tale.

"No," Danforth said, "nothing like that woman in the bar. Who walked straight to the rear of the place that night, by the way." His gaze grew distant, a man sinking back into the past. "As a matter of fact, she came so close to me a clump of snow fell off her coat and landed on mine."

Old Town Bar, New York City, 1939

"Oh, I'm so sorry," she said.

As the woman had gone by, a clump of snow had fallen from

the bundle of woolens she held and dropped onto Danforth's overcoat.

"Nothing to worry about," Danforth told her gently. He noted her face, how young it was, the tragedy of her derangement doubled by her youth.

The woman frantically brushed the snow from the shoulder of Danforth's coat. "You got a nice coat," she said. Their eyes met. "It ain't ruined, is it?"

"Not at all," Danforth answered. "Really. Nothing to worry about."

A crooked little smile appeared. "I thought I got that snow off me," she said with a quick, self-conscious laugh. "But it ain't easy to get off you once you got it on you."

"No harm done," Danforth told her. "It's just snow."

Her smile struggled for and lost its place, a string by turns taut and slack. "Anyway, sorry."

"Nothing to worry about," Danforth assured her again.

With that, the woman turned and made her way to a table in the far corner. She sat down and fussed with her things, her scarf, her coat, a cloth bag with a long strap, all of which appeared to fight her, making her movements grow more frustrated, almost comically so, as she labored to subdue them. During all of this, she seemed the victim of some vast, inner disarray, one of the city's future street grotesques, a young woman prematurely sinking into the idiosyncrasies that would doubtless overwhelm her middle years.

"That one will end up in Bellevue," he said sadly.

"Do you think so, Tom?"

"I do indeed," Danforth answered firmly. "My God, Robert, that woman couldn't—"

The glimmer in Clayton's eyes stopped him cold.

"What?"

"Her code name is Lingua," Clayton said.

26

"Code name?"

Clayton glanced to the back of the room. The woman had removed her scarf, revealing a disordered mop of dark, curly hair. "She's had a rather hard life."

Danforth's eyes shot over to the woman in question, her small body still jerkily grappling with an assortment of gear that appeared at every stage determined to thwart her.

Clayton returned his gaze to Danforth. "So small," he said. "Not even five two. Perhaps a hundred pounds." He lifted his hand, and when the barmaid came over, he ordered another round for the two of them. "She's a genius at languages," he added once the barmaid had stepped away. "Hence her code name."

Danforth leaned forward. "What are you telling me, Clayton? That this woman is a . . . I don't even know what to call her."

Clayton crushed out his cigarette and lit another one. "Her assignment for this evening was to come to the Old Town Bar at precisely seven forty-three. I would be smoking a cigarette. If I wasn't wearing a red scarf, she was to take a table, have a drink, but in no way approach me or draw attention to herself. If I was wearing the scarf, however, she was to sweep by my table and on some pretext or other get a good look at whomever I was with." He leaned forward. "And she was to do it in such a way that the person I was with would notice her, so that at any point in the future I could say, 'Remember that woman in the Old Town Bar?' and my companion would know instantly whom I was talking about." He took another draw on his cigarette. "If you hadn't been here, that convenient clump of snow would simply have melted." He glanced at his watch and when his eyes lifted toward Danforth again, they were quite grave. "Let's take a walk, Tom. I want to speak to you very seriously now."

They got to their feet, left money on the table, and headed for the door. Before going out, Danforth glanced toward the back of the bar, where Code Name Lingua sat; her profile was now blocked by the barmaid, so he could see only a chaos of black curly hair and the small, still madly flitting hands.

Outside, the snow had lightened, but enough had already fallen to cover the sidewalks. A trail of gray footprints followed them westward, then north on Park Avenue, until they reached the wintry stillness of Gramercy Park.

Clayton drew the red scarf more snugly around his neck. "Have you ever heard of Geli Raubal?"

Danforth shook his head.

"She was Hitler's niece," Clayton said. "She was found shot dead in a room in her uncle's apartment in Munich. She used her uncle's Walther. But Hitler was clearly not in Munich when it happened, and although Geli was shot in the chest when her head was perfectly available to her, the death was ruled a suicide."

They moved along the border of the park, the snow-covered sidewalk now empty.

"The smart money had been betting that Hitler would self-destruct in some way like this," Clayton continued. "They thought he was a buffoon and that some scandal would destroy him." His laughter was laced with irony. "But he hasn't self-destructed . . . and he's not a buffoon."

They reached the eastern edge of the park just as the snow began to increase, falling in large, silent flakes that quickly outlined their coats and hats.

After a long silence, Clayton turned and looked squarely into Danforth's eyes. "There's going to be a war, Tom. It will start in Europe, of course, but we'll be drawn into it eventually. And we're not ready, that's the point. We're weak and disorganized. Everything the Germans aren't. We're going to need time to build up our war machine." He paused, and Danforth understood that he was choosing his words very carefully. "There may be a way to get that time. Something no one has thought of. The woman in the bar can be of great help in this . . . project. But she will need to be trained in various skills. She'll need a place for that. I was thinking of your house in Connecticut. It's very remote. As you know, my own country property isn't."

They had reached the other side of the park. The snow was now falling in great curtains of white, covering sedans and settling like powdered wigs on the tops of traffic lights.

"This woman is willing to risk her life," Clayton said emphatically. "I'm only asking for a place where she can be trained."

They walked on for a time, then stopped again. Clayton nodded toward the lighted windows of Pete's Tavern. "O. Henry wrote 'The Gift of the Magi' in that bar," he said. He exhaled a long breath that seemed extraordinarily weary for so young a man. "What will be your gift of the magi, Tom?" he asked. "Another rug from Tangier, or a project that could help keep your country safe?"

Century Club, New York City, 2001

"That's an odd reference," I said. "O. Henry. 'The Gift of the Magi.' Are you religious?"

"Not then or now," Danforth answered. "But we lived in a culturally coherent world, Clayton and I, a world of shared symbols and references. Old Testament. New Testament."

"A coherence our current enemies now have in abundance," I added coldly. "But which we have somewhat lost."

Danforth shrugged. "True enough, but would you want it back if you got the Duke of Alva with it too?"

I had no idea who the Duke of Alva was but saw no need to demonstrate that lack of familiarity, and so I said, "Meaning what?"

"That it's easy to become what you once abhorred," Danforth answered.

This struck me as rather windy, and probably a quote. I returned to the more relevant subject at hand. "So, Clayton had made his proposal," I said. "What did you do then?"

"Despite the snow, I started walking uptown," Danforth answered. "On the way, I thought about the young woman, about what she was willing to do. And I thought about myself. I even thought about O. Henry. I was still turning all that over in my mind when I got to the Plaza."

Pulitzer Fountain, New York City, 1939

Danforth paused briefly at the fountain in front of the Plaza and thought over his conversation with Clayton. Something had changed and he knew it. A small door had been pried open in him. Perhaps that was Clayton's gift, that he could sense the locked door inside you and find a key to it.

He fixed his attention on the horse-drawn carriages that slowly made their way in and out of the park. The rhythmic beat of the hooves was muffled, and yet the sound was compelling, a soft, romantic dirge. Most of the passengers were young, and Danforth supposed a good many of them were on their honeymoons. He believed the world was indeed hurtling toward cataclysm, just as Clayton had said, but it would not occur tonight, not for these well-heeled newlyweds in their romantic haze. Soon he would be among them, he thought, newly married and in a carriage with Cecilia, a settled man in a profoundly unsettled world.

He'd walked the entire distance from Gramercy Park, and as he'd walked, a little seed grew in his mind, its roots sinking down and down until he could feel its feathery tendrils wrapping around him.

Abruptly he recalled Razumov, Conrad's dazed and fumbling revolutionary, how he'd been drawn into a deadly intrigue accidentally, his fate entering his room, he said, because his landlady turned her head. Danforth knew that he was not at all like Razumov. If he chose to be an actor in Clayton's project, it would be his choice, not one that the blind play of circumstance had thrust upon him.

His mind shifted again, and he imagined the young woman at the Old Town in quite a different bar, a little Bleecker Street dugout with sawdust on the floor, the woman surrounded by what he assumed must be her type of friends: would-be writers, painters, musicians, all of them young revolutionaries, probably Communists, the entire lot wriggling in the fist of hard times, talking life and art and politics, quoting Marx, Engels, Lenin while they sipped cheap beer and ate whatever the bar provided. He wondered if she was in any way different from such starry-eyed idealists, if she had remotely glimpsed the executioner's wall through the fog of their windy dialectics, sensed, whether she'd read Saint-Just or not, that revolutions devour their children.

There could be no answer to this, of course. He'd seen only the crazy show of this young woman, and now he doubted if even the curls of her hair were real. Perhaps she was all performance, enjoying the night's little vignette but in the end lacking the stuff needed to carry out the mission — whatever it was — that Clayton had in mind.

As if he were pushed by an anxious hand, he stepped away from the fountain, crossed Fifth Avenue, and headed toward his apartment on Park.

His father lived in the same building, and as had become his custom, Danforth looked in on him before going to his own apartment.

His father answered the door immediately.

"You shouldn't have bothered coming here tonight," he said when he saw Danforth. "You need your rest. You have a meeting with Akmet tomorrow at seven."

Although the elder Danforth had increasingly removed himself from the daily affairs of the business, he kept a close eye on how it was run, especially any dealings with Akmet, whom he considered little more than a Bedouin trader with a knife up his sleeve.

"The appointment was changed to ten," Danforth told him.

"So Akmet is feeling his years at last," the senior Danforth said with a small laugh. "Would you like a drink?"

Danforth nodded.

His father stepped out of the doorway and motioned him inside.

They walked into the front room of the apartment. A large window opened onto the night-bound city. The twinkling lights of its distant buildings looked like a rain of stars halted in their fall.

Danforth's father poured two scotches, handed one to his son. He was a tall man, lean and fit. It was easy to imagine him as a figure in ages past, the captain of a great vessel, standing on the bridge and plotting his course by the stars; this was precisely what the first Danforth men had been, and by their intrepid scouring of the world, the family fortune had originated. They had sailed the roughest seas, hacked their way through jungle depths, staggered across desert wastes, been shot by muskets and arrows and even poison darts, and suffered all manner of tropical fevers. Compared to these intrepid forebears, Danforth had lived a pampered life, as he well knew, safe and secure in his Manhattan apartment, a student of languages, for God's sake, with no claim to being different from a thousand other rich boys. A line from Pope crossed his mind, something about how much son from sire degenerates.

"You seem a bit tired," his father said. "Long day?"

Danforth turned to face the window. Below, the sweep of Central Park gave off an eerie glow in the streetlights. "I was thinking of the Balkans," he said. "Those thieves who stopped our train."

His father took a sip of scotch. "Why would you think of that?"

Danforth recalled the young woman at the Old Town Bar, the peril she would be in should she really go to Europe. "Maybe it's because I haven't made any memories in a long time," he said. "You know what I mean? Real memories. Something searing, that you'll never forget."

His father laughed. "Count yourself lucky," he said. "Most lasting memories are bad."

Count yourself lucky, Danforth repeated in his mind, and he knew he should do precisely that, but he also knew that in some strange, inexpressible way, he couldn't consider his good fortune entirely good.

He left his father's apartment a few minutes later, slept uneasily, went to work the next morning. Outside his office, the file clerks and secretaries busied themselves as usual. Dear old Mrs. O'Rourke was as attentive to him as ever, filling out his itinerary, screening his calls, making the appointments she deemed necessary, handing off various salesmen and solicitors to Mr. Fellows, the office manager, or Mr. Stans, the chief shipping clerk, doling out Danforth's time frugally, as she knew he wanted.

In that way, the week went by, the weekend arrived, and he met Cecilia at a restaurant across from Gramercy Park, not far from the corner where he'd spoken to Clayton the week before and then been left to ponder his friend's final question.

"Snowing again," he said almost to himself as he glanced out the window toward the park.

Cecilia unfolded the menu and peered at it closely. "I think I'll have a Waldorf salad," she said. "What about you?"

"Caesar salad," he told her.

The waiter stepped up, and they selected their entrées, Cecilia her fish, Danforth his chicken.

"And to drink?" the waiter asked.

Danforth chose a pouilly-fuissé, then handed the wine list back to the waiter.

"Very good, sir," the waiter said as he stepped away.

Cecilia reached behind her head.

Danforth knew she was checking for errant strands of hair.

"You look perfect," he assured her.

She dropped her hand into her lap. "The Vassar reunion is on Saturday. Do you want to come?"

"Of course."

"It'll be the first time I introduce you as my fiancé."

She seemed pleased and happy, and her happiness made Danforth happy too. For a moment, they smiled at each other, as happy couples do, and in that instant Danforth reaffirmed to himself his love for her, his commitment to the life they would share.

The wine came and they toasted their future together, and everything seemed perfect until Danforth glanced out the window, where he saw a young girl fling a handful of snow at a passing stranger; at that instant, he thought of the woman in the bar and found himself imagining her somewhere in the dark grove beyond the window, a lone figure moving away from him until she disappeared . . .

Century Club, New York City, 2001

". . . into the snow," Danforth said softly.

He paused and looked toward the window, the snow now

falling a little heavier than before. "When is your flight back to Washington, Paul?"

"Not for a few hours," I answered, though I feared that even this generous stretch of time wouldn't be enough to finish what was turning into a much more leisurely interview than I'd planned.

"So," I said crisply. "You were at Gramercy Park again. In a restaurant with your fiancée. You were looking out the window of the restaurant, out into the park, thinking about—"

"Thinking about myself, actually," Danforth interrupted. He took a sip from his glass. "Have you ever read *The Riddle of the Sands*?"

"Yes," I answered.

"I suppose I was a bit like Carruthers in that book," Danforth told me. "Youth can be a cruel lash, you know. Sometimes a lash you suffer. Sometimes a lash you wield." He looked for some response to this, but when I gave none, he continued. "Anyway, I called Clayton later that night, after that dinner with Cecilia. I told him that I was interested in the Project. He didn't seem surprised. But I wasn't entirely convinced, I told him. I wanted to meet with Lingua. He arranged for us to get together at one of those dimly lit grog houses they still have down on Fourth Avenue."

"And when you met her," I asked with a sly smile, "was she . . . Mata Hari?"

"She was pretty, if that's what you mean," Danforth said with perfect seriousness. "But that wasn't what I most noticed about her."

"What did you notice?"

Danforth paused, then said, "How shall I put it?" Once again he appeared to retreat to that earlier time. "That she already seemed to be looking back at life from the bottom of her grave."

Dugout Bar, New York City, 1939

Danforth arrived first and proceeded to a booth at the far corner of the bar. He'd come to have serious reservations about the meeting, along with even greater ones about getting involved with Clayton's no-doubt-inflated idea of influencing history. What scheme could possibly do that?

But for all that, he couldn't deny that he felt a certain anticipation with regard to this meeting; when he saw her come through the front door of the bar, he felt a quickening.

"Hello," she said when she reached him.

She sat, drew her arms out of her coat, and let it fall behind her back, then she folded her scarf and laid it beside her on the bench, all of this done as if she thought herself alone in the booth. Her gaze was still cast down when she said, "No snow this time."

There was an olive undertone to her skin that made her look faintly Sicilian; her features were at once delicate and inexpressibly strong, and there was a penetrating sharpness to her gaze.

"My name is Thomas Danforth," he told her.

"Anna Klein."

Klein, Danforth thought. It meant "small" in German, and therefore seemed quite appropriate to the woman who sat across from him. He recalled that Clayton had said she was a genius with languages, and he decided to test the waters. *"Können wir Deutsch sprechen?"* he asked.

"Wie sie wunschen."

For the next few minutes they spoke only German, Danforth's considerable fluency matched by hers.

"Where did you learn German?" Danforth asked her when he returned to English.

"I pick up languages very easily," Anna answered without elaboration.

"And you speak French too?" Danforth asked.

"Yes," Anna said. *"Voulez-vous parler der Français?"*

Danforth nodded and they switched to French, and after that to Spanish, and after that to Italian, and in all three cases Anna spoke with a fluency that astonished him.

"How many languages do you speak?" he asked in English.

"Nine," Anna answered but did not list them.

"You live in the city?"

She nodded crisply. "The Lower East Side."

Danforth's father had called her neighborhood "the squalid kingdom of the Jews," and as she lowered her eyes, Danforth considered the long history of her people's persecutions: the false accusations made against them—that they poisoned wells and sacrificed Gentile children—the hundreds of sacked and burning villages they'd fled, the wintry forests in which they'd hidden, boiling tree bark for their soup.

The barmaid arrived. Danforth ordered a scotch, but Anna merely waved her hand. "Thank you, nothing for me," she said.

"Not a drinker?" Danforth asked.

"No," she said.

"I admire your discipline," Danforth said, meaning it half as a joke. He shrugged. "I suppose you know that I've been asked to provide a place where you can be trained."

One of her tiny brown hands inched over and covered the other. "Yes," she answered, then suddenly leaned forward. "Why did you want to meet me?" she asked quite determinedly and in a way that radically shifted what had seemed a secure balance of power: Danforth was now the one being evaluated, she the one with favors to grant.

"To satisfy myself, I suppose," he answered. "I wanted to make sure you were a serious person."

"And are you satisfied that I am?" she asked.

Her frankness surprised him, as did her impatience to get on with whatever task lay before her.

"Yes," Danforth answered quickly, though it was not until that moment that he realized he was. "I'm not being asked to do very much, after all."

"So we'll use your place for the training?" Anna asked.

Danforth nodded.

She rose and began to gather her things, her movements quick but precise, not at all like the antic twitches of the character she'd played when he'd first seen her at the Old Town Bar.

"I thought we might have dinner," Danforth said.

She shook her head. "I have work."

With that she reached for her coat, drew out an envelope, and offered it to Danforth. "I'm to give you this. It's from Clayton."

Danforth took the envelope from her, and as he took it, he noted how small her hand was, how nearly doll-like and delicate, the slenderness of her bones. "Do you know what's in here?" he asked.

She nodded as she put on her coat. "The next step," she said.

Century Club, New York City, 2001

Here Danforth paused and drew in a slow breath.

"There are symbolic gestures, Paul," he said. "They may be small, like taking that envelope from Anna's hand, but they have the force of moral commitment."

"Like that line Travis drew in the dust at the Alamo," I said.

"There's no actual proof that that ever happened," Danforth said. "But it doesn't matter. And yes, my taking that envelope from Anna's hand was like that, a gesture that states quite clearly that from this moment on, there will be no turning back." He paused again, then added, "With that simple gesture I committed myself to the Project. Not just to the rather unspectacular thing I'd been asked to do for it, provide a house in the country, but to the Project as a whole. It turned out to be a good thing, since Clayton was already asking me to take another step — to provide a cover identity for Anna — which I did after I read the note inside the envelope." He took a sip from his drink. "And so the next day, following the instructions in that note, I put an ad for a special assistant in the classified section of the *New York Times*. The applicant's only requirement was that he or she had to be available for extended service abroad and be familiar with several languages." He smiled softly but warily; he briefly appeared to me like a child being led into a dark wood.

"Then I waited," he said.

Danforth Imports, New York City, 1939

Over the next few days, applicants for the special-assistant position came and went, mostly young men with sparkling credentials, some of whom were quick to mention their distinguished families and the prestigious schools they had attended. Fraternities were brought up, as were summers in the Hamptons or on Cape Cod. It was clear to Danforth that some of the applicants viewed importation as an attractive career choice, perhaps even, oddly enough, a step toward acquiring a position in the State Department. Several of these young men had traveled extensively, and all spoke at least one foreign language, though their proficiencies varied widely. Most were eager to be employed, though Danforth knew that very few of them would go hungry as a result of being out of work.

But a few less well-heeled applicants also showed up, always in suits they'd bought off the rack. These were first-generation men who had no claim to any distinctions they had not won by their own efforts. Danforth admired them in a way he could not admire the others or himself, and he would have hired them to fill other positions if any had been available. He liked the cut of them, their modest style, even the slightly beleaguered quality they tried to hide.

There were no female applicants until Anna showed up a few days after the ad appeared, a delay Danforth thought ordered by Clayton and for which no explanation was requested or given.

She wore a surprisingly professional ensemble: tweed suit, white blouse, a single gold chain at her neck, and a pair of matching earrings.

"Miss . . . Klein?" Danforth asked when he looked up from her perfectly typed resumé.

Her smile was quite bright, as were her eyes. "Yes," she said. She thrust out her hand energetically. "Pleased to meet you, sir."

The transformation was stunning. There was no hint of either the frenetic female who'd snatched at her things in the Old Town Bar or the curiously aggressive young woman who'd slid into his booth at the Dugout Bar four days earlier.

She was more than an actress, Danforth thought; she was a chameleon.

For the next few minutes, they did the dance of prospective employer and prospective employee. Danforth asked the usual questions, and Anna gave the expected answers. He showed no hint that he'd ever met her, and neither did she. He maintained a strict professional air, and she an eager one, as if anxious to be offered the job.

Cautiously, as they neared the end of the interview, he asked a question he would have considered vital even if he'd had no knowledge of the woman before him.

"Do you have a passport?" he asked.

"No."

"You'll need to get one." His smile was coolly professional, as he thought it should be. "If you get the job, of course." He glanced at her resumé. "I suppose that will be all for now."

With that, she left the office, but something of her lingered through the day, an awareness of her that surprised Danforth as he went about the usual business routines. From time to time, he looked up from his desk at the chair she'd sat in during their brief meeting, and strangely, its emptiness created a hunger to see her again. It was a feeling he found curiously new and faintly alarming, like the first sensation of a narcotic one knew one must henceforth avoid.

At six he packed his briefcase with the evening's work and stepped out of his office.

Mrs. O'Rourke, his secretary, was sitting at her desk. She handed Danforth a small envelope. "This came by messenger."

Once in the elevator, Danforth opened the envelope and read the note: *Six o'clock. Sit near the fountain at Washington Square.*

He'd thought he might find Anna seated on a bench near the fountain, but she was nowhere to be seen, and so he took a seat and waited. For a time, he simply watched various Village types as they strolled beneath the bare trees: professors and students with briefcases and books, a bearded artist lugging paints and easel, two workmen precariously balancing a large piece of glass.

The man who finally approached him was short and compactly built, a little steel ball of a fellow. Danforth had noticed that he'd cruised twice around the fountain, then broken from that orbit and drifted along the far edge of the park, and then around it, until at last he'd seemed satisfied of something. That Danforth was the man he'd been sent to meet? That he wasn't being followed? Danforth had no idea. He knew only that as if in response to a radio signal, the man had suddenly swung back into the park, walked over, and sat down.

41

"My name is LaRoche," he said, then laughed. "Clayton thought I might scare you off, so I have to be nice so you will not be afraid of me."

Danforth had no idea if this was true, but he suspected that it might be and felt himself challenged by Clayton's evaluation of him.

"You don't look very scary," he said, though Danforth did find something frightening in this man, an edginess that made Danforth slightly unsettled in his presence.

"Not scary at all," LaRoche said. "Just a round little man."

He wore a faded derby, and his body was loosely wrapped in a brown trench coat, his hands sunk deep in its pockets. Despite the French name, he was, Danforth gathered from the accent, anything but French.

"I am to teach the woman the skills she needs," he added.

Skills was *skeels* and the *w* in *woman* had not been pronounced with a German *v*, linguistic characteristics that made it difficult for Danforth to pinpoint LaRoche's accent.

"Clayton says she is small," LaRoche said. He followed a lone bicyclist's turn around the fountain. The cyclist made a second circle, and that seemed to add an uneasiness to LaRoche's manner. "Your house is far away," he said.

"Yes," Danforth said. "And very secluded."

LaRoche nodded crisply, then looked out over the park, his attention moving from a woman pushing a carriage to an old man hobbling slowly on a cane. His expression remained the same as his gaze drifted from one to the other. It was wariness and suspicion, as if both the woman and the old man might not be what they appeared to be. "This weekend," he said.

Danforth nodded.

LaRoche glanced toward the far corner of the park, where a man leaned against a lamppost, reading a newspaper. "I should go now," he said.

With that, he was gone, and for a time Danforth was left to wonder just what sort of man this LaRoche was. His accent had been impossible to determine, which could only mean that he'd never lingered long enough in one place to sink ineradicable linguistic roots. There had been a nomadic quality in his demeanor as well, rootlessness in his twitching eyes and in the way he was constantly alert to every movement around him. Had Danforth known then the dark things he learned later on, he would have seen that LaRoche suffered from a paranoia of the soul, the same fear that would later be experienced by the huddled masses that were crowded into railway cars and the creaking bellies of transport ships and whose cries he would hear in many as-yet-unknown dialects.

Century Club, New York City, 2001

Dark things he learned later? Paranoia of the soul? Huddled masses? The creaking bellies of transport ships?

I couldn't help but wonder where Danforth's tale was headed.

"Clearly, your story doesn't end in New York," I said.

Danforth shook his head. "No, not New York," he said. "We have decades to go, Paul, continents to traverse. Lots of sweep for a little parable."

"A parable?" I asked.

Danforth shrugged. "Nothing more."

Now my journey here truly seemed a waste of time.

Danforth saw the impatience that seized me and quickly acted to relieve it. "Tell me a little about yourself, Paul."

"Well, my father was a professor, as you know," I answered.

"And your mother?" Danforth asked.

"A professor's wife," I said. "A listener. We had faculty dinner parties, the academics always holding forth. My mother hardly

43

ever spoke on those occasions. I think she felt inadequate." In my mind, I saw the car swerve on the ice, tumble into the ditch. "My parents were killed in a car accident."

"I'm sorry to hear it. And your grandparents?"

"They're gone too," I answered. "The last of them, my grandfather on my mother's side, died just last year."

Danforth's demeanor abruptly changed. "Life can be very treacherous, can't it?"

I assumed that he was speaking of the accident that had killed my parents, though I could sense a more obscure undertone; it seemed as if I were gazing at a painting that revealed one thing on the canvas but hid something darker beneath it.

"Yes, it can," I agreed.

I saw the shadow of one of those dark things pass over him.

"A young man adopts a terrible ideology, and after that, there is nothing but destruction," he said.

I wondered if he was now speaking of the young men in the planes, and for the first time I allowed myself the dim hope that his story — his parable — might offer something of value in regard to my assignment. If so, I hoped to reach it speedily.

"So, you agreed to provide a place for Anna's training," I said coaxingly.

Danforth nodded slowly. "A place for her training, yes."

Winterset, Connecticut, 1939

LaRoche's car was a rattling old Ford, dusty and with a badly sloping running board on the driver's side, the conveyance of a tradesman, exactly the sort of car no one would notice. For a moment Danforth wondered if it too was part of the plan, a tiny screw in the mechanism that was apparently much more meticulously assembled than he'd thought at first.

"Good morning," Danforth said as Anna stepped out of the car.

"Hello," she answered softly.

"Nice place," LaRoche said, though with little interest, as if he were indifferent to anything beyond his reach.

Anna drew an old, badly frayed coat from inside the car and put it around her shoulders so that it hung like a ragged cape. Her curls were held in place beneath a black scarf, and Danforth noticed that she now wore the scruffy shoes and black stockings he'd seen on the women of the Lower East Side. In such Old-World garb, she looked not only foreign but deeply so, a Moabite like Ruth of old, alone in alien corn.

"May I take your bag?" Danforth asked.

He would have asked this question in just the same gentlemanly way of Cecilia or of any of the other young women he'd squired to nightclubs and fancy restaurants, but he felt certain that Anna must see such courtliness as foppish. What a prissy little wedding-cake figure of a man she must think him, he decided, she who would be on the front line while he remained in America, having brandies at his club, his life compared with hers almost grotesquely free of care.

And yet she said, "Thank you," and handed the bag to him.

His smile was more a self-conscious twitch. "Good. All right . . . well . . . let's go in."

He had built a fire and it was crackling nicely as they entered the main sitting room.

"Would you like something to eat?" he offered.

Anna shook her head. "No," she said, then looked at LaRoche. "I think we should get started."

"Okay," LaRoche said, then, with what Danforth found a shockingly casual movement, he drew a pistol from behind his back and handed it to her. "Take it."

Anna did, and for the next few minutes Danforth watched

45

as LaRoche acquainted her with the pistol's heft and the simple mechanics of its use.

"First, you feel it," he said. "Get a good grip." He grabbed Anna's right hand and placed the pistol firmly inside it. "Lift up, down. Get the feel of it."

As instructed, Anna lifted the pistol, then let her arm drop, then lifted it again.

Such small things, Danforth thought, both the woman and her weapon, so small in comparison to the forces against which they would be used.

"See, not so heavy," LaRoche said.

Anna nodded.

"Like a bottle of milk," LaRoche added.

Anna turned the pistol over, looked at it from each side.

"It's a Smith and Wesson three-fifty-seven-magnum revolver," LaRoche told her.

Danforth glanced down at the gun as LaRoche continued his description of its technical superiority, a recitation that seemed designed to convince Anna that it was the finest pistol ever produced, one in whose performance she could feel the greatest possible confidence. It was small and black with an elliptical design on the side and a three-inch barrel that Danforth assumed would be called snub-nosed, and which he guessed would make the gun easy to conceal.

LaRoche drew a box of cartridges from the pocket of his overcoat, and in three simple steps taught Anna to load, unload, and reload it, timing her efforts with an old pocket watch until her juggling of cartridges and pistol became sufficiently smooth. He closed the lid of the watch and peered out into the woods behind the house.

"You try it now," he said.

With that lackadaisical instruction, he led Anna out the back door, Danforth following behind, feeling very much a fifth wheel and yet undeniably curious as to how this diminutive young woman would handle the weapon.

LaRoche stopped a few yards out into the grounds, then pointed to a small tree in the distance. "Walk there."

Anna did as she was told, her feet leaving gray tracks through the snow.

"Stop," LaRoche called.

Anna halted.

LaRoche looked at Danforth. "No need for you to stay," he said in a voice that made it clear that Danforth's continued presence was both unnecessary and unwanted.

Danforth nodded and headed back to the house. He'd reached its back porch when he heard LaRoche call, "Aim."

He turned and saw Anna, small and still, standing before a slender maple. From where he watched, she appeared to be very close to the tree, so close that when she lifted the pistol, its barrel seemed only a few feet from the trunk.

Would she be that close to peril? Danforth wondered. Would danger come so near? He imagined her trapped in a garret in some foreign town or village, men coming up the stairs, pounding on her door, then bursting through it; Anna reaching for the pistol at her bedside, aiming, firing again and again, though knowing that the men would keep coming, whole armies of them streaming through the door.

"Fire," LaRoche said quite casually, the way he might have asked her to pass the salt.

Anna fired; her shoulder jerked backward slightly, and she gave what seemed to be, at least from a distance, a quickly contained shudder.

"Anna?" Danforth whispered before he could stop himself.

She didn't turn but stood facing the tree, her arm stretched out, the report of the pistol still reverberating through the surrounding woods.

"One step back," LaRoche called. "Fire."

She stepped back and fired a second time.

"Step back," LaRoche said. "Fire."

Again, Danforth envisioned a dreadful scene: Anna rushing about some foreign room, reaching for the pistol as the door bursts open to reveal a troop of German soldiers or policemen or some other gang of men who'd come for her. But this time he imagined the scene with no hint of his earlier inner quaking and so he felt himself, even if just in his imagination, in training alongside Anna, both of them growing more able and more ready to face her peril.

Danforth went inside. The shooting went on for several minutes, Anna emptying and reloading the gun again and again, though Danforth knew that no matter what the scenario of her discovery and capture, she would likely never get off more than a few shots. LaRoche had clearly not been apprised of this, however, so his training was all about firing and reloading and firing again, as if he expected Anna to be holed up and fending off a sustained attack. Perhaps Clayton had told him just that, Danforth thought, given LaRoche the idea that Anna was part of some larger contingent, a ruse designed to lead LaRoche's mind in the wrong direction.

After a time, the shooting stopped. Danforth glanced through the cold-misted window. In the distance, LaRoche and Anna stood shoulder to shoulder, her small hand cupped in LaRoche's disproportionately large one so that it was impossible to determine which of them actually held the revolver.

For a moment they talked, LaRoche clearly giving more instructions. Then they turned and came back into the house. By then LaRoche had tucked the pistol into his belt, as if he thought Danforth's seeing it might disturb his tender sensibilities.

"She's good," he said quietly. He looked at Anna. "To fire is easy. The will to fire is hard."

Anna sat down on the sofa, a large window behind her, and through it came brilliant morning light.

"We go back tomorrow morning," LaRoche said to her.

She nodded, then looked toward the window just as a deer emerged from the edge of the woods, rather scrawny and with a patch of hairless skin at the side of its neck.

"Beautiful," she said, her eyes trained on the deer, her gaze ever more intense, a slight smile on her lips.

LaRoche laughed. "With what you've learned today, you could kill it with one shot."

Anna continued to stare at the deer, but her expression had taken on something distantly sad and tragic. Quite inexplicably, Danforth suddenly thought of the Triangle Factory fire, the many young women who'd leaped from the sweatshop's flaming windows. She didn't speak, but as he would later recall, many times, it seemed to him that all those falling girls were in her eyes.

Century Club, New York City, 2001

Danforth fell silent for a moment, then bent forward and massaged a point just above his right knee. "In memory, most people come and go," he said. "But a few leave parts of themselves inside you." He released his leg and drew back. "Like shrapnel."

There was something troubling in his recollection of this incident, of course, and I felt a distant rumbling in his tale. Still, at that moment I found myself less concerned with Danforth's faded memories of Anna than with the Project itself, the way it was emerging as an endeavor put together by rank amateurs.

"I must say the whole thing seems rather farcical," I told Danforth. "I mean, you didn't even know what Clayton's plan actually was, or Anna's role in it."

Danforth's eyes glimmered with an eerie wintriness, like a streetlamp in the darkness, a metal blued by cold and laced with snow. "Farcical," he repeated. "Yes, I suppose it could be seen that way."

He added nothing to this but abruptly got to his feet, buttoned the middle of his three-button jacket, and waved me to the right. "The dining room is this way," he said.

I looked at him, startled. "I didn't know we were having lunch."

"Come," Danforth said. "You need nourishment."

With some reluctance, I rose and walked beside him, the two of us moving at a leisurely pace toward a far room where tables were set, all covered with white tablecloths.

"We were at Winterset," I reminded Danforth as we made our way to the tables. "Anna was being trained."

At the entrance to the dining room, Danforth grasped my arm in the manner of an old man, a gesture that showed a frailty he'd concealed before.

"So to you it seemed a farce," he said in a tone that struck me as painfully searching, like a fish striving with all its wounded power to comprehend the hook.

"But not to you, I take it?" I asked cautiously.

For a moment Danforth gave no response, merely continued forward, though now with a slight tottering, as if he were seeking purchase on a perilous ledge. Then he said, "No, but I wish it had."

"Why?"

"Because I might have grasped the truth."

"What truth?"

"That the question was never whether she would live or die," Danforth answered finally, his voice sounding cracked and worn with use, like the pages of old books, "for that had been decided long ago."

PART II

The Point of
a Spoon

Century Club, New York City, 2001

I had learned by then that Danforth strolled in and out of his story rather fluidly, as a man might drift from one room to another in a sprawling house. There was no fanfare attached to these transitions, nothing to signal a new chapter save a sudden play in his eyes, a tiny light going on or off. Anna seemed always a lingering presence in everything he said, a ghost that followed him no matter where he went. Or was he following the ghost, shifting here or there whenever she beckoned him with some gesture only he could see?

For all that, once we reached the table reserved for him, Danforth made no mention of her but talked of the club's furnishings until the waiter arrived. He ordered the beef Wellington and a glass of Bordeaux. I ordered prime rib and said no to the wine.

"I need to keep my wits about me," I explained.

"Indeed you do," Danforth said, and added quite pointedly, "especially now."

His words seemed darkly instructional, and he followed them with a brief speech about "desperate times" and "dangerous circumstances" that could easily lead to some rash action one might later regret, a disquisition that was quite broad and without specifics and yet still seemed intimately connected to his story. "One should never embrace a mental process that is a wall rather than a gate," he said cryptically at one point. At another, he said, "The tragedy of human history is that it takes too long for gods to fail."

These were windy epigrams, but I dutifully wrote them down, a gesture he noted but didn't seem to trust.

Our lunches arrived. Danforth touched his wine to my water. *"Bon appétit,"* he said.

We ate with little or no further discussion of the Project. Instead, Danforth rather insistently kept our conversation on my background. He wanted to know if I spoke any foreign language fluently. None fluently, I told him. I'd taken German in high school, as I'd mentioned, and picked up a little Spanish during visits to my grandfather in South America. For a time, Danforth tested what remained of my skills, but my Spanish proved so rudimentary that he finally said simply, "Well, back to English," and from there inquired about my studies at Columbia and the career track I saw for myself in the future. Then, rather oddly, he commented on how life seemed to be a landscape marked by what he called "moral fault lines" to whose "subtle trembling" we should remain alert.

Then, with lunch behind us, Danforth put down his fork and returned to the past.

"To love not wisely, but too well," he said. "That's a moral fault that has many different aspects."

"A caution that comes from Shakespeare," I said, rather obviously making the point that I'd read *Othello*.

"To love a woman and not know who she is," Danforth went on. "Or a man and not know what he did." His gaze briefly intensified. "To love a cause but not know where it leads. They are different in many ways, but in one way they are the same."

"In what way the same?" I asked indulgently.

"In that one simple parable can contain them all," Danforth said.

This was the second time Danforth had referred to his story as a parable, though now his reference seemed more complicated, as if he were trying to convince me that this would be a multilayered tale, at once sweeping and intimate, by turns adventure story, morality play, and God knows what else, but at its end a narrative worth my time. His need to make his case seemed rather sad to me, making me feel that, rather than being an intelligence analyst on assignment, I was a volunteer at an old-age home, sent to sit by the bed and feign rapt attention to some old duffer as he recalled the many Chevrolets he'd owned.

Danforth appeared to see all this and so returned to the concrete aspects of his story.

"After the war began, we could do it differently," he said. "There was no need for secret training. We simply dropped people out of the sky."

He seemed still in awe and admiration of these night-bound, behind-the-lines jumpers, the courage their actions had required, and his voice began to show the old grief he felt, that so many had been lost.

"It was amazing how little they carried, the ones who were dropped behind the lines once the war began," he said. "An entrenching tool for burying the chute, a compass for finding your way. A pair of glasses for disguise. It's quite surprising how well they work, Paul. Just a pair of spectacles with clear glass lenses. It gives you a totally different appearance." He rolled his eyes upward slightly. "False identification, of course. One needed that. A map. Matches for secret writing. A little chocolate for energy. A razor. A dozen or so detonators if you were going to blow something up. A wireless to make reports." He thought a moment, then added, "Oh, and a revolver . . . for that tight spot you dread."

I found this a rather impressive display of insider knowledge, but more important, it raised the question of Danforth's own wartime activities.

"Were you dropped?" I asked.

"Yes, but that was several years after my work with the Project had been completed," Danforth answered. "My target was Sète, a little fishing village between Marseille and Barcelona, on the Mediterranean. The poet Paul Valéry was born there. He said something I've often recalled over the years, that a poem is never finished, only abandoned. It's the same with an ideal, I think, or a quest." He shrugged. "Anyway, Sète was quite lovely, with its canals."

"Why were you sent there?" I asked.

"To find out if Spain was truly neutral," Danforth answered. "Which it was. Spain had already been bled white by its civil war. Besides, the Germans had nothing but contempt for the Spanish, and the Spanish knew it. 'For the Germans, Africa begins at the Pyrenees,' my Spanish contacts used to say. Meaning that Spain was Africa to them, impoverished and inept, unworthy of consideration."

"Spanish contacts. You crossed into Spain?"

"Yes," Danforth said. "I pretty much kept in the vicinity of Saragossa. My mission was to watch for any sign that arms were moving out of Spain and toward Vichy France."

"Were you still with Anna at that time?" I asked.

And suddenly it was there, that little light going off, then on, then off again, and that seemed to flash distantly but insistently, like a warning signal at the entrance to a place Danforth both did and did not wish to go.

He lifted his glass, but rather than drink, he swirled the wine softly, gazing at its ruby glow. "No, I was not with Anna," he said. His hand stopped and the wine's surface calmed again. "Blood red," he said, and appeared lost in that thought.

"The training," I said in order to bring him back. "We were last at Winterset during Anna's training."

"Oh, yes," Danforth said. "There was a good deal more training, of course. LaRoche was a genius at destruction."

"Destruction?" I asked. "But he was only teaching her to use a pistol for self-defense, wasn't he?"

"At first," Danforth said. "But there were other skills to be learned."

"What skills?"

"Those of a saboteur," Danforth said. "The word comes from the Dutch, you know, from when Dutch workers threw their wooden shoes, their sabots, into the cogs of the textile machines that threatened their jobs."

"So you never lost your interest in languages," I said.

"No," Danforth said. "Because words are important, Paul. Do you know how Sartre defined a Jew?"

I shook my head.

"As someone whom someone else calls a Jew," Danforth answered. He looked at me sharply. "It was all in the word, never in the person." He let this sink in, then added, "A word like that, *Jew*, is an explosive."

The way Danforth pointedly made this remark gave me the impression that he had long been planning it and that other such remarks lay like mines in the road ahead.

"A word is an explosive," I repeated, with no hint that I found the comment a trifle overdramatic, as well as trite.

"Yes," Danforth said. "Which brings me back to Anna."

Winterset, Connecticut, 1939

Danforth had watched during the past few weekends as the cellar of the house was converted into a sinister laboratory. LaRoche

57

had set up tables and covered them with an array of materials. There were scores of glass bottles filled with various powders and liquids. He'd brought in brass scales as well, along with a black marble mortar and pestle. To these he'd added a large collection of items he thought might prove useful: a briefcase with a false bottom, a clock and several wristwatches, samples of European electrical switches, sundry dyes and polishes, and a supply of detonators. Each weekend had brought another lesson, and with each weekend, Anna had grown more adept in the secret arts of sabotage. There'd been more shooting lessons, as well as a great deal of training on the wireless LaRoche had unloaded from the back of his car the last week of February.

With each stage of Anna's training, LaRoche grew more confident in her abilities, so in the last days of winter, he decided to take the final step.

"Today we'll make a bomb," he told Anna on that particular day.

He directed her over to a table on which he'd set various materials.

"This is potassium chlorate," he said. "You can kill slugs with that, but it's good for a bomb too." He pointed to a glass jar filled with a white powder that looked as innocent as confectioners' sugar. "That's potassium nitrate. Plenty in fertilizer." The next exhibit was potassium permanganate, which LaRoche said could be found in a common throat gargle. After that, he picked up a can of what appeared to be ordinary wood stain. "Ferric oxide in this." The next can was silver paint. "In here you've got ground aluminum." He gave an almost comic shrug. "It's easy to find stuff for a bomb."

But it was not enough merely to make a bomb, LaRoche added. For, once it was made, a bomb had to be hidden, and the best way to do this was to disguise it as something else.

"Like this," he said as he picked up a large lump of coal. "Coal is soft. Very easy to carve out and place a bomb in. There's coal everywhere in Europe. Big stacks in the basement, right by the boiler. Blow a building sky-high."

Danforth envisioned the moment when Anna's new courses of study all abruptly came together in a fiery explosion, a building shuddering somewhere in the heart of Europe, great tongues of flame climbing charred walls and leaping out of shattered windows; Anna would be some hours away at that point, he hoped, perhaps already set up in another town, connecting other fuses to other timers, preparing the next action.

By then he would have settled back into his work at Danforth Imports, he thought, be taking the usual calls, making the usual decisions. He'd be married to Cecilia, settled into the Connecticut house, perhaps with a baby on the way; he'd lounge in a spacious living room reading the latest report on the war in Europe while outside workmen raked fall leaves and plowed under the last of Cecilia's summer garden.

Danforth couldn't pinpoint why he found this vision of his future unsettling, though he knew it was more than simply his familiar sense that the most adventurous part of his life had already passed. There was something in the deeply serious nature of Anna's training, as well as her tirelessness in learning LaRoche's dark arts, that made him feel small and insignificant. He thought of the Apollonius statue of a pugilist at rest, its battered face and body. Here was a man who'd known the worst of it, who'd been seasoned by grave experience. It was not for nothing, Danforth admitted to himself, that there was no statue of the man who'd held his towel.

This was a troubling thought, and so he was relieved when a ringing phone took him out of it. He turned away from Anna's training and rushed up the cellar stairs. The phone rested on a stand near the front door.

"Hello," he said.

"I've sent you a client," Clayton told him. "He's interested in French Impressionism. He thought you might have contacts in Paris. Be at the town bandstand. Two thirty. He'll be wearing a light brown jacket. There'll be a sprig of lavender in its lapel."

"Lavender?"

Clayton laughed. "You remember those fields, don't you, Tom?"

"Yes," he said.

"The bandstand," Clayton repeated. "Two thirty."

Danforth returned the phone's hand set to its cradle, walked out onto the broad front porch, and peered into the forest. Soon the trees would be bristling with green buds, and here and there the first leaves would begin to rustle in the warming air. Where, he wondered, would Anna be when the first flowers bloomed?

Suddenly a noise came from the cellar, a small pop, tightly controlled and heavily muffled, followed by LaRoche's hard laugh.

Danforth wondered if Anna had laughed along with him, or at least allowed herself a smile, pretending for that brief moment that it was all a game.

The drive to the town park was short, and it was only two o'clock, but Danforth saw no reason to remain at the house. He could take the valley road, the one that wound along a cold blue stream, and approach the town from an unexpected direction, as if his mind were now focused on surprise attack.

On the drive into town, he thought of Anna. They'd had few conversations at work, and all of them had been on business matters. They never met outside business hours, save for the weekends at the house, during which LaRoche had kept her almost entirely to himself, teaching her skills that she then had to demonstrate over and over until the most complex procedures flowed from her with the technical fluidity of an old hand. From time to time the three of them shared meals together, but even

60

then LaRoche focused the conversation on her training, asking her questions, noting her answers, sometimes nodding with satisfaction but otherwise keeping his opinion of her to himself, though Danforth supposed that he was reporting his evaluations to Clayton.

So what did he know about this woman? Danforth asked himself now. Little beyond her steeliness and the fact that she was very bright. At the office, she quickly grasped every element of her training in imports, an intelligence Mrs. O'Rourke had mentioned on several occasions. At Winterset, she'd mastered Morse code and how to operate and repair a wireless with the same effortless alacrity with which she'd learned to fire a pistol and was now learning to make a bomb. He'd already noticed her astonishing ability to slip in and out of identities and to do it so quickly and completely that she seemed briefly to lose herself within them.

But it was her skill at languages that had most impressed Danforth. In conversation with her, he enjoyed the way she could move seamlessly from one to the other. Once she'd told him that it was impossible to know a people if you did not know their language and that if she were granted many lives she would spend them learning yet more languages. *But you will have only one life,* he thought suddenly as he was driving into town, and then, with a sense of distress, he added, *And perhaps quite a short one.*

Years later, as he stood in the bombed-out remains of Plötzensee Prison, Danforth remembered these thoughts, the way they'd come to him on the drive into town, and it occurred to him that love is, at bottom, simply the deepest of all sympathies, and that perhaps his love for Anna had begun the morning he'd watched her by the window and thought of all the immigrant girls like her, the arduousness of their labor, their limited prospects, and seen Anna as somehow their representative in his life. Still later it had been her tenderness that called to him, as he remembered

61

on that same bleak occasion, the shattered walls of the prison perfectly symbolic of his own shattered life; after that it had been her resolve that drew him, and following that, her sacrifice, so in the end it seemed impossible that a love built on such a multifarious foundation could ever crumble and then boil up again as ire.

He reached the town in a few minutes. It was moving at its customarily slow pace as he drove down its single main street. There was a grocery store and a gas station, along with a clothing store and a five-and-dime. The town was typically American, quiet for the most part, and very neighborly. Danforth thought of the moment he'd committed himself to Clayton's project and allowed himself to believe that by giving himself to that effort — even if only by providing small assistance — he was doing something to preserve and protect this little town and all the others like it. It might even be enough, though this possibility paled when he thought of Anna, the deadly skills she was being taught and would at some point employ. Providing a country house for her training was hardly at the same level.

The bandstand was surrounded by a small park, and as he approached it, Danforth saw a man in a brown jacket make his way toward it from the opposite direction. The man wore a dark hat pulled down low, like the figure he'd seen outside his apartment window, and Danforth felt certain that it was, in fact, the same man.

"So, French Impressionism," Danforth said when he reached him.

The other man appeared darkly amused. "These little games will seem silly to us one day." His tone was nostalgic, as if, like Anna, he too had already glimpsed his fate. He offered his hand. "I'm Ted Bannion."

Bannion, Danforth thought, an Irish name. Unlike LaRoche, this man seemed well suited to his name, with his light hair and blue eyes, along with something in his manner that made it easy for Danforth to picture him in the execution yard of Kilmainham Gaol, shoulder to shoulder with Connolly and Pearce.

"Clayton has never mentioned you," Danforth said.

Bannion plucked the sprig of lavender from the lapel of his jacket and tossed it onto the ground, as if to demonstrate his distance from such foolish trappings.

"I'll be in charge of Anna once her training is finished," Bannion said.

"She's being trained for lots of things, it seems," Danforth said cautiously, hoping he might get some hint as to what the Project actually was.

"So that she can train others," Bannion said by way of explanation. His smile was bleak. "Our Joan of Arc."

This seemed a hint that the Project was much broader than Danforth had previously imagined, Anna not one of a small cadre but the spearhead of a large force.

"Train them in several different languages," Bannion added.

His accent was very faint, Danforth thought, and it seemed layered with other inflections, like a voice behind a mask.

"That's her greatest asset," Bannion said.

"Not her courage?" Danforth asked.

Bannion shrugged. "There's never a shortage of courage," he said. "It's skill that's hard to find." He appeared sad that this was the case, that humanity was very good at meeting danger, very poor at knowing what to do about it. A realization of this fallen state, mankind nobly brave but helplessly incompetent, swam into his eyes, and Danforth thought it gave him the look of a disappointed god.

"Where did you meet Clayton?" Danforth asked.

"At one of his talks at the library," Bannion said. "He seemed to think that the wealthy had an obligation to do something. I had an idea of what that might be."

"I still don't know what the Project is, by the way," Danforth told him.

"With any luck, you never will," Bannion said flatly.

"It's very ambitious, I'm sure," Danforth said. "Clayton's not one for small measures."

"Very ambitious, yes," Bannion said, clearly refusing to reveal any part of the Project. "Has he told you that I was a Communist?"

"No."

"Oh, yes, I was a great singer of the 'Internationale,'" Bannion said with edgy bitterness. "One of *those* kind of Communists." He appeared still seared by the experience, a man cheated by a clever swindler. "I wasted years of my life marching under that banner." Those lost years were obviously a source of deep resentment; Bannion seemed raw and charged with violence, a man who'd caught the only woman he had ever loved sleeping with another man. "Clayton prefers people whose gods have failed," he added.

"What god failed Anna?" Danforth asked.

To that question, Bannion gave the saddest answer Danforth had ever heard.

"Life."

Danforth felt that this was true and wondered if it was in this terrible failure she had found the steeliness he saw in her.

"Anna's going to be brought in earlier than we thought," Bannion told him. "Clayton wanted me to tell you this in person. So that we could meet. You won't have further dealings with her once she leaves for Europe."

So she would be a bird in his life, Danforth thought, a bird for whom he had briefly provided a nest and who would soon take flight and then simply disappear over the horizon.

"When is she leaving?" he asked.

"We'd like her in place within a few weeks. No later than mid-May."

"Why the hurry?"

"Because things are heating up, as I'm sure you're aware," Bannion answered.

"Where is she going?"

"There's no need for you to know that," Bannion answered. A disquiet surfaced in his eyes, as if he'd suddenly spotted trouble in the distance. "And once she's gone, you should never mention her to anyone."

"I understand," Danforth said. "I'll never say her name again."

Bannion gave no hint of how he received this declaration, only glanced to the right, where a beat-up sedan had come to a halt at the far end of the park. There were two men in the front seat and one in the back, a configuration that appeared to draw Bannion's grim attention. He waited until one of the men got out and walked into a nearby store, then he turned back to Danforth. "You should be aware that they may already be onto the Project," he said. "And if so, they'll stop at nothing. So right now, all of us have to watch our backs, because they could be anyone, anywhere."

Danforth found this assertion slightly paranoid. "Who is this mysterious 'they'?" he asked doubtfully.

"German sympathizers, of course," Bannion answered. "The type who break up anti-German rallies. If they find out what we're doing, they'll do whatever has to be done to stop it." Bannion looked at Danforth in a way that made Bannion's doubts about him quite plain. "So the point is to get Anna in place before anyone has a chance to betray her."

"I would never betray her," Danforth said firmly.

Bannion's smile was hard to read. "Let's hope you're never tested."

With that he turned and made his way across the wintry park.

There was something both comforting and scary in his determined stride, Danforth thought, the robotic severity of a man who could be trusted to do whatever had to be done, no matter how extreme. Such was the way of men whose Great Ideal had failed them, he supposed, and in that failure left scar tissue on their souls.

With Bannion gone, Danforth had no reason to remain in the park, but he found himself compelled to linger there awhile. He did not know why, save that the park gave him a sense of comfort, of rootedness. The bandstand was freshly painted, the perfect symbol of a small town whose inhabitants had no reason to mistrust the world. The still-naked trees, the distant swings, the small fountain, all of it now seemed terribly vulnerable, a naive realm that had to be protected by men like Bannion, who he suddenly imagined as quite capable of anything. This had not come from what Bannion had said but from the flinty nature of the exchange, the dead earnestness he'd seen in Bannion's eyes. Danforth knew that in a less perilous time, he would have been the last to entrust any aspect of his country's good to such a man. But now history seemed to demand the Bannions of the world, men without reserve, men without limits, men who cared little for the usual dictates of governance and who made those who could be ruled by them seem weak and dithering.

Ah, so this is what it feels like, he thought as Bannion got into the car at the far end of the park, *to lose your innocence.*

Century Club, New York City, 2001

I felt a pang of disappointment. To lose his innocence? Was this to be Danforth's story, some little moment of moral quavering?

66

If so, it was familiar in the extreme. Worse, it was irrelevant, since Danforth's personal transformation, however trivial or profound, had nothing to offer in terms of useful tactical information. I could almost hear Dr. Carlson, my superior at the center, fire off the inevitable question: *Is that all you got out of him, a tired tale of lost innocence?*

"Innocence," I said blandly, "that's a hard thing to nail down, don't you think?"

Danforth picked up the dessert menu. "Not in terms of knowing who they actually are," he said. "We always know who the innocent are."

"But as a concept, it's somewhat complicated, isn't it?" I asked.

"Only when it should more accurately be called naiveté," Danforth said. "I had a contact in the French Resistance." He continued to peruse the menu as he spoke. "He was of no great value. A courier, not much more. He was arrested and taken to Hotel Lutetia. Do you know it?"

I shook my head.

"It's at forty-five boulevard Raspail," Danforth went on. "During the war it served as Gestapo headquarters in Paris, and so there were quite a few interrogation rooms. Augustin was taken to one of these rooms, of course. He was interrogated for a while. There were a lot of people screaming in his face and a few stinging slaps, but nothing really unbearable. He didn't know anything, so he couldn't tell them anything. After a time, the treatment became more severe, and before it was over he was pretty well broken." He looked up from the menu. "The apple tart isn't bad."

I nodded.

Danforth returned to the menu, studying it thoughtfully as he continued. "All of this shouting and slapping was done by Germans."

He put down the menu and summoned the waiter. "The apple tart for me. And you, Paul?"

"I'll have the same."

The waiter stepped away.

"Out of the blue, a uniformed Paris policeman came into the room," Danforth continued. "And do you know what went through Augustin's mind? *It's over.* That's what he thought. *Here is a French policeman. He will stop this immediately.* What a wonderful thing to have believed." His smile was anything but cheerful. "And how much more wonderful had it been true." He paused, eyeing me closely, then went on. "But the French policeman simply stood at attention and watched a little more rough treatment, this time with cigarettes. I'm sure you know what I mean."

"Yes."

"And when one of Augustin's torturers took out a fresh cigarette to continue the game, this same French policeman clicked his heels and dutifully stepped over and lit it for him." He looked at me starkly. "Now *that* is a loss of innocence, Paul, a loss of belief in your own countrymen that makes my slight moral twinges by the bandstand entirely laughable."

I was relieved to hear this, since it was at one with my earlier thought and gave me to understand that wherever Danforth's tale ultimately led, it would not be to some effete notion of wounded idealism.

"You're right," I said confidently. "Perspective gets lost in little moral misgivings."

"Do you think so, Paul?" Danforth asked. "I'm more of a mind to think that perspective gets lost in moral certainties." He shrugged. "Which only means that no one was ever burned at the stake by a doubter."

Before I could reply to this curious remark, Danforth eased

back slightly, and for a moment he seemed uncertain as to how he should proceed. "So much in life comes as a surprise," he added softly, and I knew he was once again moving down the twisty path of his tale. "Things we were so sure of. People we thought we knew so well but perhaps did not know at all." He added nothing to this; instead, he craned his neck slightly, so that I heard the brittle grind of ancient bones.

"Old gears," he said. "No oil can smooth them." Then, again moving down a familiar trail, he returned to that long-ago afternoon. "She was in the woods when I got back from the bandstand," he said.

Winterset, Connecticut, 1939

She was in the woods when Danforth got back to Winterset. He caught only fleeting glimpses of her as she moved through line after gently swaying line of slender trees. She was walking slowly, as he would time and again recall, dressed in a dark blouse and a long equally dark skirt that fell below her ankles. She'd flattened her wild hair beneath the Old-World babushka common to the women he'd seen toiling in the frozen fields of Eastern Europe. In that way she suddenly seemed beyond any future assimilation, a woman fiercely, almost willfully, separated from himself and that part of his country that was most like him.

And yet, it was this that inexplicably attracted him, the allure of something so foreign it called to him in the way of indecipherable languages, and that returned him to the haunting wonder of his boyhood days. She was like a city he didn't know but wanted to, a vista he'd never seen but yearned to see. Bannion had been right. There was no shortage of courage. Every battlefield was strewn with it. But he sensed in Anna a fatalism she had long ago accepted, making her seem like a woman walking toward her future just as religious martyrs walked toward their execution sites, as if there, and only there, they would find fulfillment.

"Don't get lost," he said when he reached her. "These woods are deep."

"I never wander far," she replied.

He leaned against one of the trees and glanced back toward the house. "No more training today?"

"No, there's more," she answered.

She added nothing else, her silence like a cloak around her shoulders.

"You may be going earlier than we'd thought," he told her.

She nodded, and an errant strand of hair broke free from the scarf and curled at the side of her right ear.

"No second thoughts?" he asked.

She shook her head.

With that, she turned away from him, and for a moment continued to face away, her features now in profile, her attention focused on the stone bridge in the distance.

"Do you want to walk over there?" Danforth asked.

She nodded, and together they made their way out of the grove and into the wilder woods, with its newly sprouting undergrowth, and finally to the bridge.

During the awkward silence that followed, he made a point of not looking at her.

At last he said, "What are you thinking about?"

She stared out over the stream. "Ellis Island," she said. "The view from my window."

"Your window?"

She nodded. "I had trachoma, so I had to stay on the island for a while. My bed was near a window. I could see the big buildings. It was like a make-believe city. Especially at night. The lights fell like fireworks, only frozen."

"Very different from where you came from?" Danforth asked.

"Yes."

"Why did you leave your native country?"

"To escape the killing," Anna said.

Danforth imagined the smoldering villages of the Pale, a half a million Jews crowded into small-town ghettos where they periodically fell victim to renegades of every sort, bandits and gangs of deserters. It was a vast region through which he'd traveled with his father as a boy and through which he would pass again as a man, after the war, those same crowded villages now emptied of their Jews.

She faced him. "How about you?" she asked. "Clayton says you went everywhere when you were a child. What was the most beautiful thing you ever saw?"

He told her about Umbria, the village of Assisi, the valley that swept out from the terraces of the town, how beautiful it was, almost unreal.

"When I remember it, I see it more as a painting," he said at the end of his description.

Anna's gaze fell toward the swiftly flowing water. "And what's the most beautiful thing you've *never* seen?" she asked.

It was an odd question, Danforth thought, but he had an answer for it.

"According to my father, it's the Seto Sea from Mount Misen," he said. "He saw it, and said it was like a dream."

"Where is it?" Anna asked.

"Japan," Danforth answered. "On a little island called Miyajima."

"Then you must go there," she said. She glanced toward the house. "I'd better be getting back. LaRoche is waiting."

They turned and together walked to the house; in the distance, Danforth could see LaRoche standing on the porch, watching them.

"We still have a lot of work," LaRoche said to Anna when they reached him.

Danforth saw that LaRoche had already been told that Anna was to leave quite soon, though there was no hint that this speeded-up schedule disturbed him. And yet in the following days, small cracks began to appear in LaRoche's otherwise granite exterior. Danforth noticed it in the way he grew more tender toward Anna during their sessions, and in the way his voice lost its coldness, a change in manner that made him appear almost fatherly in regard to her. He might have been teaching her to ride a bike, Danforth thought, or erect a tent, or any of a hundred other innocuous skills, and he sensed that LaRoche had come to fear for her and so had grown more gentle, as a parent might be more gentle with a child stricken by some dread disease.

Some two weeks later, Danforth and LaRoche sat alone in the front room, enjoying the final cigars of the evening. LaRoche had drunk considerably more than usual, and in that loosened state, he began to talk about the old kingdom of Azerbaijan, where he'd spent some time in the region's busy trade-route capital of Baku.

"It was all silk and saffron then," LaRoche said in a nearly musical way that suggested he'd heard these words in a song. His eyes closed with an intoxicated languor. "With towers and minarets, and plenty of oil too. Like Texas." He leaned back, more relaxed than Danforth had ever seen him. "Everybody well fed. Even the camels." He laughed. "Especially the camels." Suddenly his face soured. "Then the czar stuck in his nose. The Azeris and the Armenians started cutting one another's throats." He stubbed out his cigar with the violence of one who knew what had been consumed in these ethnic fires. "And after the czar, the Bolsheviks."

For a moment he seemed lost in a blasted idyll. Briefly, he watched a curl of blue smoke rise from the smoldering cigar. Then he grabbed his scotch and downed it in a single, tortured gulp.

"She's a good woman, Anna," he said, then rose to his feet and walked out the door.

Danforth sensed that he was being summoned, that LaRoche had something to tell him. He walked onto the front porch, where LaRoche stood.

It was an overcast evening, neither moon nor stars, and so solid darkness surrounded them. Danforth could barely make out LaRoche's features, barely tell that another body stood near his, save for the labored sound of LaRoche's breath and the liquor he smelled on it.

"Maybe I'm getting old," LaRoche said in a voice that was hardly above a whisper. "Maybe I'm seeing things."

"What things?" Danforth asked.

"Men," LaRoche said. "Never the same ones."

"Are you telling me that you're being followed?" Danforth asked.

LaRoche shrugged. "Maybe."

"Have you told anyone else about this?" Danforth asked.

LaRoche shook his head.

"I'll speak to Clayton," Danforth assured him.

"Good," LaRoche said. "Maybe you take Anna somewhere else. Someplace so I don't know where she is." He paused, started to continue, then hesitated, making Danforth sense that he was about to hear a secret LaRoche had revealed to very few. "It's easy to break a man." For a time, he didn't speak. When at last he did, the words fell like toppling headstones. "All gone, Kruševo."

73

Kruševo, Danforth thought, and it all suddenly came clear. *The ten-day republic.*

One of Danforth's Far East business associates had been in Macedonia when the Kruševo rebellion began, and he had more than once related the horrors of its suppression, Turkish atrocities piled one upon the other like bodies in a lorry. They'd razed towns and farms, cut a blood-soaked swath of terror through the region and put thousands to flight, a pitiable throng, bitter and defeated, doomed to be forever homeless, and no doubt among whose dispirited number had been LaRoche himself.

"A man will break under the lash," LaRoche murmured softly, and now Danforth was unsure of whether LaRoche had suffered the outrages of Kruševo or inflicted them.

Danforth started to speak, but LaRoche suddenly whirled around and grabbed his arm in a tight grip. "Clayton should hide Anna," he said emphatically. "He should hide her soon." Even in the darkness, LaRoche's eyes glittered with the cold sparkle of broken glass. "And tell no one where she is."

Danforth said nothing. LaRoche's voice, drunken though it was, had been so fierce and heartrending that in the wake of his words, as the two men lingered in the night, silent and enclosed, he felt himself more adrift than ever in this new, darker world where nothing seemed entirely within anyone's control.

Century Club, New York City, 2001

"Perhaps a glass of port, Paul?" Danforth asked. He'd stopped his story abruptly and now daintily touched the corners of his mouth with a napkin. "Or are you afraid it might dull your senses?"

I took this as something of a challenge, one I felt I should meet.

"I think I can handle a port," I said.

"Good," Danforth said, his smile quite bright for one who'd just related such an ominous exchange. "A port it shall be." He summoned the waiter and ordered two glasses of a port I didn't recognize but, given Danforth's refinements of taste, assumed was excellent.

"Did Clayton do it?" I asked once the waiter had stepped away.

"Do what?"

"Hide Anna."

"No, but I did tell him what Bannion had told me at the bandstand and about the conversation with LaRoche, how worried they both had been. But Clayton decided to keep to the same road at the moment. He said Anna would be headed for Europe soon anyway. Until then, he thought her quite safe. Bannion was always overstating things, he said, and LaRoche had grown ridiculously close to Anna and was acting unprofessionally. Besides, he was sure no one had caught on to the Project."

"That's all he said?"

"Yes, and he was very convincing," Danforth said. "Clayton was always very convincing. And what he said was true. You can't run an operation if you react to every fear."

In order to keep vaguely to my mission, I asked a technical question. "What should you react to?"

"Doubt," Danforth said. "If you suddenly feel a quaver of uncertainty, you should look closely at what caused it."

"Did you feel such a quaver?" I asked. "In terms of the Project, I mean."

"Yes."

"Caused by what?"

"Clayton," Danforth answered. "He was concerned about Anna, her many guises. We were moving closer to the time when she would be sent to Europe, and so he wanted to be sure of her."

"Sure of her?"

"Who she was," Danforth said. "Sure of her story. Bannion had given Clayton a full account of himself. All those years he worked for the Communists. Strikes he'd been involved in. Organizing. He'd even gone to fight in the Spanish civil war. After that, his disillusionment. He'd tried to switch sides completely, become an informer against his old comrades. Clayton had checked out every detail of Bannion's story and knew he'd told him the truth. But Anna's past was more obscure, so he wanted to make certain of her. It's the small lies that trip you up, so that was the place to start, he said. Her story about being on Ellis Island, for example, of being held there because she had trachoma. There would be records of something like that. It would be possible to find out of she'd actually been there."

"Had she?"

"Yes," Danforth answered. A mood of reflection suddenly settled over him as the waiter brought our port. "I went there many years ago," he continued when the waiter left. "The hospital had been closed for decades by then, of course. The windows were broken and everything was open to the sea air. The room where she'd once been kept was littered with debris and there were piles of dead leaves in the corners."

"You went to her actual room?" I asked.

"It was a ward, but yes, I went there," Danforth answered. "She'd remembered exactly her view from her window. She was able to describe it accurately. It was rather simple to locate the room, a matter of angles."

Danforth was not one for drawing word pictures, but I suddenly imagined the scene, an old man in a black cashmere overcoat, his hands deep in his pockets, alone in an abandoned hospital room, the ghostly image of a little girl no doubt playing in his mind: the child dressed in a hospital gown, sitting on the side of a bed, her skin olive, and with wildly curly hair.

76

"Everything is a matter of coordinates, Paul, of intersections," Danforth continued. "Standing in the room where Anna had been kept on Ellis Island, thinking in that abandoned room of that little girl, knowing all I'd learned by then, it was easy to gather the coordinates of her experience. A person is like a leaf. You pick it up. You hold it up to the sun, note the veins, how they spread out from the central stem, and suddenly, it's all there. What she was. What she did. Why she did it. Everything."

He stopped abruptly, and something in his demeanor, a raw sadness, told me simply to wait until he spoke again.

"Anyway," he said after a long moment. "Clayton wanted me to get to know her a little better and report back to him. And so I decided to see her under less formal circumstances. Not just in the office or at the house, but in a more . . . intimate setting." He took a quick sip of port. "Have you ever heard of Vera Atkins?"

I shook my head.

"During the war she ran a secret operation out of England," Danforth said. "Women were smuggled into France in order to —"

"We were talking about Anna," I blurted before I could stop myself; there was a sharpness in my tone that surprised and unnerved me a little. "Sorry," I added quickly, "I just —"

"I'm sorry too," Danforth interrupted, and he appeared to mean it genuinely; his discursive narrative was not a storyteller's tactic designed to keep the hook in place but merely the tangled product of an aged mind. "It's just that talking about Anna, it brought back how brave they were, the women of the war. They should build a memorial to them someday, Paul. A bronze sculpture in Washington or on Whitehall. Something quiet, but suggestive, to remind us of their sacrifice." A look of utter heartbreak swam into his face. "It's the lost we must remember, Paul. The ones who never had a chance to sit by the fire and lift their grandchildren into their laps and tell them the stories of their service."

"Of course," I said sincerely.

For a moment we seemed to reach another level in our understanding, not only of each other but of what was truly owed to those toward whom history had not been kind.

"Anyway, about Anna," Danforth continued, then stopped. He seemed at sea in his own tale. "Forgive me, Paul, but where was I?"

"You said Clayton wanted you to find out more about her," I reminded him.

Danforth nodded. "Yes, that's right. But without asking her questions directly. The idea was for me to insinuate myself into her life." Suddenly a pained smile formed on his lips, and a faint sadness came into his eyes. "And so I became a spy."

"Did you find anything surprising about her?" I asked.

"No," Danforth said. "The surprise was about me."

Oak Bar, Plaza Hotel, New York City, 1939

She arrived exactly on time, dressed in the business clothes she'd worn to the office. In a quick aside earlier that day, Danforth had conveyed to Anna what he called "Clayton's latest instructions" — they should be seen together in more casual settings — along with the fact that Clayton had given no reason for this. That was typical of Clayton, Danforth had added with a small shrug designed to dismiss the importance of the meetings; it was part of Clayton's "shadowy style."

Anna had nodded quickly in response, like a soldier under orders, then agreed to meet Danforth at the Plaza that evening.

"Hello," she said as she took a seat opposite Danforth. She glanced about but said nothing else, though it seemed to him that she had immediately absorbed various aspects of the room—the dark paneling, the lighted bar, the older man with his young mistress—that she had made careful note and would be able to recall these things, as a musician might remember the melody of a theme heard only once.

"Would you like something to drink?" Danforth asked. "Perhaps a glass of wine?"

"I'd rather have a cup of tea," Anna said. She drew the scarf from her head, and in the way he'd noticed many times before, she seemed momentarily uncomfortable, as if even this modest disrobing was inappropriately seductive. She reminded him of the serving girls of Ireland who kept their eyes averted even as they placed or removed plates, as if doing otherwise would somehow compromise their chastity. How old it truly was, he thought, the Old World.

He motioned the barmaid over to the table and ordered.

They talked of nothing in particular. The wine and tea came. Danforth lifted his glass in a toast. "To your success," he said.

She smiled softly, touched his glass with her cup, then focused her attention on a young couple who'd taken a remote corner table, their hands locked together, their gaze intensely fixed on each other, everything else quite invisible to them.

"They must be in love," she said.

The way she said it had an eerie inwardness to it that made Danforth recall the death of Henry Stanley, the great explorer. He'd lived near Big Ben at the end, and not long before his death, the great bell had sounded, a somber accounting that had awakened an inexpressible understanding in him. "How strange," Stanley had murmured, "so that is time."

Danforth had no idea how to say any of this, however, and so he said, "I take it you've never been in love?"

She shook her head. "No," she said. "And you?"

He thought of Cecilia, with whom he'd been out only the night before, how bright her smile was, the life that sparkled in her, the happiness she offered him, everything, everything but . . . what?

"Yes," he said, and put that *but . . . what?* aside.

"It must be wonderful," Anna said.

"I'm sure you'll know someday," Danforth told her.

She nodded crisply, as if cutting off an irrelevant discussion. "I'm leaving for Europe soon," she told him.

This news, coming to him by way of Anna herself, made her imminent departure more real, and Danforth felt the disquiet not only of her going but of the loss of some vital opportunity. It was as if he'd made a minimal offer on something small and precious but had lost it to a higher bidder.

"Would you like to have dinner?" he asked, since there now seemed little else he could give her. "We could have it in the Palm Garden."

Anna considered this a moment. "No," she said finally. "Let's have it at my apartment. If you don't mind leftovers."

"Your apartment?"

"Wouldn't you like to see where I live?"

In anyone else, the question might have been fraught with romantic tension, but coming from Anna it seemed only a closer adherence to Clayton's suggestion that they be together in more intimate settings.

"All right," Danforth said. "I'll call for a taxi."

"No," Anna said immediately. "Let's take the bus."

And so they did, a long ride down Fifth Avenue, past Saks' lighted windows filled with the clothes of the coming summer season, brightly colored bathing suits and leisurewear, the loose-fitting garb of the city's moneyed class. The clothing would be bought and bundled up and taken out to the Hamptons or Fire Island or, farther still, Wellfleet or Martha's Vineyard, the looming war in Europe causing the only change in this yearly migration, Paris and Rome abruptly no longer on the itinerary.

Below Thirty-fourth Street, the avenue darkened as they entered a landscape of closed shops, small and unlighted, the purveyors of cheap clothes and costume jewelry already home with their families in Brooklyn, Queens, or the Bronx and whose absence drained some unmistakably vital energy from the city.

The bus moved steadily southward, these same modest shops now giving way to a line of brick walkups and finally to the huddled streets of the Lower East Side.

Night had fallen by then, but if there was safety in numbers, these streets were the safest in New York. For here, the people resided in close quarters, the spaciousness of the outer boroughs still unavailable to them. And so they lived stacked above tailor shops and bakeries and small groceries. Here, in the evening, they crowded the concrete stoops and spoke to one another in old-country tongues and dressed in clothes that seemed to be handed down not from older sibling to younger but from one generation to the next.

Anna appeared as comfortable in the human current of these streets as a dolphin in the sea. Here all the world knew her and greeted her, and on the way to her apartment, she stopped many times to inquire if this child was still sick or that brother still in some far town.

On each of these stops, she introduced Danforth as her employer, then went on to speak awhile before motioning him down the street. During these intervals, Danforth stood, alien and aloof, waiting, sometimes impatiently, to move on and even slightly offended that Anna appeared either oblivious or indifferent to the odd position in which she had placed him.

The entrance to her building was over a shop whose metal staircase was covered in signs with Hebrew lettering. The shop window was filled with a curious array of objects, none of which Danforth recognized, save for the peculiar candelabrum the Jews called a *menorah* and that he knew they lit only for some holiday. Fringed prayer shawls were displayed on shelves, along with what appeared to be matching cases, and these too had Hebrew lettering. There was also a small table covered with silver-plated and ceramic chalices of various sizes. The entire display struck Danforth as typical of the Ostjuden, whose superstitions his father had often derided and whose tradesmen he'd scornfully dismissed as peddlers.

"I live on the fourth floor," Anna said as they entered the lobby of the building.

From his first step up the stairs, Danforth was aware of the odors that engulfed and swirled around him. They were flat and heavy, and they gave an oily feel to the air. He'd smelled similar food in the street stalls of the Jewish quarter in Warsaw but had never eaten anything sold there. "And they call what we eat *treif*," his father had said contemptuously, and with a quickening step, he'd hustled him back toward the far more stylish eateries of the city.

"It's really not such a difficult climb," Anna said when they reached the fourth-floor landing.

"Not at all," Danforth told her, though he found it necessary to disguise his slightly labored breathing.

Anna swung open the door of her apartment, stepped inside, and turned on the light.

The light revealed a room that surprised Danforth considerably more than anything Anna had said or done since he'd met her. For although located in what had seemed to him a sea of Eastern European Jewishness, her apartment revealed none of the ritual objects sold in the shop below, nothing to suggest anything but a secular life.

"How long have you lived here?" he asked.

"A long time," she answered.

He walked over to the window that looked out on the noisy street below, a teeming world that reminded him more of Calcutta than New York.

"Please, sit down," she said.

He lowered himself into one of the plain wooden chairs and glanced at the small table to his right, where a lamp rested on a rectangle of cloth whose weave Danforth immediately noticed.

"The mat," he said. "I saw some that looked very much like it in Istanbul. They make carpets with the same weave. They last forever, but people here don't like the way the colors aren't uniform." He shrugged. "Handmade objects aren't perfect, and customers like perfection."

She offered no response to this but instead turned and disappeared into the tiny kitchen. He couldn't see her at work, but he had no trouble hearing the clatter of pans and plates as she made dinner.

While she worked, Danforth surveyed the room, noting its spare furniture, all of which might easily have been rescued from the street. There was a table large enough for two, a few chairs, a small desk, a bookshelf bulging with old books, most with cracked spines, which she'd probably bought in one of the many used-book stores that lined Fourth Avenue below Fourteenth Street. It was a hand-me-down décor, every object bearing signs of long use, nicks and scratches, even an odd burn where someone years before had let a cigarette slip from the ashtray to char a wooden surface. Even so, he found that he couldn't say for certain whether she'd furnished her quarters with such worn-out furniture because she didn't have the money to buy anything new or out of some strange attraction to the broken and the wobbly, things cast aside or left for junk.

But it was the map that drew Danforth's attention. It was spread out over the table near him, a map of Europe with small marks along the southern coast of France. Dark lines moved along the roads and rivers of this map, and near these lines there were yet more dots, some with notations. Some of these notations were in French, some in Spanish, some in German, and there were others he couldn't read, though he recognized the letters as Cyrillic.

"You speak Russian?" Danforth called to her.

"Yes," she said. "And Ukrainian."

"I would love to study the Slavic languages someday," Danforth said.

"You can go to the table now," Anna said when she came out of the kitchen.

Danforth did as he was told, then watched as she set the table: two plates, one slightly cracked at the edge, mismatched utensils and cloth napkins, and two large water glasses, neither of which, he was relieved to see, was chipped at the mouth.

They ate a few minutes later, food clearly left over from the day before, hearty peasant food, as Danforth would have described it, and which he'd eaten during his travels when he'd been waylaid by weather or other circumstances and ended up in some small hotel that served local fare.

"Very tasty," he said at one point.

"Good," Anna said. She tore off a piece of pumpernickel bread and offered it to him. "Try this."

From time to time, he thought he was being evaluated in some way, put through an arcane test, and for that reason found himself not altogether comfortable. The less fortunate always had a way of mocking the rich. He'd seen its various forms throughout the world, the petty signals of their ridicule. It came in half-concealed winks and smiles, or was spoken in the shared idioms of both the idle and the working poor. The rich were always fops to them, always inept, protected from the storms of life and therefore assumed to be unable to weather them. Rickshaw pullers had guffawed at his approach, then bowed to him with an exaggeration that burned with comic ridicule. Ferrymen had done the same, and taxi drivers everywhere. It was class and ethnic war fought with smirks and muttered asides, and he wondered if this dinner might not be some version of it.

Then, rather suddenly, Anna said, "Does anyone know you?"

"What?" he asked, completely taken aback by both the frankness and the intimacy of her question.

"Does anyone know you?" she repeated. "At the office, no one does."

Without willing it, he ran down the list of those who might be expected to know him — his long-standing social and business associates, his few relatives, and finally his father and Cecilia — asking himself which one knew him, really, truly knew him, and arriving at a single disturbing answer: *No one.*

He started to say exactly that to Anna but stopped when his eye caught the one thing in the room that didn't appear to have been bought at a consignment shop or rescued from the street. It was a relief, made of leather. It showed a street scene, one-story buildings crowded together, almost everything in brown save for the places where the artist had carved small flowers from red leather and sewn them into tiny baskets or hung them from balconies.

"I've seen something like that before," he said. "It's from a famous leather shop in Córdoba that's been there for generations."

"Yes," Anna said. She smiled. "My father used to talk about the sunflowers in Spain. He said you could travel from Madrid to Barcelona and never have them out of view."

"That's true," Danforth said. "Your family came from Spain?"

"Yes," Anna said. "From Córdoba, as a matter of fact."

Suddenly Danforth no longer imagined Anna's ancestors

digging potatoes from the unforgiving ground of the Pale but strolling the flowered streets of Córdoba and walking beneath the red-striped arches of its famed *mezquita*. In some sense, she seemed more the daughter of that sun-baked people, darker and more physically graceful than the lowly street peddlers of Delancey.

"Córdoba," he said, and with that word entertained the possibility that the name Klein had been given to her, as so many names had been given at Ellis Island, and this, combined with the utter lack of any religious objects, raised an even more extraordinary possibility. "So you're . . . Spanish . . . not —"

"No, I'm not Spanish," Anna interrupted. "My father had never been to Spain. But he told me about the sunflowers because his father had told him about them, and his father before that, and so on down the line." A single eyebrow arched, but it was enough for him to see a not altogether cheerful change in her expression. "You'd rather I were Spanish, wouldn't you?"

She said this as if she were merely curious as to the arcane workings of Danforth's mind, but he immediately understood what she was thinking and couldn't keep back a self-conscious laugh.

"No, not at all," he assured her quickly. "I was just curious about your forebears."

He could tell that she didn't believe this innocent explanation. Nor should she have believed it, he thought, because his question hadn't come from some general interest but from the prison of his own upbringing, his father's often stated contempt for what he called "the riffraff of the East," by which he meant its black-frocked Jews, to his eyes so unsightly, with their white shirts and dangling curls, scattered across a thousand muddy villages or heaped in roiling masses in the ghettos of Warsaw and Lodz, a people he clearly loathed.

"My forebears," Anna repeated, and let the matter drop. They moved on to other subjects.

But even as they talked of other things, her gaze remained intense, and Danforth felt layers of himself peeling away, the sense that she knew what he had not known about himself until moments before but that he now accepted with a piercing recognition and repeated in his mind as the night wore on: *I am an anti-Semite.*

Century Club, New York City, 2001

"It was strange to realize this particular element of myself," Danforth said. He leaned back slowly. "Here I was, involved in a project whose mission was to thwart Germany's plan for world conquest, opening my house to this effort, and yet all the time I was in some sense a sympathizer with at least one of Nazism's frankly stated aims." The tone of his voice darkened by a shade. "I wanted to make Anna something else. Something . . . anything but a Jew. Isn't that a kind of extermination?"

When I didn't answer, he smiled quietly.

"The human heart," he added softly but with a searing word of warning, "is a twisty little thing, Paul."

With that last remark, he returned to the thread of his tale. "I must say that, except for this rather embarrassing moment of self-disclosure, we had a nice meal, Anna and I. Very modest. Some kind of stew."

He seemed once again seated in a cramped apartment, rather than in the spacious dining room of the Century Club.

"A humble life," he added quietly. "There are good things about it, believe me. Good things about a small apartment with a few books, some music."

I knew that something was going on inside Danforth's mind, that he was both here, seated at our elegant table, and there, at Anna's far less elegant one. But he was also somewhere else, beyond both places, a man standing on a bridge that joined two remote islands.

I let him remain there, suspended, holding to some imaginary rail. Then, cautiously, I said, "So, was this the first of many such dinners with Anna?"

"No," Danforth answered. "There was no time for that."

"Why?"

He took a step forward in his narrative. "Clayton," he said. "He suddenly became quite worried."

"About what?"

"That Bannion and LaRoche might have been right after all," Danforth said. "That Anna was in danger."

Clayton and he had stood under the New York Public Library's great stone portico and stared out over Fifth Avenue, he said, the usual collection of cars and buses in a noisy metal stampede, New York at full gallop, a city, he'd naively thought, that nothing could ever make, even for a single falling instant, catch its breath.

"But we know better now, don't we, Paul?" he asked.

"We do indeed," I said, surprised that my throat could still grow taut at what had been done to the city, planes hurled so unexpectedly at its shining face that they'd seemed like rocks cast at us from the distant age of stoning.

Danforth saw my smoldering anger at this barbaric outrage, and its undiminished heat seemed to press him forward in his tale.

"We met at the library," he said, like one returning a storm-tossed boat to a peaceful cove. "Looking down on those quiet lions."

"Thanks for meeting me," Clayton said. "I know you have a date with Cecilia, but I needed to tell you something."

Danforth said nothing. He had learned to wait.

"I've decided to move Anna to a different place," Clayton said. "I don't think it's safe for her to stay where she is now."

"Why the sudden change?"

Clayton glanced about in the way of a man being watched, then drew a single sheet of paper from his jacket pocket. "This."

Danforth took the paper and opened it. Inside there was a drawing of a Star of David hung in a noose, a design he would see repeated many times over the years, in an alley in Montpelier, on a wall in Bologna, splashed inside a metro station in Madrid, where a scrawl had been added: *Gracias a Isabella*.

"It came yesterday," Clayton said. "A pretty clear warning, don't you think?"

Danforth folded the paper and handed it back to him.

"I've been rather vocal in my opposition to the anti-Semitic goings-on in Germany," Clayton added. "This could have come from someone who heard me. It may have nothing to do with Anna, but I don't want to take that chance, so she won't be going to Winterset or the office anymore."

"So she's in hiding, that's what you're saying?" Danforth asked.

"Yes," Clayton said.

"When will I see her again?" Danforth asked.

"You won't," Clayton answered flatly.

In the years to come, Danforth would relive this moment with great vividness. He would feel again, often but always as if for the first time, the hollow sensation that comes with the sudden and irrecoverable loss of something secretly held dear, cherished so secretly, in fact, that he had scarcely been aware of it himself.

"So," Clayton said coolly, "I'll be in touch."

Danforth nodded, and the two men parted as unceremoniously as they'd met, Clayton back into the bowels of the great library, Danforth down its wide stairs and out onto the avenue.

He'd planned to meet Cecilia at the theater, a short walk from the library, and as he moved through the onrushing crowd, he realized that he now felt sidelined, like some rookie at a game. He allowed this resentment to mask the actual nature of his distress, which was the abrupt departure of Anna from his life, the emptying he'd felt at the news of her going, and as he walked, he worked to restore his equanimity before he met Cecilia outside the theater.

By the time he met her, his resentment at being relegated to a bit player had dissipated, leaving him with only the dull ache of Anna's departure, an unsettled state Cecilia immediately recognized.

"You look quite out of sorts, Tom," she said.

"I'm fine." He took her arm and smiled as brightly as he could. "Really."

The play was a farce, with much slamming of doors, and with each new twist of fate or identity, Danforth withdrew more from the action. He could hear the audience's laughter, but he joined in it only rarely, so that he often noticed Cecilia glancing toward him, vaguely troubled by his mood.

After the show, they walked through the unseasonably warm night to Sardi's. The crowd was young and loud, and terribly theatrical, and Danforth suddenly felt himself much older than these happy youths, so cheerful and optimistic despite the darkening times.

"What's wrong, Tom?" Cecilia asked after they'd been seated at the table for a moment.

Looking at her, he thought, *She knows.*

She knows that the life he'd foreseen with her has lost its luster and now appears to him like a ruined garden, its once-bright flowers dry and shriveled.

She knows that she could never be a part of this other life he now imagines for himself, that no matter how vague his vision of it, how lacking in detail, she, more than anyone, remains outside it.

She knows that if he were to cast aside this other, half-hidden vision and once again commit himself to a future with her, he would eventually be undone by his own painful effort to pursue that life, would give himself over to drink or squalid little affairs as her father had, and that, like her father, he would awaken each morning to the smoldering regret that he had not reached for the other life that had once beckoned him.

She knows that she had ignored the many signs he'd given over the past few weeks and that she cannot ignore them any longer.

She touched his hand. "Tell me," she said with surprising resignation, and Danforth realized that he must have long been giving off indications of whatever change had now completely overtaken him.

"I'm not sure exactly," he said, knowing that this was true, that his feelings were a mixture whose disparate elements he couldn't pin down but that he felt growing ever more volatile. He knew that he was not in love with Anna Klein, though without doubt he was intrigued by her. But love, surely, was more than curiosity, and he'd known other women who, like Anna, seemed reluctant to reveal themselves.

"You must tell me, Tom," Cecilia said. "I have a right to know."

He had no answer for her, and knew it, and so he said, "I com-

mitted to something a few months ago. Something that has . . .
I don't know . . . made me . . . unhappy."

He would always remember Cecilia's face at that moment.
She had the look of a woman who believed that Danforth's un-
happiness was but the first of many unpleasant obstacles that
lay ahead for her and who realized that the promises of life were
merely false claims; that life itself was a carnival barker's prom-
ising the wonders of the Alligator Man who turned out to be
only a boy with a dreadful skin disease.

She offered him that look for only a few seconds before she
rose.

"We should go now," she said.

Danforth got to his feet, and the two of them walked back out
into the night. The crowd had thinned by then, and so they were
able to walk shoulder to shoulder without being jostled. They'd
made the stroll hand in hand before; they were not touching
now.

They walked across town, then swung north on Fifth Avenue.
A few blocks to the south, the library gave off an eerie glow, and
Danforth recalled his meeting with Clayton, the unsettling news
he'd received, and felt again the strange pang he'd felt at that
moment.

"I really am sorry," he said to Cecilia.

She took him in her arms, held him briefly, then let him go,
turned, and moved quickly away from him, taking with her, as
Danforth would later realize, the last chance he would ever have
for an ordinary life.

Century Club, New York City, 2001

"I saw Cecilia very rarely after that evening at the theater," Danforth told me. "She married in 1941 and had a daughter about a

year later. Then the war came along. Her husband was wounded on Guadalcanal and shipped back to the States. On the way to visit him in the hospital, she swerved off the road. They were both lost."

"Both?"

"Cecilia and her daughter," Danforth said. His attention seemed directed more toward an approaching object than one in the distant past. "Her name was Audrey, and I suppose you could say she was a casualty of war." His gaze drifted back to me. "Would you say she was innocent, Paul?"

"Of course."

"Hmm," Danforth said softly.

Briefly, he looked away from me, as he might have looked away from a fact too boldly stated.

"Anna," I said, to nudge him back onto the now-familiar road we were both moving down. "She was taken to an undisclosed location, I imagine?"

"Undisclosed?" Danforth asked.

"Well, wasn't she being hidden?"

"Yes."

"But clearly you saw her again," I said.

"How do you know that, Paul?"

"Well, your story is about her, isn't it?"

Danforth smiled. "No, my story is about treachery, and the need one can feel to kill a traitor at all costs." His shrug suggested a coldness I hadn't seen before. "Killing someone who deserves killing isn't difficult," he added. "I could do it without blinking." His eyes sparkled with what seemed genuine purpose and resolve, and I saw that he meant exactly what he said. Thomas Jefferson Danforth was not a man who would waver in the face of villainy; a traitor in his hands would hang at dawn.

"But as you say, I did see Anna again," he continued. "After only a couple of weeks, as a matter of fact." He signaled the waiter and asked that his water goblet be refilled. "I get dry," he explained. When the waiter had filled his glass and stepped away, he took a slow sip, then returned to the subject at the point we'd broken off. "For as it turned out, Anna's whereabouts were disclosed to me. Bannion had been called away, Clayton told me, and Anna had to be resupplied." He allowed himself a small laugh. "That was the word he used. *Resupplied.* Like a military unit." His laughter trailed off. "Which is what I suppose she was, by then." Again he sank back into his past, sank back fully and with such ghostly ease that time seemed only a mist through which he could effortlessly pass, carried on a carpet of memory to some long-lost door.

214 West Ninety-fifth Street, New York City, 1939

He knocked softly, and waited for the door to open.

"Clayton told me you were coming," Anna said when she opened the door and saw him standing on the tiny landing. "He must trust you." She glanced at the large bags Danforth held in his arms. "You'd probably like to put those down." She stepped out of his path. "Come in."

Danforth walked into the apartment, waited until she closed the door, then followed her into the small kitchen, where he placed the bags on the table by the window.

"Do you think this is all rather extreme," Anna asked, "this hiding me away?"

"I don't know," Danforth admitted. "But you are . . ." He stopped because he felt a vulnerability he didn't want her to see.

"What?"

"Valuable," Danforth said, "to the Project." He shrugged. "Whatever the Project is."

She began to empty the bags. "How did you explain my leaving work?"

"A sick relative," Danforth answered. "No one questioned it. Why would they? It's a common story." He drew in a quick breath. "Anyway, I've brought you two weeks' worth of provisions."

"Would you like something to drink?" she asked.

"Coffee," he said. "If you have it."

"I have it."

She sent him to the front room, made the coffee, then joined him. By then, he was sitting in the chair by the window. In the distance, he could see the private school he'd attended as a child, all the boys in suits.

"You have a nice view of the children of the privileged class." He took a sip from his cup. "You'd probably find their parents rather shallow."

"No," Anna said. "Just lucky."

He wanted to tell her that the privileged were perhaps less lucky than she imagined, that for all their many advantages, they were blocked from certain of life's core experiences. They could know great grief certainly, and great loss. They could fall victim to a thousand random horrors. But there was a desperate hunger they could not know: the shaping rigor of actual need. He was not at all sure she would understand this, however, and so what came from him was a simple "I'm sorry. I didn't want you to leave without telling you that. I'm truly sorry."

"Sorry about what?" Anna asked.

"That business about your being Spanish," Danforth explained. "You must have found that very insulting."

She shrugged.

"It would never affect what I feel about you personally," Danforth said cautiously. "The respect I have for you, for what you're doing." He shook his head at the terrible inadequacy of what he was saying, how it seemed he was only digging a deeper grave for himself. "This must all sound so hollow to you." He placed his cup firmly on the table beside him. "I respect you, that's what I mean. I truly respect you, and I respect what you're doing."

She went back to the kitchen and continued to empty the bags. "You won't have to come again," she told him. "I'm leaving for France in a few days."

"France?" he said, following her into the kitchen.

"Yes."

"Alone?"

"Of course."

She continued to busy herself with the bags, but Danforth saw a quick succession of emotions flash in her eyes: first dread, then the immediate suppression of it. In that moment, she seemed carved from will alone. He could not imagine her as a child, or even as a teenager, and he sensed that during her youth, she had been aged by a hardship she had yet to reveal, aged so deeply and thoroughly that her soul was now like one of those ancient coins his father imported, so scuffed and striated no polish could ever make them shine. If she ever kissed a man, he thought, it would be beneath the Bridge of Sighs.

"Well, I should be on my way," he said, and walked to the door.

"Goodbye," she said, without offering her hand.

He lingered in a way that he thought must surely seem unaccountable to her, as if he were waiting for something to be returned.

"And thanks again," she added. "For everything."

Outside, Danforth stood for a moment in front of her building, glancing up and down the street, before turning westward, heading aimlessly toward Columbia. At Columbia Walk, he sat down on the stairs and peered out at the university library, the names of the great inscribed across its wide façade,

Homer, Sophocles, Plato, and the like. First at Trinity and later at Princeton, he had studied them all, but it struck him that they were of little use to him now, that the choices he would make during the next stage of his life would be determined without reference to his education or what his travels had taught him or even anything he'd heard in any of the languages he spoke.

Danforth suddenly thought of the cold glint in the eye of the warlord commander of those Balkan thugs, how he must have had the same look when he'd ordered the crucifixion of that hapless man, how he must have felt nothing as he'd watched him hang there, stripped to the waist, his arms and legs and feet streaked with blood. The passengers had been herded back into the train once the thieves had stolen whatever they could find. As if boarding a train at Victoria Station, he and his father had calmly reclaimed their seats, then felt the train lurch forward. He could still remember the wave of relief that had swept over him at that instant, but now he recalled something else more vividly: that in the midst of that relief, with the train inching forward, he'd glanced out the window and actually admired the beauty of the countryside until the crucified man came once again into view. Danforth had assumed him dead, but as the train dragged past, the man had lifted his head and stared Danforth directly in the eyes.

Nothing as heartrending had happened to him since, and as he sat on the stairs at Columbia, the memory of it lingered in his mind until he noticed a tall young woman with long blond hair. She was moving swiftly across Columbia Walk, her books clutched to her breast. She would graduate and marry and raise her children in a large house, Danforth knew. She would fill her middle years with works of civic charity, and in later life be many times honored with plaques and citations. In old age, she would sit in a white gazebo and oversee her gardens, minding that the irises be thinned out in the fall and that the fountain, modeled on one she'd admired in Ravello, be each week cleaned and polished.

Suddenly Danforth felt a terrible hollowness; it did not fall away as he'd expected it to but grew as the days passed, and by the weekend he seemed to be disappearing into a vast emptiness that felt, truly, like death.

Century Club, New York City, 2001

"Regret becomes self-accusation in the end," Danforth told me. "And the deepest accusation of them all is that you settled for an inadequate life."

"And for you, what would that inadequate life have been?" I asked.

"It would have been to be that blond girl's husband," Danforth answered flatly. "When you get right down to it, that was my terror. The lights were going out all over Europe, but my chief concern was that I not end up like one of those people Fitzgerald wrote about, sitting in their clubs, setting down their drinks, dreaming their old best dreams."

He had circled back to his first reference, a narrative trick I couldn't help admiring.

"What did you think I was going to say, Paul?" he asked. "What did you think I was going to tell you about my motivation at that moment?"

"Oh, perhaps that you needed to prove that you weren't an anti-Semite like your father," I answered.

"Oedipal loathing," Danforth said. "That's fueled a few tales, no doubt about it. But not this one, Paul." He shook his head. "No, my thinking wasn't complicated. You wouldn't need Sophocles to figure it out. It was the young bourgeois's dread of being bourgeois."

"The Sorrows of Young Danforth," I added, with no doubt that he would get my literary allusion.

"A precise reference," Danforth said. "And very German." He laughed softly, but it was a troubled laugh. "As you are, Paul," he added.

"Yes."

"But an American now, with an English name," Danforth added. "Working for our country's good."

I had no idea what Danforth meant by this remark, but something in his gaze alarmed me so that I suddenly retreated to the safety of my notes. "So," I said, "you were a young bourgeois afraid of a bourgeois life."

"Yes," Danforth said. "As I suspect Clayton well understood when we talked at Winterset that day."

Winterset, Connecticut, 1939

"Thanks for coming, Robert," Danforth said as he opened the door.

"You made it sound urgent."

They headed out across the wide yard, Clayton dressed in slacks and an open-collared shirt. He'd draped his Princeton sweater over his shoulders, as if he were going to the game against Yale.

"I want to go with Anna," Danforth said bluntly. "I've thought it through. I've gone over what it means. But I want to go with her. I want to be a part of this . . . Project."

Clayton watched as a breeze swept the end of the yard, sending a few long-dead leaves forward raggedly, like a column of deserters.

"I want to be a part of the Project," Danforth repeated a tad more vehemently.

He would never be sure if what he'd felt at that moment was terror or elation. He knew only that the narrow stream of his life had abruptly widened.

"Did you hear me, Robert?" Danforth asked.

Clayton continued to look away, as if trying to gather his thoughts. When he turned back to Danforth, his face seemed to have lost the last vestiges of its youth.

"You don't even know what the Project is," Clayton said.

"I don't care what it is."

"Don't be ridiculous, Tom," Clayton said. "Hard slogging's not for you."

Later, Danforth would recall Clayton's remark often. He would recall it as he tramped through the mud and snow of blasted villages, and as he sat, waylaid for hours, in storm-beleaguered airports and railway stations, although those difficulties hardly compared to those that still awaited him then.

"I also feel that Anna shouldn't go alone," Danforth added urgently.

"But that was always the plan," Clayton said. "She expects to go alone."

"But there's no reason why she should," Danforth said. "I'd be the perfect cover, wouldn't I? An importer with plenty of business reasons to be in Europe. And I have contacts. If things got really hot, I'd have the best chance of getting both of us out."

"This is not a game, Tom," Clayton reminded him. "The next step is a big one. We're talking about an indefinite period in Europe, not a weekend lark."

"I know," Danforth answered. "I have people who can take over the business. I'll tell my father that Danforth Imports is getting long in the tooth, that it needs new contacts, new sources. That maybe I need rejuvenation too."

In later years, Danforth would hear his argument with the sad amusement of an old man confronting the young one he'd once been, and each time he did so, he would remember that Clayton had not once betrayed any feeling for Anna or given the slightest indication that he expected her to survive her mission, whatever it was. Because of that, as his mind careened from villain to villain, Danforth would forever wonder if Clayton had always known that, whether on this mission or the next, Anna would find a way to die.

"What about Cecilia?" Clayton asked.

"That's already settled."

This seemed genuinely to surprise Clayton but also to move him one step farther toward considering Danforth's proposition.

"Anna is not some little spy," Clayton said. "What we have in mind is a large effort. We're not talking about her sitting around with a wireless, tapping out messages. There will be a lot of movement. Difficult logistics, once the operation is afoot." He looked at Danforth very seriously. "You could be killed."

Danforth realized that only a few weeks before, he would not have been able to tell if this was a genuine warning or just one of Clayton's inflations.

"I know," Danforth said.

Clayton studied him a moment. "I'll talk to Bannion," he said. "He was the one who actually thought of the Project. He has a right to have some say in what I decide."

"I understand," Danforth told him.

With that, they walked back to Clayton's car and said goodbye to each other. Danforth returned to the house, took a seat at the small table where he and LaRoche and Anna had shared their first meal. Then in his mind he journeyed farther back, to the tavern where he'd first seen Anna, frantic and befuddled, a street grotesque in the making, and finally back to that first bit of conversation with Clayton, the small fuse he'd lit, which was now burning more brightly than he'd ever expected. How odd that his own good fortune could prove so hollow, he thought, that the life of a secret agent could attract him so, that for him the pursuit of happiness would seek its measure in the pursuit of peril, and that in this pursuit he would feel for this new life — as he suddenly realized he did — a surprisingly charged tingle of desire.

Century Club, New York City, 2001

Desire?

The curious emergence of this word in the context of his story must have been visible in my face, because Danforth suddenly grew very still, then said, "They are strange, the erotics of intrigue."

The erotics of intrigue? I wondered if Danforth was now leading me into the boudoir of his mind.

"I would sometimes imagine myself endlessly strolling the old streets of Gion at dusk," Danforth continued, "forever strolling among the geisha and the *maiko.*"

"When would you feel this?" I asked.

"In the prisons and on the trains," Danforth said. "When I thought of her."

"Of Anna?"

He was clearly reaching for something whose touch still pained him.

"*Geisha* means 'artist' in Japanese," he said.

For a moment he seemed to dissolve into his own memory. "Love as performance, as something . . . acted."

It was obvious to me that this was too sensitive a subject for anyone but Danforth alone to pursue, and so I said nothing.

"The 'smile of smiles,' Blake called it," Danforth added. "It's where love and deception meet."

After this, he fell silent for a time. Then, quite surprisingly, he smiled. "Tell me, Paul, have you ever seen *North by Northwest*?"

This question, along with his abrupt change in mood, sent my mind spinning. "The old Hitchcock movie?" I asked. "The one with Cary Grant?"

"Yes," Danforth said. His tone took on a slight eeriness, as if his story had now become one of strange occurrences, though the sort that were more ironic than supernatural, the freakishness of real life. "It happened just like that." He nodded in the general direction of the club's entrance. "Right there."

Century Club, New York City, 1939

The rain had begun just as Danforth stepped out of the Century Club. He didn't have an umbrella, and so he turned to the left, toward Fifth Avenue, planning to sprint to the corner, find a shop, buy an umbrella. That was when he felt a grip on his arm that was sharper than any he had ever known; when he looked down toward the grasp that held him, he half expected to see black talons rather than a hand. Then he felt a similar grip on his other arm.

He saw two men, one on either side of him.

"Don't speak," the man to his left said gruffly. He was dressed in a dark blue double-breasted suit and wore a gray fedora. "You're dead if you do."

The second man wore a brown suit, also double-breasted, but no hat. He nodded toward a car that idled beside the curb just at the club's entrance. A third man, this one in a dark green single-breasted suit and wearing a brown hat, had already opened the door and seemed to be grimly awaiting Danforth's decision.

"Move forward and don't speak," the man in the fedora said.

The one in the brown suit tightened his grip but then added a slight, surprisingly warm smile. "You're too young to die, Mr. Danforth."

It was dread, and dread alone, that swept over Danforth in what he would always remember as an intense wave of heat that emptied and confused him and in an instant sucked away his will to resist these men. It was as if the sun had suddenly focused all its fiery blast upon the tiny puddle of himself, leaving him dry and dusty, and strangely dead to any sense of himself other than the physical. He was no longer mind or heart. He was only the body that encased his life, which was in dire peril.

"Move," the man in the dark blue suit said sharply.

Almost without willing it, Danforth drifted forward like a dazed creature floating in the aftermath of some shock, and seconds later he was seated snugly between the men who'd grabbed him, the man in the green suit at the wheel.

He had not spoken, and this muteness surprised him. He felt like a child between two enormously imposing and unstable parents, unable to question what they did or in any way predict their behavior.

The car headed north on Broadway, and as it moved, Danforth strung enough of his senses together to begin to contemplate the silent, stern-faced men between whom he was tightly wedged. Who were they? What were they after? Was he being kidnapped? He briefly tried to guess what his father's reaction might be to that first phone call, how much ransom he might actually pay. This idea gave way to the equally far-fetched notion that this bizarre abduction might be the result of some business dispute of his father's. The elder Danforth often handled people quite roughly, so it seemed possible that some dissatisfied client or subcontractor might have decided that the usual avenues of redress against his father's high-handedness were far too slow and uncertain.

Then, quite suddenly, it became obvious that both of these surmises were dead wrong. It was then and only then that he thought of the Project and considered the possibility that the fear Bannion had expressed and LaRoche had later seconded had been justified all along, that they were truly out there, these American storm troopers, and that Danforth was now in their hands.

The northern reaches of Manhattan faded behind him, and he suddenly felt unmoored from New York. The city had seemed permanent before, a castle that protected him, and he had thought it changeless and certain. Now it was just a place weakened by events, no longer able to provide the slightest comfort, and in that incapacity, it seemed almost to mock him, as if all his life he'd been fooled by the city, lulled into a pleasant sleep from which he had now been roughly awakened.

The Bronx came and went, and after it, the squat streets of Yonkers. An hour passed, perhaps more. They were in Connecticut, the outskirts of one of its industrial towns, an area of crumbling and abandoned warehouses, with dark brick and black roofs and everywhere a dull patina of grime and soot.

The car bumped violently over a badly pitted street, then made a sharp left toward a large brick building with a loading dock and concrete ramp that led into the black bowels of the building. Once inside, they sat in that near total darkness for a few seconds, and then, as if responding to a signal Danforth couldn't see, Fedora got out of the car and turned to Danforth.

"You can get out now," Fedora said with unexpected gentleness, as if it were an option rather than an order.

Danforth pulled himself out of the car and stood very stiffly in the darkness, fully a child now, awaiting orders, afraid that any move he made would be the wrong one.

"Come with me," Fedora commanded.

By then the other two men were at his side and behind him, and in this formation they moved toward a metal door that opened just before they reached it.

The room was very small, with an iron bed and a bare mattress. A single lightbulb hung from a black cord. The walls were bare, and the ceiling was streaked with water stains. The sweet smell of mold thickened the air and gave it a musty taste. There was no sink or toilet, and so Danforth knew he would not be held there long, that this was a kind of purgatory, the place where he was to wait.

"If you choose to be a spy," Fedora told him as he closed the door, "you should get used to the life."

He would never be sure how long he remained alone in this room, but years later, as he stood before the starvation cells of Auschwitz, he would recall the terrible sense of confinement that had overtaken him, and how much more confined the Auschwitz prisoners must have felt with not even the space needed to sit down, able only to stand and face bare concrete walls until they died.

Time passed, but the men had taken his watch and his wallet before leaving him in the room, and so he had no idea how much time had passed, though he felt sure that the sun had gone down before the door of the room finally swung open again.

"Time for a chat," Fedora said. He had taken off his suit jacket and now wore dark blue flannel trousers and a light blue open-collared shirt.

Danforth rose and followed the man down a short corridor, at the end of which he opened the door, stepped away, and motioned Danforth inside.

The look of this room was unmistakable. It had a small, rectangular wooden desk with chairs that faced each other. A narrow table rested behind the desk, bare save for a pitcher and a few white towels.

"Sit down," Fedora told him, and on those words, closed the door, walked to the desk, and sat down behind it.

"Where is Anna Klein?" he asked casually and with an almost bored air, as he might have asked after the whereabouts of a lost cat.

Danforth sat down but said nothing, and years later, first in the interrogation rooms of Plötzensee in Berlin, and later in Lubyanka, he would marvel that all such places gave off the same sweaty dread, fear like an odor coming from the walls.

Fedora peered at him grimly. "I'm not going to ask you this question over and over again. I won't have to, believe me. But before I ask it again, take some time and think things through."

Danforth glanced toward the door. One of the other men opened it, came in, and stood in place in front of it, arms folded over his chest and wearing a strange expression, like a dog eager to be fed. They must seek out and find such men as this, Danforth thought, perfect for their purposes, the sort able to relish what others abhor.

Danforth remained unaware of time, and he wondered if this too was part of the game, to remove a man completely from the ordinary signals of life, his inner bearings weakened by the loss of all outer ones.

To resist that far-from-subtle ploy, Danforth focused on his cuff links. They were gold with small sapphires, and he'd bought them in Paris, at a little shop near the Luxembourg Gardens. Now he recalled the great expanse of that garden, how it had been so very French in that the children had not been permitted to play on the grass but instead had dashed and fallen and briefly wallowed in the dust of its wide, pebbled walkways. Paris in the morning, he thought, and saw the gardens in bright sunlight. Paris in the afternoon. Paris at night. So that is what it is, he thought, time.

"Where is Anna Klein?" Fedora asked.

This was the second time the question had been asked, and Danforth knew that whatever came next would be either the making or the undoing of him, that at the end of it, he would have either the highest regard for himself or the lowest, and that either way, in all likelihood he would never be so tested again.

He felt a kind of stiffness overtake him, a leathery thickening of his skin, a hardening of his bones, as if his body were preparing for the ordeal to come. But it was the innermost part of him he sensed most physically at that moment, something solidifying at the center of himself, so that he realized that although he'd many times felt the beat of his heart, the expansion of his lungs, the banal shift and quiver of all his other organs, he had not until that moment of inward reckoning felt the palpable workings of his soul.

"Put your hands behind your back," Fedora commanded.

Danforth hesitated, less out of any genuine will to resist than as a child would hesitate before taking his place in a dentist's chair.

"Put your hands behind your back," Fedora repeated.

Danforth knew that he was being asked to be complicit in his own torture, but he could find no way to resist doing as he was told that didn't seem both futile and foolish. Perhaps this was part of the torturer's strategy, he thought, to break your spirit a little before he begins to break your body. Had all the great legions of victims cooperated with their torturers, he wondered, and instantly imagined them in the dungeons of the Inquisition, all meekly placing themselves onto the rack, lying back, positioning their feet and hands.

Even thinking this, Danforth found himself unable to refuse, though he stood, lifted his head, and manfully straightened his shoulders as he brought his hands behind his back.

The other man stepped forward and tied them, then grabbed Danforth by his shirt collar and hauled him out if the room, Fedora following behind.

Seconds later, they entered a different room off the corridor. It was completely bare save for a rope whose two loose ends dangled from a pulley.

Another push and Danforth stood with his back to the dangling ropes, waiting silently as Fedora attached the pulley's ropes to the one that bound his hands together.

When it was done, the other man stepped back and gave a hard yank on the rope.

Danforth cried out as his body bent forward and a terrible pain streaked down his arms.

"Remember the question," the man said as he yanked the rope a second time, more violently, so that the pain became a flame that shot up and down Danforth's arms, circled his neck, then hurtled like a bolt of fire along his spine, legs, all the way down to the feet.

"Remember the question as we go along," the man said.

He did not speak again for half an hour.

Century Club, New York City, 2001

"Father Grandier," Danforth said in a sudden, typically disorienting aside. "Now that was an interrogation."

I saw a memory of pain flicker in Danforth's eyes and felt the discomfort one always feels in the presence of someone whose experience of suffering is vastly deeper than one's own.

"I'm afraid I've never heard of him," I said.

Even so, I thought that Father Grandier must be some heroic priest who had resisted the Nazis during the war, as a few had. Perhaps he had aided Anna in her exploits, or helped Danforth in some way.

"Loudon, France, August 1634," Danforth added. "Satan signed a diabolical pact with him, according to Grandier's accusers. A few other demons signed it as well, Astaroth and Baalberith. The highest of the devils signed." He smiled. "But Grandier never did."

Had we been two men upon a stage, the lights would have dimmed at that moment save for the single beam trained on Danforth; it would have softened and been touched by a blue as intense as the blue of Danforth's eyes as he began to speak.

"He was accused of bewitching nuns and brought to trial by a man very jealous of his power," Danforth said. "He refused to confess to any of the charges against him, and so he was ordered to endure what is called 'the question.'"

The question.

I recalled Fedora's ominous method, his insistence on asking only one question, and again recognized the winding through and winding back of Danforth's mind, how later words were linked to earlier words, recent allusions to more distant ones, all his small stories but stepping-stones to a greater one.

"Father Grandier was a very handsome man," he continued. "His torturers were about to crush his legs. He knew that his face would never be the same once that process began. Agony would contort it. And so he asked for a mirror. The mirror was given to him and he looked at himself for a long time. According to witnesses, there was no hint of vanity in his expression. What they saw, they said, was peace."

I could not imagine that peace was what Fedora had seen on Danforth's face, a suspicion he immediately confirmed.

"What my tormentor saw was terror," Danforth said without

110

hesitation. "I was acting bravely, of course. What else could I do? But it's convulsive, pain like that. And I remember thinking how important it was for me not to vomit." He laughed. "I'd just had a nice lunch right here in this club. Lamb with mint sauce. Very good. And port. A little too much port. I had this night-mare vision of spraying it all over the floor, then looking up to see Fedora staring at me with absolute contempt." He lifted his glass and rolled it in his arthritic hands. "The root of the word *terror* is an Indo-European word meaning 'to shake.' And I was shaken, believe me, down to that root word. Because that's what terror does. It shakes you until you collapse."

"Did you collapse?" I blurted before I could stop myself.

Danforth didn't answer immediately, but instead regarded the glass he was still rolling back and forth in his gnarled hands.

"There are torture museums throughout Europe," he said fi-nally. "I visited one in Amsterdam. Very elaborate affairs, the instruments of the Inquisition." He mentioned a few of these elaborations, the virginal face carved into the iron maiden, the brightly polished wood of the Spanish horse. "Ah, but Paul," he added softly, "to break a man you need only a little spoon."

New Brunswick, Connecticut, 1939

He heard the snap of the pulley's release and felt himself collapse onto the hard floor. In the aching blur that settled over him, he could feel the chill of the concrete. Perhaps at some point the pain had simply unstrung his senses, ripped out the wiring that connected him to time.

The door opened, then closed, but Danforth didn't know if his torturer had left or if someone else had entered. He listened for footsteps but heard none, and so, after a time, he decided that he was alone. He wanted to move but couldn't.

"Get him up."

Then he was lifted from the floor, the muscles of his arms so unnaturally stretched they'd lost their power to flex, his hands like weights at the end of a burning tangle of ligament and bone.

Now he was moving down the hallway, carried like a broken toy in his torturer's arms, then plopped down in the chair before Fedora's desk.

He sat, slumped and drained, barely able to keep himself in the chair, and waited as Fedora took his place behind the desk.

"Are you passing?" he asked. "Are you a secret Jew?"

Danforth didn't answer.

"What else can explain it?" Fedora asked. "This . . . stubbornness." He seemed amused by the taunting. "Do you think England will stop the Communists? France? America?" He laughed. "Perhaps you don't want them to be stopped. Perhaps you are a secret Communist *and* a secret Jew."

Danforth stared at Fedora silently.

"Do you know what they are doing, the Reds?" Fedora asked. "They are ripping down everything. They are waiting to swarm over Europe, and then they will swarm over us." He leaned forward slightly and looked closely at Danforth, his gaze probing, a man digging through a cluttered box. "Why are you helping them? America and Germany have the same enemy. Even the English know that."

Danforth knew that the slightest movement would send sheets of pain through his rib cage, and so he sat motionlessly and stared straight ahead. After a moment, he felt sensation in his toes, then his fingers, a glimmer of power returning to the far reaches of his body. It was like the first fibrous tingling of a phantom limb, and he experienced it as an awakening, the sure and certain evidence that for all the damage done, it was not irrevocable.

"Listen to me," Fedora said sharply.

Danforth tried to focus on the man behind the desk.

"Pay attention to what I am saying."

Danforth's head lolled back slightly, but with effort he drew it up again.

"I think you believe that somehow you're going to get out of this without any real damage," Fedora said. "Get out of it and go back to your nice warm little club."

Danforth felt his muscles moving like tiny insects beneath his skin, a delicate tremble that quickened his flesh with soft, regenerative spasms, and by that movement shook him to a somewhat greater clarity of mind. The haze of pain was lifting, and in its departing mists, the room took on its familiar proportions and no longer seemed skewed and off balance. His mind was returning to him like an old friend.

"But that's not true," Fedora said.

The clouds of pain continued to part, and as they did so, Danforth steadily regained his bearings, remembering things he had forgotten, the way at one point Fedora had splashed his body with ice-cold water, the stinging feel of being slapped.

Fedora opened the desk drawer to his right, took out a small spoon, and laid it down on the table. "I'm going to scoop out your eyes, my dear fellow. First one, then the other." He allowed Danforth to focus his starkly clarifying consciousness upon the spoon, then he picked it up and pointed it directly at Danforth's eyes.

"Where is Anna Klein?" Fedora asked.

It was at that moment the gorgeous vistas of Danforth's life turned against him as insidiously as a traitor in the ranks. For he instantly recalled in scores of simultaneous images all the magnificent things his eyes had seen: the snowcapped heights of Fuji, the walls of Avila, Hong Kong from the Peak, Uluru impossibly radiant in a sunset glow.

"Tie his hands," Fedora said.

Someone stepped behind Danforth's chair, drew his hands around the back of the chair, and tied them.

"So," Fedora said when this was done. He lifted the spoon, and it glinted in the light. "So."

The first wave of panic came in an uncontrollable shaking of his legs, a quaking Danforth experienced as an inward disintegration of his will. It was as if the little island of himself had been struck by a boiling wave that instantly dissolved whatever it touched.

In a suspended instant of intensely clear thought, he saw that he could have faced a pistol without faltering. To die, given the pains that still racked him, would not at that moment have seemed so great a forfeit. Death was only darkness, after all, an oblivion that offered no reminders of what had been lost. But to lose his sight? To see nothing more of this earth forever?

It was a crazed distinction, and he was not unaware of how crazed it was. And yet he felt himself helplessly melting in the curled fist of this one engulfing dread, all that was solid, all that had held up, now evaporating in the impossible heat of a terror he had not expected and against which he could offer no resistance: the love he had for things as yet unseen.

And what's the most beautiful thing you've never seen?

The question returned to him in Anna's voice, her words so clear that he all but expected Anna suddenly to materialize before him, and the fact that it was this memory of her that most weakened and tormented him seemed the cruelest of ironies.

Fedora was beside him now, his fingers wrapped around the handle of the spoon. His fingers were long and thin; perfect, Danforth thought, for playing the piano.

Fedora drew in a long breath. "So." He pressed the tip of the spoon beneath Danforth's left eye. "Where is Anna Klein?"

Danforth thought of the Atlas Mountains, the plains of Kilimanjaro, and last of the Seto Sea from the heights of Miyajima, that storied place his father had said no man should die without seeing.

"Where is Anna Klein?" Fedora repeated.

Danforth felt the answer well up from below, like a swollen gorge rising from his belly, surging up into his throat.

"For the last time," Fedora said. "Where is Anna Klein?"

Danforth felt the edge of the spoon press down then tilt upward, and with that tiny, otherwise insignificant pinch, Anna's address exploded toward his mouth so that he could feel his lips forming them, his breath ready to release them, all of them . . . now.

"Well done."

It was a vaguely familiar voice, and as if at its command, Fedora drew back the spoon and almost immediately untied Danforth's hands, then gently turned his swivel chair toward the door, where Danforth saw Bannion standing like a guardian of the gate, Clayton beside him, both staring at him with unmistakable admiration.

There were footsteps outside the door, and at the sound, both Clayton and Bannion straightened themselves, as if ordered to attention.

The door opened and she was there, Anna, standing stiffly, like a soldier. She seemed hardly to notice the other men in the room. Her attention was entirely on Danforth, and for a moment her eyes moved over him soothingly, like fingertips.

"We'll go to France together then," she said.

As he would remind himself down all the many years to come, he had not been able to determine at that moment whether she was obeying an order or issuing it. He could only see her steeliness, and so he stared at her brokenly, still trembling with fear and rocked by the eddies of his own retreating pain, yet determined to steel himself against whatever might befall him in some future interrogation. Next time, he would keep faith with Anna no matter what, he told himself, even to the point of a spoon.

PART III

Chekhov's Hammer

Century Club, New York City, 2001

"It was a moment of knight-errantry, I suppose," Danforth said in a voice that was darkly nostalgic, like that of a man recalling a struggle he had almost won. "And it was probably the origin of my obsession."

Knight-errantry? Obsession?

This was the stuff of romantic fiction, I thought, though oddly so, part King Arthur's Round Table, part Sigmund Freud's couch.

Then suddenly I recalled a line I'd read as an undergraduate. It had been attributed to Kenneth Patchen, a Greenwich Village poet: *Boxers punch harder when women are around.* If this was what Danforth's story reduced to, his need to win the hand of a mysterious woman, then surely I was wasting my time. I glanced outside. The snow was deepening. I'd flown in last night; the hotel room was booked through tomorrow, but I'd decided to leave right after today's interview. I hadn't checked out yet, though, which was fortunate, since there would probably not be a plane this evening. Still, no doubt the Acela train would be running. If Danforth's tale proved increasingly prosaic, I could cut the interview short and be snugly back in my Arlington apartment by nine o'clock.

"The whole thing was staged, that's what you're saying?" I asked in order to return Danforth to the subject at hand.

"Yes," Danforth answered. "Bannion had insisted on it, Clayton told me later. To protect Anna. If I passed the test, I would go with her to France."

"Did Anna know beforehand that you were going to be . . . tested?" I asked.

"I don't know," Danforth answered. "I never asked her."

"Why not?" I asked.

"Probably because I didn't want to know," Danforth answered frankly. "To think that she might have been sitting in the room next door, listening to my screams. That would not have been a good thing."

"Why not?"

"Because it would have suggested that Anna was a woman without limits," Danforth said, "and wisdom is about proportion, Paul, about having a sense of proportion."

This seemed little more than a weary restatement of the golden mean, and so I glanced down at my notes, saw a gap, and sought to fill it.

"How did Anna come to the Project, by the way?" I asked. "It's not clear who recruited her."

"Bannion recruited her," Danforth answered. "At first I thought she might have been a member of one of his Communist cells. But it turns out he'd known her almost from the time she'd first come to America. He'd been a Shabbos goy, working at one of the synagogues on the Lower East Side. Anna was learning Hebrew from a rabbi there. Later, Bannion had gone off to do Party work, and after that to Spain. He'd come back quite disillusioned with Communism, Anna told me, but looking for a way to fight Fascism."

"So he was one of those men who have to have causes," I said in a worldly tone.

Danforth nodded slowly. "I've learned that ideology is a room without windows, Paul," he said. "You can only see what's already inside it." He shrugged. "It's the same with a political cause. Once you commit yourself to it, it's hard to find limits, hard to say, 'This I will not do, even for my cause.' The Project was like that, something that found its way into your blood."

"So at this point, were you told what the Project was?" I asked.

"Yes," Danforth said. "It had to do with making contact with a large group of displaced Spaniards who'd fled to France toward the end of the Spanish civil war. The French had interned them in quite a few scattered camps. The thinking was that these Spaniards who'd fought against Franco and retreated into France could now be organized and equipped to fight against the Germans in the event that France was invaded."

"To field an army," I said. "That's quite ambitious."

"Very, yes," Danforth answered. "Ambitious enough to accomplish something, which was the goal, after all. For that reason, I think you'll agree that it was an idea worth exploring."

"I suppose so."

"And protecting."

I nodded.

"Even to the point of romantic deception," Danforth added. "Bitter though that may be."

"I'm not sure I know what you mean by 'romantic deception,'" I told him,

"No, of course not," Danforth said. He thought a moment, then asked, "Do you know *The Maltese Falcon*?"

"The old movie, with Humphrey Bogart."

"I was thinking of the book," Danforth said. "But, yes, the same story. Except that in the book things go a little differently, so that when Sam Spade discovers that Brigid O'Shaughnessy pretended to love him but never did, he strips her naked. He does this literally, Paul. And then — at least metaphorically — he sends her to her death."

I sensed a curious turn in Danforth's story, a tingling that suggested the plot, as they say, had thickened.

"And such a person would be worthy of death, don't you think?" Danforth asked, his voice now very cold and hard. "A traitor?"

"Yes," I said firmly.

"Even if you loved this traitor, as I'm sure you'll agree," Danforth added. "And even if, perhaps, an innocent person was also put in danger." He leaned forward slightly. "Because what secures man's moral life, Paul, is accountability. And accountability is based on punishment, the more sure and certain, the better." Now he sat back. "Wouldn't you agree?"

"Absolutely," I said.

He was silent for a moment, his gaze very steadily upon me, then he said, "Later, I came to wonder just how many parts Anna had acted. She once told me that she'd worked for a few weeks at a French construction firm on Vandam Street, translating correspondence. It turns out that this was true. I know because I checked the records."

Checked the records? So Danforth had carried out some sort of investigation of Anna, I thought, one he'd conducted after the war. Why, I wondered, had he done that?

But before I could ask him directly, Danforth posed a question of his own.

"Tell me, Paul, have you seen much of the world?"

"Some," I answered.

"Asia? Africa?"

"No."

"The Middle East?"

I shook my head. "I'm not a world traveler, if that's your point," I said a little sharply.

A vague dreaminess came over him. "The Seto Sea," he said. "I went there three years ago. They have a rope way, a cable car that takes you up Mount Misen." Briefly, he seemed captured by that moment in his past. Then quite abruptly, he returned to the present, though not directly to his tale.

"Did you know that Kyoto was at the top of the list of cities marked for the first atomic bomb?" he asked.

"No," I confessed.

"General Groves wanted Kyoto bombed first," Danforth told me. "It was the ancient Japanese capital, so its destruction would devastate Japanese morale, he said. It was also surrounded by mountains that would concentrate the blast." He drained the last of the port. "But Secretary of War Stimson scratched Kyoto off the list. He'd been there, you see. Twice, actually. Once on his honeymoon." He looked at me significantly. "It's hard to destroy something you have reason to love." His smile struck me as a direct warning. "Travel removes places from the target list, Paul. In a way, it removed Paris. A German general refused to destroy it and lied to Hitler when he was asked if Paris was burning."

"Yes," I said, somewhat relieved that I was familiar with this story. "I read about that."

"That general made a wise choice," Danforth said. "Paris is a beautiful city. Anna and I arrived there the third week in May."

Ah, I thought, *he has, according to his style, wound back to his narrative.*

"I'd rented two apartments on the Left Bank, just off Saint-Germain-des-Prés," Danforth said.

"Two apartments?" I asked.

"You mean, did we sleep together?" Danforth asked. "Is that what you want to know, Paul? Did Anna and I have fantastic sex then enjoy a *petit déjeuner* on a flower-filled terrace with the towers of Notre Dame in the distance?"

I had to admit that his earlier mention of the "erotics of intrigue" had rather surreptitiously asserted itself.

"Something like that," I said, a little embarrassed that I had given this away so blatantly.

Danforth straightened one sleeve of his jacket. "No, we were not lovers."

What they were, or later became, sparkled briefly in his eyes, then vanished like a candle tossed down a well.

"But Paris was beautiful, a city of lights," Danforth added. "And there was the touch of intrigue I felt every time Anna presented her passport, the very American name she'd chosen: she was now Anna Collier. Everything gave off a certain dramatic charge and made my little world a tad brighter." He drew in a breath that was quick and light, yet with something heavy at its center. "Even in those dark days."

Jardin des Tuileries, Paris, France, 1939

They sat down a little distance from the L'Orangerie, both tired from the day's long walk. During the last few hours, they'd reconnoitered the city, an expedition that had taken them from Passy, where Balzac had lived his extravagant life, to the groves of Père-Lachaise, where that life had come to rest. They'd wandered the streets of Pigalle and mounted the stairs to Sacré Coeur. In that way, street by street, Paris had revealed itself as all great cities do, like an exotic dancer shedding one veil at a time.

Anna looked out over the park, gazing first at a group of children in their school uniforms, then at an old man in a black beret, and finally at a young couple strolling arm in arm down one of the neatly manicured paths.

"Our city of intrigue," Danforth said lightly.

In later years, he would consider how odd it was that he was there, how little he'd known, and he'd see this as emblematic of the decision to break free from the moorings of his former life. Despite the peril that followed, when he recalled sitting with Anna in the Jardin des Tuileries that evening, he regretted nothing about his decision to accompany her, not the complex business matters he'd abruptly left in the care of others, or even the consternation his sudden departure from New York had caused his father. The only thing that mattered to him was that he'd cast all that aside and embarked on a course whose outcome he could not foresee, a journey — the first of his life — that had no clear destination. At that moment, as he would often in the future recall, he'd felt only the sense that what he'd done was right and that to have done anything else would have been wrong.

And he'd been busy, after all. His little act of subterfuge required him to perform as an importer, and so, upon arriving in Paris, he'd met with several of his Parisian business associates, looked at the merchandise in their shops and small warehouses, with Anna always at his side, taking notes, perfect in her role as his dutiful assistant, her French flawless. By then she'd learned quite a bit about antiques and art and could tell the genuine from the fake; from time to time she even felt confident enough to suggest a price or reject one.

Toward evening they found themselves at the Place de Grève, and Danforth suddenly thought of the execution of Damiens, the unbearable torments he had suffered on this very spot. At that thought Danforth returned to his ordeal in the Connecticut warehouse, and from that point suddenly imagined Anna in the custody of such men, the insult and humiliation they would add to whatever tortures they administered, because it had always been so with torturing women. It was not a subject he could bring up, however; it would serve no purpose, and so he simply guided their walk toward the banks of the Seine, where they strolled slowly and for the most part silently as the river's boats and barges cruised by.

"It all seems like the quiet before the storm, doesn't it?" he said finally.

Anna nodded. "Unless the storm can be stopped."

The remark struck Danforth as odd since, as he'd learned by then, the Project was not concerned with preventing the coming war. The goal was to make sure that any German advance would encounter opposition from an unexpected quarter, an undertaking far more extensive than he'd imagined and whose feasibility it was Anna's — and now his — mission to explore.

He said nothing of this, however, so they walked on in silence until they reached a large hall where a crowd had gathered.

"It's Daladier," Anna said.

In the years after the war, as one by one the tiny lights went on in his brain, Danforth would try to recall the precise details of what followed next: the look in Anna's eyes as she watched the prime minister of France move through the crowd; the way the people pressed in toward him; the chaotic nature of that crowd, the women bearing flowers, the tradesmen with packages, and here and there a lone man with his hands sunk deep into the pockets of his trousers or his jacket or, as Danforth noted in one case, tucked beneath a bloodstained apron.

"He seems quite fearless," Anna said, her gaze intense as she studied the way Daladier moved through the crowd, a short, stocky man, looking very much like what he was called: the bull of Vaucluse.

"Heads of state have to be fearless these days," Danforth said.

Daladier disappeared into a building, and the crowd began to disperse. Anna, however, remained in place, seemingly still captivated by the scene that had just played out before her: a public figure publicly adored, confident in the adulation of the crowd through which he'd moved.

Was that the moment, Danforth asked himself on the countless occasions when he replayed this scene, when Anna had first thought of a quite different plot, one considerably more dangerous? Or had the Project never been anything more than a smoke screen to her, its only goal to conceal the real plot behind it? Had it always been her plan that they would appear as innocents, amateurs, Americans on a fool's errand? Years later, as he combed through everything from government records to spy fiction, Danforth would continually wonder if he had from the very beginning been a dupe, manipulated at every turn, little more than a string she'd artfully wound around her finger.

But on that evening, Danforth could think only of Anna's mood and the silence that once again enveloped her as they headed home and that was not broken until they reached her door, where, to their surprise, they found a young man waiting for them.

"I am Christophe," he said.

The man who spoke was only a few years older than they, and in Danforth's view, he hardly looked the part of a secret agent. His hair was black, and he wore spectacles, but his ragged clothes set him apart and gave him the look of an impoverished student.

"My English is very good," Christophe assured them. "I lived in America for some years." He nodded down the boulevard. "Please, come. We can talk in my room."

The walk to Christophe's room was longer than Danforth had expected, and it ended on a block considerably seedier than any he had yet visited. The front door creaked loudly as Christophe opened it and motioned them into the dank, smelly interior of the building.

"Just up the stairs," Christophe said.

His room was on the third floor, and it was a true garret, crowded with books and magazines that lay in great stacks all around the place. A musty odor came from these papers that Danforth recognized as the same one that came from Christophe's jacket, and probably his shirt and socks and hair.

"Would you like a glass of wine?" Christophe asked.

Danforth said that he would, but Anna declined, as always, a

dedication to sobriety he took to be emblematic of her seriousness, though later he would wonder if this too had only been a
show.

Christophe produced a jug of red wine, and after pouring
it, lifted his glass, and spoke in Spanish. *"Hasta la victoria,"* he
said.

"Victory over what?" Anna asked.

"Over the Germans," Christophe answered.

"We're not at war with Germany yet," she reminded him.

"I am," Christophe said. He turned to Danforth. "I have been
since Guernica."

Christophe had met Bannion when they'd been in the International Brigades, a group of young men from all over the world
who'd rallied to the anti-Fascist cause, shipped out to Spain,
fought bravely but hopelessly, and then returned to their native
lands.

"They sang an American song," Christophe told them cheerfully. "'Red River Valley.' All the time, they sang it."

Christophe had the starry-eyed look of an idealist, Danforth
thought. There was a boundless naiveté in the way he went on
to praise his fellow brigadiers, a blindness to human nature he
suspected most idealists shared since, in order to believe such
ideals, they first had to believe that all men were as innocent as
they.

"As you know, our hope is to use the great number of Spanish in France now," Christophe said at the conclusion of his
brief paean to his own lost cause. "These are republican soldiers
who escaped over the Pyrenees before Spain fell to Franco. The
French have put them in what they call transit camps. Le Vernet
d'Ariege, Saint-Cyprien, Barcares, Argeles, Gurs." He looked
suddenly toward Anna. "These men are seasoned fighters. And
they know that if the Germans overrun France, they will all be
killed or sent back to Spain." His eyes did not leave Anna's. "Es-

cape is not difficult. At Gurs, for example, the barbed wire is only two feet high, and there are no guardhouses."

None of this was news to Danforth, as he'd spent the last of his time in New York being filled in on the Project by Clayton and Bannion. Even so, he listened intently as Christophe talked about how many displaced Spaniards were currently in France, almost a quarter million. They had proven their courage, and their hatred of the Germans was intense. They were Spaniards, he said, and therefore they were brave. Surely arrangements could be made to arm and supply them if war broke out between Germany and France.

Danforth would long recall the fervent nature of Christophe's argument, his deep love for his Spanish comrades. But it was the suffering at the Spanish internment camps Christophe most powerfully described: the poor food and shelter, the anguish of their defeat and subsequent dispossession. It was a vision that Danforth found quite moving, though he saw almost no response to it in Anna's eyes. Rather, she peppered Christophe with questions that were almost entirely logistical, as if her intent were not simply to make contact and later train and supply this ghostly army, but to lead it.

"So," Christophe said when Anna had asked the last of her questions, "the next step is that you go to Gurs, mademoiselle."

The arrangements were made the next day, and three days after that, Danforth and Anna set off from Paris on a southwestern journey through the heart of France that he found utterly exhilarating and that filled him with an inexpressible joy. He recognized that this happiness was fanciful and romantic, but he could not — even later, after all was known — strip this journey of its tingling pleasure or of the sense that he would never live higher or more passionately than he lived at that moment.

At Urdos station, the mountain passes of the Atlantic Pyrenees loomed ahead, but Danforth found nothing ominous in their high, jagged walls. Oloron-Sainte-Marie lay before them, and a short time later they stood before the old doors of Sainte-Marie. It had been a smooth journey thus far, but also a long one, though Danforth didn't feel in the least depleted by it. He was on the road again, like the boy of old, only this time destined to pursue a higher goal than the purchase of Etruscan pottery or an Afghan rug.

"The Romans tramped through these ravines," he told Anna. "These were the gates of Western Europe."

But on the road that day, there was only a group of pilgrims bound for Santiago de Compostela. They were a ragged assemblage, French peasants who seemed unchanged from the Middle Ages save for their clothes. The trudging of this ancient route was no doubt a powerful act of faith, and Danforth noticed a curious sympathy for them in Anna's eyes; perhaps this ritualized Christian journey reminded her of the Hasidim of Delancey Street, the way they also went on foot to their sacred houses.

Once the little group of pilgrims had passed, she turned idly toward the church doors, and Danforth saw that she was peering at the base of one of the church's supporting columns: two medieval peasants, standing back to back, the great weight of the column on their small shoulders.

"Peasants doing their duty," Danforth said lightly. "Despite the burden, I mean." He looked at them more closely. "Contented with their place in the chain of being."

Anna's gaze remained on the two bent figures, their faces not at all strained as the vast weight pressed down upon them.

"Oppression often looks like harmony," she said.

It was a remark that seemed to come from the darkest of her experiences, her expression as solemn as her voice, so entirely genuine that Danforth would for many years refuse to consider that it might have been a mask.

"Monsieur?"

Danforth turned to see a small, stooped figure standing just beyond the church door, his scruffy brown hat clutched in both hands, meekly, like a servant.

"I Diego," he said in deeply accented English.

He was dressed raggedly, and Danforth, with his keen eye for such things, noticed every dangling thread and nodding button.

"I show you camp," Diego said.

Danforth stepped forward and offered his hand, which Diego took in the shy, uncertain way of men abruptly dispossessed.

"I'm Tom," Danforth told him in Spanish. "And this is Anna."

"A pleasure," Diego replied in his native tongue, with a quick bow toward Anna. "I have a car," he said in Spanish, and he never again reverted to English. He motioned toward the small street that led away from the church. "Please come."

They followed Diego to a mud-splattered Renault that Danforth thought at least fifteen years old. The black exterior paint had long ago lost its gloss, and the running boards were caked with past generations of gray Pyrenean dust. It wheezed pitiably as the engine turned, and the chaise shook and rattled before it finally jerked forward, heaved backward, then bolted forward again in the comic way of silent movies. Danforth could almost imagine a bespectacled Harold Lloyd fearfully clutching its worn black steering wheel.

"We should not go too close to the camp," Diego said, "but you will see it very well."

The drive from Oloron-Sainte-Marie was brief, but on the way, Danforth noticed a few straggling French soldiers, their rifles held in the loose, jaunty way of stage actors as they marched raggedly southward. They had the beards and handlebar mustaches of the typical *poulie*, the type of soldier renowned since Napoleon, rustic, undisciplined and indisputably courageous, men who at Chemin des Dames had charged from their trenches contemptuously braying in loud and profoundly mocking imitation of sheep going to slaughter.

"The guards get drunk," Diego said scornfully as the old Renault jostled past a knot of laughing soldiers. "But we Spanish, we have nowhere to go, so we stay behind the wire."

"But you escaped," Anna said.

"Yes, I escaped," Diego said wearily. "For two months I ate grass and snow. Then an old woman took me in. She lives high in the mountains." He laughed. "A crazy old thing. Very nice, but crazy. She said to me . . . in French, she said, *'Combien de Louis maintenent?'* She made a big joke. 'How many Louises have there been?'" He laughed again. "She thought there were still kings in France."

Diego was a careful driver, but the Renault was anything but compliant, and with the slip and slide of the muddy road, it occasionally veered violently to the left or right, making Danforth and Anna collide in its cramped back seat, each time with a little laugh, and, for Danforth, a small electric thrill at her touch.

Later it would seem to Danforth the height of solipsism that he had felt no dread as he approached the transit camp at Gurs. In fact, he had felt only the continuing elation of their recent journey; he was still adrift in its intrigue but more keenly aware of the physical nearness of Anna and of the increasingly intense nature of the experience they were to share.

Afloat in that phantasm, he scarcely felt the old Renault grind to a halt and barely heard Diego's whispered "Through the trees."

Diego went to the trees and motioned them forward and down, so they were in a low crouch by the time they reached him. Anna got out first, but Danforth had joined her by the time she got to the trees. "Six thousand now," Diego said, "but every day it gets bigger." He pointed. "There."

Years later, in the midst of his own dark search, Danforth would see a grainy black-and-white photo of the camp taken from the water tower by a camera aimed straight into the bowels of the site. It would appear quite expansive in the photograph, with column after column of wooden barracks that reached as far as the eye could see. In that picture, Gurs had seemed as large as Auschwitz when he'd later walked those bleak grounds, still searching for a clue as to how it had all happened, and where he had gone wrong.

But on the day he first set eyes on Gurs, Danforth could make out little beyond a scattering of ramshackle barracks hammered together from what appeared to be thin plywood sheets covered with tar paper, a muddy little shantytown that reminded him of the Hoovervilles back home. Captured like a school of fish within its barbed-wire net, the defeated Spaniards seemed defeated indeed, not an army at all, despite what Christophe had said, but a weak rabble, the lost brigade of an equally lost cause.

"No running water," Diego said. He shook his head. "Others are worse. Saint-Cyprien. Ninety thousand there. Right on the Mediterranean. They have nothing." He shrugged. *"Les Rouges a côté de la mer,"* he said sadly in French. "The Reds beside the sea."

They didn't linger for very long after that, Diego clearly jumpy and eager to leave. He was, after all, a fugitive, and if captured he would be returned to Gurs or, worse, sent back to Spain, where he would no doubt be either executed or imprisoned.

Back in Oloron-Sainte-Marie, he quickly bid them adieu, and a few minutes later Danforth and Anna went to have dinner at a small restaurant, after which they boarded the night train back to Paris.

"What do you think of the Spanish?" Danforth asked.

"I think that if war comes, they will fight," Anna answered.

In this, as Danforth would later learn, she had been right. When war did come, the Spanish blew up bridges and sabotaged factories and even managed to kill General von Schaumburg, the German commandant of the region around Paris.

But at the time, Danforth did not know any of this, and the logistics of helping to provision an army of displaced Spaniards seemed daunting, to say the least.

Even so, he said, "We have lots of plans to make."

"Yes, we do," Anna said.

And so it had seemed to Danforth that together they would take the next step in the Project, as planned: establish a network within the camps, find secret storage facilities, arrange for the clandestine provision of this most ill-equipped of armies — details that made clear the importance of their many languages.

All of this, Danforth fully expected them to do.

But they never did.

Century Club, New York City, 2001

"Never did?" I asked.

"No," Danforth said.

"Why?" I asked.

My question appeared to strike him like an infinitely thin blade; rather than answer it, he said, "Tell me, Paul, have you ever heard of Chekhov's hammer?"

"No," I answered.

"Chekhov said that at the door of every happy person, there should be someone tapping with a little hammer, just as a reminder, soft but steady, that there are unhappy people in the world."

He saw that I didn't get his point.

"On the train back to Paris, I was happy," Danforth said. "I felt that Anna and I were now true comrades in arms. We had just completed a little investigatory mission and were about to begin the further implementation of the Project. I envisioned this as a long process, with many dramatic turns. Anna would teach me the skills she'd learned at Winterset. We would teach these same skills to various contacts. We would be secret agents. We would live lives of intrigue in service to our shared cause." He smiled. "Youth is life's chief deceiver, Paul, and its chief deception is that you will somehow escape the common fate." The smile withered. "At that moment, with this vision circling in my head, I should have heard that little hammer. Because these would be the last days I would be without suspicion or look forward without fear."

He reached into the breast pocket of his jacket and produced a cable encased in plastic, preserved as if it were a rare document. He handed it to me.

It was dated May 21, 1939, and it was from Clayton. He was in London, where he'd encountered "some urgent business problems." Danforth and Anna were to meet him there as quickly as they could book passage. He was staying at the Savoy. In the meantime, they were to "take care."

"Well, what do you make of that, Paul?" Danforth asked.

"Nothing," I said. I handed it back to him.

"It wouldn't cause you any alarm?"

"About what?"

"Clayton? That he might be a traitor."

"No," I said, quite confidently. "Why would it cause me to doubt Clayton?"

"You're right; it wouldn't, of course," Danforth said. "It wouldn't cause any alarm having to do with a specific person. But in a vague way, it might make you begin to doubt everything. It might produce a sense of things perhaps being not quite right. I mean, just what are these 'urgent business problems' about which Anna and I should 'take care'? You would not doubt Clayton or anyone else. But you would suddenly feel . . . on trembling ground." He smiled.

"That is the sinister art of deceit, Paul," he said. "To make things unclear, to allow for multiple interpretations. It's very effective at disorienting even the most experienced of conspirators, because more than anything, the conspirator seeks certainty. If he is certain he is discovered, he will act accordingly, probably by getting the hell out of town. If he is certain that he is not discovered, he will act accordingly, stay put and carry on with his plot. But when he is truly unsure if he is or is not discovered, he will be in a constant state of fearful disequilibrium. He will sleep, this uncertain conspirator, but he will do it fitfully, and his judgment will be clouded by this lack of rest. He will sleep but this sleep will exhaust and debilitate him and fill his mind with unsettled thoughts and unfounded fears. He will sleep, but only as we wish him to sleep, warily." His smile was as lupine as the thing he said: "It is called the sleep of wolves." He returned the cable to his jacket pocket. "We left for London the next day."

Paris, France, 1939

But they had dinner on the boulevard Raspail the night before they left for London, and while they ate, Danforth told Anna how his father had taught him to be wily and observant. Watch for the unseen, he had told him, and listen for the unsaid.

He hoped, he said, that he had learned those lessons well.

"They are useful lessons," Anna said, and added nothing else.

After dinner, he walked her to her door, where they parted with a long, close embrace that Danforth found curiously exciting, as if he'd received a jolt of energy, one that lingered long after and finally kept him from sleep. Eventually he rose and headed out into the street.

It had rained earlier in the evening, and now a few soggy papier-mâché remnants of some sort of patriotic celebration hung heavily from balconies and trees. Posters memorializing a glorious past bowed from dripping kiosks, and it seemed to Danforth that all around the city, there was a sense that only the past could be celebrated, because what lay ahead for France, and perhaps for the world, was utterly uncertain.

The windows of the shops were dark, but even in the shadows Danforth could see how much style still mattered to the French. In a bakery, it was in the blush on little marzipan peaches. In a boutique, it was a dress with an impudent ruffle. In a gift shop, a decorative box tied with lace. These small gestures stood against the encroaching doom, Danforth thought, but at the same time he wondered if this was all that stood against it.

Surely not, he decided, and in a kind of reverie he imagined a vastly extended web of heroic conspirators, an army of courageous men and women who passed notes in Viennese cafés and exchanged signals on the Ponte Vecchio. In Budapest they hid crates of arms and loaded them into little boats and sailed them to cadres waiting along the Danube. Other arms came ashore at Marseille or Dubrovnik and were taken far inland by railway car or covered with hay and borne by horse-drawn wagons into the heart of Prague. Surely in Copenhagen and Oslo, and from Calais to Trieste, there were brave men and women who thought of nothing but how this dark tide must be stopped. Surely, Danforth declared to himself, surely at some illuminating moment not far in the future, the blustering Prince of Darkness would confront a rifle behind every blade of grass.

This was not an illusion he could long sustain, however, and by the time he returned to his apartment, his fantasy of a sweeping pan-European resistance had died a dog's death, and dawn found him by the window, peering out over the boulevard, wondering if he and Anna could still carry out their mission if Clayton's "urgent business matters" proved more perilous than he'd supposed, or if Clayton himself—the unsettling possibility suddenly struck him—was something other than he seemed.

"Other than he seemed?" I asked.

"Yes."

"Clayton other than he seemed," I repeated, now no less unsettled than Danforth had been so many years before. "So that cable *had* made you suspect that he might be a traitor?"

"That night, as I was standing at the window, yes, that thought did occur to me," Danforth answered. "But not because of anything I actually knew about Clayton. It was more general than that, and it was very vague. Later, I would come to believe that life itself—when you look it in the eye—is a treacherous thing. It isn't out to break our hearts, as the Irish say. It's out to leave us baffled and confused, to strip us of any faith we might have in anyone, even ourselves. That's what life really is, Paul, a wearing down of trust."

For the first time, Danforth appeared profoundly weathered, a landscape raked by wind and rain, part of him deeply furrowed, part of him smoothed and softened.

"It can make a man murderous," he added. "It can make a man reach for a pistol on a warm tropical day."

Then I saw it for the second time, the quiet capacity Danforth had for violence, how steady it would be, how carefully calculated and reasonably carried out, the way he would kill.

Some hint of this insight surely appeared in my gaze at that moment, because Danforth reacted to it in a way I'd not seen before. Retreat. It seemed to me he had gotten ahead of himself and knew it, and now he forced himself to step back and back and back, until we arrived in London.

The Savoy, London, 1939

"They once flooded the lobby, you know," Clayton said in what struck Danforth as a strained effort at his old gaiety. "They filled it with water, and the patrons floated in little gondolas." He shook his head. "It's hard to imagine now," he added. "Such . . . frivolity."

Danforth found Clayton's uncharacteristic solemnity worrisome. It was clearly a sign that certain things weren't going well, though in what way they weren't going well remained obscure. One thing was obvious, however. Clayton was no longer enjoying his role as lead conspirator; as he sat in suit and tie, dressed as perfectly as ever, he seemed like a portrait darkening at the edges.

"Thank you both for coming," Clayton began somberly. "This is not something I could say in a cable or letter that might be opened by some curious official." He appeared quite grave. "It has to do with a report I received not long ago. I want you to know about it in order to calm any doubts you might have." He looked at Anna. "Or any suspicions." He took a deep sip from his glass and then began.

"Bannion has a contact in Germany," he said. "His code name is Rache, and he's been very good at supplying us with highly reliable information. The latest is that some very wealthy Brits have been regularly making payments to informants in Poland because they expect that country to be invaded. Rache doesn't know who these Brits are or how many of these informants are on their payroll. He knows only that once the invasion takes place, these informants are supposed to make reports to their backers." He paused as if truly pained by what he was about to say. "But it's all a twisted conspiracy, because, according to Rache, these same wealthy men have been turning over the names and addresses of their paid informants to the SS."

Danforth was a novice in matters of international plots and counterplots, and if Clayton had asked him his opinion at that moment, he would have had to admit that he had not a clue as to the meaning or implication of what he'd just heard.

"Why would they do that?" Anna asked.

"Because these British backers are actually pro-German," Clayton answered. "They are only pretending to be otherwise."

Danforth looked at him quizzically.

"The real enemy of these men is the Soviets," Clayton said. "For that reason, they want the eastern German invasion of Poland to be smooth and fast. The idea is that after the invasion, the Brits will hand over the names of these informants, who'll be rounded up very quickly, then shot. This will happen immediately, and in a very public way, right in front of neighbors and coworkers. Scores will be killed, but hundreds will be witnesses to their executions. This, the Brits think, will send a shiver through the population and put a stop to any early resistance."

It seemed a wildly far-fetched scheme, but all Danforth said was "Does this Rache have any proof?"

Clayton shook his head. "No, and Bannion suspects the whole thing is just the usual Communist paranoia."

"Rache is a Communist?" Danforth asked.

Clayton nodded. "In the underground, yes. Still loyal to his cause, according to Bannion, which is why Bannion doesn't take this plot seriously." He looked at me. "But he insisted that I warn you and Anna anyway." His smile was anything but cheery. "And so I have."

"What do you think of this report, Robert?" Danforth asked.

"That it's probably absurd," Clayton answered. "Or at least exaggerated. Bannion doubts that it would even work. If the Germans carried out these executions, it's possible that instead of squelching resistance, they would actually intensify it."

"Then why tell us about it at all?" Anna asked, a question Danforth would consider many times over the coming years, sometimes convinced of its sincerity, other times equally convinced that she had always known the larger plot and her question was meant only to conceal that fact.

"Well, suppose you heard about it later," Clayton answered. "Wouldn't you wonder if a similar game was being played on you and Tom? Of course you would. So Bannion and I thought you should be informed." He looked from Anna to Tom. "If either of you has any doubts about the Project, then now's the time to pull out."

Anna leaned forward slightly. "How much does Rache know about us?" she asked.

"Nothing," Clayton assured her. "He's focused entirely on Germany, on resistance to the Nazis in the homeland." His smile was weak, but pointed. "And he may be quite paranoid at the moment. An underground Communist in Germany? Who wouldn't be paranoid?"

There was an odd, suspended moment during which no one spoke, and it later seemed to Danforth that it was here that each of them had fully committed him- or herself to whatever lay ahead. It was as if they had been driving down a smooth road and had hit a bump; it might have diverted them, but it hadn't. In a subtle but potentially corrosive way, the challenge had tested their confidence in each other but had not shaken it.

"So," Clayton said after a moment, apparently reassured that the Project was not in danger, "tell me about Gurs."

They told him what they'd found there and that they planned to visit other camps. They would make a quick assessment, then begin the process of contacting and organizing this army of the dispossessed.

Their report was quite thorough, Danforth thought, but as they gave it, it seemed to him that Anna was unsettled, like water slowly beginning to simmer. In the early days of her training, she had viewed the prospect of living undercover, perhaps for a very extended period, as an integral part of the Project. But since Gurs, she'd seemed uneasy and perhaps even anxious; Danforth felt she was now running on a different, and more rapid, timetable than he or Clayton, and this he found disturbing. Surely at this point, the Project required patience.

"All right," Clayton said at the end of their briefing. "So we will move forward according to plan." He took a long draw on the cigarette, then snapped up the menu with what struck Danforth as his old, youthful energy. "For your information, my dear friends, the Savoy is said to have the best steak Diane in London."

There was no more talk of spies and conspiracies, of hundreds who might be sacrificed in the east, and anyone watching the three of them for the remainder of that evening would have seen nothing beyond friends enjoying themselves. Clayton spoke of his new job in London; he was working at the British Museum, a post he had gotten on his own merit, he said, rather than through his family's name or money, a feat of which he seemed quite proud. He had always had it easy, he said, and so had yearned for what he called "some hard slogging" through which he might prove himself.

During it all, Anna seemed guarded. She watched Clayton as if she were unsure he was the man he seemed to be, and the attitude caused Danforth to wonder if his earlier sense that everyone's trust had been renewed had been premature.

It was a look that urged Danforth to feel the same, and so after Anna went up to her room, he suggested that he and Clayton have drinks at the bar. Clayton immediately agreed, and for the next two hours Danforth tried to get Clayton drunk without getting drunk himself. Clayton had ultimately noticed that Danforth wasn't holding up his end, however, and he had stopped drinking.

Was that suspicious? Danforth asked himself. Was it suspicious, or was Clayton just a man who didn't want to get sloshed while his friend was quite obviously staying sober?

Danforth didn't know, and thought he would never know, and so at around midnight he returned to his room, slept the sleep of wolves, and the next morning had breakfast in the stately hotel dining room and then took a stroll around London that took him to Trafalgar Square, then across it and down Whitehall all the way to Parliament, a route he would take many times in the years to come, always with an eye to encountering something that might shed light on the mystery that both illuminated and darkened the middle years of his life, a time when, as he later reminded himself, he might have been making money and establishing a family, as Clayton had.

Back at the hotel around noon, he went directly to Anna's room.

She opened the door to him; she'd just showered, and her body was wrapped in a loose-fitting robe, her hair in a towel.

"Tom, come in."

She padded barefoot across the floor to the bathroom, and Danforth suddenly imagined her dangling those same feet off the side of an iron bed at Ellis Island, and with that thought, he felt something tragic at the heart of things, that life was dark and entangling, everyone struggling helplessly in its invisible web.

"When are we going back to Paris?" Anna called from behind her bathroom door.

"Whenever you want," Danforth answered.

"Tomorrow then," Anna said.

A moment passed before the door opened and she came out, dressed in a white blouse and long black skirt, into the tiny living room.

"You look . . . beautiful," he said.

She glanced away, almost shyly, as if this were a remark to which she could find no way to respond. "Did you have lunch?"

"No," Danforth said. "Shall we go down?"

She shook her head. "No, let's eat here."

With that she retrieved a bag from a nearby table.

"There was a little market," she said. "I bought some things."

They were modest, the items she'd purchased: a loaf of bread, some local cheese, a few squares of chocolate whose sweetness he would — along with a thousand other sensations ineffably joined with her — all his life remember.

While he ate he spoke of his long walk through London, the bookstalls of Charing Cross, the whirling traffic of Trafalgar. She had clearly made no effort to see the city, and he wondered why this was, and even suggested that they remain a day or two in London before returning to France.

"No," she said, "I'll go back tomorrow."

She clearly meant that she would do this with or without Danforth, and because of that, he felt himself at a remove from any possibility of her affection; he was a man who had a specific purpose and who was, beyond that purpose, expendable.

"Then we'll leave for Dover tomorrow," he said.

Which they did, then crossed the Channel on a peaceful sea. On the crossing, Danforth thought of the Spanish armada, and spoke of it to Anna, how the grand ambitions of a Spanish king had sunk beneath these very waves. From this observation, he had gone on to wonder if Germany might one day hazard such a crossing and perhaps, luckily for the British, meet the same fate.

She had listened to all of this attentively, and he finally decided that she did not consider him pedantic, as Cecilia probably had, though she'd made a valiant effort to conceal it.

Still he said, "I'm going on. You should stop me."

"I would if I wanted to," she told him, then asked if he'd ever heard of the Divine Wind.

He hadn't, and so she told him that an earlier armada, this one launched by Kublai Khan, had attempted the conquest of Japan. A storm, not unlike the one that had sunk the ships of King Philip, had spelled doom for this armada too, a divine intervention the Japanese had immortalized and yearly celebrated as a Divine Wind.

"My mother told me that story," Anna said when she finished it.

This mention clearly summoned emotions she did not want, so she looked away, out toward the far shores of France, a retreat he had seen before and that, rather than putting him off, inexplicably drew him to her.

"After dinner, I had drinks with Clayton," he told her at one point. "I didn't see anything that told me if Clayton was playing some game. I wish I'd found some sign to read. But if one was there, I couldn't read it."

Neither spoke for a time, and during that interval Danforth worked to reassess the situation in which he found himself: heading back to France with Anna, but with no clear activity in mind save at some point secreting supplies for an army of interned Spaniards. Anna now seemed to have waning interest in the mission, so he felt compelled to reawaken it.

"We'll need to work out supply routes that are off the beaten track," he said.

And so for the next few minutes, they spoke of the original plan, a conversation during which Danforth realized that Anna had practically memorized the entire map of France: where each road led and through which villages, along with the routes of all the rivers, particularly the ones that emptied into the sea. It was as if she were plotting some enormous evacuation.

After that, she seemed reluctant to speak at all, her silences so long and grave Danforth later wondered if she had already embarked on a far different project, one whose dark route and fatal end she had decided long ago.

"So," Danforth said jokingly, by way of testing those waters, "maybe we will change the world."

Anna shook her head. "No," she said. "We are just little spies."

Century Club, New York City, 2001

Little spies.

There would be times in the future, Danforth said, when he would ask himself if this remark had moved Anna deeper into a plot she'd already begun to contemplate, or if it was from that grim conclusion that the plot had taken wing. Or perhaps the grave conspiracy that had sealed his fate had never been anything but a shadow plot whose goal had been to keep him utterly in the dark.

"Little spies," Danforth repeated now, in a way that suggested he had many times turned this same sentence over in his mind. "We're guided through life by a mirror ball," he said. "With only little flashes to light our way." He suddenly appeared captured by a distant terror, and he said, "The world was on fire, Paul. And Anna seemed to feel that we were doing nothing to put it out. She didn't say it outright, but I could see it building in her mind." He was silent for a time, then he said, "Bannion believed that her mind worked like a mosaic: shards of this or that, illuminated here or there, but at last forming a brilliant pattern. He believed that to the very end."

"The end of what?"

"His life," Danforth answered casually. "By then he had nothing but contempt for me."

"Contempt? Why?"

Danforth smiled softly. "Because he thought I was a lovesick fool." He drew in a long, troubled breath. "And it was true, Paul," he said. "I had quite proven that by then." He laughed gently at what he now seemed to regard as a sad fantasy. "I remember how Bannion once shook his head and looked at me as if I'd never be able to understand real commitment. 'With you,' he said, 'it was always her.' Which was true, and which I became aware of after Christophe."

"After Christophe?" I asked.

"Yes," Danforth said. "Because quite by accident he came back into the story. Not with any fanfare, but like fifth business in an opera. The little thing that moves a big thing, and sets even bigger things into motion. With Christophe, it was just a chance meeting in Paris, but it changed everything."

Paris, France, 1939

"*Bonjour*, Thomas."

Danforth turned and saw Christophe, typically bedraggled, moving toward him holding a package covered in brown paper and tied with string.

"I spend a lot of time in the park now," he said. "It's big enough to hide in."

"Why are you hiding?" Danforth asked.

"I am the new Marat," Christophe said with a self-deprecating laugh.

For a moment his eyes softened, and something in them revealed the little boy he had once been, no doubt the most restless and idiosyncratic in his class, doomed by his own nervous energy and incapacity to conform, so that he now seemed as pitiable as Marat must have, a denizen of the city's sewers.

147

He indicated the ragged package beneath his arm. "It's my book," he said. "It's about my time in Spain."

He suddenly became surprisingly talkative, relating tales of combat (a bullet in the thigh in Madrid, shattered ribs when a caisson had rolled over him during the retreat toward the Pyrenees). As he continued, Danforth found himself liking the man more and more, for he was one of those people who could narrate stories of his own self-sacrifice and personal courage in a manner that was comically self-mocking. The bullet in the leg had been his own fault for trying to piss out of view of a young nun. The caisson had rolled over him because he'd dropped his ration of bread, bent down to retrieve it, been butted in the ass by an irritated burro, and from there had slid down a pebbly slope and into the path (talk about bad timing!) of the rolling caisson. He was essentially destitute, and his faith in Communism was all but childlike, but he was also generous and funny, and to these qualities he had added courage and commitment and a willingness to sacrifice his life for the great ideal of unifying mankind beneath the fluttering banner of the International Brigades.

"Would you like to read my book?" Christophe asked.

Danforth saw that Christophe thought him a man of taste and perhaps even some influence in literary circles. To decline to read his book would obviously dishearten him, and Danforth could find no way to refuse the request.

"Of course," he said.

Christophe handed over the manuscript. "You must tell me your true opinion."

After that they talked of nothing in particular, each careful not to mention the trip to Gurs, the Spaniards interned there, any hint of the Project.

They parted a few minutes later, and Danforth would always remember the slump of Christophe's shoulders as he walked away, how they had seemed barely to support the frayed little coat he wore.

Once back in his room, Danforth sat down and began to read Christophe's manuscript. The French he found there was barely grammatical, imbued with faults and misspellings that betrayed the rudimentary nature of the author's education.

As he continued to read, Danforth came to feel Christophe's many deprivations, how much he had been shaped by want and inflamed by the prospect of relieving it. There was a starry-eyed quality to his social analysis that imagined opera houses in the vineyards and concerts in the mines. Christophe believed in Man as religious people believed in God, every word directed toward the achievement of what he called, with awkward if typical hyperbole, "a human heaven where the unshod walk in the clouds and from that height don't look down on others."

It was early evening before Danforth finished the book, and in need of a walk after so long a session, he decided to return it to its author. During the walk, he thought not at all of the odd conversation he'd earlier had with Christophe, his talk of being the new Marat and that he was in hiding; in the coming years, Danforth would find himself amazed at his utter failure to recognize the signs of peril. On that day, as he would many times recall, he'd felt not a twinge of alarm as he entered the dark corridor that led to Christophe's garret, nor was he concerned by the fact that when he reached it, the door was slightly ajar. After knocking softly and calling out Christophe's name, he had, quite without dread, stepped inside.

The room was dimly lighted, and the curtains were tightly drawn, but as he moved farther into the room Danforth saw the unmade bed, single chair, and desk scattered with papers. Christophe had placed a few family photographs on the nearby mantel, pictures that revealed the humble nature of his origins as well as a view of the Normandy landscape in which he had grown up. There was a stack of newspapers by his desk, and a bookshelf that bore exactly what Danforth would have expected: French translations of Marx, Engels, Lenin, and a collection of Stalin's speeches.

From where he stood, near the center of the room, Danforth could see into the tiny bathroom. A plain green curtain hung from a metal bar over the bathtub.

It was then he saw it, a streak of blood that ran down the side of the tub and pooled at its base, a sight that both chilled and captivated him, making him move toward it in exactly the way of a man in a movie melodrama, slowly but steadily, as if in response to music in the background.

Century Club, New York City, 2001

"Like a spy-picture soundtrack," Danforth said. "Very moody. Not that Greek tinkle you hear in *The Third Man.* But very dark and moody. A sustained C, maybe an augmented chord . . ."

"Wait!" I blurted.

Danforth looked at me, perplexed by my sudden outburst.

"What happened to Christophe?" I demanded.

"He'd been murdered," Danforth answered. "A bullet in his head. I later tracked down the weapon. It was German, a nine-millimeter Mauser. Years later, I found out that Christophe had been in contact with something called the Red Orchestra, a group of Communist students based in Berlin, and that he'd made frequent trips to Copenhagen, where he'd also established contacts. All his contacts were young, and almost all of them were dead by the end of the war."

The details Danforth had gathered on such a minor figure in his story surprised me. It also generated a question.

"Did you track down the fate of everyone you were involved with?"

"Yes," Danforth answered. "Because I needed to find out what had actually happened, you see. I needed to find out what Anna had done. But more, I needed to find out why she had done it. Because Bannion was right in what he said to me. It was always her."

A wave of barely suppressed emotion swept over him; he fought it in a way that had by then become familiar, a quick retreat into an academic tone.

"Have you ever been to Orléans, Paul?" he asked.

I shook my head.

"It's quite a lovely city to the southwest of Paris," Danforth said. "Anna and I went there after Christophe's murder. We were, I suppose, on the run. We knew we had to get out of Paris, but we had no idea where we should go, so we went to Orléans. The idea was to keep on the move. I thought it would be good practice once the war broke out." He smiled. "But as it turned out, Orléans was our last stop in France."

Orléans, France, 1939

She crossed the street that day at the height of noon, and Danforth would forever after recall that in that bright summer sun, with the grand façade of the old train station behind her, she had seemed the most improbable of spies. She had none of the studied exoticism of Mata Hari, nothing flamboyant or bejeweled. She looked like someone's daughter or someone's sister or someone's wife. The trappings of the courtesan would have embarrassed her, and Danforth could not imagine her the mistress of some powerful military or government official, gathering secrets revealed during boudoir encounters, passing them on in packets sealed with red wax.

And yet, at that galvanizing moment, Danforth found himself drawn to her as he had never been drawn to any woman before or would be after; through all the passing years, he would hear the click of her heels upon the cobblestones of Orléans and see her eyes searching for him among the assembling throng; he'd remember her sudden, sweet look of recognition when she saw him, followed by her pulling back from whatever regard for him, romantic or otherwise, she'd so briefly revealed.

"Is he still planning to be here?" she asked in French.

She meant Deloncle, who was scheduled to appear at a rally in this, his hometown.

"Yes," Danforth told her. "At Place du Martroi."

Place du Martroi was a large square, the town's central meeting place. The Hôtel de Ville rested at its far end, with the rest of the square bordered by the stately, powder-white façades common to government buildings. Ninety years before, an equestrian statue of Joan of Arc had been commissioned by the town. It showed the Maid of Orléans in full military garb. Anna paused to look at it. She did not appear to identify with Joan or think herself a force in history, and yet something in the way she stopped and gazed on the statue would return to Danforth many times, Anna not as a vision of the female warrior on the march but as a woman contemplating with a certain sympathy the visionary madness of a deluded girl.

The assembly was large but by no means filled the square. Deloncle was a fierce extremist, after all, not a figure of widespread adoration, as de Gaulle would later become. And as Danforth noted a few minutes later, even Prime Minister Daladier, for all his barrel-chested squatness, gave off a considerably more commanding physical presence than the man who now mounted a small platform to address the crowd.

So this is Deloncle, Danforth thought at this first glimpse.

Eugène Deloncle, dressed in a dark suit and wearing a bowler hat, looked more like a bank clerk than the founding member of a violent terrorist organization pledged to bring down the Third Republic. He demonstrated none of the Fascist posturing so much a part of Hitler's and Mussolini's public displays, and far from Léon Gambetta's storied vocal range, his voice would have died a few yards from the platform had amplifiers not been set up to broadcast to the far reaches of the crowd. To offset the general ordinariness of his dress and bearing, he had added only a red rosebud that winked from his lapel and that seemed as out of place as a jewel in a mound of earth.

It was a day for flags, all of them French and all of them waving as Deloncle addressed the crowd. He began with a recitation of the many failures of the present government. Danforth had read excerpts of Deloncle's speeches, and this one was no different from those, save that the speaker seemed more certain that his dire predictions would come to pass, the inevitable war doubtless the harbinger of a great struggle through which the many enemies of France would get what had long been coming to them. First among the villains he named were Communists and Jews, whom he seemed to think one and the same.

The speech went on for half an hour, the crowd cheering repeatedly as Deloncle continued his attack, his rhetoric growing more vehement with each burst of applause until finally he seemed to drown in his own vitriol and, in a kind of emotional exhaustion, turned the microphone over to another speaker.

The entire rally lasted only a few minutes longer, and once it was done, the crowd dispersed more quickly than Danforth had expected, most of them strolling to the many cafés along the square.

Anna watched them go for a time, then said something Danforth had never expected and found extraordinary.

"It's too late for the Project," she said. "And it was never enough anyway."

"Never enough to what?" Danforth asked.

"To matter," Anna said.

She looked at him in a way that made him suddenly recall a night in Paris, how he'd left her apartment and walked across the square at Saint-Germain-des-Prés, and then stopped, glanced up, and noticed her silhouette in the window. He'd thought then, and it returned to him now, that she had all her life been intent upon some purpose, that her current situation was merely the implementation of that long-imagined act.

"Then what do you propose?" Danforth asked.

"I don't know," Anna admitted.

For the first time, she seemed at sea, as if some earlier certainty had been taken from her. She was silent for a time, then, as they slowly walked the square, she began to question not only the Project but any other scheme that would reduce her to a "little spy." If war broke out, what good would it do to send reports of this troop movement or that when the point was to stop those movements? In the same vein, what would be the point of blowing up a bridge or mangling railway tracks? Another bridge would soon replace it, and mangled tracks could be taken up and replaced within hours. And finally, what was the point of waiting for the war to begin at all?

Her expression changed then in a way that Danforth would often think of in the coming years. He would remember how she'd drawn in a long breath, as if undecided about how to voice the idea that had come to her; apparently anticipating that it would be thought absurd, she'd broached the topic at a slant.

"When I was a little girl, we had a nice garden," she said. "I often played in it. One day, a snake came into the garden. My father killed it with a hoe. He showed me the remains of the snake, picking up the head in one hand and the body in the other. 'To kill a snake,' he told me, 'you must chop off the head.'"

She paused, as if the conclusion she'd just come to had stopped her cold. "Do you understand what I mean, Tom?"

He did not understand, and so he simply looked at her, quite baffled.

Very deliberately she added, "I saw a picture of him in Prague. He rides in an open touring car."

Suddenly, Danforth saw the unreality, the sheer absurdity, of what she was getting at.

"Hitler?" he asked in an astonished whisper.

She nodded but added nothing else. Danforth saw immediately that he was trapped: either doomed to be a little spy or compelled to reach for something larger than he'd ever dreamed of. The latter prospect seemed so fantastical and at the same time so alluring that he felt its dark attraction as a kind of lust.

Century Club, New York City, 2001

"Lust?" I asked.

Danforth nodded. "A lust to matter. To do something that mattered."

"But surely you knew that what Anna was proposing was completely insane," I said, no less stunned by Anna's suggestion than Danforth must have been when he first heard it.

"Insane, yes," Danforth admitted. "And to think that the idea began to germinate practically within sight of that little Fascist Deloncle." He took a sip from his glass. "It was the Gestapo who killed him, by the way."

"The Gestapo?" I asked. "Why would the Germans want Deloncle dead?"

"He had gotten a little too close to the Abwehr," Danforth answered. "There was always a great rivalry between Hitler and the German army."

With this, Danforth dismissed any further discussion of Eugène Deloncle's death.

"But we had taken a step," Danforth said. "And I have to confess that for all the fear and dread, there was also a feeling of . . . passion. Very physical. It was as if a beautiful woman had walked into the room, strolled over to me, slipped a knife into my hand, nodded toward some fat old minister of state, and whispered, 'Kill him and I'm yours.'"

I stared at Danforth, genuinely aghast that a history-transforming act could be reduced to so primitive an instinct.

"That's what you must factor in, Paul, the narcotic effect of plotting a stupendous act," Danforth added. "It produces a kind of sustained ecstasy."

I couldn't help but wonder how long Danforth had felt the erotic effects of this narcotic before reality swept in and set him straight.

"Ecstasy, yes," Danforth said, and with those words returned to his story, more tensely and a little more fearfully. But was it the fear a soldier might have as he moved into a region where enemy forces lurked? Or was it the fear of some old Lothario as he opened the door of a murderess's boudoir?

"Ecstasy, but also terror at the very thought of what was in our minds," Danforth said. His smile seemed to reflect the fate he'd glimpsed at that moment long ago. "But I knew that, despite all that, I would see it through to the end." He glanced away, then back at me. "Strange, Paul, but for the rest of my life, when I thought of that moment," he added softly, "I would recall the scent of almonds."

PART IV

The Scent of Almonds

Century Club, New York City, 2001

"Why almonds?" I asked.

"Because that is the odor of cyanide," Danforth said, and then he glanced around like a man either recalling the place where a murder had been committed or looking for a place where one might be carried out.

"We should leave here now, I think," he said.

I looked toward the window. "But it's still snowing quite hard," I warned him.

He smiled at a young man's alarm that an old one should venture out in such weather. "I have learned to be sure-footed," he said. His face took on that familiar expression of an old man teaching a young one the rules of the road. "What do you think is the most important characteristic of a predator?" he asked.

I thought of the spider, still and silent in its web. "Patience," I answered.

Danforth smiled. "Very good. And what is the prey's most important characteristic?"

I shrugged. "I'm not sure."

"Resignation," Danforth said. "Which can only be achieved if the prey understands the purpose of its death."

"You're speaking in human terms then," I said.

A hint of cruelty glittered in Danforth's eyes. "I am speaking, Paul, of revenge."

With that he rose in a way that made him seem already somewhat ghostly, a dark cloud, but a cloud nonetheless, as if he were no longer entirely alive because at his great age he was so very near to death.

"Come," he said. "I have a quiet spot in mind."

The spot wasn't very far, as it turned out, though we'd accumulated a fair amount of snow on the shoulders of our coats before we got there.

"The Blue Bar," he said with a nod to the awning up ahead. "In the Algonquin Hotel. You must have heard of the Algonquin?"

"Yes, of course," I said. "The Round Table. Those famous wits. Dorothy Parker and—"

"Yes, yes," Danforth said sharply, as if all their worldly talk had never been worldly at all. "They were Manhattan provincials, and what could be more provincial than that?" He added a sly wink, but his tone turned somber. "Cleverness is the death of wisdom, Paul."

We reached the bar, and rather than allowing me to do it, Danforth stepped briskly forward, opened the door, and let me enter first. It was an old man's way of demonstrating that although he was old, he was not dependent, and I found myself admiring his determination to assert himself in such a graceful and unoffending manner.

"Thank you," I said as I passed in front of him and gave him a courtly nod. "Most kind."

Danforth smiled. "You are a very polite young man." He said it as if he were suspicious of such formality, as if it were the knife inside the glove.

We took a table by the window, from which we could watch the city's hardworking pedestrians shoulder through this inclement day in this wounded city, a scene that played in Danforth's eyes and seemed, in the way of sorrow, to both darken and enlighten them.

160

"The tragic irony is that it is the people who seek heaven in the future who create hell in the present," he said. With that, he summoned a waiter, and we each ordered a glass of wine, he a white, I a red, both whatever the house suggested.

"Tell me, Paul," Danforth said once the waiter had departed. "Have you been to Moscow?"

"I have, actually," I was pleased to tell him. "But a long time ago. When I was a little boy. On the grand tour I made with my grandfather. He knew the city quite well."

"Really," Danforth said. "Did he happen to show you the city's swimming pool?"

"Swimming pool? No. It was the middle of winter."

"Too bad," Danforth said. "I don't know this for a fact, but I can't imagine that it isn't the largest swimming pool in the world. And it has quite a history, that pool. Quite a story of its own."

And then he told it.

In the summer of 1931, he said, *Pravda* announced that the Palace of the Soviets was to be built in Moscow. The planned physical dimensions of this palace were stupendous. It was to be six times the size of the Empire State Building, and at its completion, it would be crowned with a gigantic statue of Lenin three times as high as the Statue of Liberty. This was Stalin's answer to capitalism, and he intended it to be a very powerful one. Equally important to this aim, the Palace of the Soviets was to be built next to the Kremlin on the huge piece of real estate at that time occupied by the Cathedral of Christ the Savior, itself a monumental structure thirty stories tall with walls more than three meters thick and whose bronze cupola alone weighed 176 tons.

"All this, of course, had to be torn down before the Palace of the Soviets could be built," Danforth said.

And so various methods for carrying out this destruction were endlessly discussed. It was even proposed that the building be bombed, but accuracy was a problem, and so during the course of a single night, a huge wooden barrier was erected around the cathedral, after which the interior of the church was stripped of a half a ton of gold, along with an incalculable treasure of diamonds, silver, topaz, amethyst, emeralds, and ornately carved enamels, all of which disappeared into government warehouses or the vaults of the Soviet secret police.

"The demolition was completed in early December," Danforth said. "In four months one of the great architectural jewels of Moscow had been completely razed."

Now came the construction of the Palace of the Soviets. It was to be over four hundred meters high, weigh 1.5 million tons, and enclose an area greater than the six largest skyscrapers currently towering above the streets of New York. Lenin's gigantic statue was to crown this spectacular edifice. His index finger alone would stretch to six meters.

"But this statue never rose, nor the building to support it," Danforth continued. "Everything sank into a morass of bad planning. The foundation was dug, but then the rains came, and then the snow, and in the spring, rivers of melting ice, and so the vast foundation filled with water. The water became infested with frogs and choked with duckweed, and worst of all, the whole disaster was now quite visible because the huge wooden fence that had concealed the earlier destruction had been dismantled by Muscovites desperate for firewood."

"My God," I said. "What a mess."

"The years passed," Danforth said. "Children fished in the depths of the old foundation. Stalin died. Khrushchev replaced him, and one day he looked out over this huge stinking lake of stagnant water and decided, Well, maybe a swimming pool."

With that he laughed softly, but I didn't.

"What, Paul, you find nothing funny in this tale?" Danforth asked pointedly.

"No," I said. "No, it seems very sad to me, that people can become so deluded, destroy so wantonly out of some crazy ideology."

"It rather makes you suspect that true belief is always false," he said.

I nodded. "Yes, I think that's true."

The expression on Danforth's face relaxed slightly, as if he'd been given a signal that it was safe to go on. "Then you are ready to hear more of my story," he said.

"Good," I said with an enthusiasm that surprised me. "Well, in our last episode, Anna was in league . . ."

Danforth lifted his hand in a cautionary gesture. "Anna was in league, yes." His smile was thoroughly enigmatic. "But with whom?"

Orléans, France, 1939

Danforth would relive the sight of that morning on many occasions over the next sixty years. He would sometimes remember that they stood very near each other, Bannion's entire profile visible but Anna's face obscured by the slender trunk of the sapling in the foreground.

At other times, however, he'd remember them standing somewhat farther apart, Bannion with a scrap of paper in his hand, one he quickly—rather too quickly?—sank into the pocket of his jacket as Danforth approached. In this remembrance, Anna reaches for the paper and then hastily—too hastily?—draws back her hand so that it is covered by the folds of her long, black skirt.

But in every recollection of this moment, the two of them, Bannion and Anna, would turn toward him smoothly and in unison, both with oddly drawn faces whose expressions would seem to him, in countless grave reenactments, like those of lovers plotting murder.

"Hello, Tom," Bannion said.

He had been in England when he'd received their message of Christophe's murder, Bannion told him, and of their subsequent flight to Orléans. Clayton had dispatched him immediately with orders to find out if Christophe's death had entirely compromised the Project and, if it had, what steps should be taken.

"We could certainly attempt to carry on with our earlier plans," Bannion added. "But Anna tells me that you two have been thinking of something much more . . . grand."

"Yes," Danforth said.

"I'm not sure Clayton would approve this new idea," Bannion said.

"Perhaps it's not up to Clayton," Danforth said.

"A rogue operation?" Bannion asked. "I wouldn't try it if I were you."

Cautioning though Bannion's remark was, he seemed to understand that a great plot was like a huge stone: once in motion, it took on a direction and velocity of its own, the plotters forever running in front of it while it closed in on them from behind, urging them forward and forward until, at a certain point, they feared their own failure to act more than they feared the consequences of their action.

"But if Clayton goes along," Bannion added, "then we can begin to make our plans."

With that one remark, his use of *we* and *our*, it seemed to Danforth that Bannion had insinuated himself into what had been a league of two. It was as if he had barged into an intimate conversation and then proceeded to dominate it.

"This will have to be a very tight circle," Bannion said. He looked at Anna. "But yes, it is worth doing, I think. And I can probably persuade Clayton to approve it."

So it was really going to happen, Danforth thought; they were going to do it. Up to that moment, the actual attempt had seemed distant in the way that all peril seems distant until it is upon you. But now he saw that the spiral was tightening, that it was very, very serious, the game no longer a game, and he was reminded of a line from Bion he'd once had to memorize in the original Greek: *Though boys throw stones at frogs in sport, the frogs die in earnest.*

He said none of this as they walked to the hotel, where only days before he'd sat at the little desk in his room and written several letters to business associates in Berlin. He was seeking African antiquities he'd told them, particularly items acquired from Germany's former colonies in east and southwest Africa. He'd made it a point to express his displeasure with Germany's loss of these colonies, along with "other confiscations of Versailles." At the time, this had seemed very far from the carrying out of an assassination, though it had no doubt moved the plot along. Now the letters seemed little more than props in a high-school play.

At the hotel, Bannion shook their hands, then said, "I'll be back after I've talked to Clayton. If he goes along with this, I can get us some very useful information."

With that, he left them so quickly he seemed hardly to have been there at all.

Danforth glanced toward the small outdoor café next to the hotel. "Would you like some tea?"

"Yes," Anna answered.

Once seated, she drew the scarf from her head and let her hair fall wildly, now reaching all the way to her shoulders, a gesture that seemed intimate and that Danforth would later believe she had made on purpose, creating a mood she then used — was it cunningly? — to reveal more of herself to him.

"Did Mr. LaRoche ever mention Baku?" she asked.

"Yes," Danforth said. "He talked about how beautiful it had once been and about what the Bolsheviks did to it."

"My father once took me there," Anna said. She smiled. "I was very young at the time, but Baku is a place that leaves lifelong impressions. I remember roasted cumin seeds and the sacks of spices, turmeric, how yellow it was in that sun." The smile dissolved. "And the caravans," she added. "Some had come all the way across the Caucasus Mountains. The animals looked so tired. I remember feeling very sorry for them."

"How long were you in Baku?" Danforth asked.

"Only a day or so," Anna answered. "Then we returned to Erzinghan."

The name itself returned Danforth to one of the darkest of his father's tales. "Erzinghan? In Turkey?" Danforth asked.

"I was born there," Anna said.

Danforth felt the horror fall over him. "Erzinghan," he said softly.

She noticed the glimmer in Danforth's eyes. "You know about it then?" she asked.

"Yes," Danforth said. "One of our buyers had been there. He said that near Erzinghan, at a bend in the Euphrates, the river had become so clogged with the dead, it briefly changed its course."

"Those were terrible times," Anna said. She thought a moment, and while she thought, something in her eyes deepened and darkened, as if she were moving backward into a dimmer light. "I've been thinking about them a lot in the last few days."

"Why?"

"Because there was a man in our region," she answered. "His name was Demir. He was a writer and a scholar, but he had terrible things in his mind and he did terrible things because of it, and no one ever stopped him." She paused and let her gaze deepen further. "What I mean is that no one killed Kulli Demir. That's the point I'm making, Tom. There must have been lots of people who had the chance, but no one did. And so other men saw that Demir could do whatever he pleased and get away with it. Then they started to do the same things he did. They rounded up the men and killed them, and when the men were gone, they did whatever they wanted to the women and the girls. And the ones they didn't kill, they drove into Syria. Most of them died on the way, but a few made it to Aleppo."

Danforth offered no response to this, but years later, still seeking the truth through the bramble left behind, he would come upon this passage in the memoir of an American who'd found himself in Turkey at the time of Anna's early girlhood:

The pattern was usually the same, according to reports, and it was corroborated by the one incident I witnessed myself. The local authorities would notify the Kurdish tribes and Turkish peasants that a caravan was on the way. The caravan was women and children, and they would be set upon by these Kurds and Turks and Chetes, along with various bands of thugs and criminals. These women and girls had no defense against these men because those who would have defended them, their fathers and husbands and brothers, had already been killed, and so they could be attacked without fear of reprisal. Many times these women did not survive the tortures and rapes that were inflicted upon them. They were "guarded" by the gendarmes, but these men not only did nothing to protect the women and girls, they sometimes joined the others in tormenting them. They seemed to hate the ones who survived, and when it was time to move on, they rained blows upon them with whips and truncheons, stabbed at them with bayonets, deprived them of food, and made no attempt to return the clothing, mostly rags, that had been ripped off their bodies, so that when the caravan I personally witnessed finally reached Syria, the women were starved and naked, and many were crazed and raving. I saw a group of these poor female skeletons stagger across the border one afternoon and I thought that they could not have come from any place on earth and must have somehow dragged themselves out of hell. The last of them, stumbling behind, were the most lost of the lost, very young girls, from twelve to as young as three, bereft of both mothers and fathers, with no one to help them even among their own people. Dirty, naked, unimaginably alone at the far end of the caravan, these little girls made their way into the desert wastes of Aleppo.

Reading that passage years later as he sat in the stillness of the New York Public Library, Danforth would wonder, darkly and incessantly, if one of those lost little girls had been Anna Klein.

Blue Bar, New York City, 2001

"Because she'd had this haunted look when she spoke of what she'd seen in Turkey, you see," Danforth said. "I had seen that look a few times before that afternoon, but her personal history had never seemed so tragic as it did at that moment, which made me come to believe that she herself had suffered the outrages she described."

"This is the Armenian genocide, correct?" I asked.

Danforth nodded. "Have you read much about it, Paul?"

"A little," I answered. "But I didn't know Jews were massacred as well."

Danforth clearly appreciated my response. "Very good, Paul," he said. "That would be the question, wouldn't it?"

"Question?"

"If you ever came to doubt any part of Anna's story," Danforth explained in a coolly inquisitorial tone. "You'd have to ask yourself whether a young Jewish girl might have been rounded up and marched into Syria along with the Armenians." He took a slow sip from his glass. "Well, I looked into this very question, and I found that as a matter of fact, by the time of the Armenian genocide, Jews had lived in what later became the Armenian provinces of Turkey for thousands of years. They had probably first come in flight, some from Assyria, others from Samaria, still others from God knows where." Then, quite abruptly, he blinked a thousand years of Diaspora from his eyes and was miraculously returned to modern times. "Anna saw the assassination of the king of Yugoslavia, you know."

Danforth saw my surprise at this fact and laughed.

"Not with her own eyes, of course," he said. "But in the newsreels. He was killed in Marseille in 1934. The first assassination to be recorded on film. She once mentioned how easy it looked." He shrugged. "Maurice Bavaud probably saw that newsreel too."

"Maurice Bavaud?"

"In pictures, he never had the smile of an assassin," Danforth said. "In fact, he didn't seem to know how to smile. Or maybe it was that he simply couldn't bring himself to smile in a world as chaotic as Europe was in 1938."

This was one of Danforth's divergences, and earlier I would have been eager to get past it, but by then I'd come to realize that his asides were always closely related to his tale, and so I simply heard him out.

Bavaud was a devout Catholic, Danforth told me, a young man who had been a seminarian at Saint-Brieuc in Brittany when he was seized by the insane notion that in order for Christianity to be saved, the Romanovs had to be returned to power in Russia. He was equally convinced that killing Adolf Hitler would set the wheels in motion.

In the fall of 1938, he'd traveled first to Baden-Baden and then on to Basel, where he bought a Schmeisser 6.5-millimeter semi-automatic pistol, Danforth told me.

It struck me that Danforth had studied Bavaud's plot to kill Hitler in great detail, as if he'd been in search of some small element that might explain how his own had failed.

"After Basel, Bavaud boarded another train, this time heading for Berlin," he continued.

He had planned — if his movements and intentions could be called a plan at all — simply to shoot Hitler in his capital, but he'd later decided to do it in Munich during the annual celebration of the Beer Hall Putsch.

"The celebration always included a march," Danforth said. "With Hitler himself at the head of the parade."

And so once in Munich, Bavaud obtained a complimentary ticket to the stand in front of the Holy Ghost Church, at the western end of Talstrasse, a site that seemed quite well situated to watch the march as it turned into Marienplatz, a turn, Bavaud correctly reasoned, that would slow things down considerably because everyone would have to squeeze through the small archway that led to the square.

"But there was plenty of time before the march," Danforth continued. "And at that point it seemed to occur to Bavaud that in view of what he intended to do, a little target practice might be in order."

A few days later, Bavaud bought some extra ammunition and rented a boat on Lake Ammer, not far outside of Munich. He rowed out onto the water and practiced shooting at little paper targets he launched from his boat. Later, he practiced again, this time aiming at trees in the forest.

"Like Anna at Winterset," I blurted, as if I'd discovered the reason for this divergence, the thing that connected it, however tangentially, to his tale.

"Yes," Danforth answered crisply, then continued.

When he returned to Munich, Bavaud obtained a detailed map of the route of the march, then walked its entire length in order to ascertain whether there was any better vantage point than the one he had. He found none better, and no doubt thought that here was the hand of God assisting him. What else could explain his seat near the archway of Marienplatz, a perfect bottleneck?

"And so at last the moment had come," Danforth said. "Bavaud took his place on the reviewing stand, and shortly after that, the man he'd come to kill took his place in the line of the march."

I imagined the head of this particular snake as he proceeded in the march, lifting his arm in return salute to the crowd, but curiously indifferent to their adoration, as if determined not to let even the people's idolatry sway him from his purpose.

"Bavaud finally caught sight of him," Danforth said. "Can you imagine what that must have been like, watching the target move toward you, oblivious to the danger, distant at first, but coming nearer and nearer? And you have this pistol in your belt and your hand crawls toward it, and as you do that, a kind of tunnel vision sets in, so that everything on the periphery of the target blurs and all the cheering and horns and drums go silent, and there is just you and the one you've come to kill."

At that moment in his narrative, I believed that Danforth was describing himself, rather than Bavaud, and I felt certain that at some point he had aimed a pistol at close range and felt his finger pull back on the trigger.

"But just as the target is in range," he continued, "just as you grip the handle of the pistol and ease it from your belt — just at that moment, with the man himself so close you can almost feel his breath on your face — at just that moment, Paul, the crowd shifts and surges and a hundred arms are raised, and in that press and tangle, your target vanishes from sight, and by the time you see him clearly again, he is passing beneath the little arch and into the square . . . and into his future, and the world's."

"Is that what happened?" I asked. "To Bavaud?"

"Yes," Danforth answered.

"How do you know that?"

"Because he said so," Danforth replied.

"So he was caught?"

"Yes, but not before returning to Bertesgarten, shooting at more trees — without a silencer, I might add — and generally stalking around town. He even once asked a policeman how he might get closer to Hitler."

"And no one noticed him?" I asked, astonished.

"No one," Danforth said with a shrug. "Security is a human thing, Paul, carried out by humans, and with all the human imperfections."

"Did he ever get close to Hitler again?"

Danforth shook his head. "And so he started back. Unfortunately, he had run out of money, and so he found it necessary to stow away on a train. He was discovered and questioned. During the course of this, the authorities found his notebook. He'd taken the trouble to record his intention to kill Hitler in that notebook. They found the little Schmeisser six-point-five too. Of course he was arrested. After that, the usual stages. Interrogation. Torture. Execution. In Bavaud's case, by guillotine in Plötzensee Prison."

"He seems rather hapless," I said. "Pitiful in a way. So naive that —"

"No more than we were, really," Danforth interrupted. "And Bavaud had a more passionate reason for attempting to kill Hitler than I did. Frankly, Paul, my whole purpose by that time had become simply to be near Anna." He shrugged. "At one moment, under the sway of such feelings, a man buys flowers. At another moment, under the sway of those same feelings, he takes a step toward murder."

"So it was always her," I said softly.

"Always her," Danforth said. "Yes."

Then his voice returned to its familiar narrative tone, driving slowly forward, carrying me along with it, so that, like them, I felt the train lurch forward then move smoothly out of Orléans station.

Orléans, France, 1939

The train lurched forward, and in that movement, Danforth felt that he was no longer a little spy but a man moving inexorably toward an earth-shattering act.

Later, as his train drew ever closer to the German border, Danforth still more intensely considered the astonishing fact that he was now committed to a supremely perilous scheme. He knew this clearly, and from time to time, he reviewed the weight of the task before him, how surreal it was, along with its surpassing dangers. But for all that, he could imagine no alternative course, and years later, in the frozen wastes of his long pursuit, when he came to describe these events, he characterized his feelings as "intractable, irreducible, and adamantine." Anna's resolve had fortified his own. They were iron and steel, and he felt their strength conjoined. But there was a magic that went beyond the familiar notion of one person's courage giving courage to another. He thought of it as alchemy, a mysterious mixture made from peril and purpose and infused with a romance that every day grew more intense. For he was falling in love, and he knew it, and it seemed to him that to be in love and at war simultaneously was surely to live life at the top.

At the border, the first German official approached them, his uniform thoroughly Germanic in its starched and neatly pressed precision. He asked for their passports, opened each, then returned them.

"What is your purpose in coming to Germany?" he asked Danforth.

"We are here on business," Danforth answered in his perfect German. "I am an importer." He nodded toward Anna. "Miss Collier is my assistant."

"Herr Danforth, Fraulein Collier," the officer said with a polite nod to each of them. *"Willkommen nach Deutschland."*

"Well," Danforth said once the officer had departed, "that went well, don't you think?"

Anna returned her passport to her small leather purse. "The really dangerous border stations," she said, "are the ones where the guards are wearing only parts of their uniforms."

It was a curious comment, one that suggested to Danforth that Anna had known such bleak and poorly supplied border crossings, sun-baked and remote, as he imagined them, with sweltering guardhouses of windowless concrete, the border itself merely a dusty line drawn between two vast but equally impoverished wastes.

There were no other official inquiries after that first polite officer, and they reached Berlin, and at last their hotel just off Unter den Linden, without further intrusions.

That evening they had their first dinner in Berlin. They were both tired from the journey and so decided to dine in the hotel restaurant, a faded affair with too much drapery and crystal, little more than a sepia photograph from the belle époque.

"I've been thinking about the letters you wrote the business-people here," Anna said. "Perhaps we shouldn't make contact with any of them, Tom."

"Why not?"

"Because they might get into trouble later for knowing us," Anna answered.

It was a realistic appraisal of Germany at that moment, of course, and so Danforth thought nothing of it at the time, though later he would wonder if she'd sought to isolate him, keep him within the tight circle that enclosed her plot. If so, he hadn't sensed it then and had simply nodded and said, "Yes, I think you're right."

Anna glanced from the restaurant toward the lobby of the hotel. Two men were standing at the desk, both in long coats. "We'll need cyanide," she said. "I asked Bannion to get it for us."

Danforth thought of the Connecticut warehouse, how close he had come to betraying her. "Yes," he said. "We will. But maybe we won't have to use it."

Which seemed entirely possible to Danforth, as they had previously decided on a bomb as the best method, a device Anna had been trained to make and use and hide, so it was feasible that they might both accomplish their mission and survive it.

She drew in a long breath as she turned back to him. "You would miss it, wouldn't you?"

"Miss what?"

"Life."

"Of course," Danforth said with a sudden sense of alarm. "Wouldn't you?"

She nodded.

Danforth thought of the odd question she had asked in what now seemed almost an earlier life.

"Speaking of life, what's the most beautiful place you've never seen?" he asked her.

She smiled. "There are more of them than I can name, Tom," she answered.

"Try."

She did, and as she moved from place to place, it seemed to Danforth that she had never looked more eager to live. So much so that it would be many years before he wondered if even this — the hunger she showed for the world — had been but another of her many masquerades.

Blue Bar, New York City, 2001

I knew Danforth had related this conversation for a reason, and that for some other reason, he did not elaborate upon it but instead eased himself back slightly, as if trying to get a clearer view of some far-distant scene. "There is a little town called Dubno, Paul."

This village had enjoyed a more or less quiet life, he told me, a small town that rested along the equally tranquil Ikva River. It was surrounded by a few rolling hills in that part of the Ukraine that was sometimes Poland, sometimes Russia, depending on the politics of the time. The Soviets had seized it in 1939 and then been driven eastward by a German onslaught that, as Danforth reminded me, had seemed near invincible at the time.

"When the Germans took over Dubno," Danforth went on, "about half its population was Jewish. There were fourteen synagogues in the town. Jewish doctors, lawyers, teachers."

His voice took on the quiet intensity that marked these asides, an old-man Scheherezade.

"On October fifth, 1942, if a little girl on a certain street had looked out her bedroom window, she would have seen hundreds of people passing by as they headed out of town toward the old airfield an hour's walk away," Danforth continued. "They would have been dressed according to their class, some quite fine, some in hand-me-downs. Witnesses said they walked slowly and in great order, with only a few soldiers and dogs keeping watch."

To my surprise, I could hear the muffled steps of these hundreds; even without my knowing that the street they'd walked had been made of flagstone, I heard the rhythm of their feet over them, along with bits of indecipherable talk: the urging forward of the old, the calming down of the young.

"There was a shallow chasm three kilometers out of town," Danforth went on. "This is where they stopped and stripped. Hermann Graebe, a German construction engineer who witnessed the event, saw great mounds of shoes and underwear and clothing. He said they stood in family groups, that people too old or sick or disoriented to disrobe were stripped by their younger relatives. One man bent down to his little boy, pointed to the sky, and seemed to be telling him something very important. A young woman, completely naked, came very near to Graebe as she made her way toward the execution pit. She pointed to herself as she passed by. 'Twenty-three,' she said. Twenty-three."

I shook my head at this sad tale, though I had no idea why Danforth had now taken me so far east.

"German stock," Danforth said suddenly. "Suppose, Paul, that I knew that twenty-three-year-old girl. Suppose it was . . . Anna. Suppose I also knew the man who carried out the massacre at Dubno. Suppose that after the war I tracked him down, only to find that he'd died years before." He smiled. "But suppose he had a son, a daughter, grandchildren. Should I kill them all?"

"Of course not," I answered. "They had nothing to do with what happened at Dubno."

"But they're all I have left, Paul," Danforth said. "They're all I have left to get even with the man who killed the woman I loved."

"Perhaps so, but it would be unreasonable to kill these other people," I said.

"You're right, it would be quite unreasonable," Danforth agreed. "But vengeance is a passion of the heart, isn't it? And as Pascal said, the heart has its reasons that reason knows nothing of." Before I could answer, he added, "And in that article you wrote, didn't you say that in the current situation, our acts should flow from passion?"

"Yes," I said softly.

Danforth's eyes appeared to harden. "I agree," he said.

For a moment, he peered at me silently. Then, like a driver abruptly realizing he'd missed a turn, he swung back to his earlier narrative.

"When I heard about Dubno, heard that story of the girl pointing at herself, crying out her age as she was heading toward her death, it reminded me of Anna," Danforth said. "It reminded me of the way she was in the hotel that night in Berlin, talking about Venice or Vienna or some other place she one day hoped to see. She seemed like that girl in Dubno. Too young to die."

The stricken look on Danforth's face at that moment warned me away from asking about Anna directly. And so I said, "Where did you hear about Dubno?"

"I heard about it when Hermann Graebe testified at the trials."

"The trials?"

"Nuremberg," Danforth said. "When I was working at the war crimes trials. Graebe's testimony was particularly interesting to me because it was at Dubno that a man with the daunting name of Axel Freiherr von dem Bussche-Streithorst changed. He was a German soldier who saw the massacre at Dubno, and because of it, he decided to kill Hitler."

"So your interest is in his motivation?" I asked.

"Yes," Danforth answered. "I studied them all. Every attempt on Hitler's life."

"Why?"

"Because I wanted to know the variety of motivations," Danforth said. "In discovering them, I thought I might also discover Anna's."

"But why not just accept that she was a Jew, and Hitler was persecuting Jews?" I said.

"That motivation, or a thousand other ones, Paul," Danforth said. "It would have been easy if she had been easy." His gaze became piercing. "It's what you don't know that destroys you." He drew in a sharp breath. "And believe me," he added, "I did not know Anna Klein." Danforth seemed almost to dissolve into this fog of unknowing, then he gathered himself once again. "But where were we, Paul?" he asked. "Yes. Berlin. That old hotel. So long in the tooth. I told her it reminded me of an old woman who'd once been beautiful."

Berlin, Germany, 1939

Anna smiled. "Istanbul is like that," she said. "Crumbling palaces along the Bosporus. My father called it an 'aged courtesan.'"

It surprised Danforth that she mentioned her father, since she had spoken so rarely of her past, and many years later, he would wonder if this had been a line skillfully cast out, spare yet bearing just the sort of bait she knew would lure him deeper into the current, with its hint of the foreign, the exotic. She revealed herself in little flashes of her past in the way some lady of a royal court might allow a brief glimpse of her ankle.

"He seems to have been quite the traveler, your father," Danforth said.

"He was, yes," Anna said with so much aridness that she gave off the sense of a field scattered with his dust. "I loved him very much."

"What happened to him?"

"He died."

With that she took up the menu and appeared, in that gesture, to secrete herself behind it. "I'm talking too much about myself," she said.

"Not at all," Danforth told her. "As a matter of fact, you'd think you were some kind of criminal, the way I have to pry things out of you." He gave her a knowing look. "Or do you just want to seem mysterious?"

She lowered the menu, and he saw that she had taken him seriously. "It's not that at all. It's just that I think we should stay apart, Tom. Because of what we're doing."

"I understand," Danforth told her.

And he did understand her point, that given the nature of their circumstances, they should remain aloof from each other. And yet, just at that moment, he felt a terrible urge to touch her, one more powerful than at any time before, and he knew that the more he suppressed that urge, the more it would assert itself.

He could say none of this, of course, and so he quickly changed the subject.

"So," he said as he took up the menu. "What shall we have?"

They ordered, ate, finished with tea, then strolled out of the hotel, down the street, and into a small square. It was a warm summer night, and the lights from nearby *biergartens* flickered all around them. The crowds were large, almost teeming, and nothing in their movements seemed controlled by anything more than the traffic signals.

They found a bench and sat down together, silent still, watching the passing parade. In such a pose they might have looked like a pair of young lovers, he in pursuit, she coming near to giving in to his advances, and had their purpose not been so grave, Danforth thought, he might have reached out to her as he so much wanted to do.

It was a surge of desire she clearly sensed.

"We should start to get the materials," she said starkly, a line that returned him to the cold matter at hand.

She meant the ones for the bomb, of course, though they had never discussed where it would be planted.

"We'll also need to plan a way to get out of Germany once we know it went off," Danforth told her.

"But there's only one way to know," Anna said. "To be there when it does. To be one of those women who rush up to him with flowers in their hands."

By the methodical and unyielding way she said it, Danforth knew that such had always been her plan, that she would conceal the bomb beneath her coat or behind a great spray of flowers, and by that means die with the man she murdered, join with him in the same red blast.

Blue Bar, New York City, 2001

"So she was to be a suicide bomber," I said, almost as stunned as Danforth had described himself on the heels of this revelation.

"Yes," Danforth said.

"But why not plant the bomb," I asked, "in a piece of coal, or something like it, the way LaRoche suggested?"

"For the very reason Anna gave me," Danforth answered. "Because you can't be sure it will go off at the right moment or if the target will be in place when it does go off." He shrugged. "And she was right, Paul. We know now that there were at least forty-two plots to kill Adolf Hitler. Von Stauffenberg's plot is the most famous, of course, because it came closest to actual success. But by the time Count von Stauffenberg planted his little briefcase a few feet from Hitler, his target had already wreaked havoc on Europe, ravaged whole countries, exterminated millions. Even if von Stauffenberg's attempt had succeeded, it would have been too late to save anything but a small, shredded bit of German pride. The war was already coming to a close, with Germany in certain defeat, and so to the people who'd already gone up the chimney, it would have meant nothing. To the people rotting in death pits or buried in the rubble of countless bombed-out towns and villages, it would have meant nothing. Hitler had already done his worst." He offered a small shrug. "But Paul, imagine what would have happened if Johann Georg Elser's bomb had succeeded."

"It might have changed history," I said.

"Indeed it might have," Danforth agreed, then continued. "Elser was a cabinetmaker who'd joined the Red Front Fighters' Organization," he said. "Is that name familiar to you, Paul?"

The tone of the question struck me as almost probing, as if Danforth actually thought I might have heard of such an organization.

"No," I answered. "I'm not a student of modern German history."

"Of course not," Danforth said, as if reminding himself of that fact. "Well, anyway, Elser decided on a bomb and built one. Then the question was how to get the bomb close enough to Hitler. He chose the beer hall where Hitler always spoke during Putsch celebration in Munich. And so he went there, drank, stayed late, and as closing time neared, he hid in a closet. After everyone left the hall, he went to work digging into one of the building's supporting columns. He dug all night, then repaired the front of the column, hid himself again, and left the beer hall when it opened the next day. He repeated this process every night for more than a month until he'd made a place for the bomb. He set it to go off at precisely nine twenty on the evening of Wednesday, November eighth, 1939." He shrugged. "But Hitler wanted to be back in Berlin that night. He couldn't fly there because a dense fog had grounded his airplane, so he made his speech earlier than planned and then took a train back. He left at eight ten, and so he was nowhere near the beer hall when Elser's bomb went off."

The explosion had gone off right on time, however, Danforth said. It had been quite powerful. In fact, it had killed eight people and wounded sixty-five. As it turned out, one of the wounded was none other than Eva Braun's father.

"As for Elser, he was arrested and later executed at Dachau, on April sixth, 1945, just two weeks before the end of the war. By then he'd seen all that might have been prevented if the fog had not crowded in on Munich on that November night."

He stopped, and by the change in his expression, I knew that he had returned to some memory of Anna.

"It was true, what Anna said," he added finally. "To kill a snake, you must strike the head." He thought a moment, then continued. "But something else is no less true: you must strike early at this head, before the snake has coiled and focused its yellow eyes and done the worst it can do." He paused again, then looked at me pointedly. "And so we began to assemble the materials for the bomb."

"But you still had no plan," I said.

"Most assassins don't," Danforth said. "At least, the successful ones don't. Oswald had no plan, save to be at the right place at the right time." He thought this over, then added, "The men who killed Garfield and McKinley didn't have plans either, not beyond having an idea of where the target might be and going there."

"But surely you need a plan of some sort," I insisted. "A way to get close to the target."

"Yes, we needed that," Danforth said. "And for a moment—long shot though it was—I thought I might have found it."

Berlin, Germany, 1939

"He wanted to be a painter," Anna said. "He tried to get into the Vienna Academy of Art but he was rejected." They were walking in a small square, a summer breeze playing in the leaves. "You could say that you were interested in looking at his work."

"Interested?" Danforth asked. "In what way? He sells very well here in Germany. Why would he be interested in an American buyer?"

"Because he's vain," Anna answered. "All I would need is one meeting. You could be out of the country before it happens."

Out of the country, yes, Danforth thought, out of the country and back to America and a life he felt no desire to resume.

But it was a good idea, and so he nodded his assent, and later that same afternoon composed the letter on his personal stationery. It was simple, and very direct. There was an audience for Hitler's work in the United States, he wrote, patrons of the arts who have no interest in crude Expressionism. Hitler's painting, he said, would certainly appeal to such people. To this he added, *Of course, the chancellor's place in the world, not to mention his recent appearance on the cover of* Time *magazine, would no doubt boost interest, but I believe that the paintings would find an audience here even if they didn't carry so famous a signature.*

"Okay," Danforth said. "Now, who do we send it to?"

"No one," Anna said. "Just put it in the general mail, addressed to the Reich Chancellery. It'll be less suspicious that way."

They expected no response, of course, but while they waited they became more familiar with Berlin, walking its streets and parks, strolling through its most prominent buildings, observing places where their target might at some point appear.

There was an unreal quality to this interval, as Danforth would often recall, so that he sometimes imagined them as newlyweds on their honeymoon.

Then the honeymoon abruptly ended.

"It's from the interior ministry," Danforth said when he showed Anna the letter. He opened the letter and read it with ever-increasing astonishment. "It's from someone named Ernst Kruger. He says that the chancellor welcomes my interest in his work. A car will be waiting for us at Wannsee Station on July nineteenth at ten in the morning." He lowered the letter and stared at Anna in utter amazement. "We're going to be shown some of the chancellor's paintings."

Anna took the letter and read it, then handed it back to Danforth.

"All right," she said. "Let's get started."

For the next few days they did what they could to familiarize themselves with Hitler's work. It was on display in several places throughout the city, small galleries and public buildings, and they spent long hours peering at the paintings, Danforth trying to place them within a school he thought Herr Kruger might find favorable but without resorting to obvious undeserved flattery.

"He has talent," Anna said at one point. She was staring at a painting of a cathedral in Vienna.

Danforth nodded. "He can draw at least."

The following days included other tours, and during these quiet days of waiting, Danforth gave Anna a crash course on the sort of art Hitler appeared to favor and imitate, a style heavy on traditional representation that ignored entirely any modernist influence.

On the appointed morning, they met in the hotel lobby for the trip to Wannsee, and when Danforth saw her emerge from the elevator he nearly swooned at the transformation. She looked every bit the worldly assistant to a major American art dealer. The clothes were the same she'd worn in Paris, but she'd lifted her collar, padded the shoulders of her jacket, and added a discreet white ruffle to each sleeve.

It was the art of an actress and the art of a seamstress, Danforth thought, both now applied to the art of murder.

"You look very"—he stopped and waited until he found the right word—"appropriate."

In Wannsee, a black sedan was waiting for them, complete with a driver who was clearly not a driver at all but a security agent. A second man stood beside the military officer and appeared to be in charge. He was dressed in the long leather trench coat Danforth associated with the Gestapo.

"My name is Klaus Wald," he said in German as he thrust out his hand.

Danforth greeted him in German, then introduced Anna.

"I was expecting only one person," Wald said.

"Miss Collier is the real expert on American naturalism," Danforth explained.

Danforth was relieved to see that Wald quite clearly had no idea what American naturalism was.

"She is a great lover of landscapes," Danforth explained. "Which appear to be a favorite subject of Chancellor Hitler."

Wald nodded crisply, then turned to Anna. "Good. Well, then. Shall we go?"

They got into the back seat, then waited for the officer to take his place at the wheel, Wald beside him. Anna peered out at the station. "Quite a lovely town," she said in German as the car pulled away.

Neither of the two men spoke during the short drive from the station, but by prearrangement, Danforth and Anna kept up a steady stream of talk, all of it about art, and all of it in German.

Since it was well known that Hitler was quite prolific, Danforth had expected a warehouse, scores and scores of still-life paintings of flowers, bridges, and the like, only a small portion of which, he assumed, had ever been on public display.

Instead, Wald brought the car to a halt before a large stone building that, in a less suburban atmosphere, Danforth would have called a villa. It had two stories and was constructed of a light gray stone and included a welcoming half-circle portico, a design he'd be reminded of years later when he found himself at 56-58 Am Grossen, where the terrible decisions of the Wannsee Conference had been made and where he would once again confront the possibility that Anna's fate might have been worse than he'd previously supposed.

But on that morning, in the summer sunlight, with the lovely façade of the villa in front of him and with Anna splendid at his side, he allowed himself another slip into unreality, as if it were all a novel or a movie, this drama he was living through, he and Anna merely characters in it, neither of them made of flesh that could be torn or blood that could be spilled, beyond the grasp of such human fates. It was an unreality that had often seized him in the past and that would seize him once more in the future but then, after that, would leave him forever captive to the cold reality of things.

"Herr Danforth?"

The man who spoke stood at the bottom of the stairs outside the house, dressed in a brown double-breasted suit, on the lapel of which, as if to add color, there was a swastika pin, black on a red background.

Danforth took the man's hand and shook it.

"Welcome to Wannsee," the man said in German. "I am Ernst Kruger." He looked at Anna and offered his hand.

"Anna Collier," she said.

"Most pleased to meet you, fräulein," Kruger said. He turned and gestured toward the double doors that led into the building. "Please."

The military officer stationed himself at the door after they passed through it, but Wald accompanied them into the building and up the stairs, always at a discreet distance, so although he was often out of sight, he was always somehow present, like a noise in the woodwork.

The paintings were in a large room; upon entering, Danforth estimated that there were perhaps forty of them. They had been framed tastefully and with obvious professionalism in the sort of frames used by the best museums.

The windows of the hall were high, so exterior light streamed in with crystal clarity. No other source was necessary, and it seemed to Danforth that someone had probably thought this through, the fact that natural scenes, which most of the paintings depicted, should be illuminated by the closest one could get to outdoor light.

"You may walk about at your leisure," Ernst said. "And, please, take as long as you wish." He looked at his watch, then nodded to Wald, who now stepped out of the room and closed the door behind him.

"One has to have time with a painting," Ernst added with a courtly smile. "One cannot be rushed in such things."

"Thank you," Danforth said.

Danforth stepped forward with Anna at his side; she was now thoroughly in her role as special assistant, studying the same painting Danforth studied, saying nothing, as if waiting for him to speak.

He stopped at a small painting of a bridge, its double arches made of stone, unthreatening woods behind it, everything done in the muted colors to which the artist seemed most inclined.

As if to test her, he said, in German, "What do you think of this?"

She peered at the painting for a moment, then said, "Constable."

Danforth felt a wave of boyish playfulness wash over him. "Any Constable painting in particular?" he asked.

"The Cornfield," Anna answered with complete authority, as if she hadn't learned of both the artist and the painting only days before.

Danforth decided to press the issue. "The browns?" he asked.

Anna shook her head. "The peace," she answered. "The sense that even if things turn out badly later, still, for a moment" — she drew her eyes away from the painting and looked at Danforth — "there was this."

She said it softly, and it was correct enough as a description of the painting, but in Danforth it produced that romantic shock of recognition when a man knows with all the certainty that life allows that although he might one day love again, it will never be like this.

He knew that she was still looking at him, but he did not turn to her, instead moving on to the next painting, this one very ordinary, a vase of flowers.

She followed him as he progressed along the line of paintings: more buildings, more flowers, more landscapes, each curiously impersonal, as if the painter were determined to strip all feeling from his subjects.

They'd reached the back wall when the great doors swung open and Wald, accompanied this time by four soldiers and a woman in a long wool coat, strode into the room.

"Put your hands up," Wald ordered in German as he closed in on them. "And turn around. Face the wall."

A trap, Danforth thought, they had been caught in a trap.

"Do not move," Wald said.

Danforth obeyed instantly, Anna somewhat more slowly, though Danforth couldn't tell if her less rapid response was the product of terror, shock, or some aspect of a new role she'd decided to play.

The woman now stepped forward. She took Anna firmly by one shoulder, and with her other hand, she patted down the opposite side; she found nothing, reversed the process, again found nothing, and then stepped back behind Wald.

One of the soldiers then moved forward and did the same to Danforth, with the same result.

"Turn around," Wald commanded them after the soldier took his place with the others.

Danforth and Anna turned to face him.

"Passports," he said.

They gave them to him.

"You came by way of France?" Wald asked as he looked at Danforth's passport.

Danforth nodded.

"Your purpose there?"

"I am an art dealer," Danforth answered.

"Art?" Wald said. "You are an importer, is that not so?"

"Yes, and art is one of the things I import," Danforth said coolly.

Wald's eyes ranged over the paintings that hung on the surrounding walls. "What do you have to say of these paintings?" he asked.

"German naturalism," Danforth answered. "They remind me of the work of a great American naturalist, William Bliss Baker."

"What is this painter's most famous work?" Wald demanded.

"Fallen Monarchs."

"Fallen kings?" Wald asked as if he'd caught Danforth in a political opinion.

"No, it's a painting of fallen trees," Danforth answered. "A very beautiful painting."

Wald simply stared at Danforth a moment, then turned and left the room with his accompanying entourage.

"Don't act as if anything has happened," Danforth told Anna. "Let's just go on around the room."

With that, they continued to move along the side of the room, and though Danforth knew she must have been as shaken by Wald's interrogation as he'd been, she appeared quite calm.

Seconds later, they heard footsteps coming, the hard precision of military boots, but when they turned around, they saw only a few soldiers standing guard as a group of civilians came through the door.

As the group moved forward, its ranks thinned, and suddenly the wall broke entirely, and there he was, coming toward them. His head was turned and he was talking to Ernst, saying something amusing, evidently, because there was a very slight smile on Ernst's face when he turned to them, a smile that was still there when he made the introductions.

"Herr Danforth," he said, "it is my honor to present the chancellor of the German Reich and the Führer of the German people."

Danforth had never heard the word *Führer* spoken, but what surprised him was how profoundly serious the man seemed, despite the comical Charlie Chaplin mustache. He clearly had little time for this.

"So," the chancellor said, "what do you think of these paintings?"

There was a brusque quality to his voice, though Danforth heard nothing threatening in it, only the tone of a man who was very busy but who had found the time to drop in on these

Americans because he couldn't help but be curious about what they made of his work.

"I find them quite interesting," Danforth said, working very hard to keep his voice and manner relaxed, looking for all the world as if he weren't trembling at the very thought of the man who now faced him. "As I said to Herr Kruger, I think many Americans would find them quite to their liking."

The chancellor nodded but seemed suddenly to lose interest, as if Danforth's answer had been neither more nor less than he'd expected.

Still, Danforth had no choice but to soldier on, and so he did. "Your subjects, as I told Herr Kruger — fields and dells and the like — they are very natural, and this has great appeal for Americans." He allowed himself a nervous laugh. "Because so much of the American landscape has been taken over by cities, there is nostalgia for the countryside."

The chancellor no longer appeared to be in the least interested in what Danforth was saying; he seemed impatient with the commonplace and banal remarks, which were unworthy of any further expenditure of his time. He glanced at his watch, then turned to Ernst. "Well . . ." he began.

"The subject is you," Anna said suddenly.

The chancellor turned to her and waited.

"Not impressionistically, of course," Anna continued. "What your paintings show is your condition when you painted them."

The chancellor said nothing but listened as Anna continued.

"They are the paintings of someone struggling to live." She held her gaze on a painting that seemed to fade away at the edges. "A painter rushed . . . by hunger." She might have left it there, and Danforth, cringing inside, certainly hoped she would. But instead she turned boldly toward her target. "Were you hungry when you painted them, *mein Führer*?"

Danforth would forever poignantly recall the look in the chancellor's small round eyes at that moment, something never reported and that must have rarely been glimpsed: the sufferings of his youth, the grim poverty and the unbearable rejection, the abyss of failure that must have yawned before him during all his years in Vienna and that could be held back only by the wildly self-inflated fantasy he had hatched about himself and that later, and against all odds, he had managed to make true.

Then, in a blink, all of that passed from him like fizz from a bottle, and he was once again the chancellor of the German Reich and the Führer of the German people, the visionary he proclaimed himself to be, a busy, busy man, too busy for sentimentality, too busy even for reminiscence, and thus one who now found the musings of this young American woman a simple waste of time.

And so, with a quick nod, he turned; his entourage closed in around him, and . . .

Blue Bar, New York City, 2001

". . . and he was gone," Danforth said.

I couldn't entirely conceal my surprise at this part of Danforth's tale, and certainly not my uneasiness at how Anna had behaved.

"Was she . . . flirting with him?" I asked cautiously.

"Flirting?" Danforth asked. "Far from it, believe me."

"Then why did she speak to him that way?" I asked.

"Because she wanted him to notice her," Danforth answered. "So that if he ever saw her in a crowd, he would not feel the slightest alarm if she approached him. She knew that we would never get another audience with him after Wannsee. He had seen us and had no reason to see us again. So any further meeting would have to be in public. If he recognized her face, he might allow her to go up to him." A deep gravity settled over him, and for a moment, he seemed lost in its aching cloud. "And to win the digger's game."

PART V

The Digger's Game

Blue Bar, New York City, 2001

"What is the digger's game?" I asked.

Danforth started to answer, then stopped, clearly refusing to enter a room that had not yet been prepared to receive him. "The Landwehr Canal runs parallel to the river Spree," he said. "That's where we walked that day. It was a very popular place and there were always people strolling along the canal, but it had a grim history, as I later discovered."

"The Landwehr Canal?" I asked. "Why would that interest you?"

"Because that was where the three of us strolled the day Bannion rejoined us," Danforth answered. "And where the last of our plans were laid."

This remark sounded a deeper note, and I found I was suddenly steeling myself against the dark end that seemed always to be coming nearer as Danforth's tale progressed.

"The light was so clear it made you think you could see through it," Danforth added. "It was like the best deception in that way, made invisible by transparency."

Berlin, Germany, 1939

"Clayton has approved the mission," Bannion said.

But Clayton had left the question of how the mission should

be carried out for them to answer, Bannion told them, and to Danforth's surprise, they began to discuss various methods. Bannion had reviewed several assassinations, and although he didn't press the point, it was clear that bombs rarely worked. It was pistols that had killed Lincoln, McKinley, Garfield, the king of Yugoslavia, and Franz Ferdinand, the last having been assassinated only after an earlier bomb attempt had failed.

"So it seems to me that the most effective means," Bannion said, "is a gun."

"But none of those assassins escaped," Danforth reminded him cautiously.

"Is the point to escape?" Bannion asked him. "Or to get the job done?" Before Danforth could answer, Bannion turned to Anna. "And two assassins will be better than one," he added. "So we will do this together, Anna."

For the rest of his life, Danforth would replay the startling intimacy of those words, how clearly they excluded him, so that in the juvenile way of a challenged boy, he'd blurted, "All of us together."

"No," Bannion said.

"Why not?" Danforth asked.

"Because you don't know how to shoot," Bannion answered.

No one spoke for a moment; then, as if to close the possibility of any further discussion of the matter, Bannion looked out over the narrow expanse of the canal, the placid green waters of the Spree. His gaze focused with a curious tenderness on one of its bridges, a tenderness Danforth noticed and would many times recall.

"So," Bannion said crisply as he returned his attention to the plot, "we'll have to act very quickly." With that, he turned from the bridge, and the three of them moved farther along the canal. "We will have only one chance." He was now speaking to

Anna alone. "And we should fire at different angles with as little obstruction as possible. Not in big crowds, for example, where anyone could suddenly step in front of us."

Against every resentful impulse, Danforth admired the cool way Bannion dealt with murder, not just the tools to carry it out, but the geometrics of it, how a woman with a baby might suddenly move toward the target and in that moment be torn to shreds, leaving the target no more than inconvenienced by the blood on his uniform. It is hard sailing that makes a seaman, one of Danforth's ancestors had once written, and at this moment Danforth felt himself but a weekend yachtsman in comparison to the two others.

"Rache has provided a lot of information," Bannion said. "And he can also supply the weapons and whatever else we need."

With that, they went directly to Anna's room, and there Bannion offered the information he'd gotten from Rache.

"It's very general," Bannion said. "But it's worth knowing."

He was speaking almost exclusively to Anna, the two of them united by the deadly plot, a couple as mutually murderous, Danforth thought, as any in noir fiction.

Bannion opened a notebook and drew several concentric circles, at the center of which he made a large, black *X*.

"At the outer rim you have the SS," he said. "Black uniform. Death's-head on the cap. They patrol, stand around, do drawings of the places our friend is to make an appearance, check things like bridges and water towers. They seem to be focused on a long shot. They're convinced the British are spying on everything."

Anna and Danforth stared at his crude drawing.

"Closer in you have something called the *Führerschutzkommando*," Bannion continued. "This group is in charge of providing security at all public events. They wear gray uniforms and tend to stand around in clusters." He traced the third, most inner circle with a crooked finger. "Closest of all is the RSD. Himmler runs this group, so they can pretty much do anything they want, including wearing the uniforms of the other security forces or just dressing in plain clothes."

This was very detailed information, and it struck Danforth that Rache and his Communist comrades must surely be plotting the same murder, a conviction that buoyed him with hope. If they struck first, and succeeded, then Anna would be saved.

"But none of this matters if he's simply stepping out of a car and the crowd surges forward," Bannion continued matter-of-factly. "We'd just need to be at the front of that crowd. As a rule, aim for the back of the head. It's a more likely shot because once a target moves past, security tends to focus on what lies ahead of him, not what's behind. And if possible, we should fire at the same time."

To this last bit of rudimentary instruction, Bannion added, "So now the task is to find the right place and right moment."

And so for the next few days Danforth moved about Berlin, scouting places the target might have some likelihood to appear. There were the steps of the Reichstag, of course, but they were blanketed in security. He walked the length of Unter den Linden as well, since at any point Hitler might drive along this route in his open touring car. But the car would be moving, and the target's exposure would be limited in time and narrow in space, and there would be guards on the running boards, any one of whom might shift and in that movement receive a bullet in the thigh or stomach or wrist that had been destined for the target's head.

During the same time, Rache provided Bannion with yet more information about schedules and public appearances and how to get access to the railway station where Hitler's special train awaited his often quite arbitrary travel plans.

Years later, still working to uncover the pattern of the plot,

Danforth would come across a book that meticulously recorded the Führer's movements in September of 1939: trips to Bad Polzin, quick tours of Komierowo, Topolno, Vistula, special trains to Plietnitz, journeys to Gross-Born and Ilnau, then on to the front lines at Bialaczow, Konskie, Kielce, Maslow, on to Lodz, on to Breslau-Lauenburg, on to Danzig, Wiskitki, Davidy, Stucewice, on and on and on to the very outskirts of Warsaw, frenetic journeys into the heart of a war it had been Anna's hope — or claim of hope — to stop.

All this research was carried out in the early days of August amid yet more rumors of impending war and with a sense of urgency that continued to build until, in what seemed to Danforth a kind of exhaustion, Bannion made a surprising choice.

"There is only one place we can be sure of," he said.

They were sitting in the small pension where Bannion had taken a room and through whose tiny windows light barely penetrated.

"A place in Munich," Bannion added. "A restaurant." He laughed. "An Italian restaurant, of all things." He glanced at the paper where he'd written the name. "It's called the Osteria Bavaria. It's at Schellingstrasse sixty-two." He looked up from the paper, his gaze directly on Anna. "He goes there quite often when he is in Munich, and he will be in Munich for some sort of celebration next week."

"A restaurant?" Danforth asked. "Won't it be crowded outside?"

"It wouldn't be done from the outside," Bannion said. Again he turned his attention to Anna, a gesture that struck Danforth as a cue for her to take over.

"I would be inside the dining room, Tom," she said.

"How would you manage that?" Danforth asked. "Won't the restaurant be closed for him?"

"No," Bannion answered with complete authority. "And last April, a British agent filed a report that said he was able to get very close to Hitler in this same restaurant."

"A woman would be even less likely to be thought of as a threat," Anna said.

Now Bannion took over again. "She'll book a table at Osteria Bavaria for every night he's in Munich."

"But booking a table every night—won't that be noticed?" Danforth asked.

"Of course it will," Bannion answered. "There's an organization called Group Nine. They're responsible for checking out any foreigners who suddenly appear before or during a visit. Anna's name will certainly show up."

"But my name will already have appeared in an earlier investigation," Anna added. "As an assistant art dealer from America, a woman who met the Führer in Wannsee."

"So the plan is for him to see you," Danforth said.

Anna nodded.

"To see you and remember you as the woman who made that strange remark in Wannsee."

"That's right," Anna said. "So if I come over to his table, he won't be suspicious."

"And the pistol?" Danforth asked. He looked at Bannion. "You don't expect her to be searched?"

"Probably not," Bannion said. "According to the British agent, the restaurant reservation list is screened, but the real fear is bombs, and so whole crews go through the place before the first customers arrive."

There was a moment of silence, as each of them looked at the others and waited.

"What about you?" Danforth asked. "Where will you be?"

"In the crowd outside the restaurant," Bannion answered. "If Anna fails, they'll rush him out the front door where his car is always waiting. Things will be pretty confused, I'm sure. They'll be dashing around, and I could get an opening between the front door and the car."

"And if you don't?" Danforth asked.

"I'll make one," Bannion said. "I'll fire into his entourage. There'll be more confusion. Another chance for an opening, and even a wild shot will be better than no shot at all." He shrugged with an indifference Danforth found shocking and in which he saw the fearful courage of the truly committed. "One way or the other, we're going to die, Anna and I," he said. "We'll both have cyanide in case we're captured." Then he looked at her like a suitor at last betrothed. "Maybe this was always the plan for us," he said.

A silence fell over them, until Anna said quite softly, "Done."

Blue Bar, New York City, 2001

"And so we approached the last days," Danforth said. "We would all go to Munich. Bannion would keep an eye on Braunes Haus at Briennerstrasse forty-five, near the Konigsplatz, the Nazi headquarters where Hitler was likely to spend a good deal of his time while he was in Munich. I would station myself in a hotel room within view of the Osteria Bavaria. Anna would remain in a nearby hotel until it was time for her to go to the restaurant. The idea was that she would go there every day for lunch and dinner. If the target showed up, and she could get in range, she would shoot him."

"With Bannion always waiting outside the restaurant if she failed," I said.

Danforth drained the last of his drink. "Simple as that, Paul."

"Simple, yes." I hesitated before my next remark. "Forgive me, but it sounds very . . . haphazard."

"Does it?"

"Well, you have no specific intelligence component," I said. "Other than that information Bannion got from Rache and this unnamed British agent."

"His name was Alexander Foote, as I found out later," Danforth said. "You can look him up, if you like."

"I don't doubt that he existed," I assured Danforth quickly. "But the nature of his intelligence was so general that it couldn't have been of much use."

"It was of no use at all really," Danforth agreed. "Except that it was clear it was possible to get quite close to the target at the Osteria Bavaria because Foote had already done it."

"But that is hardly actionable intelligence," I insisted.

"Well, certainly no more 'actionable intelligence' than Oswald had," Danforth said casually. "Not much more than John Wilkes Booth had. In fact, not much more than any of those boy assassins in Sarajevo who waited for Franz Ferdinand's car to go by. Just to be at the right place at the right time."

I looked at him quizzically. "So you don't believe in elaborate planning?"

"What I believe in, Paul, is human incompetence," Danforth said. "You can simply depend on incompetence within the security system to give you an opening at some point. You wait for that opening, and then you strike." He smiled. "All the training at my country house, all Bannion's information about Hitler's layers of security, all my traipsing around Berlin pretending that I could find just the right place, all of that finally came down to one thing: a guy likes to eat at a certain restaurant, and if you're in that restaurant when he eats there, you can kill him."

Something in Danforth's demeanor darkened, and the tone of his voice became intimate, as if he were speaking not to a think-tank freshman young enough to be his grandson but to someone who was tied to this ancient conspiracy. "Which brings me to the final act of this part of my story, Paul." His gaze took on a troubled wonder. "The trick love plays in life."

Munich, Germany, 1939

The pistol was the same model and caliber LaRoche had used at Winterset, and Bannion's manner was quite casual when he drew it from his jacket and handed it to Danforth.

The instructions that followed were simple: Danforth was to meet Anna in the square outside the restaurant as the dinner hour approached. He was to give her the pistol. She would take it into the restaurant.

"She should never have the gun until she goes into the restaurant," Bannion said. "Since she's the only one of us who has a reservation at the Osteria, it would be her room they'd search."

The target was scheduled to arrive in the city that same afternoon, and Bannion had found out — either from Rache or Foote — that he was inclined to have dinner at the Osteria Bavaria on his second day in Munich, usually around seven. The British agent had even been able to provide the fact that it was the table to the right of the entrance he preferred, an odd choice, Bannion noted, since it was by a window that looked out onto the street. The final elements of the plan had been put in place that very morning, Bannion went on, a reservation made in Anna's name. The only thing that remained was for Danforth to keep the pistol in his room until the following morning, when he would transfer it to Anna.

"What about the cyanide?" Danforth asked.

Bannion patted the blue handkerchief in his jacket pocket. "In here," he said. "Mine and hers."

"You don't want me to give it to her with the pistol?" Danforth asked.

"No," Bannion said. "I'll give it to her. It's the last test. Rache says it works every time."

"Works how?"

"If the person takes the tablet, he will complete the mission," Bannion said.

In his memory, Danforth would later see Anna's tablet many times, always with wonder at how very small it was, no larger than a pea, the poison contained in a thin-walled ampoule coated with rubber to prevent it from breaking under anything less forceful than a human bite.

"What about mine?" Danforth asked.

Bannion smiled. "Giving you a cyanide tablet would just be drama, Tom. After you give Anna the pistol, you're to go directly to the station and take the train to Hamburg. Passage has already been booked for you to Copenhagen, and from there to London."

He walked to the door, started to open it, then hesitated. "I know you love her, Tom. For you, it's only her."

"Yes," Danforth admitted.

For a time they talked only about Anna, and it became clear to Danforth that Bannion had closely observed her though even he could not say what had moved her to do the thing she was soon to do.

"There's something I still don't know," Bannion said at last. Then, with a shrug, he said, "Tell her story, Tom."

Danforth had never felt so entirely diminished. He was to be the chronicler of Anna's martyrdom, and Bannion's. He was to share their plot but not their peril. But he had sworn to do as he was ordered, and so he said, "I will, Ted."

Bannion looked unexpectedly moved by Danforth's sincerity but said nothing further before he closed the door.

Once Bannion had departed, a curious drive took Danforth to the window. He looked out and felt almost as if he'd been expecting to see what was there: Anna, standing beneath a street-lamp. Bannion approached her, and for a time they talked. He was giving her some final words of encouragement, Danforth assumed, or perhaps offering his admiration for what she was to do. He would no doubt have a good speech. He'd given it often enough to miners and timber men, urging them toward the revolutionary ideal he had later so completely abandoned.

Then Bannion reached into his pocket and drew out the blue handkerchief Danforth had seen earlier. He was speaking softly as he opened it. Even from the distance, Danforth saw how intently Anna peered at the two tablets Bannion's handkerchief had concealed. For a time she seemed frozen in dread; she stood like a frightened child, her hand poised over the ampoules, unable to reach down. Then, very slowly, she drew one from the folds of the handkerchief and sank it into the pocket of her skirt.

Then Bannion stepped very near to her, apparently for an intimate communication; he spoke, and it caused Anna to glance up to where Danforth stood concealed in the darkness behind his window. The distance was long. Danforth's room was on the fourth floor; Anna's face, only half illuminated by the street-lamp, was anything but clear. And yet for all that, Danforth saw a shadow pass over her face, something grave and curiously indelicate, as if an unbearable thought had crossed her mind. Then she turned to Bannion again, and a dreadful stillness fell over her, one that lingered for a time. At last she shook her head, and then nodded, as if, exhausted and depleted, she had finally allowed her *no* to give way to *yes*.

With that, Bannion stepped away, and the two of them exchanged a look that reminded Danforth of the doomed characters in movies and popular novels who, torn apart by war or some other fearful circumstance, seemed to know at the moment of their parting that they would never see each other again. Then

Bannion turned and, like a character exiting the stage, vanished into the shadowy wings of Munich, leaving Anna alone.

She had never looked more intensely solitary, Danforth thought; she briefly seemed as if she had been driven to the most remote corner of the world. It was an aloneness that was dense and impenetrable, and horribly unfair, and it made Danforth suddenly hate Adolf Hitler, not for his aggression, his cruelty, his dreadful loathing of the Jews and the Communists, the Poles and the Slavs, not for the threat he posed to all that was kind and well reasoned in human life, but simply because the ending of that squalid, repellent life would take from him the one woman he knew, now with utter certainty, he would ever love.

Blue Bar, New York City, 2001

"You think you know the depth of selfishness when you look into your own heart and realize that you want someone dead because that person slighted you in some way, made you feel small or stupid or something of that sort," Danforth said. "Or you want someone dead because of an inheritance or because you want a higher post in some university faculty, neither of which can be achieved until someone dies." He offered a small, rather desolate laugh. "But at that moment in Munich, standing at that window, watching Anna, I learned how deep selfishness could go." He stared at his empty glass. "For me, Adolf Hitler was not a megalomaniac who threatened to destroy the world but rather, strangely and perversely, my rival for Anna, the other man in her life, the one who'd stolen her from me." He lifted his eyes from the glass and settled his gaze on me. "I was not just a romantic. I was a bourgeois solipsist, utterly incapable of seeing history as anything but a personal narrative." His laugh was pure self-accusation. "I was like the obsessed man in some cheap thriller."

He looked like that man even now, afflicted by old torments, his gaze more intense than before, and with something of self-loathing in it.

"I wanted to be like Anna," he continued. "Like Bannion. I wanted to die for some great cause. But at that instant, I knew that I was nothing but a lovesick fool who would have rushed Anna out of Munich and back to New York and let the whole world go up in flames if he could." He laughed again, this time even more bitterly. "Aristotle defined an evil man as one who cannot distinguish between what he wants and the universal good." He pointed to himself. "That was me. I wanted Anna. I cared for nothing else." He was silent for a moment, then he said, "You wanted to know what it was, the digger's game?"

"Yes."

"It came from Clayton."

Clayton had come back to New York after Pearl Harbor, Danforth went on to tell me, and by the middle of 1942, he was working in military intelligence. He'd never actually run agents, but he'd evaluated trainees for their potential as agents.

"His job was to find out if they had the right stuff," Danforth said. "Clayton was always fond of strategies and so he devised a little test. It was called the digger's game. He had a number of small brass pieces inscribed with various words and phrases: *losing your wife, losing your child, poverty, illness,* that sort of thing. These pieces were put in an urn filled with sand, and the applicant was to dig until he found the thing he most dreaded, at which point the applicant was to stop digging." Danforth picked up his empty glass and twirled it slowly between his hands. "There was only one piece that mattered to Clayton. If the potential agent stopped digging before he reached it, Clayton would no longer consider him. Do you know what that piece had written on it, Paul?" He smiled. *"Failure."* He paused, a man reevaluating an earlier conclusion. "I think Anna would not have stopped digging until she found *failure*," he said. "But I would have stopped digging at *losing Anna*." His mind turned inward, remained there for a time, then swept out to me again.

"And so I decided not to lose her," he said.

Munich, Germany, 1939

He knew that it would negate everything she had worked for. He knew that it would be abandoning his own great drive to make a mark. He knew that it would be a lost opportunity to change the course of history. He knew all this, and didn't care. He had gone over every other route he might take through life after losing Anna, and not one of them made sense or had meaning or filled the void within him that she filled. Years later, as he sought the pieces of the plot, he would sometimes tell himself that he had fallen victim to a strange form of romantic imprinting, and he would blame this on his youth and on the intensity of the times and on the mission they'd shared and the danger, and that all of this had created an overdetermined situation in his heart. He would say this to himself in icy hotel rooms and in rattling railway carriages and once as, pale and stricken, he passed beneath the wrought-iron gate with the words *Arbeit macht frei*, but he would never forget the irresistible force that had driven him to hatch so many arguments so desperately, and he would always call it love.

"Anna," he said that night in Munich as he opened his door and saw her standing there.

"I don't mean to disturb you, Tom," she said.

"No one would want to be alone . . . on such a night," he said. "Come in."

She walked into his room. She had been there before, of course, but now she seemed unsettled, as if she were uncertain what she should do next.

"Shall I call down for . . . tea . . . or . . . ?"

She shook her head. "No, nothing."

She glanced toward the bureau across the room, and he wondered if by some gift of intuition she knew that was where he'd placed her pistol, wrapped in a white handkerchief.

"Please, sit," Danforth said.

She took a seat in the little chair a few feet from the bed. Her movement was slow and graceful, and had he not been convinced of the unlikelihood of such a thing, he might have even thought it vaguely seductive.

"Actually, I was hoping to see you . . . before," he told her.

She looked away, drew the scarf from her head and draped it over the back of the chair. When she looked back at him, she smiled, but her smile was quick and formless, as if she were an actress not yet completely in character.

"We're to meet in the square," she said, as if confirming an insignificant detail. "You'll give me everything I need."

"Yes."

She said nothing else, and in that silence, the terrible solitude in her eyes swept over him, and as it swept, it reduced to dust all the arguments he might have made against her dying and left him bare of everything but anguish. This boiled up and would have burst from him had he not been able to suppress it at the last second and say only, "I'll miss you, Anna."

For a moment she seemed locked in a great inner turmoil, as if powerfully drawn in two opposite directions. Then an unexpected sigh broke from her, and she came toward him with a force that he would forever recall as tidal.

In the years to come, he would witness what happened next in countless renderings. He would see it flicker with increasing graphicness on movie screens and read of it in the increasingly clinical language of books. He would hear it sung by crooners and folksingers and rock bands, the movements of that night recounted at various times by swelling violins and by the pounding beat of electric bass guitars. He would see and hear that night's events reimagined and reorchestrated in theaters, opera houses, museums, and concert halls; in countless ways and by countless means, he would attempt to relume the rapture he felt during those brief minutes of his life . . . and each time, he would fail.

When the last shudder had subsided, he felt like a character in a Russian novel, love and death mingled in that darkly Slavic way, and he wanted to turn to her, run his fingers down the length of her naked body, and say something so profound neither of them would ever forget it.

But silence was all he could offer, a silence that struck him as sweet and tender and that, as it lengthened, convinced him she would now relent. For he was a romantic, after all, and no romantic could believe that a woman who was loved as Anna now had to know she was loved could choose to go out and die.

Then she said, "Where is the pistol?"

When he didn't answer, she rolled over and faced him, her head still on the pillow. "I should take it with me when I leave."

"I'm supposed to give it to you tomorrow," Danforth told her.

"It is tomorrow, Tom," she said.

"Bannion said not to give it to you until just before you go into the restaurant."

She shook her head. "No, now."

"Why?"

"Because this should be our last time together," Anna said firmly.

She rolled away from him and lay on her back, the sheet modestly pulled up over her naked breasts so that she seemed already enshrouded.

"Where is it?" she asked.

He nodded toward the bureau, expecting that she would immediately go to it. But instead, she remained in place, very still, her eyes cast toward the ceiling, and for a moment she actually seemed to consider letting this cup pass from her. This gave him the brief hope that in a simple, quiet way, he had saved the woman he was certain was the only love he would ever know. It was a certainty common to youth, as he would many times admit, but in his later age, it would prove in his case to have been starkly true.

"Goodbye, Tom," she said.

Her voice now held that old steeliness, and so it didn't surprise him that she rose, wrapped the sheet around her body, and began to gather up her clothes. There was a quickness in all this, however, and he saw in that quickness that she was having to fight the deep current of her own conviction. For that reason, he expected her to rush from the room, like some heroine in a film, but instead of doing anything so dramatic, she simply and quite slowly turned away, then disappeared into the adjoining bathroom.

He could hear water running, her feet padding about, then the rustle of her clothes as she dressed herself behind the closed door, and in the soft intimacy of these sounds he understood with complete fullness how deep his love for her actually ran, knew without doubt that he wanted to live his life with her, wanted them to drift together into maturity and from there into age and then move inexorably toward that moment of supreme mourning when one of them would know that it was not just a dream, that one could, in fact, love another person for one's whole life through.

She was fully dressed when she came back into the room, and he could see that she had used the time to steel herself against any further argument.

"Is it loaded?" she asked.

"Yes," Danforth said.

He turned away as she headed for the bureau and kept his face to the wall during the time it took her to open the drawer, walk to the door of his room, and open it.

"Tom," she said.

He turned to her.

"Remember me" was all she said.

Blue Bar, New York City, 2001

He would always remember the gently falling rain of that next morning, Danforth told me, how the drops had moved jaggedly down the windows of his hotel room, and how he'd heard the low rumble of thunder that rolled over Munich as he sat there alone.

"Things were dark enough without an omen, of course," he added.

"Dark, yes," I said.

He reached for the handkerchief in his jacket pocket, and I saw that his fingers were trembling.

"It's easy to hide something in a handkerchief, Paul," he said.

With that, he spread the handkerchief out on the table, took a dime from his pocket, placed it at the center of the handkerchief, folded the handkerchief neatly over it, then returned the handkerchief, peak down, to his jacket pocket.

"It's called the TV fold now," he informed me. "Because it was the sort of fold men used in the forties and fifties."

"The sort of fold you must have used then," I said.

"Yes." He patted the front pocket of his jacket. "The concealed item is at the bottom of the fold."

He was obviously speaking about the cyanide tablet Bannion had concealed in a similar handkerchief.

"What about you?" I asked. "Did you have a tablet?"

"Me? No," Danforth said. "I was to flee. I was the rat leaping from the sinking ship. There was no need for me to have cyanide." He looked at me significantly. "You know, Paul, quite a few people who tried to kill Hitler were captured. Some remained alive for years. Held in prison for years, as I later learned. But not one of them survived the war."

"So in a sense, it was just as you said at the beginning of your story," I reminded him. "The question was never whether she would live or die. For that had been decided long ago."

"Hmm," Danforth breathed, and on that breath returned me to Munich in the rain.

Munich, Germany, 1939

For a time he could only sit in the chair by the window and watch the rain cascade down the glass panes. He felt numb and deflated and without resources. Bannion had made it clear that they would have only one chance, and on the wave of that urgency, any hope for escape had closed. If Anna got close enough, she would fire, and after that, if the target was still alive and rushing from the restaurant, Bannion would fire, and then each would die either in the hail of bullets that followed or by biting down on the cyanide.

He knew that all this would transpire within a few hours, and yet he still dreamed of somehow averting it, of them all meeting at the railway station, taking the next train for Hamburg, then going by sea to Copenhagen and from there to Dover, where Bannion would go one way and he and Anna another, perhaps north to Scotland, where a great green forest would enfold them and they would live out their days in a forest fantasy, like Robin Hood and Maid Marian.

It was a fantasy that urged its false reality on him so powerfully that at one point he walked to the closet, grabbed his traveling bag, and tossed it onto a bed that still bore, he noticed, the imprint of Anna's body. The sight was so painful, that outline of his loss, that he spun away from it and yanked open the top drawer of the bureau as if to remind himself that it was all truly determined, that she had taken the pistol and the poison and would almost certainly use them both before the sun rose again on Munich.

He sat down and looked at his watch and was forced to confront a reality that slashed at him with all the violence of a physical attack, and as the minutes passed, he discovered that he simply could not allow his last sight of her to be wreathed in the shadowy darkness of his room, could not permit the last physical impression he would have of her to be the rumpled sheets where she'd lain.

On the wave of that decision, he leaped to his feet and headed out of his room, then down the corridor toward the elevator. He had to see her one last time, he told himself. He had to hold her one last time. This simple moment of final physical contact he wanted more ardently than he had ever wanted anything.

He reached the eighth floor minutes later, strode down the long hallway, then knocked at her door.

"Anna," he called softly when there was no answer.

He waited, then knocked again and again, and when there was still no answer, he went to the hotel lobby, so dazed by the need to see her, hold her, that he could do nothing but stand at the window and search the street outside, waiting for her to return.

He would never be sure of how long he waited, only that time itself seemed a malicious force that was relentlessly pressing him toward inestimable loss.

And so an hour might have passed, or two, before he saw Anna strolling back toward the hotel, and then the black car that suddenly drew up to the curb beside her. Four men got out.

They approached her unhurriedly, and the tallest of them removed his brown hat as he spoke to her. She nodded toward the hotel as if in answer to a question, and Danforth immediately shrank back into the lobby of the building so as not to be seen.

For a time, the man in the brown hat continued to question her, the other men now drawing in more closely as if expecting her to bolt away. At one point she reached into the pocket of her dress and drew out her passport, which the tallest of the men examined with a quick, desultory air, as if it were only a formality.

Then, almost like dancers, two of the men took her quite gently by the arms, one on her right, the other on her left, and in that formation, with the tallest in the lead and a fourth man behind her, they began to move toward the hotel.

The gun, Danforth thought. If they found it in her room, she would be doomed.

He raced up the stairs, bounded to her door, stepped back, and then with far more force than he'd ever applied to anything, he kicked open the door, rushed inside the room, and searched until he found the pistol in the third drawer of her bureau. *Now,* he thought as he sank it into his pocket, *she is safe.* No, she was more than safe; she had come close to discovery, and because of that closeness she would be forced to abandon the plot, as would they all. With that thought, what was to be the last great joy of his life swept over him, a surging happiness, fierce and dazzling, that he would never know again.

He was halfway out the door before he remembered the cyanide. He raced back into Anna's room, glanced about until he saw it sitting completely uncovered beneath her bedside lamp, snatched it from its place, and pressed it hurriedly into the pocket of his jacket.

The elevator was rising toward the eighth floor. He could hear it clattering upward. He would not be able to reach the stairs before it arrived at the landing. There was nothing to do but continue down the corridor. He had gone nearly all the way down it before he heard the rattling sound of the elevator door opening, just around the corner.

The men turned the corner just seconds before Danforth reached it, Anna now held stiffly by the two men at her sides. Her eyes met his as they drew toward each other. They were without sparkle and gave no hint of recognition as she swept by him. He might have been a traveling salesman for all her features betrayed, just another nameless man in a world filled with them. He kept his pace steady as he continued toward the elevator, and he did not look back when he reached the end of the corridor, just turned the corner, as he knew she wished him to, and also as he knew she wished him to, he vanished from sight.

On the street, for the first time in his life, he had nowhere to turn. There was nothing his money or his family could do for him. He was without means, without connections, powerless save for the pistol he'd snatched from Anna's room and which he now thought he should get rid of, and on that thought he hurried over to a nearby wastebasket and tossed it inside.

Now what? he asked himself in silent frenzy.

He had no idea what Anna was being asked, or of what she was being accused, but he knew that interceding might only deepen whatever suspicions had already been aroused.

He thought of Bannion and decided to go to him. It was not a long walk to the building where he'd rented a room, but when Danforth reached it, he saw another black car pulled up beside the curb in front of it, as well as two men stationed at the entrance of the building.

There was a small park across from the building, its grove of trees his only place of concealment, and so he quickly took a seat on one of its benches, careful to face away from the building, but glancing toward it from time to time. He had no idea what to do now, and it seemed to him that he'd come to Bannion in a state of total confusion, expecting that by some miracle the two of them could find a way to help Anna escape the peril she was in.

He heard a vague commotion and turned back toward the building. Bannion was being led to the car, and even from a distance Danforth could see that he'd not gone quietly. One eye was nearly swollen shut, and blood trickled from his nose. For a time, he slumped, almost casually, against the wall. Then, as if seized by a sudden stiffening of will, he straightened himself, sank one hand into the pocket of his trousers, and with no hint of hesitation, brought that same hand to his mouth.

"Herr Danforth?"

He turned to find a tall man standing before him accompanied by two other men, all of them in long leather coats.

"I am Gustav Volker," he said. "Gestapo. There are some questions we'd like to ask you."

"About what?"

"Would you come with me, please?" Volker said, and with a nod he ordered the other men to take up positions to Danforth's left and right. "I'm sure you can explain everything, Herr Danforth."

Danforth glanced back toward the building. A knot of men had now gathered around where Bannion lay face-up on the sidewalk, his body utterly still.

"This way," Volker ordered, and he jerked Danforth around. "Please."

He tried to remain entirely calm as he was escorted to the car, but once they were inside Gestapo headquarters, he felt the old terror creep over him. He had no doubt that they'd brought him here because they'd discovered the plot and were looking for him to confirm what they already knew. He recalled the earlier "interrogation" Bannion had ordered carried out, all the pain he'd endured, how near he'd come to breaking before it had been abruptly halted.

That had all turned out to be a ruse, of course, but this was not a ruse, as he well knew, and they would stop at nothing, and in the end, he knew that he would break, that their names would spill from him, along with every element of the plot.

He reached into his jacket pocket as unobtrusively as possible, fingered the folded handkerchief and retrieved the tablet that had been meant for Anna.

Later it would seem to him that his decision had come not because he feared torture or that he might break under it, but because it offered the only way to bring their deepest suspicions to himself and thus divert them from Anna. They would find no pistol on Anna, after all, or in her room. They would find no cyanide tablet save the one crushed between his teeth. He knew that his death was no guarantee of her escape, but it offered the only slender service he could render her, and as he placed the tablet between his lips and then bit down, he felt that surge of ancient knighthood he'd read about in books. This he would do for the woman he loved, the only act of true sacrifice he had ever known.

"Herr Danforth."

Danforth turned toward Volker, the severed tablet in his mouth. Why, he wondered, had he not yet felt the slightest effect of the cyanide? He was by no means a student of lethal poisons, but he'd heard that this one acted almost instantly.

"Come in," Volker said.

Danforth followed him into the office, expecting to collapse at any moment, his body rocked by seizures during the few seconds it would take for him to die.

"Sit down, Herr Danforth," Volker said.

Danforth did as he was told.

"Allow me," Volker said, and before Danforth could stop him, he lit a cigarette and handed it to Danforth.

"Now," Volker said as he opened the folder on his desk. "Let us proceed."

During the next few minutes Danforth waited for the cyanide to kill him until it became clear that whatever he'd bitten into had not been cyanide at all. By then Volker was well into his interrogation, and Danforth had learned that there was not a single element of the plot of which he was unaware save that Danforth had known of it.

"We are told she is a Jew and we know her companion is a Communist," Volker said, "but we know you are neither, and your father assures us that you are not a political person."

"My father?" Danforth asked.

"Your father, yes," Volker said. "We contacted him when we learned of your association with this woman — her real name is Klein, I believe?"

"Why would my father tell you anything about her?"

"Because your father has been a great friend to Germany for a long time, Herr Danforth."

"A friend of Germany?" Danforth asked hesitantly.

"He shares many of our beliefs, as I'm sure you know," Volker said. "That the Reds must be stopped and, of course, that the Jews are a poisonous tribe."

Danforth felt the last grain of the fake cyanide dissolve beneath his tongue. "I see."

"He sends you his best regards, by the way," Volker added. He absently glanced through the papers in the folder. When he looked up it was clear to Danforth that something darker was on his mind. "It is because your father has been such a friend to us that we are — how shall I say this? — overlooking your associations." He closed the folder. "We have more than enough information to detain you, Herr Danforth, but we see no reason to keep you from leaving Germany as soon as possible." He leaned forward with a force whose violent threat could not be mistaken. "You will be leaving our country very soon, is that not so, Herr Danforth?"

Danforth nodded.

"Very soon," Volker added pointedly. "At once, in fact."

This was an order, of course, and one about which no appeal would be tolerated. In no uncertain terms, Danforth was being spared because he was young and stupid, young and not a Jew, young and not a Communist, and most of all because he was young and the son of a man who hated both Communists and Jews. His father's support of those who would destroy those groups had reached out to save Danforth's life.

"You have been granted much good fortune," Volker told him in a voice that was not unlike his father's. "Be careful how you use it." He reached into the drawer of his desk, took out the passport that had earlier been taken from him, and returned it.

"Thank you," Danforth said. He reached to draw it from Volker's hand and then stopped as Volker's fingers clamped down on it.

"At once," Volker repeated.

"Yes," Danforth said.

Volker released the passport and Danforth placed it in his jacket pocket.

Neither bothered to say goodbye.

Once dismissed, Danforth headed down the stairs and into the building's lobby. It was an ornate affair, with the sort of woodwork that had been the pride of an older age, now almost entirely covered in bunting, the interior festooned with Nazi flags.

A car waited outside the building, and as Danforth came into the daylight again, the driver quickly pulled himself from behind the wheel and opened the back door. "This way, sir."

He was driven — or was it escorted — back to his hotel, and once they were there, the driver again got out and opened the door for him. "I am to wait for you, sir."

"Wait for me?"

"You are going to the train station, yes?" the man said. "You are leaving Germany today?"

So he would be watched at every step of his departure, Danforth realized, and after he was gone, his name would be added to a list of people no longer permitted to enter Germany.

"Yes, leaving," Danforth said quietly.

He took the clattering old elevator up to the fourth floor, packed his bags, and headed for the door. He had nearly reached it when he turned back and saw Anna's scarf still draped over the chair where she'd left it the night before. It was all he would ever have of her, he thought, and in the despair that swept over him at that moment, he drew it from the chair and buried his face in its dark folds and felt in the grimly merging way of grief the full and unbearable weight of both her presence and her loss.

Blue Bar, New York City, 2001

So what was really the point of Danforth's story? I wondered in the brief silence that fell over him now. Was it a cautionary tale about the profoundly unsmooth running of true love? Or was it a warning about the twisting course of intelligence work, how plots evolve and deepen as if by their own volition, each step in some way unwilled? Could it be that I was being lectured — however metaphorically — about the passion of youth or the fierce nature of desire? Or did his instruction touch on the injustices of class, the way his own favorable circumstances had protected him from what had no doubt befallen Anna and Bannion?

I was still considering these many possibilities when Danforth's question brought me up short.

"You've never killed anyone, have you, Paul?"

He asked this casually, as he might have asked if I'd ever eaten duck confit or sipped Meursault.

"Killed anyone?" I was obviously taken aback by the question. "No, I've never killed anyone."

"I didn't think so," Danforth said.

So was Danforth's tale a murder story? I wondered now.

"Have you?" I asked him, hesitantly.

"Oh, sure," Danforth answered calmly, revealing no sense of regret at having done so.

"Really?"

"Well, there was a war, after all," Danforth said.

"Oh, you mean in the war," I said with rather obvious relief. "Of course."

"I remember one fellow," Danforth went on in the same breezy tone, as if he were relating the story of a camping trip in the Berkshires. "A British intelligence officer. He'd tracked this Nazi bastard to a hunting lodge in Bavaria. He knew his crimes. The Nazi tried to explain himself, tell him why he'd done what he'd done, but in the end, he couldn't keep that mask in place, and with all the contempt in the world, he sneered at my British friend." He lifted his hand to get the waiter's attention, then quite casually, he added, "So the Brit shot him right between the eyes." He laughed. "The British did a lot of that sort of thing after the war, you know. We wanted trials, we Americans. We wanted due process. But not the Brits. They shot those Nazi bastards wherever they found them. They shot them in barns and animal stalls. They shot them in the woods and on deserted roads. They shot them in their little town squares and dragged them out of basements and root cellars and caves and shot them in broad daylight, with their fat wives and little milkmaid daughters looking on." His laugh was surprisingly brutal. "There are certain things a human being cannot do and still expect another human being to let him live." He looked at me with the weariness born of this conclusion. "For certain crimes, there should be no protection. Even love, as they say, must have an end."

I found something curiously touching in this last remark, perhaps because it had been so hard won, given the failure of the plot, how heart-struck he'd been by Anna, their one night of passion, her capture the next day, Bannion's too, then Danforth's own escape, along with whatever dark and bloody things he'd known after that, a whole world at war. It made for the grave mosaic one saw in his face and that returned me to his time.

And yet, suddenly, he laughed. "The Old Bulldog," he said. "It was Churchill who wanted them shot without trial, you know, those Nazi bastards. He had been in a war, you see. Roosevelt had not. Do you think that might have made the difference?"

"That, along with the fact that England had been terribly hurt and we hadn't been," I said.

"The Germans would have flattened the whole of England if they could have," Danforth said. "And even as it was, Canterbury Cathedral was lost and much of London was in ruins." He shook his head. "To see the fires burning in your own land. That fills a man with rage. And add to the bombings those other German crimes. The camps and the pits. Those bulldozers." Something in his soul appeared to sour. "We should have killed them all, don't you think, Paul?"

"I can certainly understand the rage," I said, then added a

short, admittedly nervous laugh. "Of course, my father would never have been born."

"Nor you," Danforth said. "So it was good for you that something stayed our hand."

I felt a chill, as if a wintry blast had stopped me. "Yes," I said, then glanced at my notes to avoid the icy probing of Danforth's eyes. "So, I suppose you left Munich that day?"

"I left Germany that day," Danforth said.

The events of that morning returned to me, Anna's capture, Danforth's attempt at suicide, the evidence that would have been found on him had he succeeded.

"Anna's scarf," I said suddenly. "What did you do with it?"

"I left it in my room," Danforth answered. "What, Paul, did you expect me to keep it as some sort of love token?"

"I suppose I did," I admitted.

Danforth laughed. "You've seen too many movies." He was quiet for a time, then he said, "I expected you to ask me about the cyanide."

"What about it?"

"Why it didn't work."

"Yes, I should have asked about that."

He waved his hand. "Not to worry. I was well on my way to England before I asked it myself. Sitting on the ferry, thinking everything through again. Not just the events of that last terrible day in Munich, but everything. Clayton's first approach. Anna in the Old Town Bar. LaRoche. Bannion. Everything we'd shared and endured, all of which had come to nothing." He shrugged. "And of course that last night with Anna. Then her arrest and Bannion's. The fact that I wasn't arrested at all. Then, suddenly, I thought of the cyanide, that it hadn't worked." He smiled. "It just came like a soft creak into my mind."

I expected him to go on from there, follow the linear line of his tale, but he stopped instead, abruptly stopped, as if some quite different progress had suddenly occurred to him. Then, as if deciding to take an alternative route through well-known terrain, he said, "A soft creak. Yes, it came to me just like that." He paused again, his eyes on his empty glass. "A soft creak," he repeated. When he looked up at me, his eyes sparkled icily in the room's dim light. "Like a nightingale floor."

PART VI

The Nightingale Floor

Blue Bar, New York City, 2001

The Japanese word was *uguisubari,* Danforth told me, a floor designed to make a chirping sound when anyone walked on it.

"The sound of a nightingale," he added.

Then another drink arrived, and he took a small sip before returning to the reference toward which, seconds before, his tale had abruptly careened.

"Any wooden floor will creak a little when it's walked on, of course," Danforth continued, "but in a nightingale floor, it's not the wood that gives off a sound, it's nails rubbing against clamps. That's why the floor chirps rather than creaks."

"Why would anyone want a chirping floor?" I asked.

"For security," Danforth explained. "The floors were laid in hallways that led to conference rooms and the like. If anyone tried to creep close to the rooms, the nightingale floor would give off its distinctive call, and the people in council would be alerted to a spy or, perhaps, an assassin."

He took another short sip from his glass, and I saw he was being careful now to take in only a small amount of alcohol.

"I walked the nightingale floor in Nijo Castle," he went on. "Remember, Kyoto was spared the first atomic bomb because the secretary of war had been there and knew it was beautiful."

Another circling back, I thought, to distant references.

Danforth drew in a long, recuperative breath. "Older castles had been designed to conceal the rooms of the bodyguards, but the Tokugawa shogunate, the one who built Nijo, displayed these rooms quite prominently." He smiled. "Because power that does not show itself, Paul, diminishes itself." He took another small sip from his glass. "Unless concealment is an integral part of the power in question, of course."

I looked at him quizzically.

"The success of a traitor, for example, is built on never having his treachery discovered," Danforth said. He leaned forward slightly. "Do you know who the greatest spy of all time was, Paul?" he asked.

I shook my head. "No, I don't," I confessed.

He leaned back again. "Neither does anyone else."

"I see your point," I said, then attempted my own circling back to earlier references. "But what does a nightingale floor have to do with cyanide?"

"The fact that Anna's cyanide didn't work, and that Bannion's did," Danforth said. "That's what kept sounding in my mind on the Channel crossing. It was like a creeping footfall on a nightingale floor. Chirp. Chirp. Chirp. All the way to London."

London, England, 1939

Clayton's face had never looked more deeply troubled; Danforth would later wonder, from the depths of his own steadily building suspicion, if his friend had already known what he had come to tell him.

It was raining, and Danforth had walked quickly to the tavern near Whitehall where they were to meet. He'd expected to find Clayton already waiting, but it was some minutes before he arrived. From his place at the rear of the tavern, Danforth had watched Clayton strip off his very English raincoat and close and fasten his very English black umbrella. Even so, he'd looked distinctively American, though in a way Danforth could not exactly describe save by the observation that his movements, quick and decisive, gave off a certain New-World energy.

"Good to see you, Tom," Clayton said when he reached the rear table.

"Hello, Robert."

Clayton's tone was grave. "Clearly something's happened," he said.

"There was no attempt," Danforth told him flatly. "Anna was arrested outside her hotel yesterday morning. I saw it myself. By the time I got to Bannion's place, he'd been arrested too. As they were taking him out, I saw him put something in his mouth. The cyanide. He collapsed in a few seconds."

Clayton appeared genuinely stricken by this news. "I'm sorry," he said.

"I don't know where Anna is," Danforth said. He kept his voice even, and years later, he would recall that at that moment he'd managed to be no less an actor than Anna, merging with his role as a failed conspirator, cool in the wake of failure, giving no hint of the storm inside him.

"This was always a very dangerous action," Clayton said wearily.

"Then why did you approve it?" Danforth asked.

Even as he spoke, Danforth was mindful of his own failure to stop the plot, but he remained too uncertain of his own footing to reveal that he had wanted to do exactly that. Still, he wondered why Clayton hadn't put a halt to so reckless a scheme early on.

"Because I'm as susceptible to the grand action as anyone else, I suppose," Clayton answered. "And Bannion was sure that Rache could supply the sort of inside information that might make it possible."

233

"The security system around Hitler, that all came from Rache?" Danforth asked.

"Yes," Clayton answered. He glanced toward the front of the room, where a gust of wind had suddenly sent a sheet of rain loudly against the window. "Rache had saved Bannion's life in Spain." He looked at Danforth. "You trust a man who saves your life." He shrugged. "But maybe Bannion shouldn't have trusted Rache with his life this time."

"You think Rache may have betrayed us?" Danforth asked.

"Well, he's the last one standing, isn't he?" Clayton answered. "Except for me, of course." He gave Danforth a curiously distant glance. "And you."

"Me?"

Clayton nodded. "I was just wondering why you were released."

"Because they said my father was a friend of Germany," Danforth told him.

Clayton leaned forward. "Did your father ever know anything about the Project?"

"Absolutely not."

Clayton seemed to take this at face value. "Then it's Rache we have to suspect, because he was the only one outside our circle."

"And as far as you know, he hasn't been arrested?"

"As far as I know," Clayton answered. "But they could fake an arrest. And if they thought we suspected him, they probably would, and with that he'd disappear." He shrugged. "There's nothing you can do, Tom. The Project is over." He touched Danforth's hand, as if offering condolence to a mourner. "You should go back to New York."

Danforth drew back his hand. "I can't," he said firmly. "Not until I know what happened to Anna."

That was the moment he betrayed himself, as he understood

immediately. He could see clearly what Clayton saw when he looked at him: it was not his failure to make a mark or to change history that gripped him but his desperate need to find out what had happened to Anna.

"My God," Clayton said. "You fell in love with her."

Danforth nodded. "Yes," he admitted. "Was that your plan?"

"No," Clayton said. "As a matter of fact, I didn't think you were capable of that kind of feeling."

Danforth peered at Clayton intently. "The cyanide Anna was supposed to take if she was captured," he said. "She didn't have it with her when she was arrested. But I had it when they detained me. I took it."

"You what?" Clayton asked. He was clearly astonished.

"I was taken to Gestapo headquarters in Munich," Danforth added. "I thought they were going to do exactly what you'd expect, and so I took the cyanide." He looked at Clayton pointedly. "But it didn't work."

"Bannion's worked, but not Anna's?" Clayton asked.

"Yes," Danforth said. "Did you supply the tablets?"

"No," Clayton said.

"Who did?"

"Bannion got them from Rache," Clayton answered. He suddenly looked like a man who'd just grasped the thread of a fabric he wanted to unravel. "Why would Rache have given Bannion one cyanide tablet that worked and one that didn't?" He considered his own question briefly, then said, "Obviously he wanted one of them to live, and it didn't matter which one."

"How do you know that?"

"Well, they weren't marked *his* and *hers*, Tom," Clayton said. "So how would Rache know which of them would get the dummy tablet?"

Abruptly, Danforth found himself again at the window, peering down at the little plaza in Munich, watching Bannion and

Anna the night before their arrest, how Bannion had opened his hand, the way Anna had frozen as she looked at the tablets, hesitated, then made her selection, all of which he now described to Clayton.

For a time, Clayton remained silent, but Danforth could see that his mind was working through its own dark logic.

"What are you thinking?" he asked after a moment.

"That one of the tablets might have been marked in some way," Clayton answered. "Dimpled. A slightly different shape or shade." He thought a few seconds longer, then waved his hand, as if dismissing his own preposterous idea. "It's nothing, Tom. Really. Just spy-novel stuff that starts going through my head."

Danforth leaned forward. "Tell me," he demanded.

Clayton started to speak but stopped suddenly, as if addled by the direction his mind was taking. "Okay, just now, thinking over what you told me, the way Anna had hesitated . . . isn't that the word you used?"

"Yes."

"And thinking about marked pills and all that, I just happened to remember something LaRoche once said," he went on. "I didn't think anything about it at the time. But with this business of her pill not working, it came back to me." He looked like a sea captain pondering how his ship had sunk. "LaRoche said he'd once talked to Anna about Azerbaijan. About how he'd often taken the bus from Baku to Tbilisi."

It was a route Danforth had once taken with his father, though he had little memory of it now save that it had been very bumpy, the old bus wheezing painfully as it made its way through an endless series of mountain passes.

"On the way, the bus always stopped at a little town called Tovuz," Clayton said. "LaRoche talked about how charming it was. Lovely vineyards, that sort of thing. Anna listened in that quiet way of hers, then said, 'Yes, it must have been lovely at that time in Traubenfeld.'"

"Traubenfeld?" Danforth asked.

"That's what LaRoche noticed," Clayton said. "That Anna called Tovuz Traubenfeld, which was its German name. He thought only a German, or someone raised by Germans, would have known that Tovuz had begun as a German settlement."

"What does that have to do with Anna's cyanide not working?" Danforth asked.

"Probably nothing at all," Clayton answered. "It's just that Traubenfeld has remained very German, and several people from there have risen to quite high positions in a pro-Hitler group called the Gray Wolf Society. It's based in Ankara but we suspect its funds come directly from Berlin." He shrugged. "Anyway, because the Germans in Traubenfeld have always been just an enclave inside Turkey, they need to know what the Turks are up to, and so they've gotten very good at planting moles." He paused, then added, "They start training them when they're children, and one of the things they concentrate on . . . is languages."

"What are you saying, Robert?" Danforth asked. "Are you saying that Anna was in league with Rache?"

Clayton lifted his hand to silence him. "I'm not saying anything for sure, Tom. But in this kind of thing, there are shadows, and any time you encounter something unexpected, your mind begins to eat at you, and you begin to wonder if—"

"If Anna was a traitor?" Danforth interrupted.

"Hold on, Tom," Clayton said cautiously. "Look, all I know is that Rache supplied one tablet that worked and one that didn't, and that somehow Anna got the one that was designed not to kill her." His gaze took on the paranoid glitter Danforth would later see in a thousand thousand eyes. "And now, Bannion is dead. Just like Christophe. And with them, the Project died. Only Anna, or so it seems, has survived."

And so the question had never been whether she would live or die, Danforth thought suddenly, for that had been decided long ago.

It was at that instant, Danforth later came to realize, that his whole life abruptly shifted in a way that threw everything he'd known, or thought he'd known, about Anna into shadow. He thought of his last night with her, how she'd come to his room, all that had happened, and he felt the sweetness of that encounter, the genuineness, drain away. Had she sabotaged the original project because that had been her purpose all along? Had she hatched the plot against Hitler as a diversion, then betrayed them all? Had she faked everything? Again he thought of that last night. Even love?

Clayton shrugged. "But none of this matters now. Because if Anna was something other than we thought, then she's run her game, and so she'll vanish."

"No," Danforth told him bluntly. "No, I want you to find out what you can about where she is right now. Whether she's still in custody. Whether she's alive or dead."

"All right," Clayton said wearily. "But you should face the fact that you may never know more about her than you do right now."

The last of what Danforth thought he would ever know about Anna came to him two weeks later.

He had spent part of that day at the British Museum, vacantly staring at the Elgin Marbles, wondering how his father might have smuggled such massive blocks of stone out of Greece and brought them safely to the New Jersey warehouse of Danforth Imports, and this in turn had led to other fanciful speculations as to how such devices might be employed to bring Anna safely home, should he ever find her. This, of course, presumed that all along she'd been what she claimed, a belief Danforth was finding it increasingly difficult to maintain. It was as if she were a statue he had erected in his mind, bold and solid but now steadily eroding because of his own suspicions. And yet, for all that, he sometimes dreamed of a secret train that would carry her to a secret boat that would carry her across the darkened Channel, where he would wait for her by the cliffs of Dover.

Then, on a clear fall night, in a small tavern on Oxford Street, all such fanciful speculation abruptly ended.

"Anna was interrogated for several days," Clayton told him. "Then she was executed."

Danforth would later be astonished that he had not swooned with this news but had instead abruptly straightened himself and asked for a meaningless detail.

"Shot?"

Clayton shook his head. "They use a guillotine at Plötzensee."

"A guillotine," Danforth whispered.

It would be many years before Danforth visited the execution room at Plötzensee, and on that occasion, the room would strike him as small and plain. The guillotine by then had mysteriously disappeared; it was never found. He knew that a gallows had finally been installed in the room, but that had come long after Anna, and so he'd simply imagined how the guillotine's many victims had knelt upon the wooden bed, felt its hard, flat surface beneath them, then lifted their heads and stretched their necks over the semicircular cradle that awaited them. There they had knelt with their hands tied behind them, knelt for God only knew how many seconds or minutes before the blade that hung above them finally whistled down. The floor where the vanished guillotine had once rested was bare on the day Danforth came to Plötzensee, but its place was marked, and for that reason Danforth had been able to see what the now long dead must also have seen during the last minutes of their lives: the unremarkable door, the bare walls, the arched windows that, oddly, gave the room the feel of a chapel. A single red cord had been stretched across the width of the room, and beyond it, just beneath the arched windows, a wreath had been placed, and next to it was a second spray of flowers. *"So viele Todesfälle,"* someone said just behind him, but he didn't look to see who'd spoken. *So many deaths.*

"I'm so very sorry, Tom," Clayton said.

Danforth found that beyond the three words he had already said, he could add only: "Are you sure?"

Clayton nodded. "According to my sources, she never betrayed you or Bannion or anything about the Project," he added by way of consolation. "She was a heroic woman." He was silent for a moment, then he said, "It was Rache who betrayed us."

Rache, Danforth thought. In German it meant "vengeance," and at that moment the need for vengeance seemed to him the only thing he had left.

For a time, Clayton said nothing, as if warned from speaking any further word by the look on Danforth's face.

"You have to go on, Tom," he said finally. "You have to go back to New York, put Anna's death behind you."

Which was the best advice he could have gotten, and which Danforth had briefly hoped to follow, but never could.

Blue Bar, New York City, 2001

"Never could," Danforth said now.

Though he had tried, as he went on to tell me. He returned to New York and resumed his command of Danforth Imports. In that role, he immersed himself, working long hours, then trudging home to his bed. He tried to find pleasure in the old pleasures, in reading and going to plays. He went out with this woman and that one, but with each failed attempt to rekindle that part of his life, he felt himself fall farther and farther from any capacity to do so. In the middle of a luxurious dinner, he would find himself again at the Old Town Bar, fixed upon his ghostly memory of Anna. While Amy or Sandy or Marian prattled on about this or that, he would hear her whispered voice: *What is the most beautiful thing you never saw?* And with that question, he would think of all the many places he had dreamed of seeing with her and that he now no longer wished to see because he was without her.

"It was like Eve's love for Adam in Milton's *Paradise Lost,*" Danforth said. "That simple, gorgeous line of Eve's: 'with him all deaths / I could endure; without him live no life.'"

As the months passed, he worked to ease the ceaseless ache of Anna's loss. But nothing soothed him or dulled the vividness of his incessant memories of her. At night he would sometimes awaken in the midst of reaching for her, and when he found only emptiness, he would lie on his back and stare at the ceiling and accept the hard fact that nothing could fill this void.

"It was romantic anguish," Danforth said. He looked as if that very agony had been reignited. "It was passion without an object. I was like a starving man whom no food could satisfy."

"But you can't love a dead woman forever, can you?" I asked.

The question appeared to move Danforth, and he immediately turned from it and retreated into his old redoubt of academic discussion.

"The guillotine is an interesting mechanism, Paul," he said. "It's supposed to be very fast and entirely painless." He glanced toward the window, where the snow was still falling steadily, though it had begun to lighten. "But then there's the problem of Henri Languille."

This was clearly a signal that I should make further inquiry, and so I did.

"Henri Languille?" I asked.

"A condemned prisoner," Danforth said. "He was executed by guillotine in 1905. His death was meticulously recorded by a certain Dr. Beaurieux."

"I see."

"Dr. Beaurieux's observations called the guillotine's efficacy into serious question," Danforth continued, now completely in that lecturing tone he used to escape, however briefly, from the more emotional parts of his tale. "Of course, there'd been other observers before Beaurieux. For example, when Charlotte Corday was beheaded, someone grabbed her severed head out of the basket and slapped her face. The people who saw this later said that Charlotte had glared at her assailant with what they described as 'unequivocal indignation.'"

I shivered. "That's rather ghastly."

"Indeed, but getting back to Dr. Beaurieux," Danforth went on. "He said that immediately after the decapitation, Henri Languille's eyelids and lips continued to move for five or six seconds. When those movements stopped, the doctor called to Languille in a loud, sharp tone, as if he were summoning him. At that summons, Languille's eyes opened languidly, as if awakened from a light sleep. According to Beaurieux, there was no spasmodic movement in the eyes at all. They stared at him very evenly, then, after a moment, they closed. At that point, the doctor called to Languille again, and once again his eyes opened. He looked like someone torn from his thoughts, Beaurieux said. The eyes were motionless and the pupils were focused. There was nothing dull about their appearance. Nothing vague or far-away in their look. The doctor was convinced that Languille was staring directly at him. After several seconds, the eyes closed again, this time about halfway. Beaurieux called out for a third time, but Languille's eyes didn't open, and they began to take on the glazed look of the truly dead."

All of this struck me as a gruesome excursion, a reaction Danforth recognized and immediately addressed.

"The question is why I would read about such an incident," Danforth said. "It's because I could not stop thinking about Anna, and this incessant thinking sent me off in odd, nearly crazed directions. She'd been executed by guillotine, so I read everything I could find about that process. Scores of eyewitness accounts. The history of the thing. It's called a *Fallbeil* in German, by the way. 'Falling ax.' Between 1933 and 1945 about sixteen thousand people were executed by *Fallbeil* in Germany and Austria. Hitler liked the method so much he ordered twenty new ones."

This was all decidedly off the point, I thought, save for the way it exposed the obsessive nature of Danforth's research, the fact that he'd been driven to do it as a way of . . . what?

"It was a way of not abandoning Anna or allowing her simply to be erased," Danforth said as if he'd heard the question I'd posed in my mind. "My purpose in doing all this reading was to keep her with me, keep her alive, prevent her from sinking into obscurity, becoming one of history's nameless victims." He shrugged. "But of course, reading can only take a man so far, and so, in the end, it was something else that saved me."

I suddenly feared that Danforth might have fallen to some predictable form of redemption. Religion, perhaps, or another woman.

Hesitantly, I asked, "Which was?"

"War," Danforth answered. "I was still a young man when it broke out, and so I might have used it to accomplish some noble end or do some great, heroic deed." His smile was as soft as the white flakes that fell beyond the window. "But for me it only intensified what soon became my single purpose."

"Which was?" I asked.

"To make the Germans pay," Danforth answered. His gaze darkened. "To kill as many as I could because they had killed

Anna." He let his lethal gaze sink into me. "I had left Europe as a grieving lover," he stated. "I returned to it as a murderer."

Southern France, 1942

Below him, the fields of night-bound France spread out like a gloved hand. He was falling into its darkness, the earth rising toward him like a blessing in disguise.

They were waiting for him below, and when he reached them he thanked them in their native language, then gathered up and buried his parachute as he had been taught in the long sweltering summer of his training.

They were French farmers who greeted him, and for the rest of his life, the memory of their rugged courage would remain with him, the rough texture of their hands when he shook them, the heartbreaking care in their hushed voices as they guided him across the fields and into the small house where they hid him until the next night, when he set off, alone, for the Spanish border.

On that long walk, he thought of Gurs, the train journey he had made with Anna, the ragged clothes of the withered Spaniard who'd met them, and at last the look on Anna's face as the trees had parted and she'd gotten her first glimpse of the camp. A thousand years ago, he thought, a different man than he was now.

For the next year he played the vagabond Spaniard as effectively as Anna had played the disordered street grotesque on that long-ago night in the Old Town Bar. He wandered from village to village as he'd been instructed. To appear Spanish, he dyed his hair and darkened his skin beneath the Spanish sun. From mountain outcrops and village alleys, he watched the roads and railway stations and lived as an itinerant farm hand and sweeper; he slept in barns and back rooms and storage sheds, always speaking the low Spanish of the poor and dispossessed and in every way acting the part of one of Goya's *pobrecitas*.

During these nomadic days, he killed two men, one with a knife and the other with a garrote, both German intelligence operatives, and in both cases he felt as little for their deaths as he'd felt for their lives, and he told himself as he thrust the knife or tightened the garrote that this he did for Anna.

By the early months of 1943, it was clear that his work in Spain was done. Spanish neutrality was enforced by Spain's utter poverty. As a country, it was as starved and desolate as the Spanish refugees of Gurs had been, which was exactly what Danforth reported. There was no point to his remaining in Spain, he told his superiors. They agreed, and on their orders, he'd made his way to Gijon, hired an old fisherman and his ragtag boat, and through surprisingly calm waters sailed to England.

Once in London, Danforth learned that Clayton had been shipped to the Pacific, the commander of a Marine regiment. Clayton's letters had accumulated in the mailroom of Danforth Imports, collected by Danforth's father, who with the outbreak of war had thrown all his resources into the effort. No longer a friend of Germany, he'd purchased thousands of war bonds and provided his country with every imaginable trade secret for the smuggling of supplies and information. Then, in April of 1943, the senior Danforth died in his lofty aerie overlooking Central Park, still baffled by the son who had briefly returned from Europe after a long, mysterious stay, returned distant and aloof, seeming to have lost not only his will to live, as he'd told his father one long, sorrowful evening, but also his will to love.

It was this loveless and unloving man who now occupied the tiny desk in the tiny cubicle of an otherwise nondescript building in Hammersmith, his assignment to translate messages from various sources that poured into London from Calais to Istanbul. The messages were frequently in error, and some were no doubt intended to misinform, but more often than not, they were simply of no use to those planning the invasion that everyone knew was coming and in which effort Danforth felt himself once again sidelined.

But inconsequential as his work seemed to him, Danforth remained at his desk, hoping, always hoping, to find some shred of information as to where Anna had been buried so that after the war, he might find her body and bring it home. But even as he sought such information, some crazed part of his mind harbored the hope that she was still alive, though this hope caused him to envision a still darker end for Anna: in February of 1944 he read about a number of women executed in Natzweiler-Struthof, and he could not stop wondering if she had been among them. In April he read of the mass execution of *Nacht und Nebel*, prisoners, mostly foreign spies and resistance fighters, and again imagined Anna lined up against a wall and shot or hung from communal gallows.

All of these nightmare visions continually assailed him, but it was one in particular he found he could not shake:

Escaped prisoner from Pforzheim reports seeing a small dark female, very badly beaten. Reports female chained nude outside and left through night. Reports SS officer returned and gave her more "rough treatment." Reports prisoner was kicked and beaten and was "all blood." Reports prisoner left till afternoon. Reports SS officer returned and shot prisoner. Reports prisoner was conscious when executed.

Could this small dark female have been Anna?

It was an absurd question, and there was no way for Danforth to answer it, and yet the brief record of this incident refused to let him go, continually urging him to find a way to return to Europe so he could exact yet more revenge.

But each of his requests was denied, and so Danforth continued to work in his London basement cubicle, translating more communications from which he learned more details of the much earlier Parisian roundups of the city's Jews, their herding together in the transit camp at Drancy, the terrible conditions there, the priest who'd claimed to hear the cry of children, though he could not have, from the steps of Sacré Coeur. He read about Ravensbrück, where female prisoners were gassed, about the massacres at Ascq in France and Vinkt in Belgium and Cephalonia in Greece, then farther east, where hell grew hotter in the children's camp as Sisak and the women's camp at Stara Gradiška.

But the dark preponderance of messages came from Poland, a steady stream of accounts that caused Danforth at last to lift his eyes from the most recent of them late on a rainy evening, still unable to take in a fact he was sure had long ago been accepted by others far more informed than himself, and which he finally mentioned to Colonel Broderick.

"The Germans are systematically killing all the Jews," he said. "Does everyone know this?"

Broderick nodded grimly. "Yes, we know. And so when the war is over, we're going to need German-speaking interrogators who are very skilled. Like you, Tom. Because we're going to find out everything they did and make them pay for it."

The sweet prospect of the world's revenge fed the dark animal inside Danforth's soul, and so he remained in London and there read of more and more outrages, and with each new report felt his heart harden, his spirit grow arid, and something like winter settle into him, an inner death that was deepened because in every report of torture and murder, every account of people shot or hanged or driven into gas chambers, he saw among them Anna.

The invasion came in early June, and two weeks later he at

last crossed the Channel and set foot again in France to begin his work as an interrogator. It was there he met the first of what were called the Ritchie boys, the Jews who'd fled Nazi Germany, been trained in Camp Ritchie, Maryland, parachuted or made beach landings on D-day, then slogged through the countryside broadcasting surrender offers to retreating Germans or questioning those who'd already surrendered.

His first job was to break down a Wehrmacht officer named Werner Kruger, a short, stocky little man who smoked continuously during the interrogation. By then they'd learned that the Germans were terrified of being handed over to the Russians, and so they'd dressed a couple of the Ritchie boys in Russian army uniforms on the pretense that should the prisoner not cooperate, he would be turned over to Comrade Stalin. The Ritchie boys had played their parts to the hilt, and it had been effective in a surprising number of cases, Werner Kruger's chief among them.

There'd been scores of others like Kruger, an army of prisoners from whom Danforth had sought information, sometimes successfully, sometimes not, but within each new interrogation still seeking some clue to Anna. Months passed, and summer became fall, and the army marched eastward, and France was liberated and Germany defeated, so that it was amid the ruins of Nuremberg several weeks after the end of the war that he finally met Horst Dieter.

SS captain Horst Dieter had been brought to Danforth's office for what was described as a "thorough going-over." Danforth had expected the usual SS type, still arrogant in defeat, lips locked in perpetual sneer, eyes brimming with contempt. Instead, Dieter had affected a nearly jaunty gait as he walked to the chair across the table from Danforth and sat down. He was loose-limbed and gave off an inexplicable casualness, not to say indifference, and it was this oddity in demeanor that Danforth first addressed.

"You don't seem to realize the situation you're in," Danforth told him in his unaccented German.

"I speak English, Captain," Dieter said. "I lived for two years in Virginia." He shrugged. "And I know quite well what my situation is. I'm going to be shot. So what? I'm used to executions."

This was the sort of casual remark that had opened the door on horrendous crimes in earlier interrogations, and so Danforth pursued it like a lead. "Used to executions?" he asked in as similar a tone as he could muster. "Okay, so how during the war did you happen to get used to executions?"

"I was used to them well before the war," Dieter answered with a dismissive wave of his hand.

"Before the war?"

"Because I was a prison guard," Dieter answered. He leaned back so far in his chair that its front legs lifted off the floor. "We executed God knows how many."

"Executing criminals before the war wouldn't get you shot now," Danforth said pointedly.

"They weren't all criminals," Dieter said. "Unless you call some kid handing out pamphlets a criminal."

"Are you talking about political criminals?" Danforth asked.

"Reds, mostly," Dieter said. "One day you Americans will be sorry we didn't kill them all."

Danforth was getting nowhere with this and knew it, and so he decided to do as he had been trained to do, take one small piece of information, presumably innocent, then have the prisoner expand on it.

"You were in Berlin before the war," Danforth said as he glanced at Dieter's folder.

"Yes."

"Is this where you worked as a guard?"

"Yes."

"At Stadtheim?" Danforth asked.

"No. Plötzensee."

Danforth's gaze lifted. "Plötzensee?"

"In the suburbs," Dieter added with a shrug. "It's mostly blown up now. But it was a busy place before and during the war."

Danforth gave no sign that the very name Plötzensee was like a hook in his skin.

"Busy with executions?" he asked.

"Yes."

Danforth decided to test Dieter's veracity. "These executions, they were by firing squad?"

"No," Dieter said. "They put up a gallows later." He chuckled. "But before that, can you believe it, Captain? We had a . . . what's the word in English? A *Fallbeil*."

"A guillotine," Danforth said.

"That's it, yes: guillotine."

"When were you at Plötzensee?" Danforth asked.

"From June of 1936 until the war began," Dieter answered. "That was in . . ."

"September 1939," Danforth said.

Dieter nodded.

"And you participated in executions during this time?" Danforth asked.

"Yes."

"How many?"

Dieter shrugged. "Many. I don't remember. I walked them to the room, that's all. But that won't matter, they're going to kill us all. It's going to be a big show."

Danforth worked to keep his tone entirely even despite the storm building within him. "These prisoners that you . . . walked, were there any women?"

"Sure."

"Do you remember any of them?"

250

Dieter grinned. "A man always remembers the women."

Danforth faced him stonily. "Who do you remember?"

"There were only two," Dieter answered. "Benita von Falken-hayn. She was the daughter-in-law of some big shot on the general's staff. A wild one. Divorced the big shot's son and got into bed with a Polack spy." He shrugged. "They killed her with an ax. Like some English queen."

Catching his breath, Danforth asked, "And the other one?"

"She wore thick glasses, the other one," Dieter answered. "Not very attractive, I must say." Her unattractiveness seemed to make her life less dear to Dieter. "She was the first woman they used a guillotine on. Another Red. I don't remember her name, but they called her Lilo."

"What was her crime?" Danforth asked.

"She wouldn't stop being a Red," Dieter answered. "Probably other things as well, but I don't remember what they were." He leaned back again and released a slow, relaxing breath. "That's all. Just two women, like I said."

"Just two?" Danforth asked. "Are you sure no other woman was executed while you were at Plötzensee?"

Dieter looked at Danforth closely. "Someone you knew, Captain?"

"She was dark," Danforth said sternly. "She had very curly hair."

Dieter shook his head.

"You're sure you never saw a woman like that at Plötzensee?" Danforth asked emphatically. "In the yard or in the cells?"

Dieter dropped forward in his chair. "No."

Danforth's mind was working feverishly to determine if Dieter's testimony, or even his memory, could be trusted. "Anna was her name," he added. "She might have been called Anna Collier, or maybe Anna Klein."

"Klein?" Dieter asked. "She was a Jew?"

Danforth's gaze turned as lethal as his tone of voice. "She was an American," he said.

Dieter briefly searched his memory for a moment, then he shrugged. "No," he said. "There was never an Anna Klein."

Blue Bar, New York City, 2001

There was never an Anna Klein.

It was obvious that these words had brought Danforth to a strange precipice, or perhaps to a doorway that had opened onto an unexpected land.

"If Dieter was right, then Anna had never been taken to Plötzensee Prison," Danforth said. His tone was now uncertain, as if he were still feeling the aftershocks of this discovery. "And she certainly hadn't been executed there."

"So you must have wondered who Clayton's sources had been for this information," I said.

"Very good, Paul," Danforth said. "Yes, that would have been the question. Who were they? And why had they told him what they did?" He shrugged. "Unfortunately, Clayton was still in the Pacific, fighting his way south on Okinawa. And so I went to Plötzensee Prison to see if I could find any record of Anna having been there. It was in the Soviet sector, and the Russians were completely out of control, ripping the plumbing out of the walls, toilet bowls, and sinks, and loading everything onto trucks." He waved dismissively. "But it was Germany they were destroying, so as far as I was concerned, the Russians could have a free hand."

"You hated them that much?" I asked.

"They were dust to me," Danforth said. "They had killed the

only woman I would ever love, along with millions of innocent people."

I started to speak, but the flash in Danforth's eyes stopped me cold.

"If the crimes of a people go on through time, then why shouldn't our revenge?" he asked. He seemed to realize that his arctic chill had frozen me, and to warm the atmosphere, he sat back casually, like a man about to tell a lighthearted fireside story. "Anyway, by the time I was allowed to visit Plötzensee, it had pretty much been cleared out. It had been badly damaged from the bombings. There was a lot of charred brick and rubble, and for a carton of cigarettes one of the Russian guards let me walk around the place."

I imagined Danforth in his army uniform, a pistol strapped to his side, moving through the blackened ruins, then into the old cell blocks of Plötzensee, where, as he told me, many of the doors had been blown off and left lying in the wide corridors.

He had not been sure what he was looking for, he said, but in his rambling he found what appeared to be the prison's record room. There were still file cabinets, and he searched through the papers he found inside them for quite a few hours. There were prisoner lists and execution lists, along with the usual detritus of the Nazi bureaucracy, petitions for clemency almost always stamped *Denied.*

"Most of what I found was of no value to me, but I did discover that at least one thing Dieter had told me was true," Danforth went on. "He'd even gotten the nickname right: Lilo."

As it turned out, Lilo was Liselotte Herrmann, a German Communist who'd joined the Roter Studentenbund, the Red Students League, in 1931, participated in all sorts of anti-Hitler actions, and gotten herself kicked out of the University of Stuttgart.

To my surprise, he drew a photograph from his jacket pocket and handed it to me. "This is Liselotte," he said.

In the picture, Liselotte Herrmann wore a plain white blouse and was holding a small child. She had straight hair, cut very short, and bottle-bottom glasses with thick, black frames, a woman who could not possibly have been mistaken for a dark, curly-haired Anna Klein.

"The child is her son," Danforth said. "He was four years old when his mother was executed." He drew the picture from my hand and returned it to his pocket. "Anyway, I went through the records I found—which were by no means all the records, of course; God knows how many had been burned or blown to bits or used for toilet paper by the Russians—but there was no mention at all of Anna. Which meant that although I couldn't prove what Dieter had told me, I'd found nothing to disprove it, and so for me the mystery of what had become of Anna only deepened."

"But she'd surely been killed," I said. "You had to assume that."

"Of course," Danforth said. "But a certain kind of devotion—of obsession—demands to know what really happened, and I was stricken in that way, Paul. I simply had to know."

Danforth's had been a sad passion, it seemed to me, and clearly a futile one; even now he struck me as a man with much love and no one to give it to.

"You never fell in love again?" I asked.

"No," Danforth said.

"But surely your love for Anna faded over time," I said.

"That's exactly what Clayton believed would happen eventually," Danforth said. "That in the end Anna would pass into memory, and I would find a way to make a good life without her. Which was why he'd made up the whole business of Anna's execution."

"Made it up?" I asked, astonished.

"Yes," Danforth said. "As he admitted after the war. He'd done it because he believed that I would never stop looking for her if I thought she was alive. It was the action of a friend for the benefit of a friend, he said. Then he asked me to forgive him, and I did. It was as simple as that." He shrugged. "To save a man from a fruitless passion, I'd probably do the same. After all, a passion can die. But not a mystery, Paul, unless you solve it." He smiled softly. "Odd, though, that the next clue would find me working on the war crimes trials. On the Oswald Rothaug prosecution. He'd been the presiding judge in the Katzenberger case."

Leo Katzenberger was a sixty-two-year-old shoe magnate, Danforth told me. He'd lived and prospered in Nuremberg. A friend had written to tell him that his daughter, twenty-two-year-old Irene Scheffler, was coming to Nuremberg in order to pursue her career as a photographer. Scheffler ended up taking an apartment in the same building as Katzenberger's office, and over the next few weeks, neighbors became certain that the two were having an affair.

"But this was not just some commonplace May-December fling," Danforth said, "because Katzenberger was a Jew, and Scheffler was an Aryan, and the Nuremberg laws expressly forbade this kind of association."

Once alerted to official interest, Katzenberger and Scheffler had denied the affair. And since there was no evidence for it other than the speculation of neighbors, the case had been dismissed by the first investigating judge.

"But by then a judge by the name of Oswald Rothaug had gotten wind of the case," Danforth said. "Rothaug was a rabid Nazi, and he found Katzenberger and Scheffler guilty on no evidence but rumor."

At that time, the "crime" did not carry the penalty of death. But Judge Rothaug knew that the death penalty could be imposed on anyone who used wartime regulations to commit a crime. A single witness had testified that Katzenberger had taken advantage of the wartime blackout regulations to carry on his affair, and for this, Katzenberger was sentenced to death.

"He was beheaded at Stadelheim Prison," Danforth said. "After the war, Rothaug was arrested and put on trial. By then I was working as an interpreter for the war crimes tribunal, so when it came time to interview witnesses I was transferred to Nuremberg." He took a brief pause in this narrative, as if he knew that what he was about to tell me — the next twist in his story — would surprise me as much as it had surprised him. "One of the men I was assigned to question was named Gustav Teitler," he continued. "A seedy little character. I hated him immediately." Danforth's gaze hardened. "I could have shot him without a blink."

Nuremberg, Germany, 1946

"You are Gustav Teitler," Danforth said with the unrelenting hardness of the man he had become.

"I am, yes."

Teitler was a pudgy little fellow with the mild look of department-store clerk, and as he sat down in the chair in front of Danforth's desk, he offered a smile that proclaimed his great willingness to cooperate. To this he added the usual look of hapless innocence Danforth had seen in a thousand German faces by then, all bafflement and consternation, as if their malign recent history had caught them completely by surprise.

"I am pleased to meet you, Herr Danforth," Teitler said amiably.

They took their seats in a room just a few yards away from where an American tank sat idly in the square and American soldiers lounged about absent-mindedly smoking cigarettes, a fact that was not wasted on Gustav Teitler.

"The Russians are treating Germany like a dead whore," he said. "We are fortunate that you Americans are —"

"The Russians are treating you better than you deserve," Danforth interrupted sharply.

Danforth's hatred of the Germans had been intensified by his recent visit to Plötzensee and his finding no clue of what had happened to Anna, a dead end that over the past days had caused him to conjure up a hundred dreadful fates for her. The grim speculations were made even more painful by the release of yet more terrible images from the trials, all of which had turned the language he loved and spoke so well into an object of repulsion.

"You're here because you are associated with a judge who is going to be tried as a war criminal," Danforth said sternly. "And you're going to answer my questions fully. Do we understand each other?"

This was not a pose, and Teitler seemed to comprehend that he faced something volcanic in the man who sat opposite him.

"Of course, Captain Danforth," Teitler said.

"Oswald Rothaug," Danforth said briskly. "You were a stenographer in his courtroom."

"Yes," Teitler answered.

"At the Leo Katzenberger trial," Danforth added.

"That was a terrible thing," Teitler said. "The poor man couldn't believe what was happening to him, that his life was at stake simply because —"

"Yes, yes," Danforth interrupted curtly. He was not interested in any German show of sympathy for the fate of Leo Katzenberger. He began a series of questions designed to discover any incriminating evidence against Rothaug that might have been gained by such a lowly functionary as Gustav Teitler.

There wasn't much, as the next hour proved, but Danforth slogged on through Teitler's asides, how he had only "by chance" ended up as a court stenographer, as he'd once hoped to be a civil engineer. This dream had been dashed by the Great War, in which he'd been wounded; his career hopes had been destroyed, along with the Germany of his youth, and the country had been "ripe" for what happened next.

It was an old story, and Danforth had no sympathy.

"Did you see Rothaug at any point after the trial?" he asked by way of ending the tiresome and unenlightening interview.

"Once, yes," Teitler answered. "In Berlin."

"Did he say anything about Leo Katzenberger?"

Teitler took a moment to think before he answered. "They weren't so happy with that trial, you know, the higher-ups," he said. "So they moved Judge Rothaug to Berlin. He was just a low official when I ran into him. Working for the prosecutor's office. A nothing. A rat sniffing around. Students, mostly. What they were doing. The Red Orchestra, that sort of thing."

"The Red Orchestra?"

"You know, Commies," Teitler said. "Students. They were young; they had no idea what they were up against."

Young and with no idea of what they were up against, Danforth thought. As he once had been.

"Rothaug was talking about a traitor the Gestapo had arrested," Teitler said. "'Like Katzenberger,' he'd said, 'another head cut off.' He seemed to take a particular delight in it."

"Why?" Danforth asked dryly. "They'd already cut off lots of heads."

"This was a woman, and an American," Teitler said. "Rothaug said that killing her would show these foreigners that their necks weren't any thicker than the necks of German traitors."

"When did you have this conversation?" Danforth asked.

"It was in the summer of 1943," Teitler answered. "I was only in Berlin for a few days. There was no work in the courts for me, so I went back to Nuremberg."

Danforth's pen remained still. "Did he mention the woman's name?"

Teitler shook his head.

"Did he describe her?"

"No."

"Did he say anything else at all about her?"

This time Teitler shrugged. "Only that before they chopped off her head, they should shave off her hair."

Danforth was careful not to allow himself to consider the possibility that this woman might have been Anna. And yet, over the following days, he could not stop thinking about what Teitler had told him. It was like the Spanish idiom for relentless worrying over a single thought: *dar vueltas*, "incessant circling." The prospect had led Danforth to an incessant circling of particular scenes: Anna at their first meeting; Anna strolling among the tombs of Père-Lachaise. She might have survived until the summer of 1943: this was the thought that awakened him each morning after he returned to Nuremberg following his interview with Teitler, and it was the thought that faded at last with sleep, though only after it had kept him up until nearly dawn.

For the next few days, Danforth went about his work, interviewing others distantly involved in the Katzenberger case, mostly judges who claimed to have had nothing but contempt for Rothaug, whom they described as a clown, a buffoon, a climber, and a toady. Teitler's tiny clue continued to work like a needle in Danforth's mind, consuming his every free moment, keeping him in his office until the early hours of the morning going through files, ledgers, accounting books, old newspapers, anything he could find that might hold, however distantly, a clue to the identity of the woman Rothaug had mentioned.

It was three o'clock in the morning, but the man Danforth saw when he glanced up from his desk looked freshly shaved and ready for the new day with none of Danforth's hollow exhaustion in his eyes.

The man sat down in the chair across from Danforth's desk. "My name is Edward Brock. I understand you've been looking for an American woman who you think was executed by the Germans."

Danforth nodded.

"I can save you some work," Brock said. "Her name was Mildred Harnack. She was an American who lived in Germany and spoke and wrote fluent German. She was a Communist, but— get this—she was also a member of the Daughters of the American Revolution." He drew a paper from his jacket pocket and handed it to Danforth. "The State Department kept an eye on her." He nodded toward the paper. "Here in a nutshell is what we know."

Harnack had moved to Germany with her husband in 1929, Danforth read. She'd gotten interested in Communism and later toured the Soviet Union. By 1933 she'd begun teaching English literature at night-school classes in Berlin. Still later she'd published articles in the *Berliner Tageblatt* and *Die Literatur,* but the work had dried up once the Nazis came to power. It was then she'd stepped over the line and become what amounted to a Soviet agent, a fact the Gestapo had discovered and for which both she and her husband had been arrested in the fall of 1943. Her husband had been sentenced to death, but for some reason Mildred had received a mere six-year imprisonment, a sentence that was not to Hitler's liking and which he'd ordered to be reviewed. The review had ended with a predicable result, and Mildred Harnack had been executed at Plötzensee on February 16, 1943.

Most decidedly, Mildred Harnack had not been Anna Klein.

Danforth gave the paper back to Brock. "Thank you," he said wearily. "You're right, that will save me a lot of time."

Brock folded the paper and returned it to his jacket pocket. "Who are you looking for?" he asked. "Because I might be able to help you there too. We have quite a few documents from German intelligence, you know." He lit a cigarette. "So, who was this woman?"

"Her name was Anna Klein," Danforth said. "She worked for me before the war. We were in Berlin in August of 1939. She was arrested by the Gestapo. I never saw her again."

"What can you tell me about her?" Brock asked.

Danforth told him that she was Jewish, that she was in her twenties, small, dark, with curly hair.

"That's not a lot to go on," Brock said.

"She was brilliant with languages," Danforth added. It was little more than a futile aside, and he was surprised to see that this suddenly spurred Brock's interest.

"How many did she speak?" he asked.

"Nine that I know of."

"Was Ukrainian one of them?" Brock asked significantly.

"Yes," Danforth said. "Why do you ask?"

"Because I have an intelligence report on a Ukrainian named Rudy Romanchuk. He was a forger who specialized in fake documents for people who were trying to get out of Germany. He was working for the Russians too. A low-level informant. But they began to suspect that he was working for the Germans. So they picked Rudy up and took him to Warsaw for interrogation. Rudy's Russian wasn't so great, so they brought in an interpreter. An American. In her twenties. Quite pretty, according to Rudy."

"When was this interrogation?" Danforth asked.

"A week or two before the Germans attacked Russia," Brock answered. "Which means she could be anywhere now." He let

261

this sink in, then added, "As you know, we're not that chummy with the Russians anymore, so we'd be interested in tracking down any American citizen who might be in their hands." He plucked the cigarette from his mouth and crushed it into the ashtray on Danforth's desk. "So, this woman. The one who was in Warsaw. Could she have been Anna Klein?"

Blue Bar, New York City, 2001

"I had no idea, of course," Danforth said, "and I told Brock that. I had too little to go on, and I didn't want to tell him anything about Anna he didn't already know. Which was nothing."

"So, you don't think Brock knew anything about the Project?" I asked. "Anything about Anna being in France, anything at all about her?"

"I couldn't tell what he knew," Danforth said, "other than that an American woman had been translating for the Soviets in Warsaw just before the Germans invaded Russia, which was in June of 1941." He leaned back slightly. "But if this woman was Anna, then she was still alive in June of 1941, alive and in Warsaw, which meant that she'd been turned over to the Soviets." He paused, then added, "But why would the Germans have turned a woman who'd plotted to kill Adolf Hitler over to the Russians?"

I had no answer for this, and so I simply shrugged.

"Don't feel inadequate, Paul," Danforth said. "No one knew the answer to that question. Which is why I was ordered to find it."

"Ordered? You?"

"I was still in the army, so who would have been a better choice?" Danforth asked. "By that time, I spoke passable Polish and a little Russian. Brock had a few leads. He knew that Romanchuk had later been arrested and sent to Auschwitz, which he'd survived. It was only after the war that he'd vanished. But then so had this woman, which left me no option but to assume that she was still alive."

I thought over all Danforth had just told me, then said, "But realistically, could a woman who'd tried to kill Hitler have survived the war?"

"I had the same question, Paul," Danforth answered. "And although the supposition seemed far-fetched, I looked into whether it might be possible. That's how I came across the file on Olga Chekhova."

Then he told me who she was.

She'd been born in Armenia in 1897, a niece by marriage to the great Russian writer Anton Chekhov. She'd gotten married quite young to a Jewish man, and she'd borne him a daughter. She later divorced him but she never lost interest in the welfare of her daughter. The Russian Revolution drove her to Germany. She went by train to Vienna in the company of a Soviet agent, then on to Berlin, where she managed to get work as an actress. By 1930, she'd become one of the brightest stars in German cinema. She'd also attracted the notice of Adolf Hitler, in whose company she'd been photographed. Olga looked quite lovely as she sat next to the man himself, and the picture's significance had not been lost on Soviet intelligence.

"From that picture, the Communists knew that Olga was a member of the true in crowd, familiar with all the Nazi bigwigs," Danforth said, "and since she had family still in Russia, they decided she could be pressured into the spy game."

They were right, and Olga Chekhova became a sleeper agent, Danforth told me. At one point she'd even been discussed as a critical figure in a Russian secret police plot to assassinate Hitler.

"Rather like Anna, don't you think, Paul?" Danforth said at the conclusion of this narrative.

"A little too much like Anna," I agreed. "What happened to Olga?"

"She was never discovered by the Germans," Danforth answered. "Once Berlin fell, she was flown to Moscow, where she was debriefed. Then she went back to Germany, where she lived quite well under Soviet protection." He smiled. "Her last words were 'Life is beautiful.'"

"When did she die?"

"In 1980," Danforth answered. He saw my astonishment and added, "So you see, Paul, it was quite possible for a young woman who was gifted at languages and something of an actress to survive the war. Even one with deep Jewish connections whose name was later connected to a plot to kill Hitler."

I nodded. "Well, Anna was a good actress. That can't be denied."

"No, it can't," Danforth agreed. "She acted a New York nut case and she acted the perfect assistant to an importer. She acted the art critic when the target was standing right in front of her. She acted the dedicated assassin up to the moment she was arrested." All of this appeared to build darkly in Danforth's mind, but he continued anyway. "She acted like she could kill a man," he said, and then, after a grim pause that seemed to renew every ancient ache within him, he added, "and perhaps she also acted like she could love one."

"But Olga Chekhova survived only because she'd been a Soviet agent all along," I said.

Danforth now seemed a creature formed of shadows. "True enough, Paul," he said quietly. "A Soviet agent all along. As Rache was too. Which meant that only Bannion had been what he seemed."

"Only Bannion," I said softly. "And so he was completely expendable."

"As the innocent always are," Danforth said. "Because they are

of no importance to either side. And so we can kill them without losing anything save the value we once gave to innocence."

"But you couldn't know that any of this was true," I said.

"No, I couldn't," Danforth admitted. "Because the best conspiracies work like nesting dolls, Paul. They hide inside each
other." He smiled, but it was a dark, painful smile that gave
him a rather wizened look. "It took me years and a great deal
of moving around, mostly in those rattling trains that wound
through Eastern Europe, but I finally found Rudy Romanchuk,"
he said, by way of returning to his tale. "He'd gone back to the
Ukraine, just as Brock had thought, a town the Germans called
Lemberg."

Lemberg, Ukraine, 1951

Danforth had started in Warsaw, which still lay in ruins, went on
to Radom, and then continued farther eastward in long tortur-
ous rides on belching, coal-fired trains and groaning buses, all
of them crowded with peasants who ate bread and cheese and
washed it down with bottles of *miód pitny*, which they passed
from one to another as if it were a favored grandchild.

"You speak not bad Polish," an old man said to him on the
road out of Zamość, Danforth on this occasion riding in a horse-
drawn lorry with a group of former Polish prisoners, all of them
huddled together on a layer of wet hay. The old man held up the
bottle the others had been passing around. "Vodka come from
old word," he said, "*gorzalka*. You know what means *gorzalka*?"

Danforth shook his head.

The old man placed his gnarled hands on either side of his
face, rocked his head left and right, smiled widely, and fluttered
his eyes almost girlishly. "It mean," he said, "'to glow.'"

This had been the brightest moment of Danforth's eastward

journey. The rest had been a long ordeal of bone-battering travel through a landscape he'd last visited many years before the war, and the vast sweep of its destruction amazed him, even though he'd followed the Third Army through France and walked the charred remains of Dresden and the rubble of Berlin. War is one thing, as he would later realize, but massacre is another, and in town after wasted town he'd seen the cruel arrogance of the German invasion and the cruel vengeance of the Soviet re-occupation. He'd walked the pit of death in Dubno and valley of death in Bydgoszcz, and once he'd reached Lemberg it was beneath the bridge of death he'd walked to find Romanchuk's freezing hovel on Pełtewna Street.

As he traveled along that winding way, Soviet soldiers had been anything but welcoming, and he was stopped repeatedly and interrogated in small concrete rooms pocked with bullet holes and ripped by shrapnel. But the old art of bribery still possessed its ancient power, and he'd been free in the dispensing of it, softening these war-weary men with meals and liquor and speaking his precarious Russian in ways that made them laugh and drink more and in their sad stupor remove whatever was barring his movement east.

They'd been boys, for the most part, the soldiers and border guards who'd detained him, and in their faces Danforth had seen the youth that war had taken from them. They were cynical and cunning and something in them had been deflowered so that on a whim and in an instant they could become unimaginably brutal. In every town, he'd heard stories of men slit open at the abdomen and then made to dance until their bowels unraveled, of herds of women driven down roads and across fields and over bridges as human mine detectors, of villagers arranged in towering pyramids until those who formed its base were crushed to death. But it was an old woman's tale of a teenage girl taken from her father's house near the camp at Łambinowice that he'd never forgotten. She'd been an ethnic German, the old woman said, her parents killed in the anti-German reprisals that had been unleashed by the conquering Russians and thereafter swept the eastern territories. The girl had been entirely naked and radiantly blond, the perfect Aryan victim. A rope had been tied around her neck and she'd been tugged forward like an animal on a leash and loaded into the back of a truck filled with Polish partisans, all of them, as Danforth imagined it, "glowing." She'd never been seen again.

There was nothing particularly horrendous in this tale compared to other stories of anti-German reprisals Danforth had heard by then, and yet this scene had haunted him for the rest of his journey. He'd come to realize by the time he reached Lemberg that, as with Anna, it was the unknown fate that moved him. What tormented him was not what had definitely been destroyed but what had mysteriously vanished into time and space; not someone who without doubt had been shot in a prison courtyard but that other one — lost in night and fog — who'd last been seen strolling in a park or buying apples from a stand.

Night had fallen by the time he reached what appeared to be a shoemaker's shop. A yellow glow came from the front window, a color Danforth recognized as candlelight because he'd seen so much of it radiating softly from the otherwise pitch-dark streets of the shattered cities through which he'd passed.

He knocked at the door and waited. It opened slightly and a thin shaft of light crossed the threshold. A small eye floated like a rheumy brown bubble in that same narrow slit, and to this eye Danforth presented his now-defunct military credentials.

In the German he hoped the man understood, he said, "I'm Captain Thomas Danforth. United States Army. I'm looking for Rudy Romanchuk on a matter of great urgency."

The eye blinked once, slowly and wearily and even a bit re-signedly, and Danforth saw the many crimes for which Roman-chuk now thought he was at last to pay the price.

With no word, the door opened and Danforth stepped inside a badly damaged room, precariously supported by cracked walls and splintered wood, and with a disturbing droop in the ceiling. Water marks spread across that ceiling and then down the peel-ing walls to a bare concrete floor, broken and stained, on which stood old furniture and a few crippled machines. The room's shattered appearance echoed the mood of Central Europe, Dan-forth thought as he glanced about: crumbling, torn, a thing of jagged borders, more or less idle.

"American? So far?" Romanchuk asked in very broken Ger-man, making it clear that the man had probably spent very little time in that country. Romanchuk's grin flashed like pieces of sil-ver. "You have plenty money."

When Danforth didn't answer, Romanchuk grabbed a spindly wooden chair and drew it over to the coal stove that rested in the center of the room. Beside it an old crate contained the few chunks of coal he'd managed to procure by God only knew what illicit means.

Danforth sat without taking off his coat; the room was too cold for that, as a film of ice on the window made clear. He could see that Romanchuk was frightened, as if he expected to be arrested, hauled back to the American sector, tried for some crime of which he was no doubt guilty, then hanged or sent to prison. But he could also see that Romanchuk had been in such tight spots before and that he'd grown confident in his ability to slither out of them.

"I'm not here to arrest you," Danforth told him. "I'm looking for a woman."

Relief flooded Romanchuk's face. "I can get woman," he said.

Years later, when Danforth read of the thriving sex slave trade in Moldova, he'd wondered if Romanchuk was still alive, a wrinkled old pimp who'd slipped across the border to steal Moldovan girls from their small villages and sell them in the back-alley clubs of Chisinau. It would have been typical, he'd thought then, Romanchuk at last become some version of Joseph Conrad's Mr. Kurtz, evil the undying fuel that powered and sustained him.

"Woman. Young girl," Romanchuk added.

Danforth restrained the violent urge that swept over him and said, "I'm looking for a particular woman. You may not have heard her name, but when the Soviets interrogated you in Warsaw, she was the one who translated your answers."

Danforth could see that Romanchuk was still trying to read the situation and somehow use it for his own gain. He was a criminal through and through, Danforth recognized, the sort of man who never once got up in the morning and asked himself how he might make an honest living. Danforth had encountered scores of such people in his postwar interrogations, a whole criminal class the Germans had used to carry out some of their most dreadful crimes: rapists and murderers who'd been taken from their cells in countless eastern towns, supplied with whips and truncheons and ax handles, and then unleashed to storm through streets and hospitals. During a particular atrocity he now recalled, a schoolyard full of children still in their uniforms had been attacked. Remembering the dreadful photographs he'd seen, the knots of terrified little boys and girls, hulking brutes still in their prison clothes raging among them, their truncheons in midstrike or already making contact, he found himself amazed that such miscreants, along with the nation that had unleashed them, had not been exterminated at the end of the war.

With that thought, Danforth's still-fuming hatred of the Germans spiked, and on its hurtling flame he burst forward and grabbed Romanchuk by the throat.

"Now you listen to me," he snarled. "You're going to tell me all you know about this woman, and you're going to do it because if you don't, I'll kill you." He pressed his face close to Romanchuk's and released every spark of his hatred and contempt. "Do we understand each other?"

Romanchuk stared at Danforth unbelievingly, a man who had seen many forms of hurt and hatred but never like this.

"This woman translated for you when the Soviets held you in Warsaw," Danforth repeated, still speaking German. Then, using a Ukrainian word he'd been careful to learn at the beginning of his journey, he said, *"Chutka!"*

Talk!

With no further prompting, Romanchuk told Danforth that he'd forged a passport for a man the Soviets were desperately trying to find, a German agent they believed had betrayed them. "I tell them this guy want passport and identity card just before Germans make pact with Russia."

"Did you know his name?" Danforth asked.

Romanchuk shook his head. "He was big deal, because Russian officer was wearing Order of Lenin."

"Tell me about the woman who translated for you," Danforth said.

"Small woman," Romanchuk said. "Dark. Good-looking."

"And her hair?" Danforth asked.

"It was very short," Romanchuk said. "From behind, she could be boy."

"Did you get any impression of where she was from?" Danforth asked. "Whether she was German or something else?"

"She was American," Romanchuk answered without hesitation.

"How do you know?"

"When I was sit in the room, wait for questions, there was guard. Regular clothes, but he was guard, you know what I mean."

Danforth said nothing.

"Another guard come in and just loud enough, he say, 'She here, the American girl.' And maybe in a minute she come into room with three men."

Like many others Danforth had interrogated, Romanchuk seemed lost in surreal recollection. Danforth had seen the same look in the faces of both the witnesses and the defendants at Nuremberg, in the architects of the chimneys and in those who'd barely missed going up them. It gave the sense that they believed they could not possibly have done or suffered what they had done or suffered, that it had all happened in some unreal space, all been something . . . beyond.

"She didn't say nothing to me," Romanchuk went on. "She translate. My German not so good. My Russian not so good. We speak in Ukrainian, and she translate to Russian." His eyes narrowed. "No. She was . . . saying wrong. Well, not exact wrong, she leave out important things."

"Why would she do that?" Danforth asked.

"I don't know. Maybe she protect this guy the Russians want."

"She was protecting a German agent?" Danforth asked starkly.

"Yes," Romanchuk said. "For example, she don't say it was Argentina passport he want. She just say passport. They look for this man, but she don't say where." His grin was like the slavering of a dog. "I say nothing. Maybe he her lover or something."

In years to come, Danforth would often try to re-create the storm of feeling that broke over him at that moment and that left him utterly desolate. It was as if he had seen the whirlwind from the inside, the terrible violence of its swirl.

Romanchuk laughed again. "She give Soviets false turn. They don't know that. She act different."

"How?"

"Like she was with them," Romanchuk said. "Like she was on

271

their side, a good comrade. Very friendly. Especially with the guy with the Order of Lenin. She even speak to him in Turkish."

"Turkish?" Danforth asked.

"I hear, I know. I once work in Ankara," Romanchuk explained.

"Did you understand what they were talking about?" Danforth asked. "This woman and the Soviet officer?"

"Moscow," Romanchuk answered. "She ask him about city. He say it is crowded." He laughed, then he said, "But there's always room in Adult World."

Adult World, Danforth thought, a term he'd picked up from his many interrogations, the comical Russian nickname for Lubyanka.

Blue Bar, New York City, 2001

"Adult World because there was a famous toy store across the square from Lubyanka Prison," Danforth explained. "Children's World, it was called."

"Funny," I said grimly.

"Lubyanka was also said to be Moscow's tallest building," Danforth added without the slightest glimmer of humor, "because from its basement windows you could see Siberia."

"Even funnier," I said darkly.

"It had once been the *gos strakhkassa*," Danforth continued. "The government insurance office. *Strakhkassa* means 'insurance office.' But *strakh* means 'fear' in Russian, so later people called it *gos strakha*, the 'government terror.'"

"But of course, this was something Romanchuk only claimed to have overheard," I said.

"Which meant I had nothing to go forward on," Danforth

said. "But I also had nothing to go back to, Paul." He shrugged. "And so I went east."

"East," I said, as if I'd stumbled on a clue. "Where your story always seems to be tending. A story that is sort of a haunted-house tale now, it seems to me. With the protagonist searching from room to room, looking for that ghost."

"Anna's ghost," Danforth said in a tone that gave me the impression that I was being led down a road whose end Danforth knew well, being conducted step by step, carefully and thoughtfully, toward some fateful final moment.

"From room to room, yes," I said, "but always to the east."

"Always to the east," Danforth repeated. "How right you are, Paul." His smile was paper thin. "Where you've never been, I think you said. The Middle East, I mean."

"No, never to the Middle East," I said a little defensively. "But as I told you, I've been to Moscow."

"Ah, yes, Moscow," Danforth said, and on that word resumed his tale. "I arrived there—"

"But wait a moment," I interrupted. "Romanchuk said that Anna was giving the Russians a wrong turn."

"Yes."

"So, you were now convinced that this woman was working for the Germans?"

"Completely convinced," Danforth said. "And I was also convinced that this woman was Anna."

"So why did you continue looking for her?" I asked. "She had probably betrayed you. Probably gotten Bannion killed. Maybe even Christophe. She was a—"

"She was a Nazi pretending to be a Jew," Danforth interrupted.

"Then why look for her?" I asked.

"Well, wouldn't you look for the person who had used you

and betrayed you while all the time working for a cause that killed millions of innocent people?" Danforth asked.

It was at that moment I saw the deep hatred he had harbored for so long.

"You were going to kill her?" I asked, more astonished by this notion than by anything Danforth had revealed so far.

"Yes," Danforth said brutally. "Faced with such a betrayal, nothing should stay your hand, don't you agree, Paul?"

"No, nothing," I said, in an admiring tone I hadn't used with him before.

"But it was no longer love that drove me," Danforth said. "It was hatred."

He let me ponder this stark reversal for a time, then he added darkly, "And so to Moscow, because there seemed no place else to go."

He arrived there in November of 1952, he told me, a thin, weary man who'd developed pneumonia on the way and had spent several days in a barely heated room in Kiev, then yet more time idly strolling about and working to improve his Russian before he reached Moscow.

Moscow was a long way from the rest of the world, not only in miles, but in its steadily deepening paranoia.

"Everyone was terrified of everyone else," Danforth said. "Brock's contacts in Moscow were afraid that any help they extended to me would put them under suspicion. I knew that my time was running out, but I didn't care. In fact, I had lost the capacity to care, Paul. And there is no place darker than that place." He paused a moment, then added, "So dark I was almost glad when they came for me." Suddenly he smiled, as if greeting a brighter turn in his tale. "It was snowing that day." He glanced toward the window, layers of white deepening on the streets and sidewalks. "Like now."

Moscow, Soviet Union, 1952

The snow was falling heavily as Danforth made his way toward Gorky Street that morning, but nonetheless a long line of freezing Russians snaked from the entrance of the Lenin mausoleum, as it had every morning since his arrival in Moscow. It was as if a new list were published each evening telling you, you, and you that you must pay your respects to Comrade Lenin at an appointed moment on the following day, as if hundreds had been ordered to appear at the exact same time, guaranteeing an endlessly extended line and the continuation of the absurd pretense that Lenin and the frightful society he had helped create were still universally beloved.

He had disliked Moscow from his first day. Its one majestic vista was Kremlin Square, but that majesty had been dulled by the horrendous sprawl around it. Added to this was the sheer weight of oppression that turned each minute into a dull throb and that seemed to lace the air with molten lead.

Once on Gorky Street, Danforth headed for the Aragvi, the restaurant Brock's contact had suggested, probably because it was one of the city's most luxurious, and thus hardly likely to be chosen for a meeting anyone would want kept secret from the KGB.

A squat little Pobeda drew up alongside him; it moved slowly at the same pace as him and then spurted forward and stopped. A tall man in a long overcoat got out, nodded toward Danforth, then motioned him forward, smiling quite broadly as he did.

"*Kiryukha*," the man said as he thrust out his hand.

The word meant "old friend" or "pal" or something of that sort, and it could not have surprised Danforth more.

Then in English the man said, "Get in car."

Danforth did as he was told, and seconds later found himself cruising down Gorky Street, the big man at the wheel.

"You know what *pobeda* mean?" he asked.

Danforth admitted that he didn't.

"'Victory,'" the man said. "You call me . . . Flynn, okay?"

"Whatever you say," Danforth replied dryly. "I'm Thomas Danforth."

"Thomas Danforth your real name?" the man asked.

"Yes."

The man grinned. "You spy maybe?"

"No."

The man laughed heartily. "I Errol Flynn. American movie star." He laughed again. "See, I give you my real name too. Real name and real what I do. So we always tell truth, right, buddy?"

They moved on down the street, then made what seemed to Danforth a series of random turns, Flynn whistling for a time, then humming something that sounded vaguely like a Slavic version of "Dixie." They passed the Central Telegraph Office with its great clock, and then went along Pushechnaya and onto Dzerzhinsky Square, where the gray façade of Lubyanka loomed ahead.

"You know where you are, Thomas Danforth?" Flynn asked.

"Yes," Danforth answered.

"Good," Flynn said cheerfully. "Good you should know where you are."

With that, he gave the steering wheel a violent jerk, and the Pobeda abruptly turned into the wide entrance to Lubyanka, then stopped before its forbidding steel doors. The doors were on rails, which Danforth had not known, so he watched in surreal and curiously untroubled surprise as they slid open to reveal the building's broad central courtyard.

During all this, Flynn sat silently, staring straight ahead. It was not until the doors had disappeared into the walls that he spoke again. *"Kiryukha,"* he repeated as he pressed down on the little car's accelerator. "You are here."

Minutes later, Danforth found himself in a small office looking at a man in a military uniform behind a metal desk flipping through pages of a file.

"So, you're looking for an American woman," the man said in an English that was as perfect as an Oxford don's. Before Danforth could answer, the man smiled widely and said, "Did you think we Russians are all illiterate peasants, Captain Danforth?"

Danforth shook his head.

"You know the story by Dostoyevsky?" the man asked.

"Which one?" Danforth asked.

"About a man in prison. All the other prisoners are talking about the Russian peasant. He is a type to them. A brute. That is what these men think. But the hero of the story remembers when he was a boy, there was a peasant who worked on his father's estate, and on one occasion, and at the risk of his own life, this 'peasant' had put himself between this boy and a wolf."

He watched to see if the moral of his tale had sunk into Danforth's mind. "So, what is the meaning of this story, Captain Danforth?"

"That all Russians are not the same," Danforth answered.

He laughed. "Some can read . . . and speak a fine English, is that not so?"

"Clearly," Danforth said.

"I am Comrade Stanik," the man said. "What can you tell me about this woman you are looking for?"

"She spoke quite a few languages," Danforth said. "She was described by our contact as dark, young, pretty."

"Why are you looking for her?" Stanik asked.

"Because we have some evidence that she gave false translations to your agents. We believe she did this in order to protect a German who later fled Germany."

"And you think she has information about this agent?"

"Yes."

"He must be very important to you then."

"We lost a good man because of this German agent," Danforth said. "We want him to pay for it. Her too."

"But you do not know the identity of this agent?" Stanik asked.

"We only know his code name: Rache."

Something glinted in Stanik's eyes. "Rache?" he asked. "And if you find this woman, you wish to interrogate her?"

"Interrogate her, then bring her back to hang," Danforth answered coldly.

He saw that this blunt sense of justice appealed to Stanik, and so he gathered himself in, fully playing the part now. "We Americans don't like traitors any more than the Russians do."

Stanik looked satisfied by this statement, though it was clear that something continued to nag at him. "And you think this woman is in Soviet territory."

"Yes."

"What makes you think this?"

"Because she was last seen in Warsaw," Danforth said. "With Soviet authorities. One of them was wearing the Order of Lenin."

Stanik glanced down at the file. "Romanchuk, Rudolph. Now resident in Lemberg. You spent an evening together some months ago, after which you were taken ill in Kiev." He looked up and smiled. "I like to make sure our information is up to date. Have you anything to add?"

"No."

Stanik closed the file. "Maybe you should stay here for a while," he said, by which he clearly meant in Lubyanka.

"Stay here?" Danforth feigned a dismissive laugh. "I'm an American citizen."

Stanik's laughter was not feigned. "American citizen? We have plenty of American citizens staying here." He leaned forward. "You have been in Moscow many days. Have you seen our people? Have you seen them in the lines, in the cold, holding their little bags?" He leaned forward even farther. "Do you know what they call these bags, hmm?" He didn't wait for an answer. "*Avoski*. Your Russian is not so good, so I will tell what it means. *Avoski* means 'perhaps.' Because it is their hope, you see. My people hold their little bags because perhaps they will have a little fish or a little potato or a little piece of hard bread to put in it." He opened his desk drawer and put the file inside it. "My people have learned that they can be harmed and that nothing can save them from this harm," Stanik said as if in conclusion. "And you, my American friend, are going to learn that too." He shook his head. "No eastern front for the Americans and the British. Never an Eastern Front because you wanted the Germans to kill every last one of us." He glanced toward the door and called out in Russian, a sentence spoken too rapidly for Danforth to catch anything but the *тараканий*, the Russian word for "cockroach."

With a speed he would always remember as unreal, Danforth suddenly found himself in a small room of no more than four feet by nine feet, which he would later learn was called a *bok*. It had a metal door with a peephole and a food slot, and above the door there was a naked light bulb in a metal cage, very bright and very intense and that he guessed to be no less than 1,500 watts. A wooden bench had been pushed up against the wall opposite the door, and when Danforth finally sat down on it, he saw a single eye watching him through the peephole. At intervals over the next ten hours, this same eye came and went and came and went, as if it were not real at all but a glass eye slowly spun on some mechanical device, the Lubyanka version of a lazy Susan.

During this time he was fed black bread and a thin soup that tasted like water strained through barley.

At some point he heard the metal door clang open, and a small bald man in a lab coat stood before him with a guard on either side, each of them with a cap that seemed too small for him and that bore a distinctive red star.

The man in the lab coat said something in Russian; part of it had to do with clothes, but the rest Danforth couldn't make out.

"What?" Danforth asked.

The man made a gesture of unbuttoning his lab coat and then repeated the command.

"Undress?" Danforth said. "I will do no such thing."

The man gave a quick nod, and instantly the guards stepped forward, grabbed Danforth by his arms, whirled him around, and pressed him hard against the wall.

They held him there for a few minutes, one of them pulling up on Danforth's right arm all the while, sending a streaking ache down his shoulder that seemed to settle, like a burning coal, somewhere near his wrist. Then they jerked him around to face the man in the lab coat once again.

The man repeated his earlier command, though he added the Russian version of *Do it now*, a phrase Danforth understood.

"All right," he said, and with that removed his shirt and undershirt, his shoes and socks and trousers, and at last stood in his shorts.

The man pointed to the shorts and made a sign of dragging them down.

"Do it now," he said.

"All right," Danforth said again, convinced, despite so grave a humiliation, that he was somehow the subject of an old parlor game. "All right."

Once naked, Danforth stood silent and unmoving as the man looked in his mouth. With another gesture he demanded that Danforth lift his testicles, which Danforth did, then he waited as the man peered under them as if expecting to find a folder of state secrets. A third gesture instructed Danforth to face the wall, which he also did, and after which he endured the probing he expected. A fourth gesture directed him to sit down on the bench.

As he sat, the man in the lab coat handed his jacket to one of the guards, who methodically slit open its lining and pawed about, looking for whatever might be hidden there. The second guard did the same with Danforth's shoes, slicing the soles open and digging out the heels before tossing them under the bench.

With these tasks completed, the man in the lab coat left, looking satisfied, and Danforth, still naked, was taken down the hallway, a guard on either side, to a room where he was told to shower.

He'd expected to be returned to his small room after the shower, but instead he was escorted, now by only one guard, down a long corridor with metal doors on either side. He suddenly felt the immensity of Lubyanka, how long and wide and deep it was, how easily one could disappear into its labyrinthine vastness.

Even so, he himself did not expect to disappear, and so, during the many days that followed, through all the interrogations and deprivations, the few blows and the long torture of enforced sleeplessness, he continued to believe that on this day or the next or the one after that, he would be released. It was an unreality that defied what he would later think of as Lubyanka's greatest torture: the cries of the other prisoners on his block.

They were loud and they were ceaseless, women crying for their children, children for their parents, officials for their superiors, some even for Stalin, who they seemed to believe knew nothing of this cruelty and would never have permitted it if he did. They came in such variety, these endless cries, that in the midst of his own hallucination, Danforth began to conceive of Lubyanka as the place where man's immemorial complaints were gathered up and eternally stored in its echoing maze of metal and concrete.

Just stay sane, he told himself, *just stay sane until they let you go.*

Then, on a morning he calculated was three months after the start of his detention — he never allowed himself to call it an arrest — the door of his cell opened and he was led down a different corridor and into a different room to face a man he'd never seen.

"Please to sit yourself," the man said in heavily accented English.

Danforth took a seat. "So, a new interrogator," he said.

"I Comrade Ustinov." He did not look up from the papers on his desk. "I do not have no questions," he said.

"Really?" Danforth said with a small chuckle of the lightheartedness he'd incorporated into his general demeanor. "Then why am I here?"

"To go now," Ustinov said. His pen whispered across a page in the routine way of a man who had thousands of times made the same notations on identical pages. "Please to sign this."

Danforth took the paper the man slid toward him. "What is it?"

"List what you to possess when are come here," the man said. He began to work on another page, filling in blanks, making checks.

An inventory, Danforth thought, *at last I am to be freed.* "Why not just give it all back to me?" he asked.

"We keep," Ustinov answered, and with that he slid a single page across the desk. "You go other place."

"Other place?" Danforth asked. "I'm not being released? Where am I being sent?"

Ustinov slid the paper farther toward Danforth. "Please to sign" was all he said.

Danforth glanced at the paper. "It's in Russian. I won't sign anything I can't read."

Ustinov stared at Danforth a long moment, then reached for the papers and returned them to the open file folder. "You wait unless-till time," he said, and he immediately started scribbling on yet another paper.

"Unless-till time?" Danforth asked. He laughed. "Isn't there someone who speaks English better than you?"

Ustinov's face turned bright red, and he screamed, *"Nye plozhna!"*

Shut up!

At that instant, Danforth realized that he was never going to be released, and with the abandonment of that hope, he felt what all men feel at every moment they are not free, when they are fixed in a world in which there is nothing so pure it cannot be stained, nothing so sacred it cannot be defiled, no right so inalienable it cannot be usurped, no possession so justly earned it cannot be expropriated, no part of the body so private it cannot be violated, no particle of one's identity so established that it cannot be erased.

Blue Bar, New York City, 2001

"That, Paul," Danforth said, "was Stalinism."

It was a dramatic litany and Danforth had delivered it dramatically, clearly determined that I should feel the fist that had closed around the many millions, and which I surely did. Then he suddenly said, "But freedom is nothing, Paul. Or at least, it can come to feel like nothing when all you want is to survive." He watched me a moment, letting what he'd just said sink in. Then, with a glance toward the other people in the bar to assure himself they were no longer listening, he added, "Cutlets. I will always remember that it was written in Russian, English, French, and German."

"Written where?" I asked.

"On the side of the *chernyi voron*," Danforth answered. "How would I translate that? The . . . black raven. It was black, that's for sure. A black delivery van. They ran back and forth from Lubyanka to the railway station. Sometimes they 'delivered' bread, sometimes meat, sometimes fruit and vegetables. The one they shoved me into had *Moscow Cutlets* painted on the sides." He laughed. "Not much of a disguise, but in Moscow it didn't matter if people knew what was in those vans. Nothing could be done about it anyway."

"Did you have any idea where you were going?" I asked.

"No," Danforth answered. "For all I knew I was being taken to some other prison in the area. Then the door opened, and there it was. The train."

They were rushed out of the stifling van, lined up, counted, and then herded into the waiting railway cars, Danforth told me. Though he had not known it then, he was now one of millions of *zeks*, slang he'd later learned meant "prison laborers." Once in the car, he'd elbowed his way toward the far side where he could look through one of the slats as the train pulled away. Railroad workers stood on the side of the tracks, giving signals, waving the train forward. From the cast of their shadows as the train steamed past them, he knew that he was headed east.

Over the next hours, long miles of greenery swept by, punctuated only by glimpses, first of cities, then of towns, the towns becoming smaller and shuttling by more quickly as the train surged on. The men huddled in the darkness around him wept like small children, which Danforth found surprising until he realized that they were bereft because they'd been snatched from wives and children, mothers and fathers, deeper attachments than he had or, he feared, would ever have.

Within hours the first cries for water began, and once begun they continued without letup until at last the train stopped and buckets of water were passed; a few hours later, there were cries of agony as these same men now needed to pass the water they'd drunk. He would hear of trains that had holes in the floor for such relief, but this train had had no such accommodation, and so the men had finally wet themselves, and the floor of the car was soon soaked and slippery, the air smelling — at last overwhelmingly — of urine.

He guessed that the journey to the first transit camp had taken a little over twenty-four hours, and once out of the train, he and the *zeks* had been marched to a small provincial prison, where he'd stayed for nearly a week. There he'd been interrogated again and again, almost always being asked the same questions, and he came to realize that the powers that be believed that his search for Anna Klein was a ruse, that he was actually searching for something else, either a man or some government secret they were careful not to reveal. This wasn't true, of course, as Danforth labored to assure them, but each time he denied that he was an American agent involved in anti-Soviet activities, there were shouted threats, blows, endless hours of enforced sleeplessness. Then, without warning, another train, another prison, another series of interrogations, more threats, blows, sleeplessness.

Again and again, he repeated the same cycle: a train, a journey, a different prison, the same interrogation, the same threats, blows, sleeplessness. There were so many prisons the exact number of them began to blur in Danforth's mind, though the implication of that number never had. For this was but one rail line, as he knew, and if it was like the others that stretched into the wastes, then Russia's eastern landscape sprouted prisons like the American midlands sprouted farms.

The greenery of the country entirely disappeared, first into the graying rain, then into a grayer sleet, and finally into a white so bright it throbbed from the fields it covered. The cold of these last days in transit was like nothing Danforth had ever felt. By then the ragged ranks had thinned, and so there was less body heat, making him somehow resent the ones who'd died and been pulled off the train, as if their weakness had been a betrayal to those who lived on.

But on each leg of this long journey, his Russian improved. He gathered idioms and slang and the innumerable vulgarities to describe sex and bodily functions that the Russian language possessed, as well as the bitter cynicisms to which the Russian mind seemed prone. He met priests, Orthodox Jews, atheists. He met men who believed in nothing and men who still believed in the very cause that had enslaved them, and in every transit camp he found some new, rebellious feature of a people he'd thought utterly flattened by oppression. He saw it in the way a loaf of bread or slab of smoked bacon would sail from a window into the prisoners' ranks. He saw it in the efforts of local doctors to attend to their wounds with what few medical supplies they had. He saw it in a thousand sympathetic glances, soft nods, and, in one case, in the way an old man from the Great War had taken off his frayed cap as another round of *zeks* were driven past him, taken off his cap and held it over his breast as if these dazed, bedraggled men were the heroes of Mother Russia.

With his improving Russian, Danforth began to make inquiries in the various camps and prisons in which he found himself, always in the hope of uncovering some little thread of information about an American woman whom he described as being in her midthirties, a dark woman who was still or might once have been quite pretty, a woman who spoke many languages.

In response to these inquiries, a thousand sparks flew from what Danforth called "the great rumor mill of the Gulag." He heard of a cruel interrogator who'd worked at an American camp somewhere near Dzhezkazgan, a lead he followed assiduously over the years, only to learn that no such camp had ever existed. He heard of a "very pretty woman" who'd served as a translator at Butyka, a woman known for her ruthlessness who he later learned was tall and blond. Neither of these had been Anna, of course, but even though they were false rumors, they engraved an image of her on Danforth's mind as a woman who had survived and now served the enemy she had once despised, who carried out their interrogations and roamed their prison corridors, laughed with Stalin's other minions, and smoked cigarettes with them in their communal dining rooms, and perhaps even from time to time chose some fat, drunken official who might be useful to her, went to his room, and gave herself to him as she had once given herself to Danforth.

The last transport took him through villages with names that were no longer Russian, though whether he'd entered the lands of the Kazakhs, Tajik, or Uzbeks remained unclear. But even the Eurasian steppes were not far enough; other trains and finally a steamboat took him farther and farther to the east until it seemed he had been transported, one camp at a time, to the end of the earth.

"Then my final convoy stopped," Danforth said, "and I was taken off a truck loaded with forty or so other *zeks* and marched through some thick woods to a place — according to my own grim fatalism — that surely had been determined long ago."

Though he could not have known it, he was now a hundred miles up what would later be known as the Road of Skulls, a frozen labor camp that had been cut out of a forest whose trees he would fell and chop and load onto creaking lorries, cord after endless cord of wood hauled away on trucks that groaned like weary cattle as they made their way into the Arctic night. He would hew with axes that seemed little improved since the Stone Age, and his beard would grow and his body would thin and his eyes would shrink back into his skull; with each glimpse of himself in the frosty window he saw less and less of the man he had once been, and at last that man became little more than a shadow in the snow.

Thus did Danforth pass his many seasons in the Gulag.

"You don't expect ever to climb out of that pit," Danforth said. "You work and sleep, then work and sleep. You eat the soup that Solzhenitsyn described, with the eye floating in it. You watch life and death from the shelf-bed of your barracks, just in that way Shalamov recounts it." He smiled. "Shalamov's stories are much better in Russian, by the way."

His smile held briefly, then slowly faded into a more solemn expression than any I had yet seen.

"You see honesty perish and honesty survive," he said. "You see startling acts of kindness and unspeakable acts of depravity, just in the way Bardach writes about them in *Man Is Wolf to Man*. In later years, you read these accounts from your warm little apartment and remember that you didn't have to work when the temperature fell below negative forty-one degrees and how while you were shivering in your bunk you hoped for the temperature to drop just enough so that you could stay in that frigid room a little longer. You expect this to go on forever, Paul. You expect to die and be buried in that frozen tundra. You stop believing there's a world beyond the camp because that world no longer exists for you. You watch the Kolyma River freeze and briefly thaw. You notice the return of the mosquitoes, and you hate them so much you look forward to winter. Every blessing

288

brings a curse, even the gift of another day of life. Because you are already dead, Paul."

He stopped suddenly, and his face took on the expression of one abruptly touched by a miracle.

"Then, one afternoon, just as you've gotten back from the woods, barely able to peel those wretched mittens from your fingers," he said, "you are summoned to the camp commander's office, and there, to your amazement, you see what you think must be a ghost, because it could only have come from the life you had before you died. You stare at it, speechless, blinking. You cannot believe this ghost will speak. And then it does."

"A ghost?" I asked, with a caught breath. "Anna?"

Danforth appeared to see that very ghost, though whether in the guise of a disordered young woman in a Greenwich Village bar, an art dealer's assistant speaking perfect German, an assassin, or a spy, I couldn't guess.

"Anna?" Danforth asked softly. "Ah, Paul, how different my little parable would be if that had truly been her name."

PART VII

Traitor's Gate

Blue Bar, New York City, 2001

Danforth looked at his watch. "Do you mind if we catch a cab?" he asked. "I should be getting home."

"Home?" I asked. "Now?"

I was certain that Danforth's story was drawing to an end and saw no need to interrupt it.

"One should know how another person lives, don't you think, Paul?" Danforth said quite firmly. "It helps the moral understanding."

Moral understanding?

I immediately felt the approach of a didactic remark, but before I could voice this queasy supposition or even protest the abrupt breaking off of his tale, Danforth was on his feet, pulling on his coat and twining his scarf around his neck with the determination of a man whose methods could not be questioned or his final aim deterred.

"Come, Paul," he said. "It's not far."

This turned out to be true, though it was farther than I'd expected, since I'd reasonably supposed that Danforth lived near the Century Club. But our cab turned south onto Fifth Avenue, rather than north toward the swankier regions surrounding Central Park, and a few minutes later we arrived at a rather commonplace apartment building at the corner of Lexington Avenue and Twenty-eighth Street.

"It would be a long walk to your club," I said as we approached the building's inelegant entrance.

"Oh, I'm not a member of the club," Danforth said casually. "Clayton was a member and his wife still is, so she very kindly allowed me use it as a meeting place today."

"I see," I muttered.

The lobby of Danforth's building was entirely beige with a few plastic plants sprouting from plaster vases.

"Not what you expected, Paul?" Danforth asked.

"I guess not," I admitted.

A small elevator lifted us to the fourteenth floor, and Danforth led me through an unrelentingly charmless corridor and into a cramped apartment whose one luxury was a wide southern view of Manhattan, the skyscrapers of Lower Manhattan twinkling brightly in the distance, a horrible gap separating them.

"It must be a painful view now," I said.

"And enraging," Danforth said. "Sometimes I want to kill them all." He peered out the window for a moment, then said, "But as you noted before, if we'd done that to the Germans, you wouldn't be here, would you, Paul?"

"No," I said.

"Because we would have killed that grandfather of yours," Danforth added. "Where was he from, by the way?"

"Augsburg."

"Hmm," Danforth said. "There was a subcamp of Dachau near there."

I could not deny that this mention of the Dachau concentration camp chilled me.

Danforth's smile seemed only to add a layer of deeper cold. "So how do you want it, Paul?" he asked.

"Want what?" I asked.

"Your coffee," Danforth said.

"Oh, uh, w-with cream," I stammered.

"But milk will do, I hope?"

"Yes, of course."

Danforth made his way to the tiny kitchen that adjoined the almost equally tiny living area. While he made the coffee, I sat down and took in my surroundings. They were very humble, with little to lift their ordinariness but the large bookshelves that lined the room's four walls, which, I noticed, mainly held books about spying, the tricks of that trade, along with a surprising number of titles about Germany, though not that country in the 1930s and 1940s, when Danforth was there, but during the Cold War, from its beginnings to the bringing down of the Wall. Some volumes contained an unexpected focus on the activities of the infamous Stasi, East Germany's secret police. Could it be, I wondered, that Anna had somehow used her charms and her linguistic talents to make her way up the pecking order of that evil force and then become the perfect servant of East Germany's version of the KGB? And if so, what had she been? A Nazi agent? A Soviet agent? Both?

"There you are, Paul," Danforth said as he handed me a cup of coffee, sat down in the chair opposite me with his own cup, and took a sip. "This should return me to sobriety."

"I doubt you ever left it," I said to him. "Despite your youthful adventure, you strike me as a cautious man."

"Not always," Danforth said with a telling glance at the bookshelf to his right, all those volumes of an East Germany firmly in the grip of a now-displaced Communism. "No, not always," he repeated, then sank back deeply into his chair. "Especially when it comes to revenge."

Revenge, I thought, the emotion that seemed still to inflame him and with which he returned us to his tale.

Kolyma, Soviet Union, 1964

"Robert?" Danforth asked tentatively. Many years had passed, and Clayton's face, if indeed it was Clayton's, was now webbed with wrinkles, his hair sprinkled with silver.

"Yes," Clayton said. He was clearly stricken by the figure before him, Danforth's ragged clothes and matted beard, his body so emaciated it was all but skeletal. "The commandant doesn't speak English so ask him when we can leave," he said.

"Leave." Danforth couldn't be sure he'd heard this.

"Yes, leave," Clayton said. "Go ahead, Tom, ask him."

Danforth turned to the commandant and asked the question in Russian.

"There is a supply truck to Magadan in an hour," the commandant answered. He did not seem pleased by the paper in his hand. "It says you are to be released immediately, so be on your way."

The commandant did not leave them alone and would not allow them to talk to each other, and so Danforth simply stared at his old friend until the truck arrived.

"Go," the commandant said. He looked at Danforth sternly, and then something broke in his face, something that softened him and made him look almost wistful. "Give regard Broadway," he said.

Later, as they sat on mounds of empty sacks in the back of the truck, Clayton said, "I've been looking for you for twelve years."

"Twelve years," Danforth repeated in English, a language that now seemed foreign to him. He made a quick calculation, the result of which astonished him. "I am . . . fifty-four years old."

"Yes," Clayton said softly.

Danforth realized that he had yet to ask Clayton a single question, and so he asked his first.

"Why did they release me?"

Clayton placed his finger to his lips and softly shook his head. The failure of Danforth's final mission suddenly pierced him. "Anna got away with it," he said.

"Maybe not," Clayton said.

Clayton told him that he'd invented the story of Anna's execution, but that he'd done so with the best of intentions. He'd never suspected that Danforth would return to Europe and certainly not that he would stumble upon what he called "the truth about Anna Klein."

"But we'll talk about all that in a few days," he added, bringing the subject to a close. "After you've gotten your strength back. We can't get transport out of Magadan right away, so just relax, walk around, enjoy the weather." He smiled. "It's summer in Siberia."

And so it was, with temperate days and chilly nights that reminded Danforth of the country house he'd not seen for over twenty years and whose memory now filled him with a tragic nostalgia. "Winterset," he said, as if it were a place he had only dreamed.

"Which you will see again very soon," Clayton told him.

Clayton had booked them into a crumbling hotel in Magadan, and once there, Danforth shaved and bathed; these were luxuries whose pleasure astonished him. Simply to be clean. How few people knew such joy.

During the daylight hours, he took leisurely walks through the town streets, always followed, as he noticed and reported to Clayton.

"Me too," Clayton said. "But we're used to spies, aren't we?"

They were short, Danforth's first walks, and followed by hours of rest. He ate in the hotel's spare dining room, always with Clayton, who carefully eased him away from any further discussion of his abrupt release.

As he gained strength, Danforth walked farther from the hotel, and eventually as far as the docks, where he watched fishermen at their nets and followed the slow drift of the barges and steamers as they came into port. More than once, he saw a shuffling cargo of newly arrived *zeks* tramp down the gangway and into waiting trucks, and it struck him that if this steady stream had continued uninterrupted since his own journey here, then hundreds of thousands had passed this way, a number he found impossible to imagine or forget.

Thus the days passed, and as they passed, Danforth grew stronger, though he remained thin and would often be overcome by sudden bouts of exhaustion. From out of nowhere, a great weight would fall upon him, heavy as the logs he'd carried on his shoulders, and he would drop into a chair or onto the bed and feel this same weight press him down and down until he flattened into sleep.

Nearly two weeks passed and Danforth made no further inquiry into why he'd been released. Captivity, it seemed, had taught him patience. And so he simply listened as Clayton brought him up to date on the events of his missing years. During these talks, he was surprised to learn of a young president's assassination but even more surprised to learn that he had been a Catholic.

Then one evening, Clayton appeared at Danforth's door. "Let's go for a walk," he said.

They left the hotel, walked several blocks, then turned toward the bay and continued on.

"Tom, you've been released because the Soviets want to find out about Rache," Clayton said quite suddenly.

"I don't know anything about Rache," Danforth said.

"They believe you were looking for him," Clayton told him. He drew in a breath that was short and struck Danforth as some-what labored. "They don't believe it was ever Anna."

"But it was always Anna," Danforth told him. "Because I believe she betrayed me."

"And was in league with Rache all along," Clayton said.

"In league with Rache," Danforth repeated softly.

He felt it rise again, rise then hang like a foul odor in the air around him, Anna's treachery. He thought of her veiled past, the Gray Wolf Society of Ankara, her inexplicable familiarity with the environs of Baku and the German settlements of Azerbaijan, along with other less fully elaborated clues to a life whose coordinates he still could not determine.

Clayton seemed aware that Danforth's mind was swirling with memories of Anna, and for a time he allowed his old friend to lose himself in that swirl, then said, "The Russians have long memories," he said. "They're still looking for Rache because they want to kill him. They think you can help them."

"How?"

"By interrogating Anna," Clayton said.

"Anna?" Danforth whispered.

They had reached the banks of the Sea of Okhotsk, its docks inexpressibly dreary, and which Danforth now recalled was the place he'd disembarked from a steamship all those many years before. It had been a late-night arrival and an immediate departure, and so he'd seen only a few lights as he'd been led down the boat's snow-covered gangplank and into the back of the truck that had taken him up the Road of Skulls.

"Anna's here, Tom," Clayton said. He peered into Danforth's emaciated face. "Here in Magadan," he added. "They brought her to the hotel last night. She's in room three-oh-four."

Danforth realized that his mind had been so long numbed and disengaged it now had to struggle for pathways by which it might absorb so profound a revelation.

"It's the price for letting you go," Clayton added.

Danforth stared at him unbelievingly. "I thought I was already let go."

Clayton shook his head. "They wanted you to have a taste of freedom," he said. "So you'd know what you're missing."

"What will they do with Anna?" Danforth asked.

"Nothing they haven't already done," Clayton answered. He let this settle into Danforth's brain before he spoke again. "But who cares, Tom? She was nothing but a little Nazi."

Danforth would many times recall these words of Clayton's, the bitter tone that entered his voice as he'd said them, how they'd filled him with so much of his own remembered ire.

"Yes, all right," he said stonily.

With that, they headed back to the hotel, then down the corridor to room 304.

In years to come, he would recall the dry shuffle of his feet along the faded carpet, the jumpy movement of his eyes as he'd approached the two men who stood on either side of the door, one of them clearly in command of the other.

They had been expecting him, had immediately recognized him, and in a way that was very nearly warm, the first had nodded to him as the second turned and, with a gentle motion, like a father fearing to wake a child, opened the door, then stepped back to let him in.

Danforth said nothing to either man, nor did they speak to him; he simply moved past them and into a room where a single small lamp cast a faded yellow light, and in that light he saw her, sitting at the window just as she had sat in Paris so many years before, saw her in full, dressed in a *zek*'s gray smock, her hair cut very short and salted with gray. As he drew nearer, he saw the ravages of her long detention, the deep creases along her cheeks and her cold-cracked lips, saw all the features of premature old age that mocked her middle years, and he cared for none of her sufferings because he knew what she was and what she had done, and he recalled in a single, blistering memory the deception she had carried out in Munich, Rache perhaps more her lover than he had ever been.

Now it was his time to make a counterfeit of love.

And so he said, "Hello, Anna," in the soft, lover's tone he'd decided to use.

She seemed not at all surprised to see him.

"Rise!" one of the guards shouted in Russian.

At this rough command, Anna struggled to her feet.

"It's Tom," he told her as he came forward.

She seemed to see through his deception and stared at him without the slightest spark of affection. "They told me you were coming," she said stiffly. "What do you want?"

"A favor," Danforth answered. He struggled to bring a tiny smile to his lips. "For old times."

She glared at him starkly. "Old times," she muttered.

"Munich," he added.

Her lips smiled, but her eyes didn't, and it seemed to him that everything soft he remembered about her had been replaced by the rock-hard figure who now stood before him.

"Munich," she repeated.

He thought he heard contempt in her voice but decided to ignore it. "I never stopped loving you, Anna," he lied. "And I never stopped looking for you."

He opened his arms to her tenderly, a gesture meant to draw her into his embrace, but she instantly stepped back as if from a repulsive approach, then glanced toward the still-open door, the guards who stood on either side of it, now peering in.

"Anna," Danforth said in a voice that seemed jarringly loud. "Whatever you were then . . ."

She lifted her hand to silence him and he saw how rough it was, scarred by hard labor.

"I have nothing for you," she said, then looked again toward the guards at the door.

Her eyes widened and he saw something terrible come over her, a brutal ferocity. It was as if a wholly different human being had always lived inside this other shell and was only now fully revealing itself, the old skin falling away, a different creature slithering out of it, alive and squirming before him, as frightful as Aaron's serpent.

"*Heil* Hitler," she said coldly. Her eyes glimmered with fanatical zeal as she lifted her arm in salute and stood before him as stiffly as any SS fiend. "*Heil* Hitler," she repeated.

Danforth suddenly realized how right Bannion had been so many years before when he'd told him that he was a romantic fool; he was, and so much so that even during these last seconds, he'd hoped to find a happy ending for the long waste of his life, a moment of redemption for both himself and Anna, the revelation that she had never, never been what he now knew her to be.

"*Heil* Hitler," she said a third time, words that brought back all his memories of the trials and the camps along with Anna's vile treachery, and at last the boiling wave crested, and in what Danforth knew would be his last gesture toward her, he stepped forward, and with all the force of lost romance, and with all the passion of what he'd hoped to be a kiss, he slapped her face.

Lexington Avenue, New York City, 2001

"Slapped her face," Danforth repeated. He remained quiet for a moment, then said, "Were you expecting some great love scene, Paul?"

I stared at him in shocked silence.

"A happy ending?" Danforth asked.

"I suppose I was," I admitted shakily. "I mean, one always hopes for that."

"Oh, how true," Danforth said grimly. "But false illusion is life's chief ally, don't you think, Paul?"

"I don't know what you mean," I said.

"Believing you know a person or can control the final outcome of your life," Danforth said. "I certainly know what that happy ending would have been in my case: that Anna would begin to talk, tell me all about Rache, a story that would make clear that she had never been in league with him. It didn't matter how absurdly improbable this story might be. In my romantic fantasy, I would believe it, and so would the Russians. They would be so won over by it that they would release Anna from the clutches of the Gulag, and I would whisk her back to New York, where we would grow old together, a silver-haired couple strolling arm in arm through Central Park." He released a weary sigh. "I'm afraid that was not to be." He looked at me quite piercingly. "Do you know what the one great fact of life is, Paul?"

"No," I admitted.

"How easily it is wasted," Danforth said. "All our precious little days."

An old fury rocked him, and he appeared barely able to suppress it. A few seconds passed, and during that time an uneasy calm returned to him, after which he said, "I came home at last, but there was nothing left of my old world. Danforth Imports had limped along in my absence, but by the time I got back, it was heavily in debt. I sold it, along with Winterset, and paid off the company's bills. I knew that I no longer had a heart or a head for business, so I took a job in a language school here in New York. I tutored students on the side." He glanced toward the table where two places had been set, making it clear that he'd long planned to bring me here. "And I thought of Anna, of course." A coldness came into his eyes. "But never again in the grip of a delusion, and never again with love."

"But wait," I said. "You didn't get any information about Rache out of Anna, did you?"

"No."

"Then why did the Russians let you go?"

Danforth smiled. "Ah, a chirp from the nightingale floor."

But rather than going on to answer my question, Danforth simply shrugged and resumed his tale.

And so the years passed, Danforth said, and his first students grew older and became fathers and mothers while he remained alone, moving through the faceless crowds as skirts shortened and hair lengthened, and the niceties of language, along with all that he had once called reticence, faded in the glare of new therapies, and the old verities of his class and kind proved insufficient to command the age.

"Do you know what Burke called manners, Paul?" Danforth asked. "The 'decent drapery of life.'"

I smiled at the quaintness of both the phrase and the sentiment. "So you still believe in knight-errantry?" I asked.

"Well, someone has to, don't you think?" Danforth replied. "Otherwise each generation would awaken to utter emptiness."

This might or might not be true, I thought, but it was far from his tale. "Anyway," I said, "you were at least released from Anna."

I was far from a starry-eyed romantic, and yet I couldn't help but be impressed by Danforth's long pursuit, Victorian though it seemed in an age of e-mail hook-ups and speed dating. To feel so deeply even once in the course of life struck me as a blessing, mixed though Danforth's had surely been.

"Released, yes," Danforth said. "And so I settled into an uneventful middle age that might placidly have followed its course year by year until I reached old age, then further still until at last

I was laid to rest. But something happened to change my course, something that wouldn't have happened had I not been standing on the curb at Lincoln Center one evening. A cab pulled up and a passenger got out. He wore a red fez, and the driver spoke to him in Turkish, and at the sound of that language, I recalled that when I'd loved Anna, she had once spoken of Baku." He seemed to marvel in the twists of his own mind. "For some reason, a burning nostalgia seized me, Paul. I knew what Anna was, and I no longer cared where she was or how she was being treated. And yet, for all that, I felt an overwhelming need simply to see someone she had once seen, someone who had seen her, heard her voice. By then there was only one person left in the world who'd done that." He smiled. "LaRoche."

"LaRoche?" I asked, surprised that he'd resurfaced in Danforth's story.

"After the war, he'd become quite successful as a sweets wholesaler," Danforth said. "He agreed to meet me at the same place we'd met so many years before."

Washington Square Park, New York City, 1974

"Smoke, smoke, smoke," the young man whispered as Danforth passed by, an illegal solicitation Danforth found amusing given his steel-gray hair and clean-shaven face, the conservative look of his three-button suit. Danforth was now sixty-four years old, after all, a lowly language teacher, hardly the usual customer for a park-bench pot dealer.

For a time he watched as the young man made his rounds, then, like one entering a neighborhood much changed since his youth, Danforth headed farther into the park.

This time it was LaRoche who'd arrived first, now dressed in a gray suit that couldn't completely hide his considerably expanded waistline. He no longer glanced about, no longer seemed on edge, but instead looked almost like a member of the old burgher class, well-fed and well-heeled. But for all that, something of the dispossessed still clung to him, an Old-World melancholy that both his years and his New-World success had failed to shake. De Tocqueville had called them "the habits of the heart," and LaRoche seemed proof that they were harder to change than one's country or one's circumstances.

"Hello," LaRoche said with a smile that seemed hard-won.

"Mr. LaRoche," Danforth replied with a nod. "It's been a long time."

"How did you find me? I forgot to ask."

"You're in the book," Danforth said. "LaRoche Wholesalers. You specialize in Middle Eastern sweets."

"I always had a taste for honey," LaRoche said in an English that now bore only the hint of an accent.

They talked briefly of the old days, when Winterset was clothed in snow and, later, strewn with spring flowers.

Danforth knew that LaRoche had been told of Anna's arrest and Bannion's suicide, but whether he'd been told more than that, Danforth couldn't say.

"I saw Anna only one time after Munich," he said. "She was in Russia."

He told LaRoche about the final encounter, how he'd tried to get some small kernel of information about a German agent the Soviets believed had betrayed them, how she'd suddenly transmogrified into the ardent Nazi she had no doubt always been, a narrative that still wounded him despite all the time that had passed.

LaRoche listened silently through it all and remained quiet for a time after Danforth finished, so they simply sat, speechless, staring straight ahead, looking curiously desolate, as if recognizing at last that all their riches had been spent.

Then LaRoche said, "And they let you go after this last meeting with Anna?"

"Yes."

"Why?"

Danforth shrugged. "What would have been the point of keeping me? They must have realized that all I was ever looking for was Anna. And now I had found her. I suppose they simply had no more use for me."

"Perhaps," LaRoche said, his tone cautious, like one hazarding an unlikely guess, "perhaps, unless this last meeting had a hidden purpose." He appeared quite pensive, as if turning over all Danforth had just told him.

"When you left her, what was your feeling?" he asked after a moment.

"That it was over," Danforth said. "My quest."

"Your quest for what?"

"I suppose you could call it my quest for Anna Klein."

"Hmm," LaRoche said with a slow nod.

Danforth looked at him closely. "What's going on?" he asked. "What are you thinking?"

"That maybe she was acting," LaRoche said.

"Acting? Why?"

LaRoche laughed. "It's a little mind game I play with myself," he said. "Coming up with other ways of looking at things, no matter what crazy direction it takes me."

"What crazy direction is it taking you now?" Danforth asked.

"Well, I was just thinking that maybe Anna was forced to do what she did when she saw you," LaRoche answered. "Maybe there was something she wanted to protect."

"Rache is what she wanted to protect," Danforth said bitterly.

"Unless the Bolshies were playing an old game with you," LaRoche answered casually. "It's one they know well and play very often."

Danforth could see that LaRoche was playing a game of his own, offering a wild supposition for no other reason than to demonstrate the twisted world of intrigue he'd once known.

"What game?" Danforth asked, going along with him.

"It's an old ploy," LaRoche said. "They let you find one thing in order to keep something else hidden, something more valuable to them than what you were looking for."

"I was never looking for anything but Anna," Danforth told him.

"But was it her you really found?" LaRoche asked.

"What I found was a Nazi spy," Danforth said bitterly.

"Unless they made her do what she did," LaRoche cautioned.

"You said that before," Danforth said, a little impatiently. "Why would they have done that?"

LaRoche's gaze seemed threaded with a thousand complicated plots.

"You'd proven yourself very relentless in this whole business," LaRoche said. "So suppose they were being pressured to release you. Or maybe they were simply tired of having you on the books, as they say. For whatever reason, they decided to release you. But they wanted to neutralize you first. The only way they could do that was by letting you see Anna. Once you saw she was this crazy Nazi, you could go home and live your life and they'd never have to bother with you again."

"But why would they care whether or not I stopped looking for Anna?" Danforth said.

LaRoche looked like a man explaining evil to a child. "Because in looking for Anna, you might find whoever it was they were still protecting. Some old agent of theirs. Or maybe a mole, someone who still provided information for them. Or someone who helped them long ago."

"Like who?" Danforth asked.

LaRoche shrugged, now quite obviously reaching for a wild-card. "Like Rache," he said.

"But Rache was a German agent," Danforth said. "The Soviets would only care about Rache if he were . . ." He stopped. "If he were . . ."

"One of their own," LaRoche said, as if he'd played a trump card. "But that's how this ploy works." He smiled softly. "Suppose Rache posed as an anti-Nazi German, and in that way fooled Bannion, and in fooling Bannion fooled Anna, who ended up spending her life protecting the very one who had betrayed her." He smiled at his own cleverness. "Now that would be a great game. And he would have played it perfectly. So that the Germans continued to believe he was a German agent and Anna continued to believe he was an American agent when in fact he was always a Soviet agent." He looked at Danforth knowingly. "All that worked. Only you continued to be a problem for them, Tom."

"In what way?"

"Because you kept looking for Anna, and in doing that, you kept looking for Rache," LaRoche said, clearly pleased with himself for coming up with this scenario. "If you were going to be released, they wanted you to stop searching. And so they played one of their old games." He smiled at how it all hung together. "It is called the traitor's gate."

Lexington Avenue, New York City, 2001

"And I might have walked right through it," Danforth said. His eyes flared with familiar fire. "So was Anna acting the night she came to me in Munich? Or was she acting in Magadan?" He shrugged. "It seemed to me that only one person would know the answer to that. Code name: Rache."

"Wait a minute," I said. "Are you telling me that you took what LaRoche said seriously?"

"Yes."

"But it was pure speculation," I reminded him.

"And done as rather a devil's advocate, I think," Danforth agreed. "And even if it was true, how would it be possible to find Rache? He might be anywhere in the Soviet Union. He might be in East Germany."

I glanced at the bookshelf that rose behind Danforth's chair, its ample space packed with books on East Germany, the Stasi, the whole network of Cold War intrigue that spread out from gray offices of East Berlin. I had little doubt that Danforth had pored over each of these books, studied every tiny detail, created flowcharts of countless hierarchies, looking for some clue to where in this swarming hive of agents he might find a single bee.

Danforth saw the trajectory of my gaze and took the cue.

"I had to assume that Rache was a master spy," he said. "An adroit triple agent who'd played an American agent and fooled Bannion, a German agent who'd fooled the Nazis, and all along he'd actually been working for the Russians."

A glimmer of the old Stalinist paranoia he'd earlier described glittered in his eyes, and I wondered if the sanity he had so far displayed might be an act as clever and beguiling as the kind he'd previously ascribed to Anna.

"Rache," he said. "Vengeance."

He let this word drift like acrid smoke in the air around us.

"When you need something to hate, you will find it, believe me," Danforth said now. "You will find it and you will paint it in whatever colors you choose. With no place else to turn, I turned to Rache. He became my Moriarty, my antichrist. I thought of nothing but discovering once and for all if he had betrayed us."

With that conclusion, Danforth abruptly returned to his earlier self, all reason and careful analysis, his brain no longer boiling with suppositions that fired vengeful fantasies but now trained on a method by which he might answer the last burning question of his life.

"I racked my brain to find some small chink in all this," he said, "and the one thing that kept returning to me was the fact that during Romanchuk's interrogation, there'd been an older man with the Order of Lenin on his lapel to whom Anna had spoken Turkish. I remembered that in a conversation with La-Roche, Anna had recalled Baku, which is the capital of Azerbaijan, a part of Russia that shares a border with Turkey."

"Those are rather disparate elements," I cautioned.

"Yes, but the investigation of a plot is about finding intersections within the plot," Danforth said. "Coordinates that allow you to zero in on what really happened."

As absurd as it seemed to me now, and as absurd as it had seemed to him then, Danforth had embarked upon a huge research project. It was a search to find what he called coordinates by which he might connect the Order of Lenin, knowledge of Turkish, and familiarity with Baku.

"As it turned out, Romanchuk was wrong," Danforth told me. "At least as far as the Order of Lenin is concerned. It wasn't a big deal, really. Lots of people had been given the Order of Lenin. Pilots and scientists and aircraft designers. There were engineers and nuclear-power experts. There was a polar explorer. It was even given to *Pravda* at one point, and at other times to whole regions of the country for some service that region had rendered to the state. Lots of people got it several times."

And so the research had turned into a monumentally tedious and time-consuming task, Danforth said, but he had never relented, and each day after he finished teaching, he headed for the library. For weeks, months, years, he walked between the two sober lions and entered the great reading room with its long tables and green-shaded lamps. He worked each night until the library closed, and each night as he wearily headed home, he reminded himself that he was doing this for Anna. "Love has many faces, Paul," he said, by way of explanation, "but lost love has only one."

It struck me that Danforth's quest had been driven by a need that had been momentarily fulfilled on that one night in Munich but ultimately unrequited for all the nights after that. He was a man with a chronic illness, doomed to live forever with the incurable affliction of having loved at a moment of supreme peril a woman of supreme mystery, and this love had annihilated any hope that he might ever love again.

"It took me many years," Danforth said, "but in the end I found my coordinates in a Soviet general who had dealt with the ethnic conflict that was always breaking out in Azerbaijan." He shook his head. "Bathed in blood, that part of the world."

For a moment he seemed to drift down that red river.

"You were talking about a Soviet general," I reminded him.

"Yes," Danforth answered. "His name was Sergei Lukudovich Solotoff, and after the war, he returned to Baku. When I finally made it to his door, he was eighty-six years old."

Baku, Azerbaijan, 1981

The general lived in a building that had once been the elegant townhouse of an oil baron but was now just another crumbling structure in the old part of Baku. The Maiden Tower was visible at one end of the street, and beyond it, the blue Caspian swept out to the horizon. Danforth had been here only once, so many years in the past that he was scarcely able to remember anything but the carpet merchants who'd draped their heavy wares over ancient walls, which, to his surprise, they still did. But the great castle had faded, as had the minarets; his memories were now as weathered as the little stone statue that still rested in the market square.

Solotoff had not fallen into disfavor as so many of Stalin's generals had, and because of that, Danforth was surprised that his letter had been answered at all. He suspected that the old general might well be cocooned in the loneliness of old age and so welcomed the opportunity to tell his story.

In his letter, Danforth had portrayed himself as something of a historian, a gatherer of oral histories having to do with the war. In his return letter, the general had written in quite elegant Russian of his participation in the heroic defense of Stalingrad and of his many medals and honors and decorations. He had not spoken of anything having to do with intelligence work, and given the extensive nature of the general's military service, Danforth doubted that he'd done much of it, a fact that suggested the general had become involved in the Rache investigation for some specific reason, after which he'd returned, unscathed, to his military duties.

"Ah, most welcome," the old general said in Russian when he opened his townhouse door to Danforth, his manner so pleasant and amiable that it reminded Danforth of the Russian Errol Flynn.

Danforth returned the greeting in Russian, then followed Solotoff into a small room that looked out onto what was called a woman's view in that part of the world, by which was meant an enclosed terrace where cloistered females could gaze, unseen, at a universe otherwise denied them.

"Such a long way to come for my story," Solotoff said.

He had put out goat cheese and some dried fruit, along with slivers of dried meat Danforth didn't recognize, and together they sat, facing each other, on small woven chairs. There was vodka, but Danforth politely refused it, which seemed a relief to the old man since tea was certainly cheaper. He was clearly in fallen circumstances, an old soldier whom the new order considered little more than a Stalinist relic. His pension was probably precarious, Danforth thought, if not reduced or halted altogether. He had outlived his time and his ideology, and the revolution he had served had sunk into a mire of corruption and inefficiency so deep it had begun to generate public outcry and even strikes, Russian workers at last grown impatient with the workers' paradise.

For the next three hours, Danforth listened more or less without interrupting as the old general told his war stories, mostly concerning the horrors of Stalingrad, how Khrushchev had conducted the city's defense with an iron hand.

"We set up machine guns behind our own troops," he said, "and if they tried to return after a charge, we shot them." He shrugged away the bloodcurdling horror of this. "So they either took the position they were ordered to take, or they were killed for failure to take it." His grimaced. "War is a terrible thing," he said, then asked a question that gave Danforth his entry. "Were you in the war?"

"Yes," Danforth said.

Here was the opening, he thought, and he took it.

"I was a spy."

"A spy?" Solotoff asked. He did not seem in the least troubled by this.

"And I helped plot an assassination," Danforth added. "But it failed."

Solotoff appeared no more troubled by this than by Danforth's initial answer. "Who did you fail to kill?"

"Hitler," Danforth answered flatly.

Something registered in Solotoff's eyes, a glimmer he quickly doused with a loud laugh. "I wish you hadn't failed. It was forty degrees below zero when those German bastards retreated. We went after them like wolves. The big, brave German Fifth Army. We slaughtered them like little frozen lambs. Whoever attacks you in your homeland deserves to die. That's what I believe."

Danforth smiled. "So do I, believe me." He attempted to appear long perplexed by a curious and unsolved little mystery. "As far as Hitler was concerned, we almost did it. Or at least, we almost tried. But the Germans caught on to us. I've always wondered how."

Solotoff said nothing, but Danforth could see his mind working behind his eyes.

"I always thought we were betrayed," Danforth continued.

"You probably were," Solotoff said casually. "A spy swims in a sea full of sharks."

"A certain name has always floated in that water," Danforth said. "Rache."

The name clearly registered in Solotoff's mind, Danforth saw, and he leaned forward slightly. "Tell me, were you ever in Warsaw, General?"

"I have been to Warsaw many times," Solotoff answered. "And you?"

"After the war," Danforth answered. "I saw a lot of the East after the war."

"Did you?"

"Dubno," Danforth said. "Lemberg. Kiev. Moscow." He stopped, waited, then said, "Magadan."

"Ah," Solotoff said. "That is very far to the east."

"But you can see it from Adult World," Danforth said.

Solotoff's gaze hardened. "When were you released?"

Danforth could hardly believe the answer he gave. "A lifetime ago."

"And why have you returned to our sad country?" Solotoff asked.

"Because I want to know who betrayed me," Danforth said.

315

Danforth did not mention Anna because he had reached that point when a man looks back and feels that in his lifelong quest — whatever it might have been — he has betrayed himself, squandered his days, and to reveal the nature of that squandering would expose him as a madman or a fool.

"I want vengeance," Danforth said, a motive he was certain Solotoff would understand. "For my life."

"How would you get it?" Solotoff asked.

"By killing a traitor," Danforth answered flatly.

"You are rather old for such a mission," the general said.

"I have nothing else," Danforth said.

"And so you've come all this way," the general said in a bemused voice.

"Yes."

Danforth saw a glint of the old Russian wolf in Solotoff's eyes and realized that this was a man whose past had betrayed him and whose once fierce loyalties had faded; now he was simply a poor old man in search of a score, one who had nothing left to sell but his memories.

"Tell me more about Warsaw," Solotoff said.

"There was a forger named Romanchuk," Danforth told him. "I had some dealings with him after the war. I think you may have interrogated him in Warsaw."

"Why would you think such a thing?" Solotoff asked.

"Because one of the interrogators wore the Order of Lenin," Danforth said. "And he spoke Turkish." Danforth kept his demeanor entirely casual. "I know you have the Order of Lenin and that you were once very powerful here in Azerbaijan, so you probably speak Turkish. I put that together, and you came up as the man who was most likely to have been in Warsaw when Romanchuk was interrogated."

"In the first two of these things you are right," Solotoff said, as if the facts bored him. "But why should I tell you if you are right in the last of them?"

Danforth's earliest memories of the east returned, the abyss of corruption his father had many times described, along with the eternal miseries of the Balkans. He recalled the bandits on the railway, that long-ago crucifixion, the leader of that ruthless band, how he'd walked among the terrified passengers, nodding at watches, bracelets, cuff links, the glint in his soulless eyes that Danforth now saw in Solotoff's. He was a dead soul, and dead souls can be bought.

"Because I'll pay you," he said. "I'll pay you if you tell me where Rache is."

Solotoff took a slow, meditative sip of tea. "What else do you know about this interrogation in Warsaw?"

"There was a woman," Danforth said. "An American. She was brought in to translate from Ukrainian for Romanchuk."

Solotoff slowly put down the cup and gazed at it as if he were a pawnbroker studying its every crack and chink. "How much would you pay?"

"Are you the man who was sent to interrogate Romanchuk?" Danforth asked. "Did you speak to the American woman in Turkish?"

Solotoff grinned. "Perhaps. It is a long chain that stretches back so far. I would have to make inquiries. It might take some time. And my contacts are not without needs. I would have to be generous."

Generous. By which he meant, Danforth knew, there would be many payments.

Solotoff's smile had a canine sparkle, and at that instant, Danforth recalled the soldiers at Plötzensee, the many border guards whose palms he'd greased, their drunken delight in the power they had over him, and after these, he remembered the long line of interrogators he'd faced beneath a naked bulb, the blows that had rained down upon him in the camp, always with some brute grinning as he delivered them. *Russians,* he thought with a surging hatred he could barely suppress, and he knew that at that moment, he could cheerfully have killed them all.

Solotoff drained the last of his tea, returned the cup to the table, then sat back and waited. "Twenty thousand American dollars."

"How would this payment be made?" Danforth asked.

Solotoff laughed. "Oil seeps through many holes in Baku."

It was a typically metaphorical response, and by it, Danforth understood the great sieve of Soviet corruption, General Solotoff a surly man with many conduits, a rabbit warren of little deals and old favors with an untold number of escape routes.

"I will have to be sure of any information you give me," Danforth warned him.

"There will be only one piece of information," Solotoff said as if closing a negotiation with a nervous buyer. "A name. An address. That is all." His eyes glittered like sunlight on the blood-stained snows of Stalingrad. "Once we have an understanding, you will have to wait. But in the end, you will hear from me."

Lexington Avenue, New York City, 2001

"And so the arrangements were made, and I returned to New York and waited to hear from this old hero of the Soviets," Danforth said with undisguised contempt. "I had no doubt that eventually I would."

Danforth read my incredulity as he had so often done during his narrative, and he immediately provided a corollary tale that made clear that his own was entirely believable.

"Foreign intelligence keeps track of their old agents," he said by way of proving his story. "Take the case of Engelbert Broda, for example."

For ten years, from 1938 to 1948, a Soviet spy code-named Eric had sent Britain's nuclear secrets to the Soviets, Danforth said. During that time, he'd been the Soviets' main source for information on Britain's atomic-bomb research.

"MI Five suspected him for years," Danforth told me. "They opened his mail and watched his every move."

But they had never caught him, and so it wasn't until a full seventy years later, when KGB files were finally opened, that the British found out they'd been right all along.

"Bertie Broda had even given the Russians the blueprint for the early nuclear reactor used in the Manhattan Project," Danforth said. "He single-handedly allowed the Soviets to catch up with the West and in so doing changed the face of foreign policy for decades to come." He smiled. "So you see, what you'd call a large geopolitical purpose can be brought about by a little spy."

"What happened when they caught Broda?" I asked.

"Nothing," Danforth answered. "He was already dead. And he died a very respected scientist. He has a special grave in an honored section of a Vienna cemetery." He seemed suddenly to drift into some colder region. "Odd, what a cemetery can reveal." For a moment he remained in that distant place. Then, as he had so many times during our talk, he abruptly returned to the present.

"Anyway, Broda was never discovered," he said.

"Too bad," I said, almost lightly, as if treason were a mist easily wiped from a window. "Very clever to have outsmarted everyone for so long."

"Clever?" Danforth asked. "Perhaps. But the curious thing I've discovered about spies is that they must trust so many to keep their secrets. They have handlers, but who handles the handlers? No Soviet spy was ever handled by Stalin personally. There were layers and layers of people who knew this agent or that one, people whose identity the agent never knew." The irony of what Danforth said next clearly did not escape him. "A spy may never be uncovered, Paul, but he can never be completely hidden either. Deceit always leaves a trail."

"Which Solotoff was now pursuing?" I asked.

"Undoubtedly," Danforth said. He looked at me in a way that let me know he'd read my mind. "Ah, you are looking for that big dramatic ending. Perhaps a chase over the rooftops? Or some final scene of two old men grappling with each other, like Holmes and Moriarty slugging it out at Reichenbach Falls? Is that what you want, Paul, at the end of my tale?"

"Frankly, yes," I said. "And why not? If Rache is a traitor, he deserves to die."

"Yes, of course," Danforth said. "And if vengeance cannot be exacted on Rache, perhaps there is someone else. At any rate, I end up the hero, don't I?"

"Yes," I said. "And we all need to be heroes." I glanced toward the open wound of Lower Manhattan. "Especially now."

"Indeed that's true, Paul," Danforth said. "With one small caveat."

"Which is?"

Danforth looked at me almost sadly, like a man who'd expended great effort in an unworthy cause. "That the need to be a hero is not a hero's need."

I felt that I had proved myself to be as young and callow at the end of his story as I had been at the beginning.

"So, tell me, then," I asked with a sincerity that surprised me. "What is truly heroic?"

"Facing the complexity of things," Danforth said solemnly. He looked at me as if he were making a final evaluation, a judgment that would determine whether or not I would hear the final chapters of his tale. "Collateral damage is inevitable," he said, almost to himself. He drew in a disturbingly tense breath, held it for a moment, then released it slowly; it seemed to carry with it the last full measure of his strength. "The letter that finally came from the general was in Russian, of course. It said simply *Делай с ним, как хотели.* Which means 'Do with him as you wish.'" Just below it, the old general had written a name and address. Danforth drew in yet another slow, ponderous breath that seemed to carry with it the full weight of murder.

"And so I set off to find a man I had never seen," he said. He twisted to the side, opened the drawer of the little table that rested between us, and took out an old service revolver. "And, if he had betrayed Anna, to kill him."

Buenos Aires, Argentina, 1983

He had vaguely expected to find Rache living in Krakow or Budapest, or perhaps even the old spy haven of Vienna, where Rache could sit with his pastry and afternoon tea and stare at the Plague Monument and recall the sweet days of his treachery, the best triple agent in the world because he'd gotten away with it.

But once Solotoff had provided the man's address, along with, surprisingly, a German name, Danforth had changed his earlier notion, and on the flight from New York he imagined him as all such figures had been imagined since the war: sitting on some cool veranda, listening to the call of tropical birds, the smell of fresh mango rich in the air around them; these men who had brought winter to the world safe in their sunlit splendor.

That his purpose still burned so brightly surprised him, for in every other way he felt the steady weathering of time, death's unyielding approach. Life, at last, was a stalker, waiting for the moment, and he knew that his would come soon. Perhaps this was his true freedom, he thought, that he could murder in certain knowledge that whatever followed would be short-lived.

And so, if Rache was a traitor, this he would do . . . for Anna.

He took a cab to his hotel on Avenida Florida, unpacked, then lay down on the bed for a fitful night's sleep. In dreams, he returned to his many ages: the callow youth, the shallow adventurist, the amateur assassin, the tormented romantic obsessive, and now this lonely man on his last mission, this hate-filled man who might at last personify the thing he sought: vengeance.

Morning did not become him; in the mirror he saw the deep lines, the heavy bags, the snow-white hair comic in its disarray. Time, in the end, is a drowning pool, and as he peered at his withered face, Danforth felt himself suffocating beneath the many regrets that pressed in on him. Shouldn't he have known from the beginning that it was all a foolish enterprise and that like all such exploits it would end in disaster? At the first firings of his love for Anna, shouldn't he have done everything he could to rescue her from this tomfoolery, thus saving both their lives? Had he missed some subtle sign of treachery that, had he seen it, might have saved her? Had Rache ever walked past him or sat, a silent figure behind a potted plant, peering at Bannion or Anna, or even Danforth himself, knowing full well that they were only little spies, silly in their hope and expendable for its dashing?

After Clayton's funeral, his wife had given Danforth her husband's old service revolver, a gesture his old friend had requested only hours before his death. It would be fitting, Danforth thought now, for Clayton's gun to bring down the curtain on a drama he had begun so many years before.

He had visited Buenos Aires only once, in company with his father, but he faintly recalled the old neighborhood of La Locanda, with its small, colorfully painted buildings. He had read that here, in these quaint and quite lovely streets, there were houses where the victims of the ongoing repression were kept and tormented before they disappeared, and he wondered if Rache had found a place for himself in this world of pain. He knew that certain men were drawn to life's dungeons and death chambers. He had met them during his own interrogations, and he had met them as he himself was interrogated. They were the sewer's most pernicious flotsam, and he had learned enough of the world to understand that they were as numerous as grains of sand. But he was no longer a man of the world, he thought, no longer one inclined to inject himself into its great affairs. He had given himself over to this only once, and disastrously, and now he felt at home in the concentrated measure of his need for reprisal. He had not saved the world, but he was unquestionably prepared to remove one villain from it.

And this he would do for Anna.

So it is here, he thought as the bus drew to a halt at the cross street, *that the story ends.*

The house he located a few minutes later struck him as extraordinarily modest. If life followed art, an epic tale spanning decades and continents would have an epic setting for its final scene. But the house was small and in bad repair, with a cramped, weedy yard and a roof saddened by broken tiles.

Suddenly, Danforth recalled the times he'd killed, and it seemed to him that it was his memory acting as a buttress to his courage, reminding him that he had taken life at close quarters. He was not new to murder, he told himself, and despite his years, his trigger finger remained strong. When the moment came, he would make his will match his muscles. That had always been the key to action, and as he stepped forward and drew open the rusty iron gate that opened onto the narrow pathway that led to the cottage's door, he told himself that he must be the man he'd been all those many years ago: *This I do for Anna.*

The walkway was of uneven brick, treacherous for a man his

age, but Danforth maneuvered along it slowly and carefully, his gaze on the path until he reached the door. Once there, he drew in a long, steadying breath and knocked.

The man who opened the door was pale and bald, his eyes vague and watery, with nothing of the malevolent deceit Danforth's imagination had added to them. He had imagined Rache as still in the fullness of his youth, muscular and erect. To these characteristics, his mind had lately added features that were sometimes Slavic, sometimes Aryan, but always diabolically cruel and lit with low cunning. He knew that it was his hatred that had removed age and weariness and decrepitude from this portrait, and that in a thousand thousand ways other men did this every day, shading in the demonic in accordance with their fierce need for vengeance.

"*¿Qué pasa?*" the old man asked. What's the matter?

He was squinting hard, and by that squint, Danforth realized that the old man's vision was so impaired he could probably see only a blur at his door.

"My car has broken down," he told him in Spanish. "I wonder if I might use your phone."

The old man nodded and opened the door wider.

Danforth stepped inside the house, then followed the old man into his cramped living quarters, a small room cluttered with books and papers, though what Danforth most noticed was a small table filled with an array of medications: sprays, ointments, pills, the full ordnance of old age.

There was a phone on a second table and the old man shuffled over to it, plucked the receiver from its cradle, and offered it to Danforth with a palsied hand that kept its cord dancing frantically.

Danforth faked a call, then handed the old man back the phone. "They're sending someone," he said.

The old man nodded toward a chair, a gesture indicating he

324

should wait inside until help arrived. Then he slumped down in a ragged wicker chair, indicating with a similar nod that Danforth should do the same in the chair that rested opposite his.

"*Hace calor,*" the old man said. It's warm.

"*Sí,*" Danforth replied.

"*¿De donde es usted?*" Where are you from?

"*Nueva York.*"

"Ah," the old man said. "*Tengo una hija qué aún vive allí.*"

A daughter living in New York, Danforth thought, and so he had had it all, this man: a wife, a child.

"*¿Vive usted solo ahora?*" Danforth asked cautiously, needing to make sure that the old man lived alone.

"*Sí,*" the old man said. "*Soy soltero.*"

So he lived alone, Danforth thought, with a daughter far away.

Perfect.

Danforth noticed a large drinking mug, topped with a pewter flask. "That mug with the milkmaid," he said in English. "I saw one like it in Germany."

"Germany, yes," the old man said with a smooth shift to English. "I was there during the war."

"I was there briefly," Danforth said. "In Berlin. Near the Landwehr Canal."

"Ah, yes," the old man said. "A sad place. They tossed the body of Rosa Luxemburg into those waters."

And Danforth instantly recalled that moment years before when they'd all been strolling along the Spree: how Bannion had stopped and looked out toward a particular bridge, the strange combination of rage and sorrow that had swept into his face.

"Why did you betray us, Ted?"

The old man blinked slowly, as if in all the years of his concealment he'd known that the hinge on traitor's gate would one day sound. Now, with its small creak, he would realize, as Danforth thought Bannion surely did at that moment, that whether he would live or die had been decided long ago.

"Tom," Bannion whispered.

Danforth wondered why he did not simply draw the pistol and do what he had come to do. What was the point of any further conversation, after all? What would he be looking for? He could find no answers to these questions, and as if to provide one, he felt his hand reach inside his coat, hold a moment, then curl around the handle of the pistol.

"You were a German agent all along," Danforth said. "You never meant to carry out the plot."

Bannion shifted in his chair, a jagged, achy movement Danforth recognized as the way he himself now moved, along with most men of a certain age.

"I was never a German agent," Bannion said. "And I would have killed Hitler without a blink. I would have done everything I said I would do. It was Anna's idea to kill him, remember? It was a good one, and it came from her sense of purpose, which I admired."

There was a curious confidence in him now, Danforth observed, as if his old skills were returning to him, the dead powers of his long deceit lifting from their graves, walking the earth.

"I was never a German agent," he declared again.

"Soviet then?" Danforth asked.

"Of course, Tom," he said. "And I was loyal to the end. Which is why they've always protected me." He stopped as if in sudden recognition. "Until now, that is." He seemed to understand that history had turned against him. "When a great house falls, only the rats get out alive. Which one came to you, Tom?"

"It was I who came to him," Danforth said. "Because I never stopped looking for Anna."

Bannion's smile bore something between admiration and contempt; he seemed in awe that Danforth had so relentlessly re-sponded to so empty a call.

"With you, it was always her, Tom," he said. "But with me, it was always something greater."

Then he told his tale.

Munich, Germany, 1939

Bannion parted the curtains at his window and peered down at the street. It was a gesture that had long served to calm him, a simple gazing down onto the life below. He remembered the time when he'd walked the girders above Broadway, always with men who'd walked them far longer and with more grace, and how he'd felt lifted by their simple decency, the way they laughed and told stories, the true salt of the earth. It was in these men he'd first glimpsed the world his comrades in the east were already mak-ing and that he hoped to help them create. He knew that many Americans had already made the journey to Russia, were already working there, building the new world. He'd read about them in *New Masses* and heard their praises sung by countless street-corner speakers. At some point, he pledged a new allegiance, and he was now the secret sharer of their mission. He knew he would not see the castle finished, but he also knew that in what he had set himself to do, he would add to its measure. That Anna and Danforth and Clayton knew nothing of this continued connec-tion, believing that he'd broken it and still lived in the bitterness of that break, seemed to him only a small deceit. It had been her idea, after all, this murder. He had only relayed her plan to his superiors and gained their approval to help her carry it out.

He jumped at the rap at his door, giving in to the fear that gripped him each time a stranger arrived or drew alongside him as he walked the street. It was always impossible to tell if a plot had been discovered until it was too late to do anything about it, and now that he was approaching what would no doubt be the last act of his life, he felt all the more fearful that something would stand in his way.

The second rap at the door was more insistent, but this time he gave no outward sign of fear.

The pistol was in his jacket, but there'd be no use in reaching for it. If the men on the other side of the door had come to arrest him, then arrest him they would. He had long ago cast aside the dramatics of self-defense, the idea of shooting his way out of such a spot. Such notions were for amateurs and people whose only concept of intrigue came from the movies.

And so he merely grabbed his jacket, hung it in the closet, then with studied calm opened the door.

The face that greeted him was familiar, almost fatherly, the agent who had handled him during all his Party life.

"There has been a change in plan," the man said in German.

"It's very late for that," Bannion answered in a German no less precise.

"There has been a change," the man said. "There is to be no attempt."

"No attempt?" Bannion asked unbelievingly.

He had little doubt that this decision had been made in Moscow and that the leaders in charge there knew what they were doing. He was but a small cog in that great machine, and he would move as those who drove the gears demanded.

"All right," he said, and thought this was the end of it. "But how do I explain this change to the others?"

"There is no need to explain it," the man said. "Arrests will be made."

"For what?" Bannion asked.

"They are assassins."

Bannion was not sure he had heard correctly. "But if there

is to be no assassination, then why should the others be arrested?"

"To expose their plot," the man answered. "We will alert the Germans that we have a source inside an American plot. You are that source, of course, so you will not be harmed."

"But why tell the Germans anything?" Bannion asked.

"That is not for us to ask," the man said. "It has been decided that the woman will be needed."

"Only the woman?" Bannion asked.

"Yes," the man said. "She will be . . . interrogated until she exposes this American plot." He laughed. "Then we will ask for her. They will turn her over because they don't want the world to know that their leader is constantly a target. It will all be done secretly, and at some point after she has broken, she will be released." He took a small envelope from his jacket pocket. "One is for you. The other is for the woman. Neither is real."

Bannion said nothing, which clearly alarmed the agent.

"It is important that the Germans trust us," the man said emphatically. "What better way for us to prove ourselves to them than by exposing a silly group of American adventurers?"

Bannion would all his life recall what happened next, the quiet argument the Soviet agent made, how much depended upon this plot, the dark consequences that would surely flow should it not be carried out. What was one man or one woman in the long view of history? No individual could be allowed to stand in the way of so important a mission. Later he would remember how silently he had listened to all this, and how easily he had been persuaded by it.

"All right," he said at last, and with those words accepted his role in this far different plot. He listened as the rest of it was revealed: Danforth was to be sent to Hamburg and from there to London, where he would serve as a witness to the failure of the plot. Bannion was to be "arrested," in order to shield him from later suspicion of having betrayed the plot. He was to fake his own suicide and then be carted away; later he'd be released into Soviet hands.

"So only . . . Anna," he said.

The man's smile was clearly meant to ease Bannion's lingering concerns.

"Don't look so sad," he said. "She is just a little spy."

With that, he left, and for a long time afterward, Bannion sat by the window and thought of Anna. He saw the little girl with her many languages, then the young woman she'd become, and in seeing both, he reviewed the dark past of which he was only dimly aware even as he envisioned the yet darker future that awaited her.

Buenos Aires, Argentina, 1983

"I later learned that it was the Russo-German pact they were determined to protect," Bannion said. "Moscow called off several similar plots at the same time because they needed Hitler to trust them." He shrugged. "After that, they became great allies, Berlin and Moscow, and when that happened, I finally lost hope in Russia."

But before that, he had pretended to revile a god he continued to revere, Danforth thought.

"You fed Anna to the wolves," Danforth said icily. "There was never a Rache. It was always you."

"It's an old game," Bannion said. "Get the other side to pursue a man who doesn't actually exist. And so we made him up. And made everyone believe he existed. The Russians pretended to distrust him, which made him that much more real. It was quite an effective ruse. It fooled Clayton, and it fooled you."

"It fooled Anna too," Danforth said. "She spent her life protecting this . . . phantom." He pulled out the pistol and felt his finger draw down upon the trigger. "Because she thought she was protecting you."

Bannion squinted at the pistol, then looked at Danforth. "Can you kill a man for believing in something that turned out to be terrible?"

"Yes, I can," Danforth said.

"How?" Bannion demanded. "Answer that one question, Tom. How can you kill someone for being fooled into following a false god and doing terrible things in the service of it? How can you condemn a man for that?"

Danforth drew back the hammer on the pistol and answered Bannion with the only genuine truth his life had revealed. "I can, yes," he said, "because in the end, it is a moral responsibility to be wise."

Lexington Avenue, New York City, 2001

The feeling was exactly as the cliché described it, I realized: a stopping of the heart.

"You shot him?" I murmured.

"No," Danforth answered. "But I would have, Paul, if that grandson of his hadn't appeared." His look had all the force of a barrel pointed at my head. "He came running through the front door."

I heard one of my earliest questions: *Innocence, that's a hard thing to nail down, don't you think?* Then Danforth's reply: *We always know who the innocent are.* I glanced at the pistol that rested in his lap and knew that the question had never been whether I would live or die, for that had been decided long ago.

"You do remember, don't you?" Danforth asked.

It had been a hot summer day, I recalled. I'd been tired of the heat, eager to throw myself beneath the fan that turned so languidly in my grandfather's house. My mother had stopped a block behind to chat with a neighbor, certain that I was safe once I'd gone through my grandfather's gate.

"That was you?" I asked, now quite vividly remembering the old man I'd found sitting opposite my grandfather, the way he'd turned and looked at me brokenly, like a man who'd just been told that the last small thing he'd hoped for never would be his. "You just got up and left," I said.

Danforth's hand crawled over to the pistol. "You were just a little boy, Paul," he said.

"Yes," I agreed softly.

"A child," Danforth said. He picked up the pistol with a hand that had begun to tremble and returned it to the drawer. "And so you were completely innocent."

"I don't have to believe that what you say is true," I said, with a bit of feigned bravado that I suddenly realized I must have gotten from my grandfather.

"That's true, you don't," Danforth said. He glanced at the clock to his right. "You only have to believe that it might be true." He watched me a moment, then added, "We know what to do with evil, Paul. It's innocence that perplexes us." His smile was a reed struggling to hold its own against a stormy sea. "And so I thought it was over at last," he whispered, and with those words stepped back into the past. "But I was wrong."

He had retired from teaching his classes not long after returning from Buenos Aires, he said, but had continued to tutor on the side in order to afford the few luxuries he enjoyed, mainly books and an occasional visit to the theater, what he rightly called "the semiretirement of a simple life." Several of these students were part of the influx of Russians to New York City, a very ambitious group, according to Danforth, hell-bent on learning English. One of them had been a young woman from Vladivostok who wore thick glasses and spoke very rapidly and who greatly enjoyed lambasting the old Communist regime as the crooks and thugs they were. These had been replaced by an equally repellent cadre of Party hacks, she said, men who enjoyed the fruits of the old system's vast corruption even as Russia attempted to reform itself. Still, there were good changes, she'd told Danforth, lots of entrepreneurs creating lots of wealth. In fact, she said, quite a few entirely new professions had sprouted from the soil of Communism's rot. She listed them in Russian and asked Danforth to give her the words for them in English.

"*Бухгалтер*," she said.

"Accountant," Danforth told her.

"*Инвестиционный банкир*."

"Investment banker."

"*частный детектив*."

It was this third one that caused Danforth to feel what I had felt only moments before, the silent stricture of a suddenly stopped heart.

"Private investigator," he said.

Could it be, he wondered, with all the recent opening up of files from various Russian agencies — a few even from the black maw of the KGB — could it be that it was not too late for one last quest?

"With the last of my little savings, I hired a Russian gumshoe," Danforth said with a small, sad laugh.

He had gone to Little Odessa, he said, where the immigrant Russians thrived, and there inquired at various social clubs of anyone who might know a *частный детектив* who would take his case. A name at last surfaced, one Fydor Slezak, and Danforth wrote to him in his quite exquisite Russian. The case was taken, and for weeks it continued. Bills came, and a little doubtful information that reminded Danforth of the rumors that had plagued him so many years before, tales of this woman hewing wood, that one in a quarry.

Then, on a fine April day, an envelope arrived, bearing its brief report on a piece of paper that would forever after seem to Danforth as slender as her bones.

основывать, the note said.

Found.

Magadan, Russia, 1986

He flew out of Kennedy to Moscow, and from there to Vladivostok, where he waited as one flight after another was delayed and the terminal filled with people who reminded him of the peasants of old. There was something in their patient waiting, their anticipation of delay, the way they absorbed hardship and inconvenience into their very blood that recalled his first journeys to the east, the frigid towns where the forebears of these same indomitable people had congregated beside the rails in hopes of gathering up a little coal or some miraculously tumbled sack of grain. He'd heard of trains that used frozen fish as fuel, and along the rail lines where they ran, vast crowds of the starving waited for the blackened fish heads that were sometimes belched from these trains' explosive funnels. He'd never known if this was true, but the curious thing was that at the time, it had seemed to him entirely believable.

The plane to Magadan at last took off a full three days after his arrival in Vladivostok, and by that time his old bones had seemed almost to pierce his skin.

Once in Magadan, he'd gone to the same hotel where he'd stayed after being released years before; he'd even, with the manager's permission, been admitted once again to room 304, where he sat by the window and recalled as best he could that one last time with Anna.

He'd hired Slezak to take him up the Road of Skulls, but he'd been held up for a reason he had not made clear, and so Danforth had remained in Magadan a little longer than planned. While there, he often walked down to the sea, where he sat on the once-hellish docks and watched the workers loading and unloading supplies. *Zeks* no longer emerged from the black depths of these boats, but from time to time, Danforth would see some old man or woman who had doubtless once suffered that debased condition. He could sense their long serfdom in the slope of their shoulders, the heaviness of their weary gait. The camps had closed long ago, but where could such people have gone with their closing? They had no family left, no one to whom they might return, and so, as he could see, they had become the Gulag ghosts of Magadan.

She would not be among them, Danforth had been told, and so he no longer searched for her as he'd once searched, his needful eyes trained on each new shuffling group of *zeks*, forever hopeful that she would suddenly appear within their ranks, small and brown, with such large black eyes.

Slezak at last arrived. He stopped his mud-caked truck in front of the hotel, and its engine gurgled fitfully, like an old man with fluid in his lungs.

"Long trip," Slezak warned him in Russian.

Danforth could see that he'd expected to find a younger man and now feared that the one before him would not be up to so arduous a journey.

"Six hundred kilometers to Susuman," he added. "Bad road."

Bad, yes, Danforth thought later, but nothing compared to his earlier journey up the Road of Skulls. There was mud, and the region's gigantic mosquitoes attacked with the same aggressiveness of old.

He was not sure he had ever been in Susuman. Certainly he recalled nothing of the buildings that greeted him, though their ramshackle appearance, along with a few surviving relics of that earlier time, mostly faded murals exhorting the exhausted *zeks* to work harder for the motherland, reminded him of other villages through which he'd passed. Whole towns had been lost in snowdrifts, he now recalled, a vast world locked in frigid darkness.

He had been told where she lay and went directly there, a small cemetery that rested among a grove of trees not far from town. Slezak had told Danforth that a woman would meet them at the entrance to the cemetery, and there she was, standing between two concrete pylons that had once served as a gate.

Danforth greeted her in Russian, then deposited the money into the rough palm of her hand.

"She is just through there," the woman said.

"Did you know her?" Danforth asked.

The woman shook her head, then nodded toward Slezak as if to tell him that answering questions had not been part of the deal.

"She worked at the power station in Kadykchan," Slezak said. "When the town was abandoned, some camp records ended up there. I gave her the name, and she looked through them. That's what the money's for." He grinned. "Research."

"It took much time," the woman said gruffly.

"But you're sure it's her?" Danforth asked.

"It's her," the woman said, then turned and headed down the narrow path and into an open field, muddy and overgrown but dotted with a few squat stone slabs etched with Cyrillic letters.

"How do you know?" Danforth asked.

The woman once again nodded to Slezak, clearly refusing to give any unpaid-for information.

336

"It's the woman you are seeking," Slezak said with a certainty that seemed uncertain.

As if given a signal to back Slezak up, the woman said, "It is her. I have proof."

She had spoken defensively, like one accused of a crime she had not committed, and Danforth glimpsed the terrible sense of both distrust and being distrusted that was another of Stalin's grotesque legacies.

"It's her," the woman repeated firmly, this time in a tone that was almost surly. "I don't cheat you."

They moved farther into the field of stones until they reached its far border, and there they came to a halt. The stone had toppled over, and time and the elements had weathered it badly, but Danforth could make out its faded lettering: *Ana Khalisah*. Another stone rose hard by it; its inscription indicated that it was the grave of the woman's daughter.

He felt a desolate heaviness press down on him. It was not simply that he had made a long and arduous journey only to find the grave of some unknown woman but also that he now knew he would never find Anna Klein. He had not succeeded in avenging her; he had not even managed to find her and, in one last gesture of his knight-errantry, bring her home. He had grown old in his long effort, and he suddenly felt the full weight of those many years.

"This is not the woman I was looking for," he said.

The old woman stared at him sternly. "I don't cheat you," she said. She looked at Slezak. "I have proof."

But Danforth knew that there could be no proof, that anything the old woman might produce—a death certificate, a tattered document, even some physical artifact—would be either erroneous or falsified.

"I'm tired," he said with a slight smile by which he wished to communicate to the old woman that he would not call her hon-

337

esty into question, that she had done her best, that we are all, in the end, the final products of our errors.

He turned to Slezak. "We'll head back to Magadan in the morning."

Slezak nodded, and they both turned to leave the grave, but the old woman grabbed Danforth's coat and fiercely turned him to face her. "Wait, you see," she said.

Slezak looked to Danforth for instructions.

"All right," Danforth said to the old woman. "Show me your proof."

They walked back to Slezak's car in silence, and then the old woman motioned that they should head down the barely passable road. "Twenty minutes," she said.

It took a bit more than twenty minutes, but at last they arrived at one of Susuman's larger public buildings, though it was hardly imposing. Inside, the old woman led Danforth up a flight of creaking stairs and to what appeared to be some sort of library, though the walls were lined with stacks of files, rather than books. If the proof was here, Danforth thought, who could find it?

The old woman directed him to the front of a long counter and disappeared into an adjoining room. Behind the counter, women in faded smocks, their heads wrapped in scarves, moved about the stacks of files and papers. The Gulag had been an assiduous compiler, and Danforth imagined that with the current thaw, thousands upon thousands of people were now seeking their lost kindred. In that paper graveyard and in others like it throughout Russia, the millions of dead lay in the mass coffins of filing cabinets.

"Okay, come," the woman said as she emerged from the room. She motioned Danforth down a corridor, past several rooms where children sat at small desks, making him realize that the building also served as a school.

338

When they reached the end of the corridor, the old woman led Danforth inside a room where perhaps thirty children sat facing an ancient blackboard. The lesson had to do with Russian history, but now there were no pictures of Lenin or Stalin.

"You wait," the old woman said, then marched up the center aisle and spoke briefly to the teacher. Danforth couldn't make out what was being said, but after a short conversation, the teacher, a small, squat man in a threadbare suit, walked halfway up the aisle, then bent forward and whispered into the ear of one of the students. For a moment, the little girl sat quite still, then, as if in response to the teacher's urging, she rose, turned, and walked toward Danforth. She wore a white shirt and gray skirt, as did all the other little girls, but her hair was shorter, and very curly.

"Hello, sir," she said in perfect English when she reached him. She stretched out her hand. "A pleasure to meet you."

It seemed to Danforth that he had never held so slender a hand. "Where did you learn such perfect English?" he asked.

"From my grandmother," she said.

Danforth saw her startlingly blue eyes and knew that they were his; he saw her tightly curled hair and knew that it was hers, and in seeing this, he recalled that long-lost night, and under the weight of that remembrance, he sank to his knees and gathered his granddaughter into his arms. A great seizure of weeping shook him and he cried in a way that returned him to all the many ages he had known: the young man who had loved her, the middle-aged man who had sought her, and now the old man who had found her in the only way she could still be found.

Lexington Avenue, New York City, 2001

There was a knock at the door.

Danforth glanced at the clock, and a tiny smile crossed his

lips. "Right on time," he said, then called out, "Just a minute." He looked at me. "Could you get the door, Paul?"

I rose, walked to the door, and opened it to find a woman in her early twenties. She was small and dark, with strikingly blue eyes and short, very curly hair.

"Hello," she said, giving no hint of surprise at seeing a stranger open Danforth's door.

"Hi," I answered from the curious daze that overtook me. "I'm . . . Paul."

"Yes, I know," she said. She offered her hand, and I took it. It was extraordinarily small and delicate.

"I'm Alma."

"Alma," I repeated. "That means 'soul' in Spanish."

"In Spanish, yes," Alma said in a tone of complete authority. "And in Arabic it means 'apple.'"

"So you're a student of languages," I said.

"Yes," she said. "I work as a translator."

"Come, sit down," Danforth called from behind us.

She stepped in front of me, made her way over to Danforth, and kissed him softly on the forehead. "How are you doing?" she asked.

"As well as can be expected," Danforth said in a way that attested to some grave circumstance he had not revealed to me but that I now saw in the waning strength and slight pallor that had overtaken him during the past hours.

"Sit there," he told Alma, then nodded to the seat I'd earlier occupied. "And you sit there, Paul."

Danforth waited until we'd taken our seats, then he said, "So, to Anna's story." He looked at Alma. "This part is yours," he told her.

She looked at me, her gaze as intense as that of Scheherazade. "My grandmother," she began, "was born in . . ."

Erzinghan, Turkey, 1915

She would all her life recall how distinguished her father had been, the way he'd dominated the men who gathered around him. Even as a girl of five, she'd noticed his knowledge of many languages, and how the leaders of the community often came to him for counsel. He had traveled all over the world and yet had returned to the little town in which he'd been born and in which he'd married and where she expected to live out her life as his adoring daughter.

But dark news had begun to trickle in from other parts of the country: a massacre in Van, and a roundup of what her father called "notables" in Constantinople. Fear grew and deepened, and in the midst of that gathering terror, her father had met with other men like himself to plan what must be done.

The first soldiers arrived in the village on a sweltering day when the dust was made bright yellow in the sun and swirled in gusts and pools, and it was into this dust that her father walked to meet their leader.

From the darkness inside her house, Ana watched the men on horses peer down from what seemed a great height to where her father faced them, unarmed and without defense, as it had seemed to her, his hands pointing first this way and then that, so she thought he must be telling them of the many roads by which they should leave her village. But the soldiers remained in place, staring down, hands on their sabers or fingering the straps of their rifles or the handles of their pistols. A few took the moment to groom themselves, raking their fingers through jet-black hair that had no hint of curls or drawing out their luxurious mustaches to fine, glittering points.

The dust was a swirling curtain, and as the horses pawed the ground, yet more of it lifted into the air, until her father and the soldiers seemed enfolded in the arid cloud. She could still hear his voice, speaking their native tongue, but there was now in that voice something that seemed to fill her mother with terror. She quickly drew her from the window. "Come, Ana," she said.

The grip of her mother's hand had been tighter than she'd ever felt it, her slender bones felt like talons.

"Come," she repeated. "Come."

As if spiriting someone away, her mother rushed her into a back room of the house, where Ana heard nothing but the tromping of the horses as they galloped off. There was something fierce in that sound, and frightened by it, she went to the window and drew back the curtain to see that her father's horse had departed with the others.

"Where has Father gone?" she asked her mother.

"With the soldiers," her mother answered. "We must leave, Ana. We must leave now."

Her mother quickly packed bread, cheese, dates, olives, and water into two large cloth bags, and with these heavy on her shoulders, they left the house.

"Walk slowly," her mother said. "Do not cause anyone to notice."

They walked along the dusty street, turned at the far corner, and came to a house Ana knew well. At the door her mother cautioned her to keep silent, though it was hard for her not to greet the woman who came to the door, for it was Garine, who cleaned and helped with the marketing and whose two children, a small boy and a girl somewhat older, stood at her side, fearfully clutching their mother's skirt.

"Garine, I must leave," Ana's mother said to her. She lowered the bags and placed them on the threshold. "My husband has gone with the soldiers."

"Where?" Garine asked.

"To the river," her mother said.

"Then you must go," Garine said darkly. Her hand reached for the small Star of David that dangled from the chain at her throat.

"Can you help me, Garine?" Ana's mother said.

"My brother-in-law lives in Baku," Garine said. "But he is in Aleppo now. He could meet you at the Syrian border, then take you into Azerbaijan."

"Thank you, Garine," Ana's mother said.

Garine's gaze darkened. "We will follow soon. None of us can stay here anymore."

Ana's mother grasped Ana's hand, and they quickly made their way down the street. "Come," she said. "We are going on a journey. We must go to the train station."

"Why was Father taken away?" Ana asked her mother.

"Quiet, Ana," her mother answered. Her eyes glanced about frantically. "Do exactly as I say."

The streets were dark, but Ana's mother knew them well so that they reached the railway station just as the train approached.

"Speak only Turkish," Ana's mother warned.

Many eyes followed them as they made their way from car to car until they reached one far at the back, where they could sit alone.

"Where are we going?" Ana asked.

Her mother never answered, merely stared out at the rocky terrain, so Ana had no idea where the train stopped, or why the soldiers entered it and ordered the passengers from the car. She knew only that these men were like the ones who'd taken her father away.

"This way," her mother said as the soldiers approached their car. She took Ana by the hand, dragged her quickly out of her seat and toward the rear of the train, then out of it and behind a rocky embankment, where they hid in silence until the train rolled away.

The days that followed would forever blur in Ana's mind, leaving memories of only the endless walking, the appearance of other stragglers, and the men who fell upon them. Their numbers grew into a bedraggled river that wound its way, though she did not know it then, toward the Syrian border. She would recall only that they had almost reached Aleppo when her mother spotted another gang of men moving toward them.

"Ana, hide there," she said, and pointed to a wooden cart.

Ana did as she was told, and from her hiding place she watched the men come forward and surround her mother. She could tell that they were questioning her, and she heard her mother say that Ana was dead, that her child had died on the road and been buried in a pit. Then one of the men took her mother by the arm and led her away, the other men falling behind her, pushing her roughly forward with the butts of their rifles. She did not look back, nor give any indication that she had left Ana behind, and this, it seemed to Ana, was courage.

In the days ahead, she thought of that courage as she trudged on, continuing with the bedraggled caravan until they finally reached the border, where a guard passed them through with a desultory wave. She had only walked a few paces into Syria when the man appeared.

"Are you from Erzinghan?" he asked.

Ana nodded.

"What is your name?"

"Ana."

"My sister said that I should watch for a curly-haired little girl," the man said. "Garine, you know her?"

With what seemed the last of her strength, Ana nodded again.

344

"Come then," the man said, and took her hand. "Come with me." He smiled. "You are my daughter now."

Lexington Avenue, New York City, 2001

"The man's name was Helmut Klein," Alma said. "He was a German spice trader who lived in Baku. My grandmother lived with him for two years, where she picked up Yiddish and Hebrew. A skill Klein recognized as quite extraordinary, so he decided to send her to America to be educated." She smiled. "I am told you know the rest of this story."

"He does indeed," Danforth said.

With that, he abruptly rose, and in that rising seemed to declare his long and difficult mission at last accomplished. "I am tired now, Paul. Forgive me if I must say goodbye."

I got to my feet and offered my hand.

Danforth took it and shook it gently.

I drew on my coat and within seconds stood outside Danforth's building; the snow was still falling. Alma came up behind me as I turned uptown. "I'll take the bus back to my hotel," I said. "I'm sure my flight's been canceled."

"I'll walk you to the bus stop," Alma said.

She turned, and I fell in beside her; shoulder nearly touching shoulder, we strolled toward the avenue.

"One thing," I said as we walked to our destination. "What happened to your mother?"

"She died when I was born," Alma said. "I never knew her."

I nodded, since I had nothing to say to this, and for a time we walked on silently.

Then, for no reason other than to continue the conversation, I asked, "And Ana's father?"

"He was killed," Alma said.

"By Kulli Demir, or someone like him, I suppose," I said.

"No, Ana's father wasn't killed by Kulli Demir or someone like him," Alma said. She stopped, turned to me, and with her eyes told me that we had truly reached the end of my own quest for Anna Klein. "He *was* Kulli Demir."

She saw the utter shock in my expression. "Ana's mother told her to take her mother's family name, not her father's," she said. She looked at me with an odd tenderness, then added, "My grandfather asked me to give you something." She reached behind her neck and unsnapped a silver chain from which hung a star and crescent moon.

"I wear this to honor my grandmother," she said as she dropped the chain into my hand. Her lips smiled but her eyes bored into me with the accumulated fire of Danforth's simple parable.

"Especially now," she added.

For a moment, I couldn't speak. Then I said simply, "Thank you."

"Goodbye, Paul," she said.

With that farewell, she turned and strolled southward down the avenue, her body framed by the great emptiness of where the Towers had once stood, a wound in our hearts, barbaric and infuriating, crying out for a response both passionate and reasoned, and whose grave balance now seemed more complicated than before.